D0380928

PASSION'S POWER

"Love me, Elana," Reeve whispered softly against her parted lips, "Love me and belong to me as I would belong to you."

She whispered his name softly and he could read warm surrender in her eyes. Slowly, his mouth lowered to claim hers. It was a time that was meant to be, as inevitable as the stars that lit the night sky.

Enfolding her in his arms, he began to assault her senses with hungry kisses and warm, seeking hands. She responded with a wild and vibrant passion that both surprised and thrilled him. She was no longer a delicate, fragile girl, but a strong, sensual woman whose desire blazed as high as his own.

"I love you, Reeve Burke," she cried out as she drew him closer to her, opening to him as a new blossom to the morning sun. "If I am forever damned for it, I love you!"

BESTSELLERS BY SYLVIE F. SOMMERFIELD ARE BACK IN STOCK!

TAZIA'S TORMENT	(1705, $3.95)
REBEL PRIDE	(1706, $3.95)
ERIN'S ECSTASY	(1704, $3.50)
DEANNA'S DESIRE	(1707, $3.95)
TAMARA'S ECSTASY	(1708, $3.95)
SAVAGE RAPTURE	(1709, $3.95)
KRISTEN'S PASSION	(1710, $3.95)
CHERISH ME, EMBRACE ME	(1711, $3.95)
RAPTURE'S ANGEL	(1712, $3.95)
TAME MY WILD HEART	(1351, $3.95)
BETRAY NOT MY PASSION	(1466, $3.95)

Available wherever paperbacks are sold, or order direct from the Publisher. Send cover price plus 50¢ per copy for mailing and handling to Zebra Books, Dept. 1466, 475 Park Avenue South, New York, N.Y. 10016. DO NOT SEND CASH.

Sylvie F. Sommerfield

Betray Not My Passion

ZEBRA BOOKS
KENSINGTON PUBLISHING CORP.

ZEBRA BOOKS

are published by

Kensington Publishing Corp.
475 Park Avenue South
New York, N.Y. 10016

Copyright © 1984 by Sylvie F. Sommerfield

All rights reserved. No part of this book may be reproduced in any form or by any means without the prior written consent of the Publisher, excepting brief quotes used in reviews.

Third printing: October 1985

Printed in the United States of America

I dedicate this book to all my readers for their support.

Prologue

Torquemada! A name that would bring terror to the hearts of thousands. An abstract genius presiding over a gigantic and cruel engine of its own perfecting . . . the Inquisition.

His history will prove that of all human infirmities, there is none productive of more extensive mischief to society than fanaticism.

From a benign gospel of love thundered forth a malign hatred; its divine lesson of patience and forbearance has been taught in murderous impatience and bloodthirsty intolerance.

It could never be denied that at such a time in the history of Christianity, the enlightened pagan would be justified in saying, "Behold how these Christians love one another."

Isabella is queen of Castile and Aragon. Twenty-five years of age and a jealous Catholic. The deeds of her life—with one dark exception that is the subject of this story—show an exceptional woman of great faith and character. Being of rigid chastity, she exacted the same purity of conduct in the ladies-in-waiting about her.

And so it was introduced, the Inquisition unto Spain. Also introduced was Fray Tomas de Torquemada, prior of the Dominican Convent of Holy Cross of Segoria. His influence with the queen would be vast, his eloquence fiery, and his energy compelling.

Isabella still hesitated to set into motion the extreme cause that would change the lives of so many.

Blood lust was to touch the lives of two in a way that would bind them as closely together as one. One was a handsome, unwary English sea captain who had harbored no idea of the adventure that lay before him. The other, a beautiful lady-in-waiting to Queen Isabella whose sweet innocence would not believe until it was nearly too late.

The Inquisition would first bring them together, then separate them, and lead them on a path of adventure, hate, and intense love.

The story begins, Spain, 1481.

Chapter One

The large ship drew slowly away from the English coast. It was a clear night, the moon huge and yellow. The sea was calm and a light breeze touched the full sails lifting the ship with an easy rhythmic movement that gave a great deal of pleasure to the men who stood at the wheel.

The ship was the *Golden Eagle*, and the man who stood at the wheel was her captain, Reeve Burke. The captain could have been the one for whom the ship was named, for he was a golden eagle also. Tall, well over six feet, he was broad of shoulder and narrow of hip. Powerful muscles controlled the huge ship expertly. His hair was a thick lion's mane of burnished gold and his eyes, a brilliant silver grey. Tanned skin told of days in the open air and made a startling contrast for his silver eyes, as did the white gleam of his ever-present smile.

He held the wheel almost caressingly as he would have held a woman, with the same loving care. His eyes squinted against the sun as he gazed up at the wind-filled sails, and he adjusted the course of the ship to pick up all the morning breeze.

The man who stood next to him smiled. He had always admired his captain's ability to seek out the slightest touch of a breeze, capture it, and use it efficiently to draw every ounce of speed from the *Golden Eagle*. This had made it the fastest ship on the ocean.

Ralph Drake had been Reeve's first mate for over six years, and would vow readily that he had never served under a captain he admired or respected more.

He would have liked to have questioned Reeve on their destination and the reasons for what he considered a rather rapid departure from England. He was sure they had left more rapidly than the captain had planned. They had only been in port for a month after a trip to France. It had only been enough time to refit and supply the *Eagle*.

The thoughts that were in Ralph's mind were echoed in the mind of his captain. Reeve was remembering a midnight meeting a week before that had resulted in this journey.

A rendezvous with a rather seductive young lady had ended beautifully. It was in the early hours of the morning that he left her side and started toward the one place he loved to call home: the *Eagle*, although it was not really his home.

No one but Reeve knew of the thing that had separated himself from his very rich and very influential family. It was a thing that had happened before Ralph had met him. It had been mentioned once, to Ralph's knowledge, in a barroom, by a man who would never again mention Reeve's past to anyone. Reeve had methodically beat him into insensibility.

Reeve's boots clicked sharply against the rough cobbled streets. Streetwise, he was never afraid to walk anywhere alone. He feared nothing and was prepared for just about anything. The shadowed form that stepped from an alley a few feet from him, and waited in silence, drew him to a momentary halt. Then slowly he continued to approach the man. He was prepared to defend himself. He was not prepared for a well-cultured voice to speak to him softly.

"Captain Burke?"

"Yes. Who are you? What do you want?"

"A friend, sir."

"Friends do not meet on dark streets. Do you have a name?"

"Of course." The man chuckled softly, which raised Reeve's ire a little. "I will tell it to you if we can find someplace safe to talk."

"Why should I have anything to discuss with you?" Reeve answered. "If you wanted to speak to me, why did you not come to me in the daylight?"

"It is a matter I wish to be kept secret. I can trust very few."

"How did you know where to find me?"

Again the chuckle. "Your, ah, romantic adventure is known to me, sir. I took the chance that you would choose to return home tonight, although I know you have not always chosen to leave the young ladies so early."

Reeve now became completely annoyed that this man had obviously been following him more than one night. It annoyed yet intrigued him that this man felt something was so important that he had to do so.

He did not see the other man's slight smile. He knew he had captured Reeve's attention; that was what he wanted. "Captain Burke, if we could go somewhere, I would be pleased to buy a glass of wine and explain my reasons. I feel it will be mutually beneficial."

Reeve thought for a moment, then he shrugged. "Why not? I could use a glass of wine, anyway."

"Good," the man replied. "Where shall we go?"

"To the Red Bull. I have a private table there."

"Lead the way sir, please."

He did, but the man was still aware that Reeve was prepared for anything. They walked in silence until they reached the Red Bull.

In the shadowed tavern, Reeve led the man to an alcove that contained a table and chairs. He waved the man to a seat and sat opposite him. Soon a buxom and not too clean waitress took their order and brought a bottle of wine and two glasses. Reeve poured the wine while he studied the man opposite him.

11

He was older than Reeve had first thought, well over fifty, he guessed. He had white hair and a full white mustache. His face was narrow, yet his eyes were clear. He returned Reeve's scrutiny with humor in their depths. Reeve grinned, took his glass, raised it in a silent toast, then spoke quietly.

"All right, my friend, you seem to know a lot about me, and I know nothing about you. Suppose you fill me in on two things. Just who the hell are you and what do you want with me?"

The man smiled in response, took a sip from his glass, then replied in a quiet voice. "My name is Markham, but that is irrelevant for I am only an intermediary for someone much more important."

"Who?"

"He will have to remain anonymous until I am convinced you will agree to our offer."

"Just what is this . . . offer?"

Markham sat back in his chair and held Reeve's gaze with his. "We want you to take a trip."

"A trip? Where?"

"To Spain."

"I've only just returned from France. My men are tired of the sea."

"They would be more than handsomely rewarded. My . . . employer would be happy to give them all a substantial reward."

"All right, suppose they agree . . . and I agree. Just why would we be going to Spain?"

"This is a very desperate situation. We must get someone safely out of Spain. It is a matter of life and death."

"Whose?" Reeve said softly.

"That answer awaits your word of honor that this will remain a secret and you will agree to do what we need done."

"My word of honor," Reeve repeated as if he were surprised. "What if it isn't worth a thing?"

"We know you quite well, Captain Burke, we will accept your word of honor, despite the fact that you have worked hard to hide that you are a man of honor and pride. It is one of the reasons we chose you for this mission."

"I'll be damned," Reeve muttered. He sat back and took his glass and drained it. Then he set it down firmly as if he had made a decision. "All right, you have my word of honor. Then you can tell me about what I'm going to Spain to do."

The man smiled, and the smile was so filled with relief and warmth that Reeve smiled in return.

"Come, we must go," Markham said as he rose.

"Go where?"

"Why, to meet the man who needs your help."

Reeve smiled, rose and clapped Markham on the shoulder. "Lead on, this gets more interesting by the minute. I can't wait to meet this anonymous friend."

"You might get a surprise."

"The night has sure been full of them," Reeve said, laughing. They both laughed as they left the Red Bull and walked the streets of London to a home that, in truth, did cause Reeve a rather strong shock.

When they stopped in front of the large, elaborate mansion, and stood outside the tall iron fence that surrounded it, Reeve gazed at it in surprise. "My God, this is Lord Bragham's home."

"It is."

"Then he's—"

"He's the man that needs your help. Come, let's go in so he can explain to you what he needs." They walked through the iron gates and to the huge oak door. A coded rap and the door was quickly opened.

The man who let them in was a silent, dark-clothed man who rapidly disappeared. Reeve knew he was a trusted servant who had learned not to speak of what he saw in the home of

13

his employer.

Reeve followed Markham to another door. Markham opened it and they stepped into a well-lit library with a crisp fire in the fireplace. These did not hold Reeve's attention as much as did the tall man who stood in front of the fireplace. Reeve sensed a man who held power and knew how to use it. This was a strong, purposeful man he faced, yet he could not stop wondering why such a man would need him in any way.

"Captain Burke, this is—" Markham began.

"I know who this is," Reeve said softly. He bowed slightly toward the tall, silent man. "It is a great honor to meet you, sir. Your reputation precedes you. I can't help but wonder why one of England's most able ambassadors should need the help of a simple ship captain." He saw the man's lips quirk in a half smile.

"Hardly a simple ship's captain," he said. "Your life is well known to me. In fact, I have taken a great deal of trouble to find out all about you. I hope you are not offended, but I had to find a man I could trust."

"Well," Reeve said, chuckling, "you have certainly gotten my undivided attention. I'm curious about what I could do for a man as powerful as you. If I'm not mistaken, you were ambassador to Spain for many years before you were called home. Does this have anything to do with your recall?"

"If you would make yourself comfortable, share a glass of wine with us, and I shall endeavor to explain as best as I can what has happened to bring on this meeting."

Reeve sat in a comfortable chair, and his host sat opposite him. Markham poured three goblets of wine, handed one to each, then sat in a nearby chair.

"You are right about one thing," Bragham began. "My being recalled from Spain has a great deal to do with this, but not in the way you think. It came at a most inopportune time, but there was nothing I could do about it." He smiled. "An

14

ambassador does not deliberately disobey his sovereign, even for a friend."

"This friend then, he's the reason?"

"Yes."

"What is it you want of me, Lord Bragham?"

"I need you to go to Spain. It must be done with the utmost secrecy. You can trust no one with the reason you are there. I will arrange some reason acceptable. A letter will introduce you to a man who will see that you get invited to court. Once you are at court, you must wait."

"Wait for what?"

"Someone will contact you. When he does, you are to see that this man and another person he will bring with him, are safely gotten from Spain and brought to me."

"This all sounds very mysterious. What is the reason that this man cannot just take a ship, leave Spain, and just come here himself?"

"If he tries to leave Spain, he will be dead before he can step foot on a ship."

Reeve sat back in his chair, sipped his drink meditatively, wondering why he trusted this man who seemed inclined to tell him nothing, yet was blandly asking him to risk his life to save a man, or men, about whom he knew nothing. He smiled in disbelief of his own self. "What will happen," he said slowly, "if I am unsuccessful? If we get caught before we can leave the country?"

Bragham's eyes unflinchingly held his as he answered. "A good man will meet a very untimely and vicious death. Believe me, captain, when I tell you it would be a tragedy."

Again, Reeve was struck with surprise when he realized that he believed what Bragham said was absolutely true. He remained silent while Bragham and Markham watched and waited for his answer.

"All right," he replied, "what must I do?"

Both Bragham and Markham seemed to relax visibly, then they exchanged a quick glance and pleased smiles as Bragham rose and walked to a table that sat nearby. There was a map on the table. "If you will come over here, captain, I will show you exactly what you must do."

Reeve rose and walked across the room to stand beside Bragham. Markham also came to stand at Reeve's side and they looked down on the map. Bragham's finger touched the map. "Your *Golden Eagle* is here. You will leave tomorrow morning. Down the channel and across the Bay of Biscay. Continue on down the coast to Cadiz. There you will make port and go ashore." He reached into his pocket and took out an envelope. "In here is the name of the man you will go and see. He is an exporter and importer. He will set up the pretense of unloading your ship and reloading it."

"What will I be doing while all this loading and unloading is going on?"

"Waiting," Bragham said, smiling. "Impatiently, I know, but wait you must. It won't be long before my friend contacts you."

"And from there?"

"From there you will go to the court in Sevilla. There again, you must wait. I'm sure it will not be long before you are contacted again. Then you must follow a plan, my friend, I have prearranged. If all goes well, within a month you will again be headed for English waters."

"It all sounds pretty simple," Reeve said.

"No, captain. It will not be simple. I must caution you at all times to protect yourself. They do not know my plans and I would not want them to discover you. It could cost you much."

"Don't worry. Protecting my life is a thing I do very well," Reeve said, laughing.

"Captain, you have not questioned what will be expected of you at court," Bragham said softly. "I take it you have been presented to a royal court before?"

Reeve's eyes held his. "I'm sure I can find my way about," he answered.

"Yes," Bragham said, smiling. "I'm sure you can. I have every confidence in you. In fact, I am sure you shall return a few weeks from now safe, secure, and with my friends."

Reeve held out his hand, and Bragham took it in a firm grip. They finished their wine and an hour later Reeve was again walking toward the *Golden Eagle*. Once aboard, he went to bed, but sleep was an elusive thing. It was a long time before he slept, yet with the first gray touch of dawn, he stepped on deck and gave the order to raise the sail.

Now he tasted the salty tang of the sea and felt the movement that always thrilled him, the lift of his ship as it moved from the harbor and swung into the deep ocean current. The days were bright and no sign of bad weather was in view throughout the entire trip. The huge white sails of the *Golden Eagle* filled with the breeze and pushed the ship along at top speed. Behind them was the English Channel as they headed toward the Bay of Biscay, which would put them near the coast of Spain in the distance so that he would not be sighted.

It was two weeks of smooth sailing when they sighted the harbor at Cadiz. The harbor was well crowded with ships. It was a busy, bustling town. Reeve hoped the presence of so many would make him more anonymous. They docked with minimal effort, and he allowed his men to go ashore after a firm talk and a few threats as to what he would do should any of them step out of line and cause a problem that might bring them to the attention of the authorities.

Once they were gone and only a nominal guard remained to protect the ship, Reeve went below to his cabin. There he opened the envelope Bragham had given him and found the name and address of the man he was to meet, and another sealed envelope that had this man's name on the outside. Obviously, it was a letter of introduction for Reeve. He placed the envelope inside his shirt where no thief would think to look, then he left the ship and walked the streets of Cadiz.

He enjoyed the flavor of this city with its hustle and bustle, so he took his time in searching for the man.

He stopped in front of a small shop that boasted the name he sought in gold lettering on the window: Garcia and Sons, Import and Export. He opened the door and walked inside. The shop was quiet and no one seemed to be about. He gazed about him at the assortment of things there. Reeve guessed that the man had an excellent taste in material and an access to almost every country, because things from many lands were present.

"May I help you, sir?" came a quiet voice. Reeve turned to face a tall slender man who had entered the room without a sound.

"Yes, I'm looking for Emilo Garcia."

"The father or the son?"

"I'm not exactly sure," Reeve replied. "I imagine the father."

"And your name, sir?"

"Captain Reeve Burke."

"I see. Do you deal with Senor Garcia?"

"Are you Garcia?"

"No."

"Then, I don't see that that is any of your business. I have business with Senor Garcia. Would you please ask him if he will see me?"

"Of course, Senor,"the man replied. Reeve could feel the piercing dark eyes as they tried to read him. "If you will be patient, Senor, I shall go and see if Senor Garcia is free."

"Thank you."

The man bowed a short, clipped formal bow and left on silent feet. It was several minutes before he returned, this time accompanied by another man. Reeve watched as they approached.

The second man was quite striking. He was nearly as tall as Reeve, and quite slender. A rather aristocratic face with a slim aquiline nose, dark eyes and hair, and a very warm, welcoming smile.

"Senor, I am Emilo Garcia. Is there something I can do for you?"

Reeve was aware of the intent gaze of the first man. "Yes, Senor Garcia, I would like to speak to you for a few minutes. In private if I may."

Garcia bowed gracefully. "Of course, Senor, would you accompany me to my office. I would be honored if you would accept a cool glass of wine and be comfortable while we talk."

"Thank you," Reeve replied, aware again of the shadow of disappointment in the first man's eyes.

They walked through the door that Garcia had entered. Down a short hall to another door. Garcia held it open and motioned Reeve inside. Once inside, he closed the door firmly and turned to Reeve. "Please, sit down and make yourself comfortable." As Reeve sat, Garcia went to a nearby table where he poured two glasses of wine from a decanter. He carried them back and handed one to Reeve. As they sipped, Garcia sat down in a large chair behind his desk.

"Now, Senor, how may I help you?"

Without saying a word, Reeve reached inside his shirt, removed the letter, and handed it to Garcia.

Garcia's eyes held Reeve's as he broke the seal after first glancing at it to assure himself that the seal had not been tampered with. Then he unfolded the letter and read it. Reeve could see no change in his expression while he read. Finished, he laid the letter down and again raised his eyes to Reeve. This time they were warmer and much more welcoming.

"Senor Burke," he said gently, "you are most welcome. I had despaired that anyone would get here in time. I am grateful, Senor, but have you been warned about how dangerous this adventure might be?"

"Yes, Senor Garcia, I've been warned."

"Senor, the people you will rescue are well worth every effort we can put forth. I only pray that we succeed. You must now return to your ship. I shall arrange for a grand show of energy in the next few days as we load and unload your ship."

"In the meantime, I'm just to wait?"

"Yes, for even I don't know who will contact you. It is better that we don't know each other. That way if one of us is caught and put to the torture, there is no way we can inform on the other."

"Torture?"

"The arm of the Inquisition is ruthless, my friend. I hope you never have to feel its touch."

"How long do I have to wait?"

Garcia shrugged. "Who knows, Senor. Not long, I hope, for we are rapidly running out of time."

Reeve rose. "All right, I'll wait. In the meantime, I'll see a bit of your city."

"I'm afraid not, Senor."

"Why?"

"You must be at your ship and ready. The contact may come any moment, day or night."

"Good God, man, what am I supposed to do for what might be days? Just walk the decks?"

"I'm afraid so. If you are out of contact even for a few minutes," he said and shrugged, "it might be the only few minutes the contact might have and all would be lost."

Reeve sighed, placed his glass on the desk and said, "All right, I suppose you are right. But it will be most difficult just doing nothing."

Garcia rose and extended his hand to Reeve. "What you will be doing, Senor, is saving two valuable lives."

Reeve took his hand and felt the strong grip of a very purposeful man.

"*Vaya con Dios*, my friend. I hope one day we meet under better circumstances."

"So do I, Senor Garcia."

Garcia escorted Reeve to the door. Again, he walked the streets of Cadiz.

The next day, Reeve rose early. He went on deck to find a multitude of dock workers unloading crates from wagons that, it would seem to any onlooker, were to be loaded on his ship. He scanned the docks for any sign of someone's trying to get his attention. No one. The day dragged on, and all he could do to fill his time was to have the ship cleaned from top to bottom.

Another day passed, then another, and Reeve began to chafe under the inactivity.

The third night he could not sleep, so he walked along the dark, quiet deck of the ship. The dock was poorly lighted and several of the workers still moved about. Among them moved several women, obviously ladies of the evening. He chuckled to himself, realizing he would not have minded the company of one at the moment. He crossed his arms and leaned on the rail. One of the women seemed to suddenly notice him. With swaying hips and a broad smile, she walked to the bottom of the gangplank.

"Senor capitan," she called, "you look lonely. Would you like a little company?"

Reeve smiled back. She was a surprising beauty; her hair black as night, loose and full about her. She was slim and the red dress she wore revealed rather than concealed her obvious charms.

"Come aboard," he said, "it is rather lonely up here."

With a light laugh, she climbed the gangplank, and Reeve

21

was there to take her hand and help her step to the deck.

"*Gracias*, Senor," she said. Her voice was throaty and warm, and very suggestive. Reeve found himself anticipating how she would feel in the warmth of his bed.

"I've some wine in my cabin," he said. "Would you be interested in sharing a glass or two?"

"You are most kind, Senor capitan," she replied as she leaned close to him. The scent she wore was light and captivating. Reeve slid his arm about her and she offered no resistance. They walked to Reeve's cabin. He opened the door for her. It was quite dark, but he really felt the need for no light. He swung her about and into his arms, and his mouth took demanding possession of hers.

For a moment her mouth was soft and pliant under his, then he received another shock as he felt her twist in his arms and move away from him. Reeve chuckled. "We won't quibble over price," he said. "Name what you want."

Her laughter was light and sparkly as she replied, "Light a light, captain, I am here to give you a message. One I think you have been waiting for."

Reeve quickly lighted the light, then he turned and looked at her. In moments she had changed from a dock whore to a lady. The change was visible in the look in her eyes and the way she held herself.

"So, you're my messenger. Very clever." His eyes roved over her. "But might I say, I'm a little disappointed?" Again, he heard her light laughter and he enjoyed the humorous glitter in her eyes.

"Let us talk business, captain," she said in the same warm, throaty voice. "We can always discuss your disappointment later."

Chapter Two

Madrid was warm. The first rays of the early morning sun, full and bright, touched the window of the queen's apartment. Elana de Santangel sat on the cushions of the window seat. A book lay open in her lap, but she had ceased reading quite some time before. Now her gaze was held by the beauty that lay before her and the wanderings of her always vivid imagination.

The artist's eye would have been captured more by Elana's rare beauty than by any other sight. She was small and slim, yet her body spoke woman. Soft curves that rounded the soft fabric of the dress she wore would have delighted the painter with his brush and canvas. The thick mass of her midnight black hair had been intricately coiled atop her head because of the warmth of the day. The deep black hair brought contrast to her wide, deep green eyes. Almond-shaped, they tipped up slightly at the corners. Her skin was also startling white, like fine porcelain, except for the soft pink of her cheeks and lips. Her mouth may have been judged by women as a little too wide. But many men had gazed at it, longing to taste the full, ripe lips. A slim fine nose could, when she chose, give her a haughty appearance, but this was usually belied by the glow of interest and humor that could make her lips quirk and her eyes dance.

Elana did possess a fine sense of humor, accompanied by a keen interest in life and all that surrounded her. Secretly she had always longed to be a man so that she would have been free to follow her adventurous spirit.

Now she was most thoroughly bored, and her interest had fled beyond the room in which she sat, beyond the book she held in her lap, and out among the people who crowded the streets of Madrid. How she would love to roam its streets, visit the shops, and speak with all the people she met. She knew it was impossible. Queen Isabella would not only have been shocked at such a thought, but Elana would have found herself packed and sent home. Queen Isabella would harbor no such thought in the ladies she had chosen to surround her.

Elana had been lady-in-waiting to Queen Isabella for almost two years. She had grown to love her sovereign dearly. Despite the queen's strict moral laws, Elana found her the most interesting and intelligent person she had ever known. She knew she would never do anything to get herself sent from court in disgrace. She thought of the pride her family had in her for being chosen for such a position, and all the wonderful things the queen had done for the rest of her family. Her brother had been brought to court because of Elana and was a captain of the royal guard, a very enviable and rewarding position for a young man. She and her brother loved each other deeply and she knew how proud her brother was of her. They had been close all their lives, and Elana felt he was the only one who really understood her wayward spirit. He had teased her about it often enough.

Elana's attention was suddenly drawn to the far end of the room where three girls her own age sat in conversation. They had begun to laugh, and the laughter shattered Elana's reverie. She rose, laid the book aside, then walked toward the group of women. One of the girls tipped up her head and looked at Elana.

"Beatriz," Elana said, smiling, "what is so amusing?"

Beatriz de Mendosa was Elana's best friend at court. They

were so much alike that most would have claimed them to be sisters.

"We were just asking Marianna if she was going to meet that handsome young count that was doing his best to flirt with her at the state dinner."

"Oh, Beatriz," Marianna said with a laugh, "you know I have no such intentions. Her Grace would send me home in the flick of an eye. Then," she said softly, "I would never get to see him again. I must just wait and hope Her Grace would be open to his proposal that we meet."

"Why, Marianna," Beatriz said in sincere wonder. "You actually have fallen in love with Count Marillo. I'm sorry. I would not have teased you if I had thought you felt so."

"I'm sorry, too," Marianna replied soberly. "I'm sure Her Grace will never allow it."

Elana stood silent for the moment, wondering what she would do if she loved someone and the queen refused to allow her to see him. As abruptly as the thought came she pushed it aside. She had no intention of falling in love with anyone. She was having too much fun amid the excitement of court.

"Elana," another spoke, "what are you planning to wear to the ball?"

"I haven't decided," Elana said with a smile.

"Do wear the green velvet, Elana. It makes your green eyes much prettier," the girl replied.

Maria Villada was just the opposite of Elana, and at their first meeting both had thought they would not be able to get along. Strangely, despite the obvious difference, they had become friends.

"Thank you, Maria. I suppose I shall. But it depends on what Her Grace will wear."

At that moment the sound of a small tinkling bell came from the next chamber. All the girls rose immediately to their feet. They had been awake and dressed since just before dawn.

They had gathered, as usual, in the anteroom of the queen's apartment to await the moment she would waken and send for them. The light sound of the bell did just that.

The door to the queen's apartment opened and Louisa de Susan appeared. She was the oldest of the ladies-in-waiting and as such held the enviable position of sharing the queen's quarters with her in case she should need anything during the night.

"Come, ladies," she said, "we must help the queen dress. You know how upset she will be if we are late for mass."

The four of them accompanied Louisa into the presence of Isabella, queen of Spain. Isabella, at twenty-five, was only seven years older than Elana and the other ladies. Yet she had a majestic presence that always had the capability of keeping them completely under control. Elana stood somewhat in awe of her, yet she loved her completely, as she knew the other ladies about her did.

Isabella was a fair, shapely woman of middle height. She had a clear complexion and eyes that hovered between green and blue. She had a gracious, winsome countenance, remarkable for its habitual serenity. She had such self-control that she could carefully conceal her anger when aroused, and any other emotion she felt. She was very ceremonious in dress and equipage. She was deliberate of gesture, quick-witted, and ready of tongue. She was a zealous Catholic and very charitable, yet in her judgments, she was inclined more to rigor than to mercy. She had a rare fidelity to her word and never failed to do what she had said she would do.

All four of the girls dropped to their knees before her.

"You may rise. We must be dressed rapidly. We don't want to be late for mass."

Her commanding voice and reference to the royal 'we' brought them quickly to their feet. There was not much conversation as they aided her in dressing, then followed her down the long, cold hall to the queen's private chapel. They knelt in the pew behind her and in a few minutes rose again as King Ferdinand appeared. He knelt beside the queen and in a moment, mass began.

When mass was over, the king and queen dismissed the ladies during the time they would accept the presence of two ambassadors to their court.

It was a time Elana enjoyed the most for she was free to do as she pleased for at least three hours. She and Beatriz had decided to go riding. Elana was delighted to find someone who loved to ride as much as she.

Under Isabella's orders they were not permitted to ride alone, so they had asked Elana's brother to ride with them.

It was well known to Elana that Beatriz and Elana's brother were quite fascinated with each other. Elana would not tell that to anyone, for if she did, word of it would get back to Isabella, who seemed to hear of everything that went on in her court. The days of riding free would then come to an abrupt halt.

They rode from the palace gates and out into the bright, sunlit glades that surrounded it. Once free of the prying eyes of those within the castle, they galloped across the fields to the nearby forest. It was a silent agreement between them that they would "accidentally" be separated for a half hour. A half hour was harmless in Elana's eyes, because she knew both Beatriz and her brother. Neither of them would sacrifice Elana, although Elana was sure a few kisses would be stolen, and amorous professions of love exchanged.

Free! For a half an hour! She rode along the forest path, breathing deeply of the warm morning air. She allowed the sheer pleasure of it to fill her completely. She allowed her dream-filled imagination to gain control. In her mind she rode her own estate with a tall, handsome husband at her side. The impossibility of this was certain for Elana was born of a wealthy name, but only a name, for most of the wealth was long

27

since gone. It had been Isabella's generosity, and the fact that she had felt she owed a debt to Elana's father for his loyalty, that had gotten her accepted to court at all. The possibility of a tall, handsome wealthy husband with an estate to offer her was remote.

The time fled entirely too rapidly for both Elana and the two who rejoined her. They rode back through the gates. At the stable, their horses were cared for. Elana's brother, Rodrigo, parted company with them, then Elana and Beatriz started across the lawns of the castle. They had to cross the elaborate castle gardens to do so. As they did, a young page approached them. They stopped as he came to their side.

"Lady Beatriz?" he said with a warm, open smile, for Beatriz was well loved among the castle workers.

"Yes, Ramon?"

"Lady Louisa would like to speak to you in her room. She asks that you come alone."

Elana and Beatriz exchanged a surprised look, but a request from Lady Louisa could well be construed as an order. Beatriz smiled and touched Elana's arm.

"I'll met you in the Great Hall as soon as I find out what Lady Louisa wants."

Elana nodded and Beatriz walked away in the company of the young page. Elana strolled aimlessly about the garden, still reluctant to go inside. After a few minutes, she decided to sit on one of the strategically placed benches that filled the garden. She was unaware of the man who walked purposefully toward her until his shadow fell across her. She looked up in surprise that a man would approach her unescorted in the queen's garden. She gasped in surprise when she saw who it was. Then she rose quickly to her feet, unable to keep herself from trembling as the man stopped beside her.

Don Francisco de Vargas, the next one to the king and queen, probably held the most power in Spain. Although many things were whispered about his influence in the Inquisition, nothing was truly known. He was a friend of Fray Tomas de Torquemada. No one knew the true extent of that friendship or the power that rested in the man who stood before her.

"Lady Elana," he said in a deep, controlled voice, "you are unaccompanied, Madam?"

Alarm struck her very nearly speechless. "I . . . I was walking with Lady Beatriz when Lady Louisa sent for her. I was just on my way back to the queen's apartment."

"No need to rush, my dear. The queen is quite busy. I'm sure you will not be missed if you sit and talk to me for a few moments."

She knew this was an impossible situation. No matter what she did, she would be wrong. She could not insult a man of de Vargas's stature; still she could not be found sitting on a bench in the queen's garden alone with a man. If she knew what was in de Vargas's mind, she might have had the wisdom to have turned and run.

What a delightful rose, he thought. It will be a pleasure to possess her. I must look deeply into her background and see what can be done to bring her to my bed.

Her cheeks pinkened under his intent gaze, and she shivered with the feeling he was undressing her with those hawklike eyes.

"I have not seen much of you, Lady Elana."

"I have been quite busy."

"The queen is difficult?"

"Oh, no, Don Francisco! She is the most wonderful person in the world and I am deeply honored to serve her."

"But, of course," he said smoothly, "but, surely you must have time for yourself?"

It was only then that she realized his intent. If she said yes, it was an open invitation for him to claim some of the time. It was the last thing she wanted. Fear had crept into her mind and heart, accompanied by a sense of something dark and unknown she could not understand. She rose quickly from her seat as his shoulder leaned close enough to brush hers.

"I am so sorry, Don Francisco, but I must go. I would not want the queen to be angry with me."

"Well, if I must lose your beautiful company, it will be only until the ball the day after tomorrow. You will attend, will you not?"

Of course he knew that she had no other choice. If the queen attended, Elana had no way of remaining away.

"Yes . . . yes, I shall."

"Good," he said as he rose to stand overpoweringly close to her. "I shall look forward to seeing you there. Maybe we can take a stroll in a garden not quite as light as this."

His open innuendo made her stiffen in anger. She could not fight him. But she did not want to be put in this vulnerable position again.

"I must go," she whispered, then she turned and fled, feeling his dark, hungry eyes follow her.

He watched her as she almost ran across the garden and into the castle. A violent hunger filled him. "Fly, my little rose, but not too far. I shall have you when I am ready to reach out my hand and pluck you." He walked across the garden to another door. Inside, he climbed a flight of steps to his luxurious apartment.

His apartment consisted of eight rooms. They were furnished to his taste, with every luxury money would allow.

He had entered through a rear door that led to an anteroom of his study. He crossed the study and walked into another large room. Crossing it, he came to another door. It led to a small room in which sat his personal secretary.

"Miguel," he said sharply.

"Yes, Don Francisco?"

"Come in here."

The man rose with alacrity and followed Don Francisco into the room, closing the door behind him.

"There is something you wanted, Don Francisco?"

"Yes, I've a thing for you to do. Do you know Lady Elana de Santangel?"

"Lady Elana? Yes, I do. She is one of the queen's ladies. A lovely girl. The queen is quite fond of her."

"I want you to search out all her past. I want to know everything about her and her family. Everything down to the very last detail."

Miguel had long ago learned not to question any orders of Don Francisco. He heard, he obeyed, and he never violated the silent confidence. He knew better. Men who had angered Don Francisco had found themselves touched by the Inquisitors.

Miguel left and Don Francisco poured himself a glass of wine. Then he sat in a comfortable chair and began to create a plan that would give him what he wanted.

Don Francisco de Vargas was pleased with himself. At his fingertips he had everything he desired. He had only to reach out and take what he wanted, and he was not a man who hesitated to do so. He was handsome in a dark, satanic way. Tall and well formed. He had eyes so dark they were nearly black and he had winged brows over them. His skin was dark and his smile broad. He was able to charm much of what he wanted.

But there were other ways, and what he could not get by charm and persuasion, he could get in that other way.

As if to put the truth to his thoughts, there was a light rap on the door. He smiled, for he knew who was on the other side.

"Come in," he called. The door opened and a slender man, quite short and almost fragile, stepped inside.

"Ah, Salizar, you are most welcome."

"*Gracias*, Don Francisco."

"Come here and have a glass of wine with me."

Salizar nodded and Francisco rose, poured another drink

31

and handed it to the brown-clothed monk who stood before him.

"Your, ah, mission has been successful, my friend?"

"Yes, yes, quite," Salizar said. His eyes seemed to brighten and Francisco saw again the glow of fanaticism. It was a flame he had been fanning from his first glimpse of the glowing embers to the raging fire that now burned. He was the rabid animal that Francisco could release at will on anyone who dared to cross him.

"We have questioned all the prisoners; we were even forced to persuade some to answer our questions truthfully. The wheel can persuade the sternest apostate to tell his truth. I am pleased to say we have wiped out the Devil's work in that village. We were forced to burn over two thousand, but they finally confessed. We have saved many souls this day."

"You should be quite pleased, Salizar, as I am. It is good fortune that I found out about that nest of Jews."

"Your information is always correct, Don Francisco. The church and Fray Torquemada should be grateful to you."

"I only ask," Francisco said, smiling pleasantly, "that I be allowed to continue to turn over to your office all that I have found practicing such things."

"We are grateful, Don Francisco."

Don Francisco shrugged eloquently as if to dismiss what he knew was a great service. Their conversation lasted for quite some time before Salizar left.

Francisco relaxed with the vision before him of a green-eyed beauty who would one day be his . . . no matter what he had to do to get her. He thought now of the ball that would be held and the first taste of her sweetness he would claim.

Elana returned to her duties, but the dark specter of Don Francisco lingered in the recesses of her mind. Beatriz was the first to realize something was very wrong with her.

It was bedtime. Since the queen was already in bed, they

were free to retire. Beatriz and Elana were in Elana's room talking.

"Elana?"

"What?"

"What's the matter?"

"Matter? Nothing, why?"

"Come now, Elana, we are too good of friends for that. You have been quiet all afternoon. It was almost as if you were . . . afraid of something. Can't you tell me? I would help if I could."

"Oh, Beatriz," Elana said softly as she sat on the edge of the bed beside her, "I don't think there is anything I can do, and you are right, I am afraid. I am terrified."

"Of what?"

"Not what, who. Don Francisco de Vargas."

"Good heavens," Beatriz breathed softly, "where in the name of God did you meet him?"

Elana went on to explain her confrontation with de Vargas in the garden. Beatriz's face grew pale as she listened. She, too, was aware that there was no way to protect themselves from a force as strong as de Vargas.

"I cannot go to the ball," Elana finished.

"You know you have to. How could you explain to the queen? De Vargas is a great name. You would make many people very angry."

"What can I do, Beatriz?"

"Make sure you do not leave the ballroom. If you refuse to go to the garden, he can say nothing to you. Maybe, if we put our heads together, we can find a way out of this."

"I shall try, but I'm frightened."

"So am I," Beatriz replied. "But, remember, I am your friend, and I will do anything to help you. We will stay close to each other."

"Thank you, my friend. I shall never forget."

"Now, you had best get some sleep. We have to be up very

33

early in the morning. The queen is to have her final fitting for the ball gown so we will go to mass early."

Elana agreed because she did not want to worry Beatriz anymore, but she could not sleep for a long time. She felt as if the hand of fate had reached out to touch her somehow. As if some traumatic thing were about to enter her life and change it in a way she could not see or understand. She felt helpless before a thunderous wave of fear.

As she drifted off into sleep, dreams filled her mind, strange dreams of unknown danger and a strange golden bird that flew above her and gave her protection beneath the shadow of his wings.

Elana slept, while the *Golden Eagle* entered the harbor. Fate had, indeed, stirred the cauldron of life and begun a new and violent page.

Chapter Three

Reeve could not have been more surprised by anything in his life than the seductive prostitute turned lady in front of his eyes. He tried to contain his surprise, but the sparkle of humor in her eyes defeated all his intentions.

"Don't be upset, captain," she said. "It was the only way we could get to you. Many of our people are being watched and we don't want to arouse suspicion."

"We?"

"I'm afraid I cannot name you names. I told you it is safer that way."

"Obviously, you've some instructions for me. How are you to get me into court without anyone getting suspicious?"

"Tomorrow you are to leave your ship. You will go to an address I will give to you. The man you will meet will be the one who is your link to the queen's court. You will travel together and he will open the doors for you. From there I have no idea what you will be told."

"And you?" Reeve questioned hopefully. "Will you be at court, also?"

"Eventually, captain, I shall be there, but you are not to recognize me. We will be introduced."

"It will be a pleasure to make your acquaintance, my mystery lady." She laughed a soft, delightful laugh and he had to laugh with her.

"I'm afraid, captain, it would not do your reputation or my credibility any good if I were to leave your cabin too soon. Shall we talk?"

His eyes told her that he would definitely have liked to do much more than talk, yet she could see that he would not jeopardize the mission he had been sent on.

"I have some excellent wine. If you please, I shall offer you a glass and you can tell me all about the court and what goes on there."

"Agreed." Reeve poured the wine while he watched her. Without hesitation, she walked to his bunk and sat down on it. He walked to her, handed her a glass, then lightly touched hers with his.

"Here's to the success of my mission, and the hope that we will meet soon and the circumstances will be less . . . restraining," he said with a broad smile. The tinkle of her laughter pleased him. He drew a heavy chair close to the bunk and sat down to face her.

"Now, suppose you fill me in on the court of Queen Isabella, and what kind of problems I can expect when I get there." She took a sip from her glass. Then she began to talk.

The first gray touch of dawn bordered the horizon when Reeve and his mystery lady walked to the gangplank. For whatever viewers that might still be watching, she rose on tiptoes to kiss him. His arms came about her and he drew her tight in his embrace. His mouth possessed hers for one long moment, then he released her. She offered no resistance. Then their eyes held for only seconds and she was gone. He watched the bewitching sway of her hips until she disappeared from sight. Reeve turned to his cabin. He allowed himself a few hours of sleep, then he rose, bathed and dressed in his finest clothes. He prepared a chest of clothes and personal things to carry with him.

He left his ship in the only hands he trusted, Ralph Drake, with explicit orders for its care.

"Will you be long, captain?"

"I'm not sure, Ralph. I should say about twenty days or so if nothing goes wrong. After that much time passes, be prepared to leave quickly. The minute I get back we must be ready to leave this harbor, is that understood? It's the most important thing. You must have the *Eagle* ready to fly."

"She'll be ready, sir, you can count on that."

"I know I can." Reeve smiled as he clapped his hand on Ralph's shoulder. "I wouldn't leave her with anyone else. You love her as I do. I'll be back in a little over twenty days or I'll send a message."

"Yes, sir. Good luck."

"Thanks, Ralph," Reeve said quietly. "Somehow I have a feeling I'm going to need it."

Reeve left the ship and boarded a carriage he had hired. He gave the address to the driver, then sat back to enjoy the city. They drove through the city itself and beyond to the more secluded areas past the outskirts of the city.

When the carriage stopped, it was in front of a huge house that was surrounded by a large iron fence and a gate that was elaborately scrolled in iron with a large and intricate C. Before either Reeve or the driver could do anything, the gates swung slowly open. Only when they drove through the gate did they see the two men on the other side, who had silently worked the mechanism to open the gates.

The carriage drove up the long drive to the front door of the house. Again, before Reeve could move, the door of the house opened and a tall man told Reeve he was being welcomed by his host. It was the kind of welcome the Spanish dons were famous for, warm and genial.

He was a tall slender man whose age Reeve would not have tried to guess. His face was smooth and tan, but the eyes were

37

wise. His hair was silver white and a full mustache was the same gleaming silver.

As Reeve stepped down from his carriage, his host approached him with an outstretched hand and wide welcoming smile. He spoke excellent English but with the Castilian lisp.

"Senor Burke, you are most welcome. I am Don Diego Chavez."

Reeve took his hand and was somewhat surprised again at the iron-hard strength of the grip. "Thank you, Don Diego."

"Please come in, let me give you some wine and some food." Don Diego escorted Reeve graciously into the house where Reeve was again struck with wonder both at its immense size and its fantastic beauty.

"Your home, Don Diego, it is extremely beautiful." Don Diego's eyes glowed with pleasure.

"*Mi casa es su casa*, Senor. Consider my home your home while you are in my country." He gently touched Reeve's elbow and waved his hand toward an open door through which Reeve could see a low burning fire in an immense fireplace. They walked into Don Diego's study where Reeve was motioned into a comfortable seat while his host poured two crystal goblets half full of a deep red wine. One glass he offered to Reeve who sipped it, aware that it was an extremely fine wine.

Don Diego sat in a high-backed chair opposite Reeve. He watched Reeve and waited for the questions he knew were coming.

"Well, Don Diego," Reeve said, "I guess we had best get down to business. So far I've been being led about in the dark. I think it's time to shed a little light on what is happening and what is expected of me."

"Yes, my friend, you are right. What you are doing is a very charitable bit of courage. The least it deserves are some answers. I will take you with me to Madrid. Once there we will do everything we can to blend with the court and do nothing to arouse any suspicion. When the time is right you will be approached. From there on we will do everything in our power to make the escape work."

"Don Diego, can you tell me who I am to look for?"

"I am only a small part of an organization. Most of us, at the most, know only one name. That of our own contact. It is—"

"Yes, I know, it is safer that way."

"I wish I could help you more. The only thing I can say is the man you are going to rescue is a good and respected man who well deserves to be helped to freedom."

"I hope I can live up to what you expect from me," Reeve said.

"If we had not thought so, you would not have been sent to us. You seem to come with the most impressive credentials."

"I didn't know I had passed out any credentials," Reeve said, grinning. His host's smile echoed his.

"Maybe that is why you were chosen."

"When do we leave for Madrid?"

"There is to be a Grand Ball to celebrate the king's birthday. Many will be traveling here from distant countries. It is the best time for you to arrive. No one will question your arrival. Many guests will be staying for several days. It is the custom. So no one will be surprised if a friend of my son were to stay. You will find the ball and following celebrations interesting. In time you will be approached. After that there will not be much time. You will have to escape on a moment's notice."

"The *Eagle* is ready, her captain is ready. Shall we go?" Reeve replied quietly.

"We will leave in the morning. My son, Rafael, will be here soon. He will be going with us." Reeve had to be content with this, and at first he was reluctant. Then the charm of his host and the lovely home he lived in caught Reeve in the magic of

Spanish hospitality. They were sitting at a late evening dinner when the sound of crisp, authoritative footsteps interrupted their conversation. One look at his host's pride-filled face told Reeve immediately this was the long-expected son.

When he stepped through the doorway, Reeve felt he was looking at the handsomest man he had ever seen. He walked across the room with a grace that made Reeve think of a smooth-moving predatory animal. His skin was tanned, and the smile he wore was broad. His hair was thick and black, and his eyes were a golden amber.

"Father," he said in a deep, resonant voice, "I am so sorry to be late. I was unavoidably detained."

"It is nothing, my son," Don Diego said as he rose. "Let me introduce you to Captain Burke. Captain, this is my son, Rafael Chavez." Reeve extended his hand to Rafael, who took it in a firm grip.

"I am honored to meet you, Captain Burke. Welcome to our country and to our home."

"Thank you, Senor Chavez."

"Please join us, Rafael. We were discussing a trip to Madrid."

"Ah, Madrid. To court, Father?" Rafael asked expectantly. Reeve could see a quick leap of pleasure in the young man's eyes.

"To court," Don Diego replied with a glitter of humor in his eyes. "And into the presence of the lovely court of our Queen Isabella." The young man's smile grew even broader.

"Elana," he said softly, "it will be a great pleasure to be present at court again."

"Yes," his father said, laughing. "I imagine you will enjoy it as you always have."

Rafael chuckled in response. "Father, even your expert eye could not find a flaw in the lovely Elana," he said. "You must admit she is the most beautiful creature you have ever seen."

Diego smiled and looked at Reeve. "I must admit my son is right. You have a rare treat in store. The queen's court is quite an interesting place."

"You will enjoy it," Rafael said. "I will consider it an honor to introduce you to everyone of importance."

"Except Elana," his father said with a laugh. Rafael's eyes glittered with answering amusement at his father's jibe.

He shrugged expressively. "One could not blame me, Senor Burke, if I tried to keep the loveliest flower of the court to myself. I have tried, as have many others, but I'm afraid Elana's eyes are not for anyone, to my knowledge."

"Well, I'm afraid I won't have time to stay and try to convince her otherwise," Reeve replied.

"Don't worry, my friend, if anyone can change your mind and your plans it would be Elana," Rafael replied. He returned his gaze to his father. "When do we leave, Father?"

"In the morning."

"Then if you will excuse me, I shall go and make preparations for the trip." He rose, bowed elegantly toward Reeve, then his father. In a few minutes he was gone.

"Well, Senor Burke, may I show you to your room? You might need some rest, and if we are to start early in the morning, then you must get some sleep. We will leave early and have a long, hard trip before us."

"Yes. I do feel a little tired."

Don Diego rose and the two of them walked to the room that would be Reeve's for the night.

"This will be your room, Senor. I hope you are comfortable. If there is anything you need, do not hesitate to make your needs known."

"Thank you, Senor Chavez, I'm sure I'll be fine. Good night."

"Good night, sleep well, my friend." Reeve watched Diego walk away and was again struck by the aristocratic carriage and

41

the pride that seemed to be so much a part of him.

Reeve did sleep well, and was wakened just before dawn by a silent-footed servant.

"Senor Burke, Don Diego requests your presence at breakfast. He said he would be most pleased if you would join him."

"Thank you, tell him I will be there shortly."

"Yes, sir. I have taken the liberty to prepare your bath and lay out your clothes. If you wish anything else, you need only call."

"What are you called?" Reeve smiled as he sat on the edge of the bed.

"Juan, Senor," the man replied in response.

"I think that will be all I will need, Juan, thank you." Juan left as silently as he had come. Reeve rose and walked from his bedroom to the small room that adjoined it. There he found it warmed by a small fire and a tub of hot water. His clothes lay over a chair, next to the fire to grow warm while they waited for him to dress. He did so quickly, then joined Diego for a quick but hearty breakfast.

By the time the sun began to rim the horizon, they were on their way to Madrid and to a meeting with the mysterious person Reeve had no way of recognizing.

It was to be several days of traveling, and Reeve was impressed with the attitude of the people every time they stopped, either to eat or to rest the horses. It was obvious that both Diego Chavez and his son Rafael were well loved. Of course, Rafael seemed to have a magnetic charm for the dark-eyed senoritas who were drawn to him by the laughter in his eyes and the wicked gleam of his smile. If they were drawn by Rafael's dark charm, they seemed to be awed by the golden hair and silver, gray eyes of the tall man who stood beside him.

Don Diego may have found his bed early on the nights they stopped, but Rafael and Reeve found theirs much later and found them much fuller and quite a bit warmer.

Three days later, they rumbled down the rough streets of Madrid. It was nearly dusk and Reeve knew nothing, not even the name of the man whose house at which they would be guests. That was why he was unprepared for the huge mansion they approached. It had to be the most magnificent place Reeve had ever seen outside of Buckingham Palace.

The carriage door was opened by an elegantly liveried man. They stepped down from the carriage and walked up the three steps to the door which seemed to open like magic before them.

If the outside was magnificent, then the inside was more so. It was an elaborate beginning to what was to be a memorable stay. Reeve was profoundly impressed, as for the next three days he was treated as though he were visiting royalty.

His host, Don Ricardo Alverez, was the epitome of elegant, suave hospitality. By the time of the Grand Ball, Reeve found himself quite comfortable and unable to believe anything could be more elaborate or more pleasant than his stay in the Alverez's home.

There was a much larger group that traveled toward the palace. Don Diego, Don Ricardo, Rafael, Reeve, and Don Ricardo's wife and daughter.

Catrina Alverez was obviously enamored of Rafael, who, outside of being his usual well-mannered self, seemed unaware of her. She was extremely pretty, with large dark eyes and a shy smile. Reeve knew Rafael's thoughts were on the oh, so mysterious Elana. He found himself conjuring up pictures of a woman who could capture and hold the thoughts of a man like Rafael who, Reeve knew, had many women at the tips of his fingers.

The arrival at the Royal Palace was done with much pomp and ceremony. Reeve was sure that the men who had chosen to ask him to perform this task had felt sure he would be at home in these surroundings.

A series of small dinners and parties were held for the next three days. Reeve enjoyed himself but was waiting at any moment for someone to approach him. No one made any sign that they might want to speak to him in private.

He and Rafael shared a quiet dinner in the apartment given to Reeve. It was the night before the Grand Ball.

"I have seen no sign of the beautiful Elana you spoke of. Isn't she at court now?" Reeve questioned.

"She has been away with her brother for the last two days. I believe some relative or other has been ill. I'm quite sure she will be back for the ball. All the queen's ladies must be in attendance for social functions. Since her brother is enamored of Lady Beatriz, I'm sure nothing short of death will keep him away, and I guarantee you, my good friend, nothing short of my own personal demise will keep me from being as near Elana as I can."

"My God," Reeve said, "after some of the beauties I've seen you capture, I can't believe this one can be the paragon of beauty you claim her to be." Rafael was silent for a moment as if he himself could not quite believe it either.

"It's not that she's so beautiful," he said slowly. "It's some intangible magic she has. She is the only woman who has made me want to ravage her and protect her in the same heartbeat. She's like a piece of fragile porcelain, beautiful and delicate. She's like a rose just opening to the morning sun, and I would give my soul to be the one she would reach for when the time comes for her to choose the man she would spend the rest of her life with."

"Marriage," Reeve said with mock shock. "You and marriage seemed to me to be doing your best to avoid each other."

Rafael laughed. "Until now, my friend, until now."

"I can't wait to meet her."

"Umm, I imagine you can't," Rafael answered.

"I won't be stepping on any toes?" Reeve replied with a grin.

"How can you step on any toes? She doesn't seem to know any of the men who are panting after her are even about. Although I would like to, I have no claim. I only warn you that I will fight you like hell all the way," Raphael said, grinning in return. "And," he said, his eyes growing serious, "since you have no intention of staying here, and since you plan on leaving at a moment's notice, well, I wouldn't want Elana to be the victim of a flirtation that might leave her brokenhearted. That I couldn't stand."

"Quit worrying about me, Rafael. I agree, I don't have much time here, and I have to mind the business I was sent to do. I don't have time for a fling and I have no intention of being caught in anything serious. I haven't met the lady yet who has instilled any desire within me to give up my freedom."

Rafael sighed. "You haven't met Elana."

Reeve chuckled. "I'll leave the romance to you from now on. I wish you luck with the lovely Elana. Maybe I'll come back to dance at your wedding if you invite me." They laughed together and the conversation turned to other things.

The next day Reeve was aware of the aura of excitement that seemed to linger in the air. There was a lot of expectancy that even seemed to touch him. He could not shake the feeling that some rare and eventful thing was about to happen to him. He set the feeling aside by blaming it on the secret mission he was on. He felt sometime soon the hand of the unknown would reach out to touch him.

He took great care as he dressed for the ball. It was not every day, he thought, that one met a queen.

The deep blue doublet he wore set his gray eyes to advantage. He and Rafael and their host and family rode together in a dark carriage which bore the Alverez crest on both doors. Up the winding drive to the doors. The palace that blazed with light. The sound of music drifted through open

45

doors and windows accompanied by voices and laughter.

Inside their host guided them about after they were supplied with filled glasses. He stopped often to introduce them to people. After a while, the names blurred in Reeve's mind.

On a raised dais, several feet away from where Reeve stood, sat two high-backed gold chairs. Obviously, seats of honor for the king and queen.

There was suddenly a moment of complete silence, then a trumpet blare was followed by a deep strong voice that announced the royal pair. "His Majesty, King Ferdinand and Her Grace, Queen Isabella!" All heads turned to the door. Ladies dropped in deep curtseys and the men bowed deeply as the royal couple and their company swept in.

Reeve bowed as did the others, but as they passed him, he could not resist a glimpse. He raised his head and suddenly a shock vibrated through him, and he felt as if a huge hand had shut off his breath.

Reeve had seen many beautiful women in his thirty years, but he was completely unprepared for Elana as she walked past him, close enough for him to smell the delicate scent of her perfume. His eyes followed her, unaware of what the others about him might be thinking. He was even unaware of Rafael's light chuckle. The royal couple passed them.

"So?" Rafael said softly.

"Good God," Reeve breathed, "who was that?"

"Elana, of course."

"Remember last night, when you told me you would fight like hell for her?" Reeve asked.

"Yes."

"Prepare for battle," Reeve answered softly as he walked away from Rafael to see if he could find his host and somehow maneuver an introduction to the dark-haired beauty named Elana.

46

Chapter Four

The carriage rattled down deep-rutted roads. Elana sat within in contemplative silence with her brother Rodrigo beside her. Elana had taken the first opportunity to escape from the pursuit of Don Francisco by accompanying her brother to the sick bed of a very distant relative. Although Elana and her brother had seldom seen their Aunt Sophia, still they were her only relatives, so they had been summoned.

Sophia had always been a cold and angry woman; illness had not changed her. Elana had found her difficult and the short time she had spent with her, quite miserable, yet it had been more welcome than the advances of Don Francisco.

Elana had refused to allow herself to explain her reluctance to return to the castle to her brother Rodrigo. She, of all people, knew her brother's pride and his love for her. She was afraid Rodrigo would do something irrational and foolish. To attack Don Francisco in any way would not only bring down his wrath and his expert ability to rid himself of such aggravations, but Elana was convinced the dark shadow of the Inquisition stood behind Don Francisco like an evil specter. She knew it would reach out and touch her brother, and the fear of such a thing frightened her more than the thought of acquiescing to Don Francisco's wishes.

She sat now, gazing out the window, her thoughts seeking

ways she could keep herself from Don Francisco's presence. It would be quite difficult, because once she returned to the castle she would be forced to remain at the queen's side at every function. This made her accessible to Don Francisco whenever he chose.

Elana was unaware that her brother's gaze had been on her for quite some time. His brow furrowed in puzzlement as he read the emotions that flickered across her face. He watched the light touch of fear darken her eyes and saw her hands clasp and unclasp each other in her lap in nervous agitation at whatever she was thinking.

"Elana?" His voice broke the silence so firmly and abruptly that it startled her back to reality. She turned her face to him and tried to smile.

"Yes, Rodrigo?"

"What were you thinking just now?"

"Thinking?" she questioned to stall long enough to regain her thoughts.

"Whatever you were thinking just now must have been very upsetting. Is something wrong? Is there something I can help you with?"

"Oh, Rodrigo, there's nothing wrong, really, I'm fine. I can't even say what I was thinking about. It was so unimportant that it has absolutely slipped my mind."

Rodrigo was startled with the thought that for the first time in their lives Elana was lying to him. This was such an alien thing that for a moment he was speechless. Then he was struck by another thought. What could be so wrong that Elana would feel she had to lie to him?

"Aren't you happy being lady-in-waiting to the queen? You seem reluctant to return to the palace."

"The queen is magnificent, and I love her dearly. I am proud to be lady-in-waiting to her," Elana protested. "Really, Rodrigo, you are imagining things, I do believe." She laughed.

"Being so involved with your Beatriz has set you reading emotions not really present."

"I'm sorry." He smiled. "I just had the strange feeling that you were afraid of something."

"Well, I'm not," she said, smiling in return, "so let us not speak of it again. Rodrigo, are you planning to ask Beatriz to marry you?" Knowing it was an obvious ruse to change the subject of their conversation, Rodrigo complied, but he kept the thought in his mind that he would watch his beloved sister more closely. Elana had never lied to him. That she did now made him sure there was some dark motive and he intended to find out what it was.

"I hope and pray Their Majesties will grant us permission. I'm not sure. You know the de Mendosa family might not consider it a very good thing. The de Santangels are almost newcomers to the royalty in comparison."

"I don't care what they think. You and Beatriz would make the perfect couple. I'm sure the queen will understand. You do love her, don't you, Rodrigo?"

"You know I do. How often have you given us a few moments together?"

"It's so important, Rodrigo," she said softly, "to love and be loved. How dreadful it must be to be forced to live with someone you did not love." Again, Rodrigo was caught by the note of fear in her voice.

"Elana, has someone asked to marry you?"

"Not that I know of, why?"

"Have you met someone . . . someone you're not quite sure would be approved of?"

"No," Elana replied. She turned to look at him and a note of defiance filled her voice. "But if I did, Rodrigo, if I wanted to run away with someone I loved, would you stop me?"

"If he were the one you wanted, if I knew he would make you happy. No, I wouldn't stop you."

"Even . . . even if someone . . . anyone of the court were to condemn me as immoral, would you stop me?"

"You! Immoral. Elana, what a ridiculous thing to say. Who would ever accuse you of such a thing?"

"Immorality is often in the eye of the beholder. Things can often be made to seem the way they are not, and there are those who have the ability and the power to twist things to their own liking."

"I don't understand you, Elana. What are you talking about? Immorality, the use of power . . . what is wrong?"

"I'm sorry, Rodrigo, I seem to be in a mood today. Pay no attention to me. Things will be all right. I am just nervous . . . you know, getting back to all my duties. Of course, after Aunt Sophia, they should be a pleasure."

They laughed together, and Elana again turned the conversation from herself to other less dangerous subjects.

They arrived at the castle. Rodrigo went to see if he could find a moment he could share with Beatriz. Elana went to her room where she washed and changed her traveling clothes to more suitable garb in which to arrive in the presence of the queen. She opened the door of her apartment and looked down the long hall to the queen's door. It was empty. It was strange to Elana to be afraid to walk the halls of the castle for fear of meeting Don Francisco in one of the corridors.

She closed the door behind her and made her way as rapidly as she could to the queen's door. There she knocked lightly and in a few moments Louisa de Susan opened the door and admitted her.

"Elana," Louisa said, "I'm glad to see you are back. The queen has been asking about you."

"Is anything wrong?" Elana asked anxiously. "She is not angry with me?"

"No, Elana! For goodness sake don't be so alarmed. I don't think the queen has been angry with you since the day you arrived. You know she is very fond of you. She is choosing her jewels for the ball tonight and wanted to ask your opinion, that is all."

"Oh." Elana sighed.

"Come, let's go and join the others," Louisa said. They walked across the anteroom to another. They crossed this room and opened the door to the adjoining one. There they found Queen Isabella surrounded by most of her ladies. Elana's quick eye knew who was missing . . . Beatriz . . . she also knew why. Again, as she had many times before, Elana prayed silently that her brother and her dearest friend would be careful.

Elana went to where the queen stood and dropped to her knees before her.

"Elana," Isabella said in a pleased voice. "It is good to see you back. Did you leave your Aunt Sophia in good health?"

"Yes, Your Grace, she has fully recovered."

"Excellent. We were concerned not only about her but your welfare, as well. She had nothing that you were in danger of catching, did she?"

"No, Your Grace, I am quite well. I am flattered, Your Grace is concerned."

"You have pleased us quite well, Elana de Santangel, and you have been a lovely addition to the court."

"Thank you, Your Grace."

"You may rise," the queen said. Elana rose to her feet and the hustle that had filled the room at her coming resumed its laughing and chattering hum.

"Elana?" Isabella questioned.

"Yes, Your Grace?"

"You were not betrothed to anyone before you came to us?"

"No, Your Grace, why do you ask?"

"I think you were being discussed today."

"I, Your Grace?"

51

"The king and Don Francisco. They are also impressed with you. The king would like to see you marry well and stay with us. I'm sure Don Francisco agreed." Elana could feel the blood drain from her face and the thunder of terror course through her veins. Don Francisco was discussing her with the king! She suddenly felt like a moth caught in the web of an enormous spider. There was no possible way of escape.

"I . . . I had not thought of marriage for quite some time, Your Grace. I should prefer to stay with you for as long as I can."

Isabella had sat in a high-backed chair, and now Elana dropped to her knees beside the chair and took Isabella's hand in both of hers.

"Please, Your Grace," she pleaded, "don't ask me to marry now. Give me some more time to spend with you. I have never been happier in my life than I have been as part of your court. I would cling to it a while longer."

Isabella's astute gaze caught the fear in Elana's eyes and she felt a touch of sympathy. She knew Elana had no control over her life or whom she would marry. She also knew when Ferdinand and she chose, Elana would marry that choice.

"Elana, my dear," she said softly, and her eyes held a wisdom beyond Elana's, though she was only seven years older than Elana. "We have to perform our role in life. For women, there is nothing more than to marry well and to bear children."

"Yes, Your Grace, I know that. It's just—"

"Just that you are young, and you are a romantic. Do you believe in the old tales that into a woman's life will one day come that perfect man, the one that will make her happy just to be with him?"

"I suppose you are right. Is it wrong to want to love the man you marry?"

"For the poor, it is easy to choose the man you love. For the nobility," Isabella said with a shrug, "we must do what is expected of us. Your family has prospered because of your position. An advantageous marriage would make their position even better." Elana knew it was impossible and futile.

"Does . . . does His Majesty have someone in mind?"

"At this moment, no. What was discussed was just a thought. Do not worry, child. I'm sure the king will choose a nice handsome young man who will set your heart aflutter and make you desire to be married. Now, let us forget this. Come, help me choose the jewels to match my gown. I have always relied on your excellent taste."

Elana rose trembling to her feet. There was no escape, no way out of the sacrifice she would be called on to perform. Silently she prayed that some unforeseen hand would reach out and lift her from this life she faced.

The afternoon was spent helping the queen choose her jewels. Then Elana and the others were sent to prepare themselves so that when they were finished they would rejoin Louisa and the queen to put the finishing touches on her toilette.

Soft strains of music could faintly be heard in Elana's room as she stood in front of her mirror and examined herself. The gown of emerald green velvet she wore accented her matching green eyes and gave her an even more striking look of delicacy. The flow of the gown seemed to cling to her and denied nothing about the fact that she was utterly feminine.

Slowly, with resignation, she rejoined the queen and the other ladies. Within an hour the entourage was descending the huge staircase to greet the guests.

Elana had eyes for no one. Her mind was centered on one thought. She must get through this night, then she must speak to her brother. She had to work this distracting problem out in her mind. How to get her brother's help without involving him with Don Francisco. If worse came to worse, she vowed, she would go to a convent.

The king and queen took their seats and the ladies of the court gathered at the foot of the dais. It was only then that the crowd resumed its murmur of conversation and subtle movements. It was then that Elana turned and surveyed the crowd, and it was then that she saw him. He stood out from the crowd like a golden lion amid dark, tamed cats, and to her he looked just as dangerous. Yet, she could not seem to draw her eyes away from his as they touched and held for a breathless moment. She felt a fierce warmth surge through her, leaving her breathless and trembling.

She watched him leave Rafael Chavez's side and push his way effortlessly through the crowd. He stopped beside Don Ricardo Alverez and spoke to him. Don Ricardo looked in her direction and her heart began to beat furiously as they began to make their way toward her.

She could not seem to break the flowing current that seemed to join them. His amazing silver-gray eyes held hers. She could feel the flush touch her cheeks, and her hands, if she had not clasped them together, were shaking.

When they reached her side she gazed up at him and felt a sudden warmth reach and enfold her. Suddenly, she felt as if a protective shield had been placed between herself and all the others in the room. He smiled a broad smile, and she found herself smiling in return.

"Lady de Santangel," Don Ricardo said, "it is a pleasure to see you again. I have been told you were at the bedside of a relative who is ill. I'm sure your lovely presence brought sunshine and good health back rapidly."

"Thank you, Don Ricardo. It was my aunt who was ill, but she has recovered."

What a lovely creature she is, Reeve thought. Her voice was almost as soft as the velvet she wore. Rafael was right. She was like a delicate flower. He was right about another thing. He felt a definite protective urge, and another urge that had nothing to do with protection. He waited impatiently for an introduction, first to hear her speak again, and then to get her attention from Don Ricardo and directed toward him.

"May I introduce a friend from England, Elana? This is Captain Reeve Burke. He is a friend also of Rafael Chavez. I promised Reeve I would introduce him to the loveliest lady in the room. Reeve, this is Elana Margurita Inez de Santangel." Elana extended her hand to Reeve. He held it and slowly raised it to his lips to gently touch.

"I am most honored, Senorita de Santangel. I agree with Don Diego on all but one thing. You are not the loveliest lady in this room. You are the loveliest lady I have seen in this country since I arrived." Elana could feel the warmth in his eyes as they held hers. Neither could deny the tingling current that seemed to leap between them. Her hand trembled in his for a long moment before she withdrew it.

"Thank you, Captain Burke, you are most gallant. Welcome to our country. I hope you have enjoyed your stay thus far."

"It was pleasant until now. Now it has become most interesting." He watched in fascination as a dimple appeared at the corner of her smiling lips. He felt the pleasant sensation of expectation, as if at any moment some new facet of her would appear. What a fascinating woman, Reeve thought. He desired very much to have her smile again and wondered what the protocol of the Spanish court would be to be able to ask her to walk with him in the garden. He was about to take the chance and ask her and damn all protocol when Rafael's voice came from just behind him.

"Elana, how good it is to see you again."

Reeve watched her eyes sparkle in pleasure and at that moment he wished Rafael was anyplace else in the world.

"Rafael," Elana said, "welcome back to court. I have missed you."

"Had I thought that for a moment, Elana," Rafael said with

a laugh, "I would have returned much sooner." Both Elana and Rafael laughed in pleasant camaraderie and Reeve found the sound unpleasant. They were much too relaxed and easy with each other to suit him.

"Elana," Rafael said, "would you mind if I joined you and your brother again for an early morning ride? I have missed riding with you."

"You are most welcome, Rafael, as always." Rafael smiled smugly, his glowing eyes catching Reeve's for a moment of satisfaction. It was short-lived as Elana turned to Reeve. "Would you care to ride with us, Captain Burke? We would be pleased to show you a little of our country. You do ride, do you not?"

"Yes, I do, and I should enjoy nothing more. But I insist on one condition." Her eyes seemed a little startled.

"Condition?"

"Yes. You must cease calling me Captain Burke and begin calling me Reeve." Again the quick smile appeared and Reeve enjoyed it as much as he did Rafael's scowl. He was about to speak again when a young man came to Elana's side.

"Lady Elana?"

"Yes, Tomas."

"Your brother wishes to speak to you in private."

"Where is he?"

"He is waiting by the fountain in the garden."

"Thank you, Tomas." Elana smiled warmly and the young page flushed in pleasure as he bowed deeply. Both Reeve and Rafael bowed deeply as Elana excused herself and watched the enticing sway of her slim hips as she walked away from them. The stood in silence for a moment, then their eyes met and both smiled. Each knew they were in for quite a battle for the affections of the elusive and lovely Elana de Santangel.

It was several minutes later, and Reeve was slowly working his way about the room, making his name and presence known to whoever might want to talk to him. He found himself beside a tall handsome young man who looked vaguely familiar to Reeve. After a short conversation, Reeve was startled to hear his name.

"Rodrigo de Santangel?" he said in surprise.

"Yes," the man answered, "why are you so surprised? Do I know you from somewhere?"

"No, no," Reeve said quickly. "You are Elana de Santangel's brother?"

"Yes, why?"

"One of several, I suppose?" Reeve smiled.

"As far as I know," Rodrigo replied with a grin, "I am the only brother Elana has."

"Your sister is a very beautiful and fascinating young woman."

"So I've been told." Rodrigo chuckled. "I guess a brother looks a little differently at his younger sister. To me, she was always the little devil who plagued my growing years." They laughed together, and as soon as it was politely possible, Reeve excused himself and made his way rapidly toward the garden. If Elana's only brother was still in the ballroom, Reeve was curious as to the identity of the person who used her brother's name to lure her to a dark garden. If a ruse was necessary it must be someone with whom Elana did not choose to meet.

He made his way slowly down the dark garden path, listening intently for the sound of the fountain or voices. In a few minutes he was rewarded. The voice of Elana, though it trembled with shock and a touch of fear, was firm and angry.

"Please, Don Francisco, I must return to the ballroom. Her Majesty will be angry with me." The voice that replied was to Reeve cold, arrogant, and quite sure of itself.

"You needn't worry about the queen. She will not question if I say you were with me."

"Say . . . say I was with you! She will think—"

uld I deny that you fascinate me? You are a most
child. Many women would give anything to share
their ... me with me." There was a rustle of movement and a soft
cry followed by a muffled sob of distress. It was the last touch
that raised Reeve's anger. He stepped from the shadows of the
dark hedge and walked toward the two who were struggling
together near the fountain. Don Francisco had Elana bound to
him, and though she struggled, he casually took her mouth
with his in a ravaging kiss.

Reeve was only a foot or two away from them when he spoke.
Both of them turned at the sound of his voice, Don Francisco
with anger on his face, and Elana's touched with relief.

"Senorita de Santangel?" Reeve said.

"Yes," Elana replied quickly.

"Sir, what do you want?" Don Francisco snarled. "Why do
you disturb us? Who are you?"

"My name is Captain Reeve Burke," Reeve replied. "I'm
sorry if I came at an inopportune time, but Her Majesty is
asking for Senorita de Santangel, and since I saw her walk this
way, I thought I might tell her."

"I . . . I shall go right away," Elana replied, and Reeve could
hear the relief in her voice. She turned quickly and nearly ran
from Don Francisco. Both men watched her disappear, then
they turned to face each other.

"You interfere, sir," Don Francisco said softly. "Is it a habit
of yours to interfere in things that are not your concern? If so,
it could be a very dangerous habit. One that could cost you
much."

"I don't usually interfere . . . if both people are willing. It
seemed to me the lady was not. I did not think," Reeve replied
in a hard voice, "that a man of honor forced himself on a
woman who was not willing. In my country such a man is
looked upon as a disgrace to his position and his name. Is it

58

different in your country?" Don Francisco's face flushed, and he stiffened with anger.

"You needn't believe all you see. Elana makes a pretense. She has not always been so unwilling." Reeve's anger rose at the casual way Don Francisco blackened Elana's name and tried to make him believe Elana was receptive to a casual affair.

"I find, after all I've heard of the unblemished de Santangel name, that is very hard to believe."

"You call me a liar, sir?"

"No, only you know if what you say is a lie. I just said I found it hard to believe." That Don Francisco might be a dangerous enemy, or that he never forgot offenses, did not occur to Reeve. But his anger would not be controlled enough to back away.

"You are a fool, Captain Burke," Don Francisco said in a quiet voice. "You will regret interfering in my business. I would suggest, for your benefit, that you board your ship and leave Spain as soon as you possibly can. It might prove to be a dangerous place to spend much more time." With these words he brushed past Reeve, and the sound of the sharp click of his boots on the stone walk diminished as he walked away.

Reeve cursed himself for being an idiot. He had drawn attention to himself when he was supposed to remain inconspicuous. But he knew he would do it again, if just to see the relief in Elana's eyes.

Reeve sat on the edge of the stone fountain. He began to wonder if Don Francisco were not the reason the person he was to meet had not presented himself . . . . or herself. No matter, he had to stay put until he was approached. He knew from this moment on he had to watch his back. He felt that was where men like Don Francisco struck from.

A rustling sound drew his attention and he looked up. Elana stepped from the shadows of the hedge and walked slowly toward him. He rose as she came to his side. She was still shaken by what had just transpired. He could tell by the way she clasped her hands tightly together.

"Captain Burke," she began.

"I thought we had agreed on Reeve," he replied softly. He watched a hesitant smile touch her lips.

"Reeve, I . . . I want to thank you."

Chapter Five

There was a clear golden moon that rose high in the sky and lit the area in its glow. It touched Elana and Reeve felt he had never seen a vision quite so beautiful.

"You needn't thank me. It was what any other gentleman would have done."

"No, Reeve, not many would have crossed Don Francisco. Most would have heard us and quietly left. You should be warned."

"Of what?"

"You have made a very powerful enemy."

"And I have pleased a very gracious and beautiful lady." He smiled. "One more than balances the other. It was worth it to see you smile."

"How . . . how did you know?"

"That you had been tricked into coming here?"

"Yes."

"It was supposed to be your brother who sent for you."

"Yes, but—"

"But, I met your brother a few minutes later and he showed no sign of coming to meet you. I put two and two together. I felt it was someone you might not want to see, so I decided to come out and see if I could be so lucky as to rescue a beautiful lady in distress."

"I am grateful," Elana replied softly, "but I am afraid I have caused you more trouble than you know." Reeve stepped close enough that Elana had to look up into his startling silver-gray eyes. Eyes that held her spellbound and stirred a strange new emotion into life.

"I don't frighten easily, Elana," he said. He watched awareness fill her eyes. Awareness of an emotion he knew she had never known before. With a gentleness she could feel deep within, he reached to touch her cheek. He caressed its smooth texture, then let his hand touch the silken softness of her dark hair.

"Do you know how very beautiful you are?" he said in a soft whisper. Elana was mesmerized by the deep warmth in the silver-gray eyes. Held by a deep stirring of warmth within her that wanted her to move closer . . . move into the security of those strong arms. Her lips parted slightly and she trembled as if in a violent wind. His hand moved slowly to the nape of her neck where it caressed for a moment then drew her slowly to him.

Gently his mouth touched hers. A violent storm lifted them and carried them beyond the moment. Slowly his arm enclosed her and drew her against him. He had meant the kiss to be a light touch, a gentle moment. Now it was as much beyond his control as it was hers. Suddenly, with a gasp, she stepped back. Her eyes were startled, yet unafraid. It was as if she had discovered a rare and beautiful thing and didn't quite know how to handle it.

"I won't say I'm sorry," Reeve said softly. "I'm not. It was too sweet a pleasure to apologize for."

Elana was caught between two violent emotions. Torn between the pleasure she had felt and the fear that touched her now.

"Elana, come sit with me, talk to me. I swear I won't touch you again. I only want to know you better."

"I can't . . . I . . . what will be said?"

"By whom?"

"Everyone. The queen."

"What are we doing wrong? I only want to talk to you. Don't be afraid, Elana." Suddenly it seemed as if Elana regained complete control of herself. She inhaled deeply and stood very erect.

"I believe I was wrong, Captain Burke. It seems all men are something alike. It looks as if I have gone from the kettle to the fire."

"No, Elana, what you are thinking isn't so."

"Of course it's so," she said coldly. "I thank you for what you've done for me, and I'm sorry if it causes you any future difficulty, but I shall not see you again, Captain Burke." She turned to leave. "Good night, captain."

He watched her walk away and was surprised at the emotions he felt. Without doubt she had stirred him in a way no other woman had, and he wanted her more than he had ever wanted a woman before.

It was several minutes before he walked down the path to return to the ballroom. It was to return to a ball that had lost much of its glow. It was quite obvious to him that Elana made a special effort to keep her distance from him. It was also very obvious that Don Francisco's eyes were on him the balance of the evening. Eyes that were filled with a dark, cold glow.

It was very early the next morning when Reeve was wakened, and it was then he remembered that he was to go riding with Elana's party this morning. He wondered if Elana expected him to come, or, after the night before, expected him to hide as if he were guilty of something. He knew he wanted her, and he knew he was going to do everything he could to get her. What surprised him was that the only thought that connected itself to Elana, in heart and in mind, was wife and future. He dressed and went to find Rafael who was already dressed and waiting for him.

Elana had left Reeve in a state of confusion. What distressed her most was not only had she enjoyed the encounter, but the desire deepest within her was to return to the strong arms that had held her and made her feel so safe, and surrender to the warm lips that had sent her senses spinning. Grimly she was determined to put Reeve Burke from her mind, but the evening drew to a close and she found it impossible.

Although she deliberately avoided any further contact with him, she could still feel his eyes upon her and she could still feel his touch, the masculine scent, and the taste of his lips on hers.

Although Beatriz was aware of her silence and knew something was weighing on her mind, she had no time to talk to Elana alone.

Curled in the warmth of her bed, Elana lay unable to sleep and resisted the silver gray eyes that haunted her. It was worse when she closed her eyes because then her senses took over and unfamiliar sensations filled her with unrest.

It was several hours before she slept and only after she had firmly gripped her thoughts, brought them under control, and vowed to herself she would not see Reeve Burke again. She had forgotten completely her invitation for him to ride with her in the morning.

Dawn found Elana already awake. She had risen while the sky was still dark and the last flickering star was just disappearing. She dressed and made her way down to the kitchen to see if she could find something to nibble on before Beatriz and Rodrigo were to join her.

She chatted aimlessly with surprised cooks who were not

used to royalty in their kitchens before dawn. After she ate a little and dawn had begun to touch the sky, she walked from the kitchen toward the stables. She heard someone approaching her from behind. Turning quickly she saw Rodrigo running to catch up with her. He stopped by her side, breathing deeply to regain his breath.

"Good morning," he said with a grin.

"I thought for a minute you might not come." She smiled in return, her eyes sparkling mischievously.

He chuckled. "You know well, dear sister, I won't be late. How could I stay abed when this will probably be the only chance I can see Beatriz alone for the rest of the day?"

"I wish it were any other way. Oh Rodrigo, why can't people just marry whom they choose?"

"Neither of us has a choice, Elana," Rodrigo replied grimly. "I wish it weren't so, too. Maybe the fates will allow Beatriz and me to marry."

"And if they don't?" she replied softly.

"I won't let her go, Elana," he said in a tense, quiet voice. "You don't understand yet, Elana, maybe you will one day. But when you meet someone who makes everything in your world glow, whose touch makes every sense you own come alive . . . just being with her a little while makes the whole day worth living. She makes me feel," he said with a shrug, "as if I'm the most important thing in her life. I love her, Elana," he added softly. Elana listened with her mind, but her senses reached for Reeve and the wild tumultuous emotions he had roused in her the night before. It was the first words that she had ever heard to describe what she had felt.

As if thoughts of him had conjured him up, Reeve seemed to suddenly appear. Accompanied by Rafael, he walked toward them with a purposeful stride. Elana suddenly felt frightened, as if she were caught in a maelstrom from which she could not escape. Warmth crept through her veins and touched her cheeks with rose. She found it suddenly difficult to breathe.

They stopped beside her. Reeve was silent as Rafael lifted Elana's hand to his lips to kiss it gently, yet Elana could feel Reeve's eyes on her intently.

"Elana," Rafael said, "you are even more beautiful today than yesterday."

"Thank you, Rafael." She had no idea why Rafael's flowery words annoyed her. She wanted Reeve to smile at her, to speak to her, yet she knew she had told him the night before she did not want to speak to him again.

She lifted her eyes to silver-gray ones that were immediately warm and seeking. Her pulse raced as his smile grew warm, and his gaze reached for her almost physically as his arms desired to do.

"How many will be in our party?" Reeve asked.

"We're waiting for Beatriz and then we'll go," she replied.

Before Reeve could speak again, a voice called to them and they turned to see Beatriz running across the lawn toward them. After she joined them, they made their way toward the stables. Before they could reach them, another voice called to them. They looked for the source of the call and saw Catrina Alverez coming to join them. The group was bright and cheerful as they mounted their horses and rode toward the rising sun. Elana and her brother had been taught to ride almost before they could walk. Reeve had to admire the way Elana seemed to have control over both the horse she rode and herself.

Elana knew that Rodrigo and Beatriz were looking for any opportunity to separate themselves from the group, but she had no idea how she was going to supply that opportunity.

They came to a narrow path that gave them room to ride two abreast. Rodrigo and Beatriz were first through followed by Elana and Reeve with Rafael and Catrina behind them.

They were coming to a sharp curve in the trail when the idea occurred to her. As Rodrigo and Beatriz turned the curve and were just out of sight, Elana drew her horse up so sharply that it reared, pawing the air with its forefeet. Still she had control of it and deliberately took several minutes to calm the horse, knowing that Rodrigo would know what she had done and take advantage of it.

The four of them held their horses immobile, waiting to see if Elana was all right. The sparkle of amusement in Reeve's eyes was missed by her as she assured them she was fine.

They moved their horses slowly around the curve to see Rodrigo and Beatriz far ahead just entering a wooded area. Elana smiled in satisfaction, a look that Reeve read accurately.

Well, my lady, he thought, what is sauce for the goose is sauce for the gander. He grinned as a devilish thought took form in his mind. Deliberately, Reeve let his horse fall back and Rafael took the advantage to ride beside Elana. Engrossed in conversation, neither of them saw Reeve bend close and whisper in Catrina's ear, nor did they see the smile of agreement on Catrina's face.

Trained in gallantry, Reeve knew just how Rafael would react to the situation he was about to produce.

Catrina's horse reared and she screamed, then the horse leapt from the path and dashed wildly toward the woods.

"Runaway!" Reeve shouted. Without thinking, Rafael wheeled his horse and dashed after Catrina. Elana watched in fear as they entered the woods. Reeve rode up beside her.

"Oh, I hope Catrina is all right."

"She'll be fine," Reeve said with a laugh, "as soon as she's led Rafael far enough to make it safe to catch her." Elana turned in surprise to Reeve and could not miss the laughter in his eyes.

"You planned this," she exclaimed.

"I just followed your example," he said innocently.

"My example! I don't know what you mean."

67

"Now, Elana, don't tell me you didn't plan your little game to let your brother and Beatriz have a little time alone."

"I . . . I never . . ." She stopped when she saw the laughter return. Then she could not help but smile, too. "Was it so obvious?"

"Only to me."

"I suppose it is best we wait here."

"Why? Let's continue our ride. We certainly can't go back without them. I told Catrina we would meet them here in an hour. I'll bet that's just what you told your brother."

Elana nodded and they rode along slowly. Eventually, as Reeve had planned, the path entered the border of the forest. When they rode into a sun-touched glade, Reeve drew his horse to a stop. Once he stopped, Elana stopped and turned to look at him.

"Elana, I want to talk to you. Can't we walk for a moment?"

"Maybe," she said softly, "I'm afraid."

"Of me?" he said in surprise.

"You don't think you're dangerous, Reeve?"

"Not to you, Elana. I would do nothing to hurt you. You need never be afraid of me . . . never." They sat for a moment in complete and utter silence, then Elana nodded. Reeve dismounted and went to help Elana. He reached up to grip her slim waist with his hands. She braced both her hands on his shoulders and gently he lifted her down, letting her slide slowly to the ground. They stood for a moment in this gentle, touching embrace.

Elana knew what she was feeling was a forbidden thing. One day she would have to marry another, yet she did not want to break the warm, magical spell Reeve held over her.

With effort, she turned from him and walked a little away while he tied the horses. He came up behind her and though he did not touch her, she felt him with every sense she had. She was amazed at her own self that she suddenly felt so alive.

"Elana," Reeve said softly, "look at me." Slowly Elana turned. Reeve was so much taller than she that she had to tip up her head to look at him. Their eyes met in a moment of truth neither of them could deny. For Elana, it was a sense of coming home to a place she had always been searching for.

"Why do you try to run and hide from the truth, Elana?" Reeve said in a voice that was a gentle caress.

"It is an impossible truth," she replied.

"Why impossible?" he said. "Is it impossible for Lady de Santangel to love a common sea captain?"

"Reeve, you know that isn't so." Distress filled her voice and tears touched her eyes. She turned from him and walked a few steps away. "It does not matter what I want or what I feel. My future is already planned and I have nothing to say about it."

Reeve went to her, took her shoulders and turned her to face him. The tears on her cheeks made him angry at the forces that had caused them. "It matters to me, Elana. I need to know what you feel, and I need to tell you what I feel."

"Don't, Reeve, please. This is too difficult to bear. Don't you know I have no choices to make?"

"Then just tell me," he said gently, "if you could choose, what would you do? Where would your heart lead you?" Tears fell helplessly down her cheeks and her eyes were filled with anguish.

"Tell me," he insisted as he reached to grip her shoulders and draw her close to him.

"To you," she whispered, "to you."

"Elana," he said softly as he bent his head to touch her lips with his. Salty tears mingled with sweetness to rouse his passion as it never had been before. Reeve had always felt he

69

had complete control over his emotions . . . until now. Now there was no reality but Elana and the sweet magic of love for her that lifted him beyond reason. He bound her to him, molding her slim body to his, savoring the warm, soft curves.

Elana was lost to the emotions that she felt. A flood of warmth from the center of her being reached to enclose Reeve and hold him even if it were only for one stolen moment. It, at least, would be a vibrant memory to cherish.

Her slender arms came up about his neck and she pressed herself closer to the source of all consuming warmth. Her lips parted under his searching ones and for that one precious moment she surrendered completely to the need that filled her and left her shaking and weak.

Reluctantly, Reeve released her lips, but he held her close to him while his eyes sought to read in hers the truth in the fiery response of the kiss. He smiled, a warm pleasure filling him, for it was there for him to easily read.

"We can't deny it, Elana, neither of us. There's no way we can ignore what we feel. Say it, Elana, for I can read it in your eyes. Say it . . . I want to hear you say it."

"That I want you?" she replied with a sob. "That I never felt anything like this, and probably never will again? That I would give my life to say I love you and belong to you from this moment? Yes! Yes, I would, but I can't! I can't, Reeve!"

"Why? In God's name why? I know you felt what I felt. We could have something very rare and very wonderful. Don't let it slip away, Elana."

"Why do you refuse to understand?" she cried.

He gripped her shoulders and shook her. "I understand that you are someone I can't turn and walk away from. I understand that what I feel for you is as new to me as it is to you, and I understand it's too precious to let it slip away."

Elana wept miserably at his anger, and bent her head to rest against his chest. His arms came about her and he rocked her gently against him regretting his anger, knowing it wasn't really anger at her but fear. Fear that he had found this rare thing only to have it slip from his life.

"I'm sorry, Elana," he said gently. "I didn't mean to shout at you." He held one arm about her and with his other hand he tipped her chin up. Gently he touched her lips with his. Slowly he warmed them, tasting gently the sweetness. He heard the soft moan as her lips softened and became pliant under his. She could not fight a losing battle . . . and she was losing.

He knew this was not the place to bring the warm beginning kisses to the conclusion he desired, and the ground was no place to take the woman you loved. Yes, loved, he thought. With Elana it must be perfect and it must be right. He knew that he had to persuade Elana that when the time came, she would leave with him. He began his campaign of persuasion now.

Very reluctantly he released her, then he took her hand and led her to a fallen log that made an excellent seat. There he sat down and drew her down beside him.

"Tell me about you, Elana," he said. "Tell me all I need to know. Then when you've given me all the reasons you have against us, I will set about destroying them. When I've gotten them out of the way, we can get down to the only reality that exists . . . I love you . . . and I think you are beginning to love me. That is the only real thing of importance."

"I . . . I must make you understand, Reeve," she began softly, "it is important to me that you know why I shall never be able to be with you; why I must . . . marry another."

"No, Elana," he said firmly. "That will never happen."

"But—"

"No buts, that will never happen." He smiled to break the harsh words.

"If it were me, if it were only me, I would go today, this

71

minute, but I have others to consider. There are many things that are beyond my control, and beyond yours."

Reeve bent toward her and took both her hands in his. "I have a ship, Elana, the *Golden Eagle*. She's beautiful. She'll take us anywhere you want to go. I'll take you to places you've never seen before. I'll show you all the beauty this world has to offer. Elana, we can leave everything and everyone behind. We can live a life together and be happy. I'll make you happy."

"Leave everything and everyone behind," she repeated softly. "If it were only that easy. The one thing in this world I cannot do is to seek my own happiness when others will pay the price for it."

"Others? What others have a claim on you?"

"I didn't say they had a claim on me. There are forces alive in this country now—wicked forces that have a power—a power to make lives bend to their will. They use people like children use toys, and they destroy lives like a dark plague. Queen Isabella and King Ferdinand will be the ones to say who and when I will marry. If I refuse, the arm of that dark power will swoop down and destroy, if not me, then my parents, my brother, my friends."

Reeve's deepest desire at the moment was to tell her he knew the dark specter of the Inquisition, that he was here to rob that specter of two victims he did not even know yet. He had to have time . . . time to find out the names of the mysterious people he was to save, and time again to do something to protect the people that Elana loved. When he did, he would come and take Elana away. He resigned himself to the one inevitable fact: He had to wait.

"All right, Elana." He raised her hands to his lips and kissed them gently. "I won't pressure you now, but I will tell you this. You are mine, and when I find a way, you will belong to me. This I vow. You will never belong to any other man for I will

72

never let you go."

"I have this," she replied gently. "If I never have anything more, I have this. To know I am loved, and that I love."

"Elana," he whispered. His eyes glowed with a fierce flame. The words he wanted to hear had finally come. Before he could speak again, a voice called to them. They turned to see Beatriz and Rodrigo riding toward them.

If Rodrigo noticed the glow of Reeve's eyes or the heightened color in his sister's cheeks, he wisely kept silent. He, too, knew the despair of wanting something one could not have. He liked Reeve, but he of all people knew Elana's situation. There was no way the lovers would be able to share their lives together.

"We finally found you," Rodrigo said. "Has either of you seen Catrina and Rafael?"

"No," Reeve replied. Quickly he explained how Catrina's horse had bolted and Rafael had gone to her aid.

"I'm sure they are both all right," Elana replied. "Rafael is an excellent rider. Shall we go and see if they are waiting for us?"

Reeve brought Elana her horse. With gentle hands he lifted her to the saddle and for one brief moment their eyes held. It spoke a million silent words, and Rodrigo heard them, for they reflected his thoughts. It took Reeve only a few moments to retrieve his horse and mount. They rode back to the predesignated meeting place in silence, each caught up in their own thoughts.

Reeve was impatient to find out who his mysterious refugee would be and Elana was resigned to a fate she did not want to think about. Both Rodrigo and Beatriz realized something had happened between these two, but neither felt this the proper time to ask questions.

They arrived at the meeting place but found no sign of

Catrina or Rafael.

"We had best wait for them," Elana said. "If we ride back alone, there will be serious repercussions later."

They waited, discussing everything but what they would really have liked to discuss.

It was over an hour before Rafael and Catrina were seen at the edge of the forest riding their way.

Chapter Six

Catrina's horse had leapt forward under the sharp jab of her spur. Rafael, taken completely unprepared, and spurred into motion by Reeve's shout, gave no thought to question either why Reeve had not gone to Catrina's defense, or why he did not follow him to the rescue. Nothing was on his mind at the moment but to keep Catrina from being seriously injured, maybe killed.

Catrina smiled as they entered the edge of the woods. This was as far as she had intended to go before she let Rafael catch her. The smile turned to shock and then to fear as she tried to rein her horse in and she realized he had gotten beyond her control.

She uttered a sharp scream as he lifted effortlessly over a fallen log and entered the dark shadows of the forest. She could hear the thudding hoofs of a horse that followed. She knew it was Rafael and prayed he would catch up with her quickly. Low hanging branches very nearly unseated her and succeeded in ripping her hat from her head and loosening the coil of her hair to let it flow behind her. Desperately, she gripped the horse's mane. He had the bit between his teeth, and Catrina knew she did not have the strength to stop him.

They thundered through a darkened wooded area, Rafael slowly closing the distance between them. Tears of genuine fear filled Catrina's eyes and blurred her vision. All she could seem to see was a whir of green as she thundered by. Then terror replaced the fear and she felt her strength wane. She began to lose her grip. Again, the horse made a leap over a rotted log, and it was enough to unseat her. With a scream she felt her grip loosen. She tumbled to the ground and darkness met her.

Rafael drew his horse to a skidding halt, leapt from his back, and ran to Catrina's side. He knelt beside her. Fear turning his heart cold, he reached with tender hands to turn her over. Her dark lashes lay against tear-stained cheeks. Her face was pale and her dark hair lay in wild profusion about her.

Rafael laid his ear against her breasts to seek some sign of life. To his relief he was rewarded by a steady throbbing beat. He took off his jacket, folded it, lifted her head to rest it on the jacket, and cradled her neck gently to make sure it was not broken.

Not too far from them was a small trickling stream. Rafael ran to it and, taking his handkerchief from his pocket, he knelt to moisten it. Returning to Catrina, he again knelt beside her and laid the folded wet handkerchief across her brow. Still she did not waken. Rafael sat close to her and took one of her hands in his.

"Catrina . . . Catrina," he said softly. He rubbed her hand gently and repeated her name again. After a few minutes, her eyes fluttered slightly and she moaned softly. Then her eyes opened completely to see a very relieved Rafael smiling down at her. She tried to stir, but Rafael laid his hand against her shoulder.

"Don't move, lie still. Let your body have a chance to recover. You've just had a very nasty fall." Catrina ceased to move for two reasons: One, she seemed to hurt over every inch of her body, and two, Rafael was still holding her hand and she wanted him to continue to do so.

Ebony dark eyes looked up at Rafael who was startled by a sudden realization. He had known Catrina all his life, and this was the first time he had ever really looked at her . . . and the first time he realized how beautiful she was.

Catrina was delicately formed, rather small in build and very slim. Her skin was a clear, smooth texture and the color of coffee with heavy cream. Her hair, black as a moonless night was thick and lustrous, and her eyes were large dark ebony pools.

They had been playmates for as long as either of them could remember. Rafael had been so close in their growing years that he had not seen Catrina as a woman. He looked for the first time and was completely shaken by what he saw.

"Catrina, you have ridden since we were children. What happened? I have never seen you lose control of a horse before."

Catrina had been reared with strict discipline and had the Spanish innate regard for honor. It was difficult for her to tell a direct lie. She closed her eyes and hot tears slipped from beneath them. Her pain was caused by the knowledge that she had to tell Rafael the truth, but Rafael misread it and thought it was physical pain she felt.

"Catrina!" he said in alarm. "Are you in pain? Are you hurt?"

"No," she said, "I am not hurt. I am not in pain."

"Then why do you weep?"

Catrina struggled to sit up. They sat close, their shoulders brushing each other. Still thinking that she was shaken and hurt, Rafael put his arm about her. "Catrina?"

"Oh, Rafael, you will hate me when I tell you the truth."

"Hate you?" He laughed. "Come, Catrina, I know you too well. It would be impossible for you to do something to make me hate you."

Her eyes turned to his. "Even if I deliberately deceive you?"

"I truly don't understand what you are talking about, Catrina, and I've never known you to practice deception in your life. Now, why don't you tell me just how you think you have deceived me."

"Rafael, I . . . I wanted to be alone with you. I pretended to lose control of my horse so you would follow. I meant to stop sooner, but then I really lost control. I'm sorry. I guess deceit is always met by disaster. Now I'll understand if you think I'm a stupid silly child reaching for something I know I cannot have." Fresh tears touched her eyes and spilled down her cheeks, and she clasped her hands together in her lap.

Rafael was, probably for the first time in his life, taken completely by surprise. This lovely and seemingly helpless beauty was telling him she cared for him and had given in to deceit to be alone with him. He was stirred so deeply that for a moment he was speechless. He was also spellbound by dark innocent eyes into which he had never looked before.

The silence was broken only by the soft call of birds as their eyes held for those few breathless moments. Pale beams of sunlight filtered down through green leaves of the trees, casting a pale glow over the small glade in which they sat.

Catrina had taken Rafael's stunned silence for the anger and disgust she thought he was feeling. She buried her face in her hands and tried to control her humiliation.

Rafael reached out and gently drew her hands from her face. Her dark eyes again lifted to him.

"Catrina," he said gently, "how can a man possibly be angry when a beautiful woman finds him attractive? I consider it a great compliment from one as lovely as you. Besides," he said with a chuckle, "how could I call you stupid when you have paid me such a marvelous compliment?" His eyes grew intent as he studied her closely. "You are very far from a child," he added softly.

A new awareness touched them both. To her, as he had

always been, Rafael was the dream that had always filled her life. To him, she was a lovely creature, gentle and vulnerable. Her lips parted slightly as her cheeks grew pink under his warm, seeking gaze. He reached out with gentle hands and brushed the tears from her cheeks only to let his fingers linger to caress the smooth texture of her skin. Slowly, he let his fingers trace the line of her jaw to the slim column of her throat. He let his hand roam to the nape of her neck where he buried it in the thick mass of her silken hair. Slowly, he drew her toward him and then gently bent his head to touch the moist, sweet texture of her parted lips.

Of the two, Rafael was more startled by the result than she. Catrina had always been aware of him and her love for him. Rafael's senses were suddenly and overwhelmingly stormed by the new and vibrant emotion that suddenly filled him. Forgotten were his thoughts of any other woman. Suddenly and miraculously Catrina seemed to fill a place within him that had been empty all his life. Just as suddenly he felt a feeling of wholeness and completeness swell within him.

They looked at each other in absolute wonder for a breathless moment. He was still shaken from the suddenness of the emotion that filled him.

"Catrina," he whispered, "all this time, all these years, I never—"

"Never knew I existed," she finished for him. "I know, Rafael. It has broken my heart many times to see you smile at other women and know you thought of me like a young sister. You will never know how many dreams you have shattered."

"God, what I almost missed," he said. "Why didn't you tell me?"

Catrina laughed softly. "What would you have thought if I had thrown myself at you as so many others have done? I saw the result of such things. You had a habit of turning your back on them. But I prayed every night and every day just to have you see me."

"You prayed for me, Catrina?" he asked in wonder.

"Yes, Rafael," she whispered, "always I prayed for you."

Rafael reached for her. Putting his arms about her slender waist he drew her against him. He felt her arms creep up about his neck. His heart throbbed rapidly as he held her against him and possessed her willing lips with a passion that tilted her world and sent it spinning beyond any control she might have had. The one thing in the world she had always wanted was here in her arms, and no matter what, she would hold him for as long as she could.

Her lips parted under his questing ones and he immersed himself completely in the warm sweetness that flooded his being with desire. Catrina was aware of nothing else but the lean, hard body that sent trembling fingers of molten flame through her.

Slowly, they moved to the soft grass and lay clinging to each other, sharing a new and blinding need.

She closed her eyes as she felt his hard mouth trace a line of light kisses down the column of her throat to the valley between her breasts. She made a soft sound of pleasure and twined her hands in his thick, dark hair to press him even closer.

Seeking hands caressed a rounded breast beneath the constricting material that kept his touch from the softness of her flesh. His hand continued down the curve of her waist to a slender hip. A bent leg had let her petticoat rise above her knees, and she gasped in surprise as his hand found the soft warmth of a smooth thigh.

He raised his head and looked into the depth of her dark eyes. His eyes questioned her need and hers answered with the depth of love and need she felt for him. Complete surrender, complete fulfillment were the only emotions that possessed them both. His heart leapt with the pleasure of knowing she wanted him as much as he wanted her.

With gentle hands, eyes holding hers to search for any resistance, he loosened the buttons on her blouse and slid his hands beneath to caress the smooth skin. He slid the constricting blouse away and gazed in wonder at the rare beauty before him. Her skin had a fine translucent glow and her breasts were small and taut. She shivered in pleasure as he reached a tentative hand to caress lightly. He drew her close to him and bent to let his lips gently caress a soft rounded shoulder and drift in warm light kisses across the rise of her breasts, feeling her tremble under his touch.

Catrina's eyes closed and she let her senses absorb the gentleness of his touch, let him rouse her passion until she knew no other desire but to surrender to the flame that licked to life in the depth of her being.

The cool grass beneath her cradled her as Rafael bent above her to again claim her mouth with his in a kiss that blended them both into the one entity they would remain for always.

But Rafael's passion was to be temporarily thwarted by the multitude of voluminous petticoats that formed the skirt of the riding habit she wore. His hands sought the smooth texture of her slim legs, only to find the confining petticoats between himself and his goal. He was sure this was to be the end of what had promised to be a bright beginning. It was Catrina's trembling fingers that reached to undo them and push them away.

He knew she was frightened, yet he knew the fire within him was matched in her. He fell into the depths of her eyes and heard the soft murmur of his name as he drew her cool body close and bound her to him.

Restraint was something Rafael had learned to practice long ago, and he used it now, though every sense he had begged him to possess her immediately. With every ounce of expertise he possessed, he sought to rouse and please Catrina and was

81

rewarded by the flame that leapt to consume them both.

As quickly as possible, and with practiced ease, he left her side for only a moment to remove the clothes he wore. Catrina's eyes widened at the magnificent man that knelt beside her. His body was bronzed and muscular. He was slim, yet his taut muscles spoke of control.

He was beside her now, drawing her cool, slim body close to him. His seeking hands caressed her, finding a soft, taut breast and eliciting a soft moan of pleasure as he followed his hands with a path of burning kisses that trailed across her skin to find the hardened peaks of passion.

She stirred in his arms, her body lifting to seek his, to find the release for this need that possessed her. She cried out to him, wanting, but not knowing what or why.

They were lost to any other touch, any other taste, any other emotion, but the violent, flowing need. Rafael did not want this miraculous, wonderful moment to be shattered. He knew he was going to hurt her, just as he knew the moment of pain would pass. He caught her mouth with his as he pressed himself deeply within her.

He heard her muffled cry, felt her body tremble and stiffen in his arms. He did not move until the moment had passed and her body adjusted to his intrusion, then slowly he again began to lift her senses and renew the pleasure.

She was alive and vibrant in his arms, responding to the heat of his desire with a wild and abandoned passion that made his senses soar until they were lost in the magic of a passion-kissed dream.

He possessed her completely and filled her with a flame that consumed every thought and every move until her world consisted of nothing but Rafael and the glow of love that filled her.

They soared like two winged flames, searching for the peak of pleasure, and they found it to stand trembling on the edge, then to tumble together into the crashing waves of the sea of completion that washed over them and left them shaking and clinging to one another.

He held her close to him, gently caressing her silken hair and slim, trembling body until they had regained control over their breathing. He lifted his head to look down into limpid eyes filled with love for him. Gently, he brushed the sweat and wayward strands of hair from her brow. Then he touched the tears that lingered on her cheeks. With infinite tenderness, he touched her cheeks and lips with feather-light kisses.

"Catrina," he whispered. "Catrina, my love."

"Rafael," she sighed, "I love you so."

"Such a truth I would never have seen, never tasted. Oh, Catrina, how could I have been such a fool? I almost let you slip out of my life without ever knowing this beautiful thing we share."

"You have been my dream always. I have never wanted anything more in this life than to belong to you. If I never have anything more, I shall still be happy. You need not feel obliged to me, Rafael. I would not force you to remain with me. I am happy now. If you choose to go—"

"Go!" he said in alarm. "Catrina, are you telling me you would not want to marry me? After this, can you send me away?"

"Marry. I . . . I thought you—"

"What?"

Her head dipped so he could not read her eyes. With gentle fingers, he lifted her chin to search her eyes with his.

"What?" he repeated gently.

"I thought you wanted someone else," she replied.

For a moment Rafael gazed at her in silence. All thought of any other woman had completely fled his mind and his heart with the touch of Catrina. Now his mind floundered in the search of what she was talking about. All other women had been the joy of a chase or conquest for Rafael.

"Love . . . who?" he asked in wonder.

"Elana?" she questioned with a note of fear in her voice.

Now, he was brought to startling awareness that he had made it obvious to everyone that Elana had interested him. He had very nearly flaunted it in Catrina's face, not realizing the hurt he was causing her. He held her close to him for a moment, searching for words to make her understand.

"Catrina, look at me," he said firmly. She raised her eyes to his and he knew she was willing to believe whatever he said. "I will admit that many beautiful women have attracted me and Elana is very beautiful. But, I am no fool. I know something very true and valuable when I have found it. In you I have found that very wonderful and special thing that makes two people one. I am not going to let it slip away from me. I am not going to let you slip away from me. If you are willing . . . if you will come to me and marry me, I will try to make you happy." He smiled. "I will not swear I will never look at another woman, but it will always be to compare them to you, and," he added in a soft whisper, "I am sure I will always find them wanting in your sweetness and gentle giving love. Oh, Catrina, say you won't leave me now. It would darken my world and make it unbearable."

The tremulous smile that touched her lips and the shining light of love in her eyes told him her answer before she spoke.

"Rafael," she said. The words, "I love you," were drowned in his searching lips. They surrendered themselves to the new and intense emotion that filled them both. It was new, yet as old as the world itself, and it consumed them both.

This time was different. It was no longer a tentative reaching but a cry to each other for the fulfillment they now knew existed only in each other. Sometime later when realization of the intrusion of the rest of the world was accepted by both, they rose from their soft bed of ecstasy. With lingering hands, soft muffled laughter and innumerable kisses they helped each other dress. Neither wished to return to the world but both knew it was inevitable.

"You will have to ride double with me," Rafael said. "I am sure your horse is home by now."

"What shall we say?"

"That you had a nasty fall," Rafael replied, his eyes sparkling with laughter, "and I had to stay with you until you were able to ride again."

Rafael went to retrieve his horse that was grazing nearby. He mounted and rode to Catrina's side. She lifted her arms to him and effortlessly he lifted her before him. She nestled against him and both would have been content had the ride taken a lot longer than it did. Rafael walked his horse slowly through the forest. With his arm holding Catrina close to him, he savored her slim body cradled against him.

Much too soon for them both, the edge of the woods was reached. For a moment, they stopped at the edge of the trees. In the distance they could see the four others who had waited for them. With a reassuring squeeze of her slim waist, Rafael reluctantly urged his horse forward and rode toward them.

Chapter Seven

No one else seemed to notice, in their concern for Catrina, but Reeve's astute gaze did not miss the arm that encircled her waist and the way it lingered there, the warmth in Catrina's eyes as she looked up at Rafael. Some instinctive thing within told him, to his pleasure, that there was much more between Catrina and Rafael than a simple rescue. He was glad and hoped what he thought was true. If so, it would remove one small obstacle from his path to Elana.

They rode back to the stables and left their horses. Rafael retained his gentle solicitous attention to Catrina by insisting he keep his arm about her waist to help in case she had been hurt more than she had thought.

Once home, they urged Catrina to her room for a hot bath and some relaxing sleep so she would be in good shape for the evening meal which the queen insisted all her court and guests should attend.

Reeve went to his room feeling the idea of a hot bath and something quick to eat was not a bad idea. On his way to his room, he was stopped occasionally by people who spoke a few words or asked about his welfare. It took him some time, but he finally reached his room. He opened his door, stepped inside, and closed it behind him. Immediately a sixth sense told him someone was either still in one of the two rooms he had, or someone had been here recently.

Without moving anything but his hand that he rested on the hilt of the knife he wore in his belt, Reeve scanned the room. Nothing seemed disturbed, but he knew better. The huge doors that opened to a huge balcony stood open, one thing he did not remember doing. When he had left in the morning he thought he had checked them carefully to make sure they were closed. Now the breeze fluttered the curtain.

Slowly and silently he moved across the room and stood by the window. His view of the back lawn of the palace and part of the garden told him no one lingered about outside. He turned to the adjoining bedroom and walked quickly to the door and pushed it open. Again, the prickling sensation at the nape of his neck told him someone had been here.

Again, he quickly scanned the room, then he stepped inside. Although he saw no sign of anyone he felt something, and Reeve was one to trust his instincts. He moved about, checking his things, and discovered someone had been searching his personal belongings. He knew he must have interrupted the intruder, for the signs told him some things had been disturbed and some had not. Whoever it was had heard his footsteps in the hallway and had escaped quickly through the open windows. It was only then that Reeve's eyes fell on the bed and the folded paper that lay in the center of it. His mysterious intruder had left him a message. He walked to the bed and picked the paper up, keeping himself alert in case someone was still in hiding. He unfolded the paper and read. He realized immediately someone was suspicious of the reasons he was here.

It would be much better for your health should you decide to leave court as soon as possible. Don't interfere in affairs that might cost you your life. If you do, you may never leave Spain at all. Be wise and leave now before a force you cannot withstand decides to eliminate you. Remember, you have all to lose, and nothing to gain. There is nothing here for you. Go! Now!

> A Friend

Reeve chuckled at the signature. With a friend like this, he certainly did not need an enemy. He folded the paper and put it away for the moment. Before he could move again, a light rap on his door brought him from the bedroom quickly and to his door. He opened it abruptly, startling the two young maids who stood in the hall.

"Oh, sir," one said in a flustered voice. "We were sent to see if there was anything you might need."

"Yes, can you get me some water for a bath?"

"Yes, sir."

"And something to eat."

"Sir, we were also sent with a message from Don Esteban. He would like you to join him in his apartment for lunch."

"Don Esteban?" Reeve questioned. "I don't believe I know him."

"He said to tell you he spoke to you the night of the ball and that there is something he would like to discuss with you."

"All right, tell him I will be there as soon as I change."

"Yes, sir," they chorused.

"And hurry up with that water."

"Yes, sir," they repeated. They were gone, but not before one cast an appreciative look over her shoulder. Dark eyes told him she would more than be willing to help him bathe should he need it.

He closed the door, laughing at his own self. Before Elana, such an invitation would not have gone unanswered. Now, his heart sang Elana and could hear no other.

The water came, carried by two young men who placed the wooden tub in the center of the floor. Reeve bathed quickly and dressed. He had asked the whereabouts of Don Esteban's apartment, and in less than an hour, walked down the hall toward his door. He rapped once or twice on the door and it was opened by a man he quickly remembered from the night of the ball.

"Don Esteban?"

"*Si*, Senor Burke. Do come in, please."

Reeve stepped inside and Don Esteban closed the door behind them. There was a table set for two on the balcony. Don Esteban touched Reeve's elbow and waved toward the table.

"Come join me, Senor." He smiled warmly. "Lunch is hot and the wine cool." They walked to the table and Reeve sat opposite Don Esteban. His host poured the wine and Reeve studied him closely.

Don Esteban was a dark man with a thick mustache and heavy-browed eyes. He was a good bit shorter than Reeve and rather stocky in build. Reeve had the sudden thought that this man was connected to the note he had found on his bed.

His host had been correct: The food was not only hot, it was excellent, and the wine was not only cool, but of the best quality. They ate, laughed, and chatted aimlessly while they enjoyed the meal. Reeve waited patiently for Don Esteban to come to the point of their meeting.

When they had finished their food, Don Esteban sat back in his chair and smiled at Reeve.

"You like our country, Senor Burke?"

"Yes, Don Esteban, I do. It is quite beautiful, and I have never been treated with such gracious hospitality."

"Good, good. You are a very appreciative man, and I might say, very intelligent." Reeve suddenly became alerted. He sat relaxed but every sense he had told him he was about to get the first objection to his presence here . . . or rather the second, since his anonymous letter was the first.

"Thank you, Don Esteban."

"You are a Christian, Senor Burke?" The question was asked softly.

"A Christian . . . yes, I think so."

"A Catholic, Senor?"

"No, does that make a difference?"

"It might help you to understand what I am about to try and explain to you."

"Explain, Don Esteban. I shall do my best to understand."

"There are factions in our country, Senor Burke. They are fighting a silent war. Her Majesty and Fray Torquemada have joined forces to eliminate our society of an evil."

"Evil?" Reeve questioned quietly.

Esteban leaned forward, bracing his elbows on the table. This was the first time Reeve noticed the intense glow in the dark eyes. For some reason that shook him more than what Esteban said.

"The Jews," he hissed. Unleashed violence clung to the words. "Fray Torquemada has urged on Her Majesty to notice the spread of Judaism. He has pointed out that these people make mockery of the Holy Church and defile her sacraments. He has urged the queen to punish these defilers."

"The Inquisition?" Reeve questioned.

"A noble crusade, Senor. It will rid our country of an evil that is trying to devour it."

"What does this have to do with me?"

"It was only a friendly warning, Senor Burke. There are people who would like to take advantage of you and your ship and use it to escape justice. We wouldn't want that to happen."

"I am here to visit friends, Don Esteban, and I shall take special care not to be taken advantage of . . . or to be afraid." He walked to the door and left, not seeing the cold eyes of Don Esteban follow his broad back until the door closed.

91

Reeve walked slowly back to his room. Twice in a few hours he had been warned to leave Spain. He hoped whoever was to contact him would do so soon. He wondered if Esteban and whoever had sent him had any idea of the identity of the people he was there to rescue.

Reeve again left his room. He intended to wander about and make himself accessible in case his contact wanted to reach him. He knew it would be impossible for them to contact him openly, and completely out of the question if he stayed in his room. He wandered about freely, striking up conversations with many, but no one gave any sign that they wished to speak to him alone.

There was no sign of the queen in the gardens where she usually spent the afternoon. When he asked, Reeve was told she had chosen to remain in her quarters to write some letters. He also knew that Elana must remain with the queen. He was disappointed to know there was no chance of seeing Elana.

He was about to return to his room for an afternoon siesta, and as he walked across the garden, he was surprised to see Beatriz seated on a stone bench. Beside her sat an older man, and they were in animated conversation. His feet made little sound as he walked toward them, and he heard the fragments of conversation before they knew he was approaching.

"Beatriz, no, I cannot let this happen," the old man said.

"We have no choice," she answered. Her voice was very nearly pleading as she bent toward the old man and touched his hand with hers. "You are too valuable, you cannot be lost. I will not let it happen. Neither will he. He will make sure that—" She turned suddenly when she heard Reeve approaching.

"Captain Burke," she said as she stood up.

Reeve smiled. "Beatriz, are we not friends enough now that you could stop calling me Captain Burke?"

She returned his smile and gestured toward the old man who

92

had been watching Reeve closely. "Reeve, this is my grandfather, Emilo de Mendosa. Grandfather, this is Captain Reeve Burke. He is a friend of Rafael Chavez. They have come for the queen's ball."

"Good day, young friend," the old man said. His smile was warm and open and Reeve liked the way his eyes sparkled with amusement.

"Good afternoon, Senor de Mendosa, it is a pleasure to meet you."

The old man chuckled. "So, you are our English sea captain? I have heard of your visit. Will you be staying with us long?"

"I'm not sure of my plans yet. I suppose when Rafael goes home, I shall go also."

"Tell me, captain, do you play chess?"

"Yes, I do."

"Good." The old man smiled warmly and Beatriz laughed. "My grandfather is looking for another victim. Beware, captain, he has beaten everyone so badly, few will play with him."

Reeve had to laugh at the twinkle of mischief in the old man's eyes. "I would be pleased to try my hand," he replied.

"Would you care to join me in my room for a game before dinner?"

"Yes."

"I have to return to the queen," Beatriz said. "Be wary of him, Reeve, and good luck. I shall see you both at dinner."

"Beatriz," Reeve said, "will the queen be present with all her court?"

Beatriz proved her relationship with the old man when her eyes sparkled with devilment. "You mean," she said, smiling, "will Elana be there? Yes, she will."

"Thank you." Reeve smiled in return.

Beatriz bent to give her grandfather a light kiss, then she left the two men together. The old man rose slowly and Reeve accompanied him on the walk to his apartment. They walked slowly as Reeve shortened his stride to match the old man's.

"You and Rafael have been friends a long time?"

"No, not really," Reeve replied.

"Are you enjoying your visit to our country?"

"Yes, I am, very much."

"From what my granddaughter said, I take it you are impressed with the Lady Elana."

"She is a very beautiful woman."

"I agree my son, not only physically, but she is beautiful inside, as well. Were I a young man such as you, I would be quite tempted to steal the lovely Elana away from the court."

Reeve walked in silence for a few moments. The instincts were again nudging his conscience. Was this old man offering a warning, too?

"I imagine, many would like to steal Elana," he offered.

"Yes," the old man said, "but, I am not too sure the ones here would be what she needs."

"And what does she need?"

"What do we all need? Freedom, security, love."

Reeve was about to speak again, to question more closely, but they had arrived at their destination. The old man ushered him inside. Before long the chess table was set up and they were facing each other across it.

The first move was Reeve's and he made it with assurance. In silence his opponent moved. They contemplated the board and one move slowly followed another. Reeve was quick and alert, but he realized the old man was both cautious and very, very good.

"Your ship is in Cadiz?"

"Yes, she's being loaded."

"Umm." The old man made a strategic move that startled Reeve. "What is she called?"

"The *Golden Eagle*."

"'Tis an appropriate name for a ship."

"Why do you say that?"

"It reminds one of the flight of the bird for which it is named."

"She is a remarkable vessel," Reeve agreed as he reached across to move a chess piece that made the old man look at him with admiration.

"Very good," he said. He contemplated the board in silence. Reaching out, he moved again. "Check," he said softly. He gazed up at Reeve from under his thick, white brows, and Reeve could have laughed at the look of cherubic innocence on his face.

Reeve could have moved again, but he saw the trap and knew he was beyond his depth in challenging this man. He smiled and raised his arms in surrender. The old man chuckled again.

"Would you care for another game?" he asked pleasantly.

"Not until I've practiced for a few more years, say ten or twenty or so." They laughed together.

"Can I offer you a drink, my son, some wine?"

"Thank you," Reeve replied. He watched the old man pour two goblets of wine. When offered his, he sipped it slowly. "Senor de Mendosa," Reeve said quietly, "what can you tell me about the Inquisition at court?" The old man's face paled and his hand trembled slightly before he brought it under control.

"The Inquisition. From what I hear it is only an arm of the church seeking out answers from those who would deny her."

"If a man wanted to talk to someone of influence in this matter, who should he approach?"

The old man's eyes read Reeve slowly, then a half smile touched his lips and the same mischievous twinkle reappeared. "I should think Don Francisco and Don Esteban would be of interest to you. I'm sure they could tell you much about the church's influence at court."

"Thank you," Reeve replied, knowing the old man knew exactly what he was thanking him for . . . the names of the men who were his enemies. He also felt the old man was another who knew more about his presence here than he thought.

Reeve rose and set his goblet on the table. "I am afraid I must go. I have things that need attending to before dinner. If you will excuse me."

"Of course. Thank you for a most interesting game. I wish you good luck, my son . . . in all you do."

"Thank you." Reeve bowed and left the room and went back to his room. Discarding his coat, he sat in a comfortable chair and tried to figure out just who among the people he had met could be Bragham's friend. No one so far seemed to fit the idea, and no one had done any more than to warn him off as Don Esteban had done or to urge him on as Emilo de Mendosa had done. Reeve had to admit, he was most thoroughly confused. Disgusted with this train of thought, he cast it aside and let his mind dwell on what he enjoyed so much more . . . Elana.

Reeve knew one thing for certain. He had no intention of leaving this country without Elana. He would try his best to convince her, but if it came down to finalities, he would kidnap her if he had to. He knew she was afraid, and it was Don Francisco and the power of the Inquisition she was afraid of. There was no way he would leave her here to face those two alone.

Reeve dressed very carefully for the evening. He would see Elana again, and that was enough to excite him. He wondered if the opportunity would come to get her alone again. If it did, he certainly did not intend to let it escape him.

He dressed in deep blue which enhanced his golden hair and intensified the silver-gray of his eyes. He felt he was prepared to meet whatever might be offered, and he was anxious to see

Elana, so he left his room and made his way down the huge winding stairway to the formal dining room.

Many of the guests had already arrived, but the queen, as usual, would make her appearance last, so Reeve had to be content to wander about the room, speaking to many. But he kept his eye on the door through which the queen would come.

Reeve was also aware of the presence of both Don Francisco and Don Esteban. He could feel their eyes on him often.

Reeve sipped some cool wine and watched the faces about him. It was a diversified and a very interesting group. It was made up of some of Spain's top royalty. It amused him to try and guess just how many might be prepared to leave the country of their birth.

A great stir among the guests told him the king and queen had arrived. Although most eyes sought the queen, Reeve searched for Elana. With a sharp intake of breath, he found her. She created a sensation within him Reeve found hard to believe.

Dressed in rose-colored silk, she looked so vulnerable, young, and sweet that he had to fight the urge to go to her and drag her from the room. He was delighted to find her seated opposite him at the table, and he immersed himself in her smile and the glow of her green eyes during the meal.

What he ate never entered his mind, and the conversation he held with the people next to him would never be remembered an hour later.

The meal was long, consisting of so many courses that Reeve grew tired of eating. After the meal, they adjourned to another more spacious and comfortable room where some entertainment was arranged.

Outside of sharing a look or a smile, Reeve could not get close to Elana. It was nearing midnight when the queen decided she was tired and chose to retire. Of course, to Reeve's distress, it meant that Elana would be forced to leave too.

After they left, Reeve felt the brilliance of the room had dimmed.

He stayed as long as possible, drank a little wine and conversed with as many people as he could, but still there was no sign of anyone trying to approach him either to slip him a message or to whisper words that would complete his mission.

Finally, he decided that he was tired, needed some sleep, and would leave it up to this unknown person to contact him. He left the room unnoticed by most of the remaining guests.

He was aggravated at the person who should have contacted him by now. He should, or they should have come forward long ago. He had given every opportunity possible.

He walked up the stairway and down the hall toward his room, his mind preoccupied with thoughts both of his mission and how he was going to convince Elana that she must go with him.

He thought of the threat of the Inquisition that could hang over Elana's head as well as others. The thought chilled him for he had heard some very frightening stories of the method of the inquisitors in finding out whatever it was they wanted to know.

He reached his room and put out his hand to open the door. His hand froze. The door stood slightly ajar. He had a nocturnal visitor. He wondered if his ghostlike friend was still inside. Very gently, he pushed the door open far enough to step inside.

It was too dark to see a thing, so he stood absolutely still until his eyes began to adjust to the dark. He could see the dark figure bent over his trunk. His intention was to capture the elusive night visitor and question him about why he was searching his room, what he was looking for, and why he did not approach him in the day. That was his intention, but his boot struck something and quickly alerted his visitor who leapt

98

toward the doors that led to the balcony. Reeve was only a room length behind him.

During the time Reeve had been in the mansion he had taken care to find the exact location of everyone's room. His shadowy friend was running down the stone patio, and Reeve decided to stay far enough behind to see just where he would run to.

He pressed against the wall in the shadows, hoping his visitor would think he was not being followed. Keeping to the dark shadows, he trailed the shadow figure past room after room until he saw him pause before one and look over his shoulder to see if he were being followed. Reeve again pressed against the wall, holding himself breathlessly still. The dark figure ahead of him opened the door he was standing in front of, stepped inside, and pulled it closed after him.

Reeve stood in stunned amazement. He knew well who this room belonged to and it took him completely by surprise that his visitor would enter here.

He made his way down the stone patio and stood outside the dimly lighted windows. Inside, seated in front of a low burning fire, slowly brushing her long dark hair, sat Elana de Santangel.

There was no sign of any other person in the room, but Reeve could not see how any one could have crossed the room and left it without Elana's seeing him. Still, she seemed relaxed as if no one had entered. She wore a loose white gown for bed. It was drawn loosely at the neckline and revealed one ivory shoulder. She created a vision Reeve could not draw himself away from.

Slowly and quietly he opened the door and stepped into an alcove about six feet in depth. He stood in the shadows and watched her. Her dark hair flowed about her in brilliant confusion as she brushed it methodically. He heard her humming softly. Her delicate beauty drew him like a magnet, and he took another step from the alcove into the lighted room.

Startled green eyes lifted to him, filled first with fear, then with questions.

"Reeve," she breathed softly, "what are you doing here?"

"I," he said, smiling, "am chasing whoever it was who passed through here a few minutes ago. Suppose you tell me the truth, Elana. Who is he . . . and why was he searching my room . . . better still, why did he run to you?"

Chapter Eight

Elana stared at Reeve in disbelief. Her wide eyes no longer showed fear, only a seeming lack of understanding.

"He? I don't understand. What are you talking about? No one has come in here."

"Elana, don't lie to me. I followed him to these windows. I saw him come in here." Elana had never been called a liar to her face in her life. Pink tinged her cheeks, and her green eyes began to sparkle in anger. She stood up, and when she did, it nearly took Reeve's breath away.

Unaware that the fire was behind her and that the gown she wore became nearly sheer in its pale glow, she stood and glared at him.

"I have no need to lie to you," she said angrily. "You are the intruder here. Please leave before I scream," she demanded.

Reeve had put his intruder to the back of his mind. He would walk that path later. For now, Elana drew all his attention. He knew she was unaware that his eyes were absorbing her near naked loveliness through the translucent gown.

"I'm sorry, Elana, I didn't mean to say it like that. Maybe I misjudged the room he entered. Who's in the room next to you?" Although he knew well who was the owner of the next room, he asked just to pacify her and hopefully to keep her mind off her state of undress.

"Rodrigo, my brother."

Reeve was completely certain the man had entered Elana's room. Hers was the corner room. To enter her brother's, one would have taken him out of Reeve's sight and into full view of the palace guards who stood below. Both were impossibilities.

"Are you accusing Rodrigo of something?" she asked, her anger barely under control.

"No, I didn't say it was Rodrigo." Her cheeks flushed a darker pink and he could have bitten his tongue as he realized how the words would sound to her.

"Are you suggesting that someone has free access to my room, can come and go as he pleases? How dare you!"

She turned her back and he was treated to the sight of a straight slim back and soft round buttocks. She gazed at the fire as if hoping he would disappear. It was then she realized the effect the fire was creating. She gasped and fairly leapt away from it.

"Get out of here!" she demanded, turning her back to him. In a few quick steps, Reeve was behind her. He slid his arms about her waist and drew her back against him. She wriggled in vain because her strength was no match for his. He had both arms about her waist and the pressure nearly spilled her out of the loose neck of the gown, giving Reeve a view that held him in breathless expectation. The scent of her touched his senses and stirred his blood until it raced heatedly through him. His cheek brushed her silken hair, and he would have been content to hold her for a while if her cold voice hadn't intervened in his thoughts.

Elana had been fighting her own battle with her wayward body and knew she was losing. The strength of the arms that held her, the lean hard body that pressed against her stirred a flame of need deep within. It awakened the memory she had tried in vain to erase.

"Let me go, Reeve, please let me go," she said softly.

"Elana," he whispered against her hair, "ceasing to breathe would be an easier request." He turned her in his arms and held her slim body molded to his. Her eyes burned into his. "Whether you will it or not, you feel as I do. Don't you think I can feel it in your touch, see it in your eyes? Don't fight it, Elana. I'll not go away until I convince you to love me as I love you."

Her eyes fought him and she tried to turn from him, but he was much too strong. Relentlessly, he drew her even closer. Holding her with one arm he tangled his other hand in the mass of her dark hair. Slowly, his mouth lowered to claim hers. It was a time that was meant to be, as inevitable as the stars that lit the night sky. A violent need coursed through her at the touch of his lips on hers.

Time seemed to slow as he caressed her lips with his. His hungry mouth searched hers for the honey sweetness well remembered. Her lips softened and parted beneath his questing ones and with a surge of joy, he felt her arms go about him, and her warm body willingly molded itself to his.

His effect on her was total and devastating. He released her lips only to claim them again and again, then touched her cheeks and eyes and slowly journeyed down her slender throat. He slid his hand down the curve of her back to soft rounded hips and pressed her against him, and her body, roused by the heightening flame within, responded to the heat of his. Her world careened beneath his demanding lips, and her breath seemed to cease within her. She was swept away and lost to all but his passion.

She gasped and sighed a ragged sigh as his gold head bent to taste even sweeter nectar. He lifted his head and their eyes met. She was stormed by the intensity of his gaze and knew without doubt she was irretrievably lost. The need for him swelled within her until it filled her so completely that nothing existed but Reeve.

Elana filled Reeve's mind, his heart, his senses. She swirled and danced within him and he allowed himself the pleasure of savoring her possession of him. He sank deeply into the sea green pools of her eyes and cared not if he ever left their depths. He wanted to remain bound with her forever and to hold her in the innermost depths of his soul.

He caught her face between his hands and with infinite gentleness, he kissed her again, trying to tell her the wild and deep emotion that filled him. In this tumultuous sea, Elana was lost. She could not deny the flame that licked to life within her and refused to die. It consumed every thought she had and sent them spiraling beyond her control or her command.

"Love me, Elana," he whispered softly against her parted lips. "Love me and belong to me as I would you." She uttered a soft sound of his name as the final defense was breached. He could read warm surrender in her eyes.

With a quick bend, he lifted her in his arms. Her head on his shoulders, her slim arms about his neck, he walked to the bed where he stood her close to him. With gentle hands he slid the already loose gown from her shoulders and let it fall to a tangled heap about her feet. He found her beauty so vibrant that he gazed at her in breathless disbelief.

"You are so beautiful, Elana . . . so very beautiful."

He wanted her now with a passion that could be dimmed only by the brilliance of the sun. He moved rapidly to remove the constricting clothes he wore, tossing them carelessly aside. Her gasp of surprise and the glow of admiring warmth in her eyes was the beginning of his reward, the reaching of her slender fingers to touch his muscular chest and slip up to his shoulders was even better.

He drew her cool, soft body against him and they stood so for a moment as his hands explored the soft sensitive flesh that trembled beneath them. He sat on the edge of the bed and drew her down into his arms, then he fell backward, taking her with him.

She was enfolded in his arms, pressed against the bed, and he again began to assault her senses with hungry kisses and warm, seeking hands. She responded with a wild and vibrant passion that both surprised and thrilled him. This was no longer a delicate girl to be treated as fragile. This was a warm and vibrant woman whose desire blazed as high as his.

Their blending was an explosive thing that fused them into one. It was the bliss of knowing each was where he belonged. The surrender to each other was an aching, sweet thing. She took him within her almost eagerly, for no pain could touch the ecstasy that filled her and tossed her emotions into soaring flight.

All will she might have possessed, crumbled and soft sighs of pleasure escaped her unnoticed.

"Elana . . . sweet lovely Elana," Reeve's voice rasped softly in her ear. His kisses touched her, warm and devouring, and filled him with a passion and love for her.

Their hearts beat together a wild passionate song that would be the music of their love for all time, and they tumbled together into a glorious tide of completion that left them silent and stunned with the tide of pleasure that had swept them away.

Thundering hearts slowed, breathing returned to normal, and the violence of the trembling passion ceased, yet they clung silently to one another.

Again their eyes met and an overwhelming sense of completeness and contentment filled them both. Reeve caressed her tangled hair and smiled down into her eyes. Hers were warm, limpid pools, gentle and filled with the wonder they had shared.

"Elana," he said softly, "tell me. I have to hear you say it."

"Is not this enough to tell you?" she smiled.

"It is a wonder, it is a beauty beyond anything I have ever

known. But, I need to make it complete."

Elana reached up and took his face between her hands. "I love you, Reeve Burke," she said. "If I am damned for it, I love you."

"Would you be damned because you love? If so, I would share it with you. If it is to be damned to love, then I shall be damned forever, for I love you beyond reason, beyond anything I have ever known."

"You don't understand, Reeve," she said. Her eyes were soft with love. "This is all I shall ever have."

His brows drew together. "I don't understand, Elana. This is just the beginning for us. We have a whole lifetime, and I want to share it with you. I need you in the rest of my life to make it worth living. How can you say this is all we'll ever have?"

"I . . . I tried to tell you, you just wouldn't listen."

"Then tell me again," he demanded.

"I cannot leave here."

"Cannot or won't?"

"I would go to the end of the world with you," she whispered, tears forming in her eyes, "but, I cannot. There are other things, other people I have to consider."

"What about us?"

"I don't know," she replied.

"Well, I do. When I leave this country, you are going with me if I have to drag you by force."

"Oh, Reeve," she said, smiling, "I do love you, and I sense with every shred of my being that you are a man of honor. Given choices to defend those you love, even if it were with your life, I know which way you would choose. I also know I cannot do any less. I cannot go while others might pay the price for what I do."

"Tell me what is going on, Elana."

"I . . . I can't yet, Reeve, I'm not even sure myself. I only know there is a great deal at stake. For now, I must remain here, at least until I know I am free."

A sudden thought flashed through Reeve's mind. Was Elana involved with the people who were trying to contact him? Was he to be the avenue of her escape and she had not been told what the plan would be? He felt sure his being here was connected more with Elana than the fact that he loved her. He was frustrated, yet sure there was more to it than he knew. He could read the distress and pain in her eyes. Since he hadn't been contacted yet, he felt he could ease her mind and wait until he was. Then he would decide what to do. He knew he would never leave the shores of Spain without Elana, no matter who or what he had to sacrifice. He refused to let the sacrifice be Elana.

"All right, Elana. For now I'll wait. But if you think it will ever make a change in what I feel, you are mistaken. I love you, my absolute beauty, and I shall continue to love you as long as there is a breath in my body."

He watched the trembling tears sparkle on the edges of her lashes, saw the tremulous smile and felt the warmth of his need for her renew itself within him.

He bent his head to taste the salt of her tears, then the moist, inviting lips. His mouth played upon hers, one gentle kiss after another until the flower of passion began to blossom again.

She opened to him as a new blossom to the morning sun. His kisses now were warm and devouring, filled with love and passion. His hands sought to renew the magic that had claimed them before. Her breasts were soft to the touch of his lips, her skin like satin beneath his questing hands. Their hearts began a new and frantic beating. He heard the soft breathless cries of pleasure and was caught in the flowing tide of joy that filled him.

They were live twisting flames that matched each other in need and ecstasy.

She could feel the hard muscles of his back tense as he

surged deep within her in a glow of spreading rapture. Every nerve was aglow as she savored the bliss of his caress.

Complete surrender for both lost them within each other and they surged upward and outward to fly into the cauldron of passion that engulfed them in the flame.

In exhaustion, Reeve held her close to him as they tumbled back to the world of reality. Elana's body, eased by the fulfillment, grew warm and relaxed as it nestled close to Reeve. After a while, she fell asleep.

One hand lay possessively across his waist as if she would refuse to let him go. Her head rested on his shoulder and he held her until her breathing was slow and regular.

He waited until he knew she was in a sound sleep, then he eased himself from her arms and from the bed. He tucked the covers close about her slim form and bent to kiss her lightly. Then he dressed and walked to the alcove through which he had passed to come in. They were lined with heavy tapestry that covered one wall. He pushed it aside to find what he had thought he might find: a narrow door. He knew without doubt Elana knew nothing about it and it filled him with anger and fear that someone did indeed have free access to her room without her knowledge.

It was nearing dawn, too late to follow the passage to find out where it led to. He planned to explore it the following night.

He slipped from Elana's room after first checking to make sure the area was clear. He made his way to his room. After he closed his windows, he decided to get what sleep he could.

His mind was a tangle of thoughts. Why had he not been contacted? He had been told it was only a matter of days. What did Elana know of his presence here? Was she involved or was her innocent love being taken advantage of? Who was his mysterious intruder, and what was he looking for? He had none of the answers, but he was determined to find them. It was some time before he found the sleep he sought and when he did, it was filled with a tangled web of dreams.

Reeve was wakened by the patter of rain against his window. The sky was a lead gray and a steady downpour was in progress. There would be no riding today. He was disappointed for he knew Elana would be surrounded by people and under the watchful eyes, not only of the queen, but anyone else who might want to see Elana and Reeve be discovered.

Reeve lay on his back, his hands folded behind his head, and allowed his thoughts to dwell on Elana. Elana, his beautiful Elana. She was his, and he had no intentions of ever letting her go. Any adversary he might face would never succeed in separating them while there was a breath in his body and strength in his arm.

He closed his eyes and allowed warmer and more interesting memories to fill his mind. He thought of taking Elana home, of her beauty gracing his home, of the days and nights they would share together.

Elana, too, was stirred awake by the falling rain. Slowly her eyes opened, and at the same moment she felt the emptiness of her huge canopied bed. She could still see the indent in the pillow next to her where he had lain, and still could feel the warmth of him. She took the pillow and held it close to her. Closing her eyes, she relived the beauty of the past night.

It is temporarily a dream, her mind told her, but her heart told her differently. She knew Reeve did not truly understand yet the power of the Inquisition, and she prayed he would never be touched by it. He would go, her logical mind said, and she would be left to live with the sweet memories he had left behind. She knew one thing for certain: She would never belong to another. There would never be another Reeve to waken the magic within her, to make her body sing as he had done. She knew she could never willingly go to another man.

Elana knew her vulnerable position. She knew the queen had absolute power over whom she would marry, but Elana would always have the choice of the marriage or the convent, and she would choose the cloistered life if it were necessary.

For now there were others who depended upon her, and she could not desert them in their hours of need. Much as she would have desired to go with Reeve, to be part of his life, to build a future with him, she knew at this time it was not possible.

A light rap on her door, and her soft answer allowed her visitor to come in. She sat up in bed and smiled.

Don Francisco and Don Esteban sat opposite each other at an early morning breakfast table.

"What do you really believe he wants here?" Don Esteban questioned.

"One thing is certain, he did not come with Rafael Chavez, just to visit the court. He was sent here for a reason and I intend to find out just what that reason is."

"What do you think, Don Francisco?"

"I believe," Don Francisco said, "that he is here to try and help someone leave our country."

"Who?"

"I'm not sure, but I have a suspicion. If I am right, Fray Torquemada and the queen would be upset with me should I let the escape happen. I am not remiss in my duties of the church."

"He seems to be quite interested in Lady Elana," Don Esteban said. The glow of malicious humor lit his eyes. Although he respected Don Francisco's power, he was still somewhat afraid and harbored a dislike for him. Don Francisco was absolutely silent for a moment. His dark eyes held Don Esteban's and Esteban could feel the perspiration form on his brow.

"Captain Reeve Burke will take nothing from this country

he did not bring. If he continues to interfere in any of my plans, he will not leave this country at all. I have plans for Lady Elana and they do not include Captain Burke."

"I must admit she is a very beautiful woman," Don Esteban said, smiling. "What do you know of her family's background?" he asked softly.

Don Francisco smiled. "Everything. He is much too proud. He reaches for things that do not belong to him. When the time comes, we will correct his wayward nature."

There was no doubt in Don Esteban's mind what those words meant. Elana's brother had brought himself to Don Francisco's attention. It was a very dangerous thing to do.

"Tell me, Don Esteban, you are still . . . entranced by Lady Beatriz? Has she returned your interest?"

Don Esteban frowned. "The lady is not only obstinate, she does not seem to understand the honor I pay her. My family is as ancient and wealthy as hers. She would do well to join my family."

"It would be the joining of great wealth," Don Francisco said. His eyes held Don Esteban's. "I am sure you would give much to have your families joined. You would have control of much wealth and power."

"Yes," Don Esteban said. The realization of what Don Francisco was offering him came to him quickly. He would have Beatriz and all the influence at court, wealth, and power her family possessed. "I would give anything that was asked."

"Good. I shall remember that."

"I have heard Fray Torquemada is going to pay the court a visit."

"Yes."

"It will be soon?"

"In the next few days."

"Is there something that draws his interest here or is it just to visit the queen?"

111

"I think it is a little of both."

"I wonder what interests him here," Esteban wondered aloud.

"That is not for us to question. He looks after the welfare of our souls and seeks to weed out the apostates. This Jewish disease that spreads among us must be cleansed. They infiltrate into places of power. One day they shall try to destroy the church. Fray Torquemada places himself between us and that disaster."

If Don Esteban had not known Don Francisco better, he might have believed those words. But he did know Don Francisco, maybe even more than he knew. He knew that it did not matter if Don Francisco's opponents were Jewish or not. If they stood against him, or his enemies, Don Francisco's enemies had a way of meeting with misfortune . . . and disaster.

"I am afraid you must excuse me, Don Esteban. I have an audience with Her Majesty this morning and you know she will not tolerate tardiness."

"Of course," Esteban replied. He rose from the table and with a slight bow toward Don Francisco, walked to the door and left.

Don Francisco checked himself before the mirror to make sure he was appropriately dressed, then he walked to the door, left the room, and started down the hall toward the queen's quarters.

The hallways were dimly lit on the best of days, but the morning's gray skies and the rain made them even dimmer.

He walked silently. It was a thing he had consciously practiced, for one never knew when he was going to walk into a situation where silence was necessary.

He was contemplating plans he had, not only for the destruction of people who stood in his way at the moment, but plans he had for Beatriz de Mendosa. He would use her as a reward for Esteban and with this he would bring the de Mendosa family under his power. Esteban would control the wealth and power, and he would control Esteban.

His thoughts now went to Elana de Santangel. He would have her. The thought of it sent a flow of heated blood through his veins. He knew many small details about her family, but none that were incriminating enough. He would search until he found some leverage that would bring her to him.

He let his mind shift to Reeve Burke. He was a nuisance at the moment, but Don Francisco knew if Captain Burke constituted any real danger to his plans, he would eliminate him. There were many methods at Don Francisco's command, and he would not hesitate to use them.

Don Francisco was just about to turn the corner that led to a short, even darker hallway between his quarters and the well-lighted hall that led to the queen's. It was well guarded but this short darker one was not.

He heard the soft whisper of voices and stopped. He held himself close to the wall and looked around the corner. A slow smile touched his lips as he stored in his memory what he heard and what he saw. Of course, he recognized the two that stood so close together and talked in low whispers . . . Beatriz de Mendosa and Elana's brother, the tall, handsome Rodrigo de Santangel. He also recognized immediately that these two were lovers. It was a tidbit of information he might use with the queen if it were necessary. Rodrigo's arms were about Beatriz and he was holding her close while they spoke.

"Beatriz, there has to be a way, and I shall find it. Just have faith and remember, I love you. We will find a way to escape without harming others."

"Oh, Rodrigo, I am so frightened. I am afraid we cannot keep it secret much longer. What will happen to him and to us if the truth is discovered?" Rodrigo kissed her forcefully and hungrily.

SYLVIE F. SOMMERFIELD

"I will find a way," he whispered. "I love you Beatriz, with every beat of my heart. I will not lose you. We must have faith, we will find a way."

Her muffled sob was silenced by Rodrigo's searching lips and soon they were engrossed in sharing the few stolen kisses they could share.

Francisco watched them, entwined in each other's arms. Beatriz's arms about Rodrigo's neck and her slim body molded to his tall, lean frame. Francisco smiled. Into his hands had been placed another tool to use when the right time came.

Silently he backed away, then he walked toward the dark hall again, letting his boots make as much noise as possible as he did. As he thought they would be, when he turned the corner both Rodrigo and Beatriz were gone. He walked on and exited the darker hall into the well lighted one. At the far hall was the queen's door, in front of which stood two of the guards.

He went to the door and was admitted into the antechamber. Four more guards stood in front of the queen's door.

In the antechamber, he found Beatriz de Mendosa.

"The queen is expecting you, Don Francisco," she said. He smiled at the awareness and fear he saw lingering in her eyes.

He walked to the queen's door, but just before he entered he turned to Beatriz and smiled. "You look chilled, my dear," he said softly. "You should not linger in these cold halls."

He saw her face pale and her eyes fill with something near terror. Satisfied, he opened the door and went inside, leaving a worried Beatriz staring after him.

Chapter Nine

Rafael was a happy man. He wondered how Catrina's beauty had ever escaped him. He also wondered how he had ever considered any other woman. The fact that they had grown up together still amazed him, probably always would. He had prided himself on being a connoisseur of women, and yet, he had never realized the rare and beautiful rose that grew in his own garden.

Now, he hummed softly to himself as he dressed. He was preparing himself to be his best, for he had requested to see the queen and the request had been approved.

He had spoken to his father and told him of his desire to marry Catrina, a desire his father was delighted with. Now he had only to ask the queen's permission for he wanted to marry immediately . . . here . . . in the glamor and excitement of the royal court. He felt it would make Catrina happy.

He looked at himself in the mirror, satisfied that he looked his best. He was a handsome figure, tall and dark. His scarlet doublet accented his dark hair and skin. He was every inch the handsome, almost arrogant, Spanish grandee. He left his room. His plan was to see the queen first, then to find Catrina and let her know the queen's decision.

He walked past Reeve's door just as Reeve was coming out. "Ah, Reeve, good morning," he said, and Reeve had to smile at his obvious good spirits.

"Rafael, you look uncommonly happy today."

"I am, my friend, I am. I can't remember a time I have felt better. Have you had breakfast yet?"

"No, I was just about to have some. Come and join me."

"Thank you, I was about to ask if I might. I have something to tell you." Rafael's eyes sparkled. "And I think it will please you almost as much as it has me."

"Almost?" Reeve laughed.

Rafael's laughter joined his. "Almost," he answered. "Believe me, friend, it has pleased me more than anything else in my life."

"Now, I am truly interested. Let's go and eat so I can hear about this wonderful news." They sat opposite each other on a sun-touched patio. Their food was served by a delighted young maid who was disappointed when neither of the handsome young men noticed her open smile and the sway of her hips.

"Now," Rafael said, "what did you want to talk to me about?"

"No, you go first," Reeve said with a smile. "Tell me what news will make me *almost* as happy as it has you."

"I have an audience with Her Majesty today."

Reeve looked at him expectantly. "Well?" Rafael asked, "aren't you going to ask me why?"

"You're going to tell me even if I don't," Reeve said, laughing.

"You are right, my friend. I am going to ask Her Majesty to permit me to marry here at court."

Reeve's smile faded and his gray eyes registered his surprise. "Have . . . have you asked her yet?"

"The queen?"

"No, the lady you want to make your bride."

"Yes, of course I have. You don't think I would ask the

116

queen if I hadn't asked her first?"

Reeve's heart slipped like lead to the pit of his stomach. Would Elana go so far as to marry someone she did not love just to remain here and sacrifice her life for some unknown person? No, his heart said. Yes, his mind argued.

"And she agreed to marry you?"

"I'm proud to say she has." Reeve felt as if someone had swept the floor out from under his feet.

"If the queen allows, I hope the wedding will take place as soon as possible," Rafael rambled on while Reeve half listened. "I can't believe I have known her all my life and never saw her before. It is impossible to believe I have been that stupid. We will join the—"

"Rafael," Reeve interrupted. The words Rafael had just said had brightened his eyes. "Stop talking about the wedding and tell me," Reeve said, bending toward Rafael, "just who are you planning to marry?"

"Why," Rafael said in surprise, "Catrina, of course." Reeve smiled, then chuckled softly, and the chuckle grew until he threw back his head and laughed heartily.

"You find my marriage to Catrina amusing?"

"No, no, Rafael." His laughter choked to a halt. "It's just . . . I thought it was Elana you were talking about. I was ready to cross swords with you."

"Elana?"

"Yes."

"But I told you once before that Elana has never looked in my direction. I was reaching for something that would never have been mine. I sought a mirage when a beautiful woman was close enough for me to reach out and touch, and she loves me."

"And I couldn't be happier. Dancing at your wedding will be a pleasure."

"*Gracias*, my friend. Now tell me what you wanted to say to me."

"Well," Reeve said, smiling broadly again. "I was going to

tell you to forget Elana. She and I are very much in love and I intend to take her with me when I leave Spain."

Rafael laughed in pure delight. "Wonderful! Why don't you marry her before you go? It would be a grand affair if you were to marry at the same time as Catrina and I." Reeve's silence caused Rafael to frown. "Reeve?"

"We can't."

"Why?"

"First . . . Elana . . . Elana hasn't said she would marry me yet."

"You have asked her?"

"Not exactly."

"What does that mean? Either you have or you haven't."

"Rafael," Reeve began, "there are things Elana can't or won't tell me. You are one of the few who know why I am here. I believe Elana is part of the group that wants to contact me." He went on to explain about his intruder and the searching of his room. He left out the secret door in Elana's room. That was something he intended to look into himself.

"You haven't been contacted by anyone yet?"

"No, I haven't."

"You think Elana knows who it is?"

"I'm not sure what I think yet. I'm only sure of one thing. When I leave these shores, Elana will be with me."

"I don't know what you are fighting, Reeve, my friend."

"The Inquisition is part of it," Reeve said softly. Rafael's face paled and he gazed at Reeve in stunned disbelief.

"The Inquisition . . . Santa Maria," he whispered and crossed himself rapidly. "How do you know?"

"Elana as much as told me so."

"What are you going to do?"

"All that I can do for now is wait, so I shall wait. When I am contacted, I shall do my best to do what I was sent to do. The one thing I swear I will do, I will have Elana. I will take her away!"

"You have much more courage than I, friend. The Inquisition could make the strongest man weak. I wish you luck. If there is ever any help you need, do not hesitate to call on me."

Reeve knew what kind of courage this took. "Thank you, Rafael, I shall remember."

Both men had been up just before dawn, and now the sun began to rise on the horizon. Rafael rose to his feet. "I must go. My appointment is early. I shall see you later. Good luck, amigo." He clapped Reeve on the shoulder and walked away.

Reeve sat very still, his mind drifting to Elana. He wondered if she still slept. The thought of her warm and vulnerable lifted him to his feet.

He walked down the steps of the patio they had been sitting in and around the side of the palace. He gazed about him. There were no guards or anyone else in sight. Quickly he walked up the steps that led to the long stone patio outside his room. To any viewer he was going to his room via the patio. But that was not his destination. He passed his door and moved quickly to Elana's. Gently he tried the large glass doors. They opened.

He slipped inside and closed the door behind him. Quickly his eyes went to the door of her room. It, too, was unbolted. He moved soundlessly across the room and slid the bolt home. Then he turned his eyes toward the bed. He slowly moved toward the bed and looked down on her.

Her dark hair spread across her pillow, gleaming like satin in the early rays of the sun. Long, dark lashes rested on rose petal cheeks and her slightly parted lips looked moist, warm, and very inviting to him. He bent and touched them lightly, tasting their sweet nectar. He slid his hand gently down soft warm curves and felt her stir and slowly come awake.

Deep green eyes looked up into his and he felt himself tumble in their depths, lost again to the sweet intoxication of Elana. He sat down beside her on the bed and lifted one of her hands and pressed them gently with his lips.

"Good morning," he said softly, and watched with fascination as her eyes turned warm and loving and her mouth softened with a smile.

Sliding both arms under her, he lifted her into his arms. She was warm from sleep and she curled close to him, enfolding her arms about his neck. This, he thought, was the way he planned to start each day of their future.

"I love you," he whispered against her slender throat as he pressed warm kisses against soft skin. He let his lips wander to more vulnerable places and heard her sigh with pleasure.

"Oh, Reeve, you are insane. If you are caught here there will be such a scandal. The queen would be outraged. She would banish me from the court."

"Good." He grinned. "Then I would get no more arguments from you about taking you home with me."

"Reeve, please—"

"All right, I said I would wait. But I didn't say I'd not try to break your defenses."

"Oh, you are a stubborn man."

"My dear love, you have not seen stubborn yet. Elana, I know I must go. I don't want to cause you any problems, but—"

"But?"

"Tonight, I may wander from my room. I might find the need for a safe place to go."

"Then come here," she answered. "This will always be a place made for you. Come here." Her voice lowered to a soft whisper. "Love me, Reeve. I need all your strength and warmth to hold me through the days to come."

Reeve could resist no longer. He bound her to him with iron-hard arms and searched her willing mouth for the sweet promise, and she returned it and offered him more than he had ever hoped! Her gift of all consuming love washed through him, setting a fire that would never again be extinguished.

When he released her, they both knew there would never be an end to the magic they found in each other. A silent promise was exchanged. Reeve was about to speak again when footsteps could be heard in the hallway. They stopped before Elana's door and were followed by a light rap and a voice that called to her.

"Elana, are you awake?"

"It's Beatriz. I must get up and dress. The queen will be rising soon and I must be there."

"Say you love me."

"Reeve!"

"Say it or I'll stay," he said, grinning.

"I love you, I love you." She laughed. He kissed her again with a soft, hard, and very possessive kiss, then in a minute he was gone and suddenly Elana's arms felt very empty.

When the knock and the call was repeated, Elana swung her slim legs from the bed and went swiftly to the door and flung it open.

"Elana," Beatriz said with a puzzled frown on her face as she looked about. "I thought I heard voices."

"Really, Beatriz," Elana said in mock surprise, "just who could I be talking to this early in the morning?"

"No one, I suppose," Beatriz replied, but she had a feeling something was very different in Elana and she couldn't figure out what it was.

Elana made herself ready as fast as she possibly could. She washed, dressed, and turned her long hair upon her head and pinned it securely. Both women went rapidly to the queen's quarters only to find that she had risen, dressed, and was enclosed in a small room with Rafael.

They waited in silence with the other women of the court, until the door opened and Isabella came out followed by a happy Rafael. He had achieved permission to marry Catrina in two days at the royal court.

121

Isabella's presence filled the room as all her ladies dropped in deep curtseys. Isabella bade them rise and turned to Rafael, who immediately dropped to one knee and pressed the hem of Isabella's skirt to his lip.

"Your Grace," he said almost reverently, "I shall be forever your cavalier. I give you my life, Your Grace, for you have given one thing that makes my life worthwhile." Isabella smiled down on the man kneeling at her feet. For a moment the smile seemed almost envious.

"You will wed a lovely and very gracious lady. Treat her well, Rafael, and grace our country with children of strength and courage."

"Yes, Your Grace."

Isabella left the room majestically with her ladies in her wake, leaving behind a man who gazed after her in deep awe and respect. They had talked for only a half hour . . . or rather she had questioned and he had answered. Then she agreed to the wedding and wished him Godspeed.

Isabella sat at her desk writing. The room she sat in was large, and Elana, Beatriz, and the rest of her ladies were scattered about, doing assorted things. Mostly they were making an effort to keep silent for Isabella did not like distractions when she was writing.

It was obvious she was following a routine she had set some time before. Beatriz knew she would be engrossed for over an hour. She bent close to Elana and whispered.

"Elana, I must leave for a few moments."

"Are you meeting my brother?"

"Yes."

"Oh, Beatriz, you both must be more careful. It could mean disaster if you were found out."

"There is something I must tell him. It is important, Elana. I will not be gone long, I promise."

"All right, if she asks for you I shall think of something. Do hurry, and do be careful."

Beatriz bent forward and kissed Elana's cheek. "You are like a sister, Elana. I shall never forget what you are doing for me."

"My brother loves you, Beatriz, and with the grace of God, one day we will be sisters. Go, and hurry and give Rodrigo my love."

Beatriz slipped silently out a narrow side door without anyone else seeing her. Quickly she ran toward a hall to the door of another. She slipped inside, turning to close the door softly. A hand came across her shoulder and slid the bolt home. She whirled about and with a soft cry, she was in Rodrigo's arms and his lips were claiming her in a heated, passionate kiss. His lips claimed hers in kiss after kiss as she murmured his name over and over and clung to him with a passion born of desperation.

"Beatriz," he said against the softness of her skin, "your message said it was important. What is wrong? You're trembling. What has frightened you?"

"He knows!" she moaned.

"He? He who? Knows what?"

"Don Francisco, somehow he knows about us!"

Rodrigo took her by the shoulders and looked deeply into her frightened tear-filled eyes. "Beatriz, calm down and tell me what you are talking about."

With supreme effort, Beatriz tried to control her trembling body. She inhaled deeply, then began to explain why she felt Don Francisco knew about them and what he had said to her. Rodrigo, too, felt she was right in her suspicions, but he knew he had to say something to comfort her. He held her in his arms.

"Beatriz, maybe he does suspect somethng, but he has no proof. Isabella will not believe just rumor." He took her shoulders and held her a little away from him. "Beloved, the time is close, very close, when we will be away from here and

123

safe. Trust me a little longer. I would never let anything happen to you. My heart, you know I love you more than my own life."

"I do trust you, Rodrigo," she shivered. "It is just . . . his eyes . . . when he looked at me."

"*Querida mia*, he'll never touch you. I swear he'll never touch you. It is only a matter of a little more time and we'll be safe to be together for the rest of our lives."

Beatriz moved into his arms. "Hold me, Rodrigo, hold me and tell me you love me. I will try to be strong for all of our sakes . . . only hold me."

He bound her to him, silently cursing the situation they were in. He kissed her and very reluctantly, moved her away again. He found it very difficult to hold her this way and know he could not possess her. She read his eyes and smiled.

"*Amado mio, amado mio*," she whispered.

"*Bella adorada mia!*"

"I love you."

"You must go, *muchacha mio*," he said, "much as it fills me with pain, you must go. Remember, it will not be long. Have strength and courage."

"I will try," she whispered. He opened the door and she left. After closing the door behind her, Rodrigo left the room by way of the windows.

That night dinner in the grand dining room was a loud and rather boisterous affair, and Reeve found it nearly impossible to get close enough to say even a few words to Elana, although it took every ounce of control not to go to her. Tonight she seemed even lovelier than she had at any other time. He controlled his impatience only by telling himself that soon he would be with her, soon he would push the gown of green silk away from her golden skin and possess her. The thought of it made the hand that held his glass of wine tremble.

The evening, to Reeve, dragged on and on and it was made

worse when he found out through random conversation that all the queen's ladies went with her to assist her in preparing for bed. It might be a long time before Elana would return to her room.

It was nearing midnight when Isabella left. It was completely against protocol for anyone to leave before she did. Reeve decided to go to his room and wait. Again, he had been disappointed that no one had tried to contact him. He was getting both disgusted and worried.

He walked up the steps to his room. Pale moonlight lit the room, casting dark shadows in the corners. From one corner came a soft voice.

"Don't turn around, captain. I want to talk to you."

Reeve remained still, knowing that if the man had wanted to kill him he could have, and he believed finally this was the person who was to contact him.

"So, you have finally decided to come out of hiding, my friend," Reeve said with a chuckle. "It's about time. I had given up hope you would come forward at all."

"I had no choice but to keep silent for a while. There are people who watch closely and too many lives are at stake now."

"I'd like to know why you searched my room. What were you looking for?"

There was a deep and prolonged silence, and with sinking heart, Reeve knew his shadowed friend was not the one who had searched his room.

"Search your room, Senor Burke? I did not do such a thing to a man who has come to save the lives of people I hold dear. I know we are being watched . . . to search your room," the worried voice continued, "they must have expected to find some proof . . . evidence to connect you to us. Do you have any such evidence?"

"Do you think I am a fool, Senor? There is no incriminating evidence in this room. I carry all things in my head."

"Excellent! I must ask you, Senor Burke, to have patience. It will be a little time yet before it is safe to try and put our plan in motion. There is no margin for mistakes. If we fail, some very good people will pay with their lives. I do not care for myself . . . but the others . . . there are those I love dearly."

"I have had patience. Can you at least tell me the plan?"

"No! If you should be questioned, all would be lost."

"Questioned by who? I have been welcomed at court. Who would ask the questions?"

A low laugh sounded. "Stop trying to make me believe you are naive, captain. I know you better than you think."

"That's more than I can say. Why don't you let me light the room and talk to me face to face? We could make plans together. They might be more workable."

"The plans have already been made."

"And I'm only a small part."

"Hardly, you are our only avenue of escape."

"Then why don't you trust me?"

"Trust, captain," the voice sighed softly, "is a luxury we cannot afford now. I do not want to offend you, captain. You are desperately needed, but we cannot reveal more to you at this moment." A slight pause. "Will you trust us?"

"I came here, didn't I?" Reeve said softly. "I have waited and been patient and I will still wait, not because I trust you, but because I gave a promise to a man whose honor I respect."

"And," the voice said softly, "you have found someone who also needs you?"

"Elana," Reeve breathed. "Is Elana connected to this? Is she part of this plan?"

"She is and she isn't. Elana has a heart that is open to her friends, but she does not know anything except that she is protecting someone she loves."

"I want to know one thing."

"Yes?"

"Elana was included in the escape."

"Without her knowledge, yes. We would not have left her behind to pay the price."

"Then," Reeve said, smiling in relief, "I will have all the patience required as long as I know she will be safe, too. I have another question to ask you. This Don Francisco, I want to know about him and his connection to Elana."

Silence.

"Are you afraid of Don Francisco? Is he the one who is connected to this . . . this Inquisition that seems to have everyone paralyzed with fear?"

Again silence.

Reeve turned slowly to face the corner, and even though he could not see into the shadows he knew by instinct his nocturnal visitor was gone. He had not heard the door open or close and the wild thought struck him that there might be a secret passage in his room, too.

He lit a lamp with difficulty and examined the room. It was completely empty. He tried to make a thorough search but found no sign of a door anywhere.

He extinguished the light and went to the doors of the patio. Outside he looked closely but there was no one about. Quickly and soundlessly, he went to Elana's room. It was still dark. Obviously, she was still with the queen. He stepped inside the door and closed it behind him. The room was silent, dark, and empty.

He felt for the edge of the tapestry that hung before the hidden door. Pushing it aside, he felt to see if there was a handle to open it. There was a light click as his fingers traced an indentation and the door moved silently open. Reeve stepped inside. As the door began to close he stopped it and left it slightly ajar.

The passageway was narrow. So narrow he could touch the walls on both sides. He began to move slowly forward. Slowly, step by careful step he moved. He passed a door that had a dim light beneath it. Still he moved on until he felt the edge of steps. Tentatively, he stepped down one after another until his feet could trace no more steps. Again he walked along a passage to another door and tried to push it slightly ajar until he could look into the room. He was not surprised to see Don Esteban entangled in his bed with a young maid.

He let the door close and walked on until he came to the end of the passageway. Another door presented itself. Again he pushed it ajar and looked in to find . . . Beatriz sleeping peacefully in her bed. Reeve let the door close and started back. As he passed it, he tried to check the first door. It remained firmly closed, bolted from *within*.

He made his way back to Elana's room. Before he pushed the door open he saw the room was already bright with light. Elana was here. He stepped into the room quietly. Elana stood with her back to him. It was obvious she had thought he might not come and was preparing for bed.

Her long dark hair was loose about her and she had just stepped out of the last of her clothes and was reaching toward a chair over which her bedgown was draped.

"Elana," he said quietly. She froze for a moment, then recognized the voice that had spoken from behind her. Slowly she turned to face him, well aware of her effect on him by the glow of profound admiration in his eyes. He could not seem to get his breath. It had been snatched from him by the slim golden vision that stood before him.

"God, you are beautiful," he said.

Elana raised one hand toward him and her eyes softened and grew warm with invitation.

It was an invitation no man would have been able to refuse, but after his first taste, Reeve was filled with a deep hunger. He moved toward her. Without a word he drew her into his arms and kissed her hungrily.

Chapter Ten

Elana lifted her arms and folded them about Reeve's neck, moving her body slowly and seductively against his. Her thighs were bare against his and her breasts caressed his chest. Elana had learned quickly from Reeve and now she used all she had learned to set him ablaze with desire. It was enough to intoxicate Reeve and turn the strength of his body to water.

Elana could feel his heart thundering against her flesh, and savored the power of giving such pleasure. His hands pressed her body to him as if he could make her a part of him. Her lips flamed with the touch of his. Elana drew back, her eyes smiling up into his. He held her still, nestling her close to him.

"You are a witch, my love," he said, chuckling softly, "and if you are trying to seduce me, your effort is a complete success."

Elana made a soft throaty sound of pleasure as his lips sought hers again. His lips tasted again and again the sweet nectar of which he had dreamed all day.

He bent down and in one lithe movement lifted her into his arms to rest against his broad chest. He walked swiftly to the bed and sat upon it, then lay back, holding her close to him.

He turned to pull her beneath him and again, his lips began a heated journey that roused her senses beyond reason.

He filled her world and a soft sigh of contentment urged him to further his need.

It took him moments to rid himself of his clothes.

Sea-green eyes drew him back to her and with a wild and fierce passion, he possessed her. The fierce and beautiful agony of their surging need filled them both. She arched beneath him to draw him deeper within and she felt the wild abandoned heat fill her and lift her with him to the highest pinnacle. His body responded to the silken touch of her body. She was his, and she gloried in their mutual possession. Once again they tasted their own special joy of their union.

When thundering hearts calmed to a steadier beat, when heated blood cooled and they regained some minimal hold over their senses, they lay silently together, each caught in the wonder of the rare and beautiful thing they had shared.

Her head lay nestled in the curve of his shoulder and he absently caressed her silken hair and savored the feel of her warm curves pressed close to him.

She was content as she had never been before and she sighed deeply as she curled even closer, twining her slim legs with his. He chuckled as his arm tightened about her and he heard her soft laugh. For a strange reason he could not fathom, the relaxed and happy laughter stirred some strange depth in him. He wanted her this way always—content and ready to laugh.

He turned to face her and braced himself on one elbow. He looked down into her eyes and saw the reflection of his own contented peace. Bending his head he tasted her lips, softly playing them gently, feeling the velvet texture.

"Elana, sweet, sweet Elana," he whispered softly.

Elana reached up and slid her fingers through his thick gold hair. Her eyes were soft and filled with love for him.

"I never thought there could be anyone as exciting and beautiful as you. You're so very special, Elana, you're like part of my body."

"I love you, Reeve," she replied quietly.

"And you ask me to leave you? You ask me to go and not look back? I would be leaving part of me behind, Elana, a part I could not survive without."

"I ask you only to take moment by precious moment. Only God knows if we were meant to be together. I only know that I cannot sacrifice others."

He wanted to tell her just why he was here, how he was to be the instrument by which people she loved would escape the dark specter of death. But there was a need within him to have her trust, to have her come to him with the truth, to have her need him as much as he needed her. "I suppose," he said gently, "that as much as I hate to admit it, I understand. Moment by precious moment, Elana," he added softly, "and they are precious to me, as you are precious to me. For now, I want you every precious moment you will come to me. Try to remember, Elana, that I will always be near you should you need my help in whatever scheme that beautiful head of yours thinks up. Will you remember that? Come to me if you need help or if there is anything that frightens or grows too big for one alone to handle."

"I'll remember, Reeve. It is good to know you feel that way and are not angry with me for being stubborn."

"I didn't say I wasn't angry with you for being stubborn," he said, grinning. "If I thought it would do any good, I would try to shake some sense into you. But I'm sure the only effect violence would have would be to take you out of my arms, and that, my sweet, is one thing I won't take any chances on."

"Reeve . . . I—"

"Shh, Love," he said gently, as his lips again caressed hers gently. "This is not the time for us to care about the rest of the world. This is our time. For these few precious moments, we will forget everything that stands between us but the love we share. I have faith that one day we will be together for always. Until then . . . until you feel safe in your heart that I would never be the cause of pain to you, until you feel free to let me share your secret . . . I will be here, and I will wait, and," he added softly, "I shall go on loving you."

Tears sparkled in her eyes, and she found words incapable of expressing the choking, filling emotion that burned within her. But she did not need words for they were lost as his lips possessed hers again. All thought of words fled her mind as passion surged again and she surrendered unconditionally to the force of it.

Elana slept, content and safe curled against Reeve, but Reeve did not. His mind was still on the hidden passage and the door that could admit a mysterious someone to Elana's room. He worried over one thing. Would the door admit friend or foe? He had to do something to bar the door from the inside. If it were friend, it wouldn't matter and if it were foe at least he could protect Elana from a surprise visit.

Before dawn could light the sky, he rose and moved slowly about the room. For a while, it seemed as if he would find nothing that would be effective in barring the door. Then he noticed a small alcove. On the wall within was a display of some ancient weaponry most likely having belonged to a previous owner and forgotten about. What caught his eyes were two crossed sabers.

He took them from the wall and carried them to the door. It pleased him to find that the door opened by sliding. He pushed the blade of the saber into the crack of the door and wedged the handle down against the frame. Then he took the second and reversed the procedure. He tried the door and smiled to himself when it refused to slide. At least from this one particular danger, Elana was temporarily safe.

He returned to the bed and tried to rejoin Elana without wakening her. She stirred and turned within the circle of his arms, and he drew her warmth close to him.

"Reeve," she said sleepily, "where have you been? You're cold!"

"Just looking to see if there was anyone outside. It's time for me to leave," he whispered.

With pleasure he felt her arms tighten about him, and he enjoyed the thought that she did not want him to go any more than he wanted to go.

"So soon?" she murmured. Her lips brushed his throat. "Time only seems to fly when we are together. Why does it seem to stand still when I am waiting for you?"

Elana sat up, still half drugged with sleep. She made a vision Reeve would remember for the rest of his life. Her hair tumbled over soft, creamy shoulders and shielded her from his view. Gently, he brushed her hair aside so his gaze could feast more leisurely on her soft rounded charms. There seemed to be a luminous glow about her, and he could no more resist reaching to touch than he could have ceased breathing.

His hand brushed gently down her soft skin and he watched the glow in her eyes. She sighed deeply and lay down across him, her dark hair enclosing them as she pressed her lips to his. It was a kiss that would have melted the snow of the poles and for Reeve it was the final seal in his determination that Elana would be his forever, no matter what he had to do to get her.

Despite the fact that leaving her side would be the hardest thing he had ever done, Reeve knew the time was growing short. Already there was a gray cast to the sky. The dark corners of the room were beginning to lighten.

"Elana, there's no help for it, love. I hate it, but I've got to go."

He pushed her back against the pillows, kissed her with a fierce possessive kiss, and rose from the bed. He tucked the blankets firmly about her and began to dress.

Elana watched him closely, her eyes storing each memory of

his golden aura. He was bronzed and heavily muscled, yet he had the lithe grace of a jungle animal. To her he seemed like a tall, golden god from the stories of her youth. She felt the warmth only he could stir come alive within her. She wanted, with every ounce of her heart, to go to him and tell him that, despite everything, she would go with him. She wanted to—but knew she could not.

Reeve returned to the bed, bent to kiss her lightly again, caressed her hair with a gentle hand, then was gone, and Elana felt the emptiness he left behind.

Elana stood in the queen's apartment with the rest of the ladies who served her. There was laughing conversation whirling about her and yet, her mind drifted to the night and the joy she had shared with Reeve. She wondered if he would return when night came again.

Her mind had been filled with a nagging thought that Reeve Burke was much more than she knew. Question after question had begun to fill her mind. How long would he stay? How did he and Rafael become friends? Why did he come here at all? Would he just leave one day never to return? Would she be able to let him go?

Her reverie was so deep that for several minutes she did not know she was being spoken to until Beatriz repeated her name several times.

"Elana . . . Elana?"

"Oh . . . yes, Beatriz. I'm sorry. I was daydreaming."

Beatriz smiled. "About anything . . . or anyone I know?"

"Shhh, Beatriz, please. Someone will hear you."

"Don't worry, they're too busy chattering about the guests for the wedding."

"Wedding? What wedding?"

"Goodness, you *have* been daydreaming. Her Grace has given Rafael and Catrina permission to marry here at court. She has sent messages and some guests are already arriving."

"How wonderful! Rafael is a wonderful person."

"Well, there will be a great many guests. As I said, some have already arrived."

"Who?"

"Don Francisco's nephew, Diego Sandoval."

For some strange reason, Elana felt a tingle of fear touch her. She had never met Diego Sandoval and she didn't want to.

"When will the wedding be?"

"In a week or so I'm told. There has to be time for many guests to arrive. You know how insulted some of these families can be if they think they are overlooked. Especially if it is an invitation to court, no matter what the occasion."

They both laughed, but Elana still felt the soft touch of a warning hand that made her shiver.

"Beatriz," Elana said softly, "has your grandfather heard any news at all?"

"No, Elana, he hasn't."

"How much longer can this go on before someone finds out?"

"I don't know. I only pray and hope that news will come soon, and we can find a way to safety."

"Where is there safety from that dark hand, for you, your grandfather, or," she added softly, "for any who have dared to help you?"

"There has to be a way to escape. Somehow we will find it. Rodrigo has some plans."

"How do you know?"

"I . . . I don't for sure, but I feel he will find us a way to safety. All we really need is a method to get out of the country quickly when the time is right."

Elana's thoughts jumped immediately to Reeve. Reeve, the golden god of her dreams, Reeve, the captain with a fleet ship. A ship that could take them all to safety.

She wondered if he would dare to get himself involved with

the Inquisition just to save a few people who must mean nothing to him. No, her logical mind said. Why would any man with any sense deliberately stand against the Inquisition? It was too much to ask of anyone. Yet, maybe she could trust him. Maybe he would at least give them passage were they to reach his ship. Could she go to him? Could she ask? Could she trust?

Dinner that night was a gala affair as guests began to arrive from nearby estates. It would be several days before all the invited guests would arrive.

The guests began to file forward to pay their homage to the king and queen. Elana and the ladies about her stood to the side and watched them come forward.

Elana could feel Reeve's eyes upon her from across the room. She did not look at him, for fear her love would show in her eyes for all the court to see.

She tried to keep her eyes focused on the approaching guests, and that was when her eyes met first, Don Francisco's, and then Diego Sandoval's.

He was tall, slim, and very dark. He wore a short black beard and the winged brows over his dark eyes gave, to Elana's startled eyes, an almost satanic look.

His eyes caught hers and she knew that he had been searching for her. His smile gleamed white against his dark skin and the gaze was both avaricious and self-satisfied. He gave a short silent bow toward her and Elana felt a shiver both of distrust and fear.

"She is a lovely creature, is she not, Diego?" Don Francisco said softly. "Do I not keep my bargains? Did I not promise you the choicest taste of the court?"

Diego chuckled. "*Si*, Uncle, she is beautiful. Have you made all the arrangements? I should hate to wait very long."

"I have made everything ready. The king will announce you betrothed at the wedding. In the meantime should you feel the necessity to . . . ah . . . court the lady, do so discreetly."

"I shall. I am not averse to a little pleasure before the marriage. She is young." He grinned. "I'm sure she is unlearned. She will respond to my experience. It will be a pleasure to teach a beauty such as she the fine art of love."

"Come, I shall introduce you to your future bride."

They walked to Elana who stood with Beatriz in conversation with Rodrigo. After Don Francisco had introduced Diego to them all, he smiled pleasantly at Elana.

"My dear, would you do me the enormous favor of introducing my nephew to the other ladies? I'm sure Rodrigo and Beatriz would not mind keeping me company while you do." He smiled broadly and there was no choice left for any of them. Diego took Elana's elbow and they left the group.

Diego could feel Elana's tension and the light touch of his hand could feel the tremor of her body. It excited him as helplessness always did. He could feel the desire for her begin to broil within him. He planned on making it known to her quickly that she would one day belong to him. He planned it because he fully intended to sample her charms as soon as possible.

Elana had started toward another group when Diego's hand restrained her. She stopped and looked up at him in surprise.

"I would really prefer talking to you than these others." He smiled. "I had not thought to meet someone as lovely as you or I should have appeared at court a long time ago."

"Thank you, Senor Sandoval."

"Oh, you must call me Diego. I think you and I shall get along famously. Come, walk with me." Again, he took her elbow and moved toward the open doors to the garden.

Elana wanted to refuse, but it was done with such smooth manners that outside of creating a scene, she could hardly

137

refuse. And he was the nephew of a man of whom she was deathly afraid, Don Francisco. Her eyes caught Reeve's as she passed him. If it had been anyone else, the whole situation might have passed him by. But Reeve was too attuned to Elana not to read the fear in her eyes. He watched them walk through the open doors down into the garden. Then he followed them. He had no idea who Elana's companion was, but whoever it was, Elana was afraid of him.

Diego and Elana stood in the garden. From where Reeve was, he could see them conversing together. He saw Diego reach out to take her hand and watched Elana withdraw it immediately. He would have moved then, but someone spoke from behind him.

"Captain Burke?"

He turned to see Beatriz standing in the lighted doorway. Since he was standing in a darkened area, he knew she was guessing his identity.

"Yes," he replied, and Beatriz walked out to join him.

"Have you seen Elana?" she asked. Her voice was filled with worry and he suspected Beatriz had seen Diego and Elana and had come out with the same plan as he—to rescue Elana.

"Yes, I have," he replied as he motioned toward the two who stood in the garden below them. Her eyes followed his motion. Beatriz watched the two below in conversation, and Reeve watched Beatriz. Her lips narrowed and her face seemed to stiffen.

"You know him?"

"Yes," she replied, "Diego Sandoval."

"I'm afraid I don't know the name."

Beatirz lifted her eyes to him and her voice was quiet. "Would it help if I said he was Don Francisco's nephew?"

"I see," Reeve breathed quietly. "Lady Beatriz, would you care for a walk in the garden?"

"I would be delighted, Captain Burke. Why," she said,

smiling with devilment in her eyes, "we might even run across friends."

"Yes, we might at that," he said, chuckling as he extended his arm to her. She took it and they walked down the stone steps.

They heard the fragments of conversation as they approached unnoticed by both Diego or Elana.

"Senor Sandoval, that is impossible. Please, I must go back."

"One moment, my beautiful Elana, we must become better friends. It is destined for us to be . . . good friends. What is the harm in a little quiet conversation here where we are alone?" Again he reached out and this time gripped both of Elana's arms and drew her toward him.

Reeve and Beatriz were not far from them and both would have gone to Elana's aid, but neither had the opportunity. There was a sharp yelp of surprise and pain as Elana kicked out with her foot, followed by another sound, a ringing slap that jolted Diego and made him step back quickly from this wild woman he had thought to be a docile child-woman.

Diego gazed after a rapidly departing Elana, shock and disbelief written on his face. Elana flew past Reeve and Beatriz so angrily that she barely saw them.

It was a difficult thing for Reeve to bury his laughter. The soft chuckle struck Diego harder than Elana's hand had done. It struck his pride. He drew himself erect, his eyes blazing with hatred. Stiffly he walked past Reeve and Beatriz, marking them both in his mind, to be remembered later.

"Captain Burke," Beatriz said softly, "what are we to do?"

"Do? He got what was coming to him." Reeve laughed. "I haven't seen Elana angry before. I must be careful to tread easy. I don't think I want to tangle with her, should she be angry with me."

"You don't understand," Beatriz replied. "One does not

embarrass Diego Sandoval, not the nephew of Don Francisco. And you, to laugh, they will never forget. Oh, Captain Burke, you have made a deadly enemy, and I'm afraid Elana and I have also."

"Surely it would embarrass him more should he try to do something about this?"

"He will say nothing in public. He will wait and watch and when you least expect it, he will attack. You would be advised to walk carefully, captain, and to beware of dark corners."

"I can take care of myself," Reeve replied. "What about you and Elana? There is no way he can harm you, is there?"

Beatriz's face was pale. Her lips trembled and her eyes seemed to see some distant thing. "I don't know," she replied in a rasping whisper. "I don't know."

Reeve would have questioned her more but she suddenly seemed to become aware of what she had said and to whom she was talking.

"We must go, captain," she said firmly and started to walk back toward the lighted dining room. Reeve had no choice but to follow.

As they entered the room, Reeve saw Diego and Don Francisco in animated conversation, then both pairs of eyes turned toward him. He smiled, bowed, and turned away, aware that their eyes were following him. He could feel them burn into his back. He promised himself he would never turn his back on either should they ever be alone. Some instinct told him that was the direction they usually struck from, and Reeve was one to follow and trust his instincts.

He was right, and would have done well had he overheard the conversation between Diego and Don Francisco.

"Calm yourself, Diego. It is a matter of time. Elana will be your bride, and I shall find out just what Captain Reeve Burke is doing here. Then I shall have all my birds in one nest, and I shall pluck their feathers."

140

"I will kill him," Diego grated angrily.

"Maybe you shall have the opportunity when the time comes."

"What is it that you wait for, Uncle? Why do you not eliminate him now?"

"Because I want him to lead me to another, another that I want even more than him. Until then, you will have patience and wait. Do not worry, Diego, you will get all that I have promised you."

"The wedding is in a few days. Then you will have the betrothed announced. After that, there is nothing Elana can do unless she commits treason," Diego said.

"She will not do that. She worries too much about her brother and her family. She would do nothing to jeopardize them. Patience, patience, she will be yours soon enough, and Captain Burke will be unable to do a thing about it."

More than one person watched the confrontation and saw the conversation and hate-filled looks of Diego and Don Francisco. Another watched the procedure with interest. Without a doubt, the onlooker read well the anger in the eyes that watched Captain Burke. He smiled and was about to cross the room to speak to Reeve when someone touched his elbow. He looked around to see a young man standing beside him. He smiled again.

"I have been expecting you. You have a message for me?"

The young man nodded and slipped a folded piece of paper into the other's hand.

"All is well?"

"Yes," the young man replied, "the plan goes well."

"Good. It is best you leave soon. *Vaya con Dios*, may we meet again soon."

The young man smiled and then left. The onlooker slipped the piece of paper beneath his jacket, smiled, and rejoined the party.

Chapter Eleven

The days before the wedding were days of assorted tensions for all involved. Rafael and Catrina were the only two who seemed to be content. Elana did her best to stay out of the vicinity of Diego or Don Francisco. It was a condition that made her nerves raw with anxiety. It was only the nights spent with Reeve that made the days bearable at all.

Reeve found it difficult to ease Elana's nervous state, and there was even a night or so when she was so unnerved that he held her and talked to her until she slept. He would tell her of his past, of his family, of his likes and dislikes until her mind was taken from her worries.

No one was more grateful for the day of the wedding than Reeve. It started well, but it was to end on a completely different note.

Reeve had anticipated another encounter with his mysterious employer and it came the night before the wedding.

Elana was completely involved in the preparations for the ceremony, so involved that she and Reeve could not share time until the small hours of the morning, which left him at odds with himself. He shared a late snack and a few drinks with Rafael and Rodrigo, then made his way rather unsteadily to his room.

He sat on the edge of his bed and laboriously removed his

boots, then he lay back across the bed. It might be hours, he thought before he could go to Elana. It was the first taste he was to have of the emptiness that existed when Elana was not beside him.

He allowed his memory complete freedom to wander through his time with Elana and realized the depths of the emotion he felt for her. She had grown to be a part of him he could not do without. Dark hair that felt like silk when he tangled his hands in it and smelled like soft spring blossoms. Slim, warm body that had the power to raise to him in a height he had never touched before. A smile that could alternately make him quake with expectancy or melt under its warmth. Eyes that could lift his heart like a bubble of air or send it plummeting should they fill with tears. All was Elana, his beautiful Elana.

He was tired of this seemingly endless waiting. He was exasperated with it and wondered as to the reason that this escape was so important, and why it had not already happened.

The need for Elana tugged at him and he sat up again. He walked to his window, stepped out on the patio and looked down its length to Elana's room. It was still dark. He left his windows open and walked back into his room.

He paced, worried, and cursed to himself, vowing he would take Elana and leave, promising himself he would shake answers from his shadow the next time he appeared; and still the time seemed to stand still.

He went to a small table where a decanter of wine sat. He certainly didn't need any more to drink, but he poured a glass and lifted it.

"Good evening, Captain Burke."

Reeve did not turn around, he simply took a sip from his glass. "It's about time, my friend. Where in God's name have you been, and what is holding you up?"

"I know you are impatient, captain, as I am. But the wait

144

was necessary."

Reeve set the glass down and turned around. The tall shadowed form stood in a dark area, and Reeve knew his first inclination had been right: There was a door that led to his room through which his shadow moved freely.

"This place seems to be permeated with hidden doors and passages," Reeve said, grinning. "Do you spend all your time spying on people?"

"Hardly, captain," the shadow answered with a chuckle. "There are only a few in this palace that interest me . . . or you. I take it you have been exploring?"

"Some."

"But you haven't found your answers?"

"To tell the truth," Reeve said, "I'm as much in the dark now as I was when I first arrived here."

"Well, captain, our time grows short. I have come to tell you that we must be ready the night after the wedding. Loose ends have been tied and we are almost ready to leave."

"Tell me your plan so I will know exactly what I have to do."

"Listen closely, captain, I have only a few minutes. The night after the wedding celebration it will be quite late. You will return to your room, make yourself ready, then go to Elana's room and bring her here. We will be waiting for you."

"And then?"

"We will tell you the rest then."

"Don't you trust me yet?"

"To tell you the truth, I do, but I will not put other lives in your hands, in case someone should discover what you are doing. I wouldn't want too many names at your command."

"I see."

"It will be over soon, captain. If God is willing, we will be gone for hours before anyone knows we have left."

"Then," Reeve added quietly, "it's a race to my ship."

"That's right. We will have six or seven hours start which

should be enough."

"If we're caught?"

There was a moment of complete silence, then the voice came again, solemn and restrained.

"God forbid, captain. God forbid."

"We'll be ready," Reeve said firmly.

"Thank you, captain. Until then." The door before him slid quietly closed and Reeve gazed at it in surprise, wondering why he had not been able to find it before. He was tempted to for a moment follow, but he knew it would kill any trust they had for him should he be discovered.

A sudden urgency to see Elana filled him. He had to hold her, to feel her in his arms, know she was safe. Again he went to his patio and saw, to his relief, a light from Elana's window. He extinguished the light in his room after bolting the door, and nearly ran toward Elana's.

Elana walked from the queen's apartment with Beatriz. Both were exhausted, and there was little conversation. The halls were dimly lit and both women were gratified they did not have far to walk.

"I have promised my grandfather to say good night to him," Beatriz said. "Shall I walk with you to your room first?"

"No, Beatriz, your grandfather's room is not too far from mine. A few steps up and I will be at my own door."

"You're sure?"

"Yes, I'm sure." Elana smiled.

They stopped in front of Beatriz's grandfather's door. "Good night, Elana, I'll see you early tomorrow."

"Good night," Elana replied. She watched Beatriz step inside her grandfather's door and close it after her. She had to walk down a hall, up several steps, and down a shorter hall to her room. She turned from the door and took a few steps, then she stopped. Her heart froze as some instinct told her she shared the hall with someone else.

She looked back over her shoulder along the dimly lit hall and could have screamed when she saw a tall form that stood at the far end of it. Her heart in her mouth, she turned and began to move rapidly toward the stairs that led to her room and safety. She heard movement from behind her and her heart began to thud furiously. The stairs seemed to be miles away.

Finally she reached them. She lifted her skirts and ran up the stairs, hearing the sound of footsteps not far behind. Tears of real fear burned her eyes and she was shaking in fright.

She reached her door and pushed it open, turned and slammed it shut, throwing the bolt home as she did. She was panting and her hands shook so badly she had trouble lighting the lamp. She sat on the edge of her bed, her hands clasped before her and tears falling helplessly down her cheeks. That was how Reeve found her when he stepped inside her door.

Her eyes lifted to his tall, golden figure as he stepped inside. She breathed his name, ran to him and threw herself into his arms.

"Reeve, Reeve," she cried, "thank God."

"Elana!" he said in alarm as his arms closed about her trembling form. He could feel her heart beating furiously. "What's wrong?"

"Some . . . someone in the hall. I . . . I'm sorry, Reeve, I was just frightened for a moment. It was probably just someone on their way to their room. It . . . it was just dark, that's all. I feel like a silly child, but I was always afraid of the dark."

Reeve moved her aside and went rapidly to the door and unbolted it as silently as he could. He opened the door slowly and stepped into the hall. He looked both ways and saw no one at all. Coming back in he closed and bolted the door again and went back to Elana who sighed contentedly as he took her into his arms and captured her lips with his.

When he reluctantly released them, the fear in her eyes was gone, replaced with a warm look of love and security.

147

"You most certainly do not feel like a child to me, silly or otherwise," he said with a chuckle. She watched the gray eyes sparkle with laughter, and he was pleased to feel her relax completely. "And if you are afraid of the dark, I certainly would not mind staying until it's light to make sure you're safe."

"Stay," she whispered softly. "In your arms is the only place I have ever felt so safe."

"Will you be here alone and afraid of the dark when I'm gone, Elana?" he asked softly.

"Reeve."

"The thought of someone else keeping you safe drives me frantic."

"There will be no one else, Reeve, never. I love you. I have never said that to another, nor will I. Don't you know if I could go with you, I would?"

Reeve realized that whoever it was she was protecting was someone she loved very much. He knew time was short, and didn't know why it was so important that she come to him in trust and tell him what he already knew—that there was a plan set in motion for the escape of the person she was protecting.

"Don't fret, love," he whispered against her hair. "Maybe you are right and things will all work out. For now you're here, and I love you."

Elana reached up and slid her fingers into his hair and drew his head down to her more than willing lips.

His mouth slanted open and hungry across hers as if he wanted to devour her, and indeed he did. He wanted to possess her as he never had before. He wanted her to surrender to him completely and turn to him with enough love and trust that nothing else would ever stand between them. It was savage, yet it was tender intoxicating savagery that swept them up and carried them beyond reality.

His hands caressed her slim body leisurely, exploring,

148

rousing. With deft fingers he found hooks to release and scattered her clothes about them at random, neither caring when or where they fell.

A whispered sigh escaped her as she pressed herself against him. He drew her with him to the bed where they fell among the blankets. It was a renewal of the beautiful magic that blended their individual desires into one soaring ecstatic fusing. Elana closed her eyes, breathless and warm beneath him.

It was blossoming magical madness that stirred her to a flaming desire. She arched against him with a passion that matched his.

He clasped her to him with hard, binding arms as if he could draw her within him. She could feel the roaring thunder of his heart and the harsh rasp of their mutual breathing. Her hands caressed the rigid muscles of his back as they flexed spasmodically beneath her touch. Sheathing himself in the velvet depths of her they stood on the edge of eternity and shared the beginning of a spellbinding ardor that was so intense that it stunned them both with its wonder and left them gasping in amazed pleasure.

Time seemed to stand still as they gazed at each other, mute with the wonder and intensity of the supreme joy they had shared.

Reeve smoothed her rumpled hair and his lips gently touched hers.

"Elana," he whispered, "there has never been a wonder such as you. You have a way, my love, of filling every part of me until there is nothing in my world but you."

Elana sighed contentedly and nestled close to him. Her lips touched his throat with butterfly kisses as her slim arms held him to her. Absently, Reeve let his hands caress her body, lightly savoring the feel of her silken skin.

They were silent now, lost in the warmth that enclosed

them, both aware that there were no words that could be said that would touch the wondrous sense of sharing and belonging.

Pale beams of moonlight bathed the room in a misty glow. The candles sputtered and went out as a breeze touched them. Within the room peace and contentment reigned, but outside nature began to stir her own cauldron.

Elana slept curled close to Reeve. He slept holding her close . . . and time slowly moved on.

It was in the wee hours of the morning that Reeve stirred. Half awake, he immediately felt something was wrong. He reached for Elana and realized what that something was. Elana was not beside him.

He sat up at once, coming fully awake, and his eyes searched the dark room. He saw Elana standing by the open windows looking out. At the same time, he heard a rolling sound of thunder.

Elana had wrapped a lace shawl about her and her slim form wavered vaguely beneath it. She held it together between her breasts, but it had slipped from her shoulders.

To Reeve she was a pale vision of loveliness as he had seen in many of his dreams. Her dark hair fell in a soft cloud nearly to her hips. Quietly he rose and left the bed. He walked across the room to stand behind her. Gently, his arms came about her and he drew her back to rest against him. He did not speak, and they both stood spellbound at the storm that was evolving before them.

The mountains in the distance appeared vague and insignificant below a dark and sultry sky. The air had suddenly become hot and still. A great black primordial cloud began to broil and from it shot blinding bolts of brilliant light. Then came the sound of rumbling thunder.

Then the rain began, first large plump drops falling with a rapid splashing, and lightning flickered over the countryside as the thunder began to howl.

The storm approached rapidly and in a moment a cool breeze blew across them. The wind became heavier and the rain began to fall in earnest.

Trees bent under the wind and some fragile branches broke and fell to be tossed about.

They watched as nature unleashed a passion that was the only thing that matched their own. They breathed the new cooler breeze together and even enjoyed the few drops of rain that fell on them.

Slowly he turned Elana in his arms. From the depths of him, a soft moan of pure pleasure beyond his control whispered against her skin. Again he looked down into her eyes, sensing some intangible difference.

"Elana?" he questioned softly.

"Oh, Reeve," she whispered, "what a fool I have been."

"Why?"

"I have told you I love you. I have loved you, and you have driven me to near madness with the gift of your loving. I have asked you to trust me . . . can I do less for you?"

His heart leapt and joy tingled through him like a touch of the brilliant lightning they had just witnessed.

"Oh, Reeve, I might have let you go, I might have been insane enough to really believe I could not trust you. You are a part of me, like my heartbeat or the course of the blood in my veins. Can you forgive me for not seeing, for not believing?"

Tears lingered on the edge of her lashes and glimmered in her eyes.

"Elana, there is nothing for which I could not forgive you, but I don't understand. What made you realize the truth?"

"I have stood here watching the storm, and you were holding me. I realized then that with you, I am no longer afraid of anything. I am safe. I am loved." Her voice dropped to a whisper. "You have given me love and trust and hope, all the things I was without. You gave so completely. I would put my

151

life and the lives of those I love in your hands. I would trust . . . I would ask for your help."

He drew her within the circle of his arms and held her, rocking her tightly against him. "Elana, don't you know I would give you my life if you asked?"

She looked up at him. "That is what it could cost you if I asked."

"Ask," he said gently. He took her hand and led her to the bed. They sat down side by side. "Ask," he repeated gently.

"Reeve, you have a ship."

"Yes, in Cadiz Harbor."

"Would you help me if I told you someone has to get away from Madrid safely and secretly?"

"Yes, I would. Do you want to tell me who?"

She knew now that she must trust him completely or turn away from him completely. Reeve waited, knowing her decision had to be made without force from him. He needed her to come to him finally and completely.

"Yes," she said in a firm voice. "Beatriz de Mendosa and her grandfather."

Relief flooded him. She was his, completely his. He put his arms about her and lifted her onto his lap. Gently his lips brushed the soft skin of her throat.

"I love you, Elana. As God is my witness, I love you more than my life. Tell me what I must know and I will help you in any way you need."

She clung to him and in a quiet voice she began to explain just why she needed him. "The Inquisition is a terrible force in Spain now, Reeve. You have never seen it or never felt it and I pray that you never do. For most of us it is a fear that we have learned to live with. If we are careful and do not offend the wrong people, then we will be safe."

"People like Don Francisco?" he asked.

"I feel that, but I do not know it for sure. I know that he has

152

many friends within the Inquisition."

"Go on," he urged.

"There are others who are not safe."

"Beatriz and her grandfather, why?"

"Because," she said hesitantly, "because they are Jews and the Inquisition has a terrible hatred for them."

"Jews . . . de Mendosa . . . it doesn't sound Jewish to me."

"It is not their name. Reeve, it has taken much to hide their identity. Beatriz's grandfather would not even have agreed to it if it hadn't been for her safety. He would face whatever they could do with that magnificent pride of his, but he could not bear to see what they would do to Beatriz."

"What has happened that they aren't safe now?"

"We have a feeling Don Francisco and others are suspicious. We think they are conducting an investigation into Beatriz's background. We feel sure it is only a matter of time until the information he wants is in his hands."

"Elana, I will help them get to my ship. I will see them safe in England. But I will do it only on one condition."

"What?"

"You must come with them."

"It is their safety we are worried about," she exclaimed.

"It is yours that worries me," he replied.

"It is not me they will harm."

"Little fool! Do you think Don Francisco or the rest of his followers would hand you to the Inquisition? They would use it to get you, and when they did, they would keep you for themselves. Elana, he would have you, and I could not let that happen."

"And Beatriz?" she said in shock.

"I'm sure they have the same plans for her. You have asked for my help and I would give it gladly, but you must come."

"It . . . it was not planned for me to go yet."

"Then tonight it is part of the plan. I want to talk to

153

everyone involved."

"Reeve, I can't do that unless I tell them first."

"Then tell them at the first opportunity. Elana, listen to me. If I left here with them, if I left you behind, it would be very nearly impossible for me to get back. Do you really believe I could walk away without knowing you are safe?"

"Then, we will change our plans," she said softly. "If I can, I will go with you."

"Now," he said smiling, "you're talking logically."

Reeve was content. Elana had come to him with complete faith and trust. He would help them all escape, and he would take her home to become his wife. Then he would never let her go again.

He also knew the identity of his shadowy visitor. There was no doubt in his mind who it was. All he had to do now was wait for the right time, and he knew the best way to make those long hours short.

All was quiet now. The storm had died away. A soft cool breeze filled the room and Elana shivered with the touch of it. Reeve stood up, lifting her with him. He laid her on the bed, then lay down beside her, pulling the blankets over them both.

"You're cold," he whispered against her hair as his arms drew her closer. "Come here and let me warm you."

"Yes," she sighed, "warm me, *mi amour*. Hold me, Reeve, love me."

"There is no command sweeter, my heart," he whispered as his mouth swept down to possess hers in a deep, demanding kiss.

Clouds skittered past a now full moon. The room was touched only by its light. The two who shared the room knew nothing but the ecstasy they shared.

There was a newness, a fuller giving, a deeper possession of each other than had ever been shared before.

Elana was secure, feeling that Reeve was the source of all she would need to sustain her. Reeve shared this and the grim determination that he would protect Elana, no matter what the cost.

It was in the pale gray of the dawn that Reeve kissed a sleeping Elana and left her room. He moved quietly and quickly across the patio to his room. Inside, he closed the windows but didn't bother to bolt them, knowing with all the secrets of the palace, there was no safety in a bolted window.

Then he sat down to consider some plans of his own.

Chapter Twelve

The storm seemed to have cleared the air and washed the entire country clean. The day dawned with a bright sun that was to herald the day Catrina and Rafael were to marry.

Elana was involved with Catrina's preparations as were the other women, which left Rafael, Rodrigo, and Reeve somewhat at loose ends.

The wedding had been planned for late in the afternoon and was to take place in the queen's private chapel after which a reception would be held.

Excitement filled the entire palace, and Reeve was amused to see the usually unflustered Rafael, the man who seemed to be calm and assured in the face of all things, stricken by a severe case of nerves. Rafael paced the stone patio where he, Reeve, and Rodrigo had shared breakfast.

Of course, Reeve, too, missed any opportunity to be with Elana. The day seemed much dimmer and he would have welcomed any opportunity to share a moment with her. To touch her, to have one stolen kiss would have brightened his world immensely, but it was not to be, so he resigned himself to the fact that he would not see her until the time of the wedding.

Reeve had no way of knowing, nor did Elana, that the festivities of the evening would be a near calamity for them.

Now Reeve rose from the table. "Rafael, let's go for a ride.

Some strenuous exercise would do us all some good."

Rafael agreed immediately as did Rodrigo. Once their horses were saddled, they rode rapidly from the palace grounds and into the wooded area. Horses and men seemed to be in the same mood, so they rode rapidly until the urgency seemed to be relieved.

They rested the horses for a few minutes and while they walked along slowly, they had time for some very constructive conversation. It began with some laughingly exchanged banter and some suggestive tormenting of Rafael which he took with an amused grin.

"Rodrigo," Reeve said, chuckling, "we had best not let our young friend ride too long. We want him to be in good condition for the . . . ah . . . celebration tonight."

"Of course, you are right," Rodrigo said innocently. "We would not want him to be too tired to enjoy all the pleasures of the occasion."

"You," Rafael said, "are just jealous, both of you. Tonight you can sleep in a cold and empty bed alone. If I have a moment, I shall think of you, but I doubt it. Both of you deserve it."

Reeve reserved his thoughts, knowing that when the night was over, he would be with Elana. He knew exactly how many hours stood between them, and had to control both his words and expression. There were other more important thoughts he still kept to himself until the proper moment presented itself.

Rodrigo was also thinking of another, and for a few minutes all three walked in silence.

"I never asked you, Rafael," Reeve said, "who have you chosen to stand with you?"

Rafael smiled as he clapped Rodrigo on the shoulder. "Rodrigo de Santangel, a man who has been my friend for many years."

"It is an honor, Rafael." Rodrigo grinned. "I should be

pleased to be standing near should you lose your courage and begin to tremble in your boots."

Rafael laughed. "Were it any other woman but Catrina, that might be a possibility. But gentlemen, I ask you, have you looked into those lovely eyes? Have you seen that beautiful smile? How can you look at Catrina and believe a man could ever lose the desire to have her? I would be insane to let her get away, and I assure you, gentlemen, I have all my wits about me."

They laughed together. "Well," Reeve said, "I suppose we should turn back." They agreed. All three men turned and remounted. They were not really in a hurry, so they walked their horses back toward the palace.

As they crested the last hill, they could look down to the borders of the palace grounds where a long retinue was winding its way toward the palace.

Even where they were, they could tell the new arrivals were out of the ordinary. Reeve turned toward Rodrigo to ask about them and was shocked at Rodrigo's face. It had gone deathly pale. The hand that held the reins of his horse trembled. Beyond Rodrigo, he could see that whoever the new arrivals were they were a threat to both Rodrigo and Rafael, for Rafael looked as upset as Rodrigo did.

"I take it," Reeve said softly, "that both of you know the new arrivals?"

"Torquemada," Rodrigo breathed softly as if were he to say the name too loudly, some great disaster might strike him.

"Torquemada? Who is Torquemada?"

Both men looked at him as if he had said something unbelievable.

"I'm sorry if I've said something wrong, but I've no idea who Torquemada is. Is he some great dignitary?"

"No," Rafael said quietly, and he and Rodrigo shared a look that Reeve could not interpret. To him, it looked like a transfer of similar thoughts: fear. What surprised him was that men the caliber of Rafael and Rodrigo would be afraid of anything or anyone.

"Well then, who is this Torquemada?"

"He's a monk," Rafael replied.

"A monk?" Reeve was really surprised now. "Why would a monk be invited to the wedding?"

"That," Rodrigo said, "is what I would like to know, and I'll bet I know just who really suggested he be asked to come."

"Don Francisco de Varga," Rafael said firmly.

"Can you think of any one else?" Rafael asked. Reeve felt as if some unsaid thing had passed between the two men.

"Rafael," Rodrigo said, "why don't you circle around and find our friend? Maybe he does not know."

"Yes, it is a good idea," Rafael replied. "Reeve, I will see you later."

Rafael kicked his horse into motion and in minutes was dashing at breakneck speed. Reeve felt it was inevitable he would be inside the palace before the seemingly unwelcome visitors.

"Rodrigo," he said quietly, "do you want to explain what's going on here?"

Rodrigo sat silent for a moment. It was very obvious he was reluctant to say anything at all. "Reeve . . . I . . . I cannot . . . not yet. I—"

"Rodrigo," Reeve said in a gentle voice, "would it help, my friend, if I told you I already know it was you in my room the other night?"

Rodrigo turned to look at him.

"I wouldn't have said anything until you were ready to come to me, but, I think the arrival of this man has changed your plans. If you need any help . . . if you're ready, we can leave any time you choose."

Rodrigo's shoulders slumped. "How did you know? I must

have made a mistake for you to find me out so soon. If I have," he said desperately, "how many other mistakes have I made . . . and who else knows?"

"No, Rodrigo, you did not make any mistakes. How I found out? Well . . ." Reeve did not want to include Elana's name or to let her brother believe their relationship was less than it was. "I found you in my room. I followed you. You went into Elana's room. But when I mentioned the next day that you had visited her late at night, she was surprised. I knew then somehow she had not known you had come in. I suspected a secret passageway."

"My God," Rodrigo said softly. "They should never have trusted me. I am a fool."

"No! Those words would make you a fool. You are doing your best in a bad situation. Why don't we have a long talk this afternoon. It is time you tell me the truth and time I did what I was sent here to do."

"Yes, we must talk. But we cannot go yet."

"Why?"

"Let us go to my room. Rafael will join us there later. I will explain the whole thing to you, and I will explain why we must wait a little longer."

"Even if it endangers everyone more?"

"Even if it costs my life."

"And Elana's?" Reeve said softly.

"If worse comes to worse, Reeve, you must take Elana and escape."

"She would never go without you."

"You love her?"

"Yes, I do."

"Then, you would take her!" Rodrigo said firmly. "By force if necessary. Do you understand, Reeve? If a tragedy does happen, there will be no time to think. You must at least get Elana away safely, swear it!"

161

"Rodrigo."

"Swear it, Reeve. I need your promise."

"I swear it, Rodrigo. I will take her, and I will keep her safe the rest of her life. I love her very much."

"Good, my friend, good. Now, let us talk." Reeve nodded and they kicked their horses into motion and rode toward the palace.

By the time they arrived the new guests had already been settled in and there was no sign of them.

"I imagine they are being presented to their Majesties?" Reeve said.

"Most of them," Rodrigo answered, "but I would wager my soul that there are some new visitors in Don Francisco's room."

They did not speak again. Reeve followed Rodrigo to his room. They were aware of the sense of excitement that pervaded the palace yet they had an urgency to build an understanding between them and to make some tentative plans. Reeve had to find out why they could not leave yet, what held them immobile.

Inside his room, they decided to wait for Rafael before they discussed the situation. He arrived a half hour later. There was one sharp rap on the door and Rodrigo let him in.

"You have explained?" Rodrigo asked.

"Yes, and received the answer I thought we would. Instructions to leave them and go at the first opportunity."

"As if we would leave them."

"He is a brave man, Rodrigo. He asks only that we take Beatriz."

"We will, but we will see to the safety of all."

"Gentlemen," Reeve said, "I'll pour some wine, you two tell me exactly what is going on and what your plans were. Then we shall see that they're carried out."

"We?" Rodrigo said.

162

"Well," Reeve said, smiling, "if you are going to be my brother-in-law, I can't just walk away and leave you in trouble, can I?"

"Brother-in-law?" Rafael questioned with a grin.

"As soon as possible," Reeve answered.

"You are a lucky man, my friend."

"No one knows that better than I."

Reeve poured three goblets of wine, handed one to each, then took his own. The three sat about a table.

"Now," Reeve said, "suppose you let me know just how we can complete your plans, who is involved, and what you expect me to do." Rodrigo sighed deeply and exchanged a look with Rafael.

"Rodrigo, you know much more than I," Rafael said.

"All right, I'll tell you how this situation came to be. To explain, I must go back some time." Reeve remained quiet, waiting for Rodrigo to continue.

"Beatriz de Mendosa's great-grandfather married a woman named Anna de Silva. It was a happy marriage and from it came Benjamin de Mendosa. From that a son, Bartoleme and from his marriage, Beatriz." Reeve wasn't sure just what all this was meant to prove, but still he waited in silence.

"Reeve, you, as an Englishman, are unaware of the black shadow of the Inquisition."

"I know it's enough to frighten Elana to death. She told me a little about it. It is hard to believe."

"You must believe," Rodrigo said softly. "Listen closely and I shall tell you some rather grim details."

Rodrigo went on to try to explain the purpose, intent, and tragedy of the Inquisition. Reeve listened, first fascinated, then appalled, then sickened by the senseless deaths and punishments it conceived.

"I can understand it a little better," Reeve said, "but I don't understand how it can be connected to you and Elana. Surely

163

you have nothing to fear."

"Oh, but we do," Rodrigo replied. "Beatriz's great-grandfather was Bernadino Coria. He had a second cousin who became the wife of Roberto de Santangel."

"So you are very, very distantly related. Surely this is not some offense to the church."

"Not to the church, not in the eyes of God. But in the eyes of some, it is dangerous."

"How?"

"There is great wealth in the de Mendosa family, a wealth that is coveted by some people in strategic places. Besides desiring the wealth, they desire something more—the prestige of the de Santangel name and the force it can carry at court. They want to dispose of me and marry Elana and Beatriz so that that wealth and prestige can be completely controlled."

Now Reeve became silent again and his eyes grew cold. "Surely they have to have some reason to use to be able to do this. They can't just arrest you and . . . burn you if they can't claim some offense."

"You are right," Rodrigo said softly, "but you see, before too long they will have the proof they need to do exactly what they want."

"What proof? What offense could two innocent women like Elana and Beatriz have committed?"

"Several."

"What? Tell me, what?"

"First, let me tell you one other thing," Rodrigo continued. "The Inquisition has a special hatred for the Jewish people. They claim they have committed sacrilege of their teachings and beliefs." He shrugged. "At least that is what they use for an excuse to kill and confiscate land, wealth, and anything else they desire to possess."

Reeve felt he knew the balance of what Rodrigo was going to say. "And?" he prompted softly.

"And," Rodrigo answered in a voice equally soft, "the wife of Bernadino Coria was a Jewess. You see. Elana, Beatriz, and I have Jewish ancestry. That is enough to leave us open to whatever they decide to do."

"Who is behind this?"

"Don Francisco de Vargas wants Elana, no matter how he has to get her. He also wants the de Mendosa wealth, so he will do whatever he wants to Beatriz to get it. As for me," Rodrigo said with a shrug, "I am expendable."

Reeve breathed deeply as a thick wave of pure rage overcame him. They sat in silence for several moments while Reeve digested what had been said and had brought his fury under some control. "Now," he said angrily, "tell me what has kept you from getting them away safely before this?"

"Don't you think I would have if I could? It was all prepared with your ambassador when he was suddenly recalled. We suspect who had a hand in that. There is another thing, our parents, Elana's and mine, we had to see they were safe and well. How could we run to safety and leave them to pay the price?"

"I take it they are safe now?"

"They are, I received a message. It was what we were waiting for."

"They you are free to go?"

"It is not quite that simple. We must move very carefully. We would never reach your ship should we just break and run. It has to be done so that no one knows what is happening until it is too late to stop us."

"And you have some plans?" Reeve questioned.

"I shall explain to you what we plan, then maybe you can find its faults. Whatever we do must be done quickly. I have reason to believe Don Francisco has intentions of moving. Our new guests would not be here if he had not."

"Explain."

Rodrigo set his glass down and bent forward to rest his arms on the table. His eyes held Reeve's intently. "Don Francisco suspects you, there's no doubt about that. The first place he will search for us is your ship. Right after the wedding, Rafael will say he is taking his wife to his home. Instead, he will go directly to your ship with a message from you. Your ship must leave the harbor immediately and go to another small harbor we have chosen. There it will wait for us.

"The next day Beatriz's grandfather will profess illness and say he will remain in his room the balance of the day. We will then take him from the palace by way of the secret passage."

"How will we do that? If we go with him, any one of us, we will be missed."

"No, I have someone I can trust to take him to our meeting place."

"Then what?"

"Then we shall go riding as usual. We will not be able to take anything along with us except as much money as we can carry. Anything we need will be bought along the way."

"We will be travelers easy to follow."

"No, we are going to join some friends of mine. We will be traveling with what looks like a band of rather disreputable Gypsies. They know this country very well and can very nearly vanish if they choose to do so."

Reeve grinned. "Rodrigo, you are a very capable man, but I must say you have a very wide range of friends. How did a man of your background run across such people, much less acquire them for friends?"

"I learned a long time ago that it pays to make friends everywhere. The way things are in this country now, one never knows when one will need them."

"And besides," Rafael said, chuckling, "there're some rather pretty girls among them and until Rodrigo knew Beatriz, he had an eye for all of them. I hope when we join them, some of your friends don't get too talkative. Beatriz might turn out to be more than you can handle should the green-eyed monster perch on her shoulder."

Rodrigo was effectively silenced for a moment. It was obvious to a rather amused Reeve that he had not thought of that situation. Finally, he shrugged and grinned amiably. "I shall just have to take that chance. Besides, Beatriz is very sweet-natured and understanding."

"I wouldn't count on that," Rafael replied with a wicked glow in his dark eyes. Rodrigo chose to ignore it.

"Well, Reeve, what do you think, will it work?"

"It sounds just wild enough to work, but it will be a matter of careful timing. Maybe it would be better if Beatriz's grandfather were to take ill at the reception. He is older and I don't believe he will travel well. If he leaves the night before, he will have a good start."

"Excellent, excellent! I shall see to it."

"Another thing, you must caution the women to wear warm cloaks. We will have to ride early while it is still cool. By dinner, they will be looking for us, and it's best we have as many hours as possible."

"I will."

"Where will the ship be? How long will it take us to get there?"

"The ship will be in a small out-of-the-way harbor not far from San Sebastián. We will meet Pedro Garcia near San Lorenzo de el Escoral. He will guide us from there. We will be traveling long, and in many out-of-the-way places."

"It will be hard for Elana and Beatriz."

"But they will be safe. They will be protected from men such as de Vargas and the plans he has for them. They will be with the ones who love them. That should help to balance the discomforts of traveling."

"I'm sure," Rafael offered, "you will not hear a word of

complaint from either of them. Both are women of stronger caliber than anyone realizes. They are strong enough, and they know what is at stake."

Remembering Elana's fiery flash of temper with Diego, he was struck with the thought that there were quite a few facets about Elana he did not know. The idea thrilled him that he would have the pleasure of learning them day by day as they shared the rest of their lives together.

"Then it's settled. The plans are as good as we'll ever find. Rodrigo, you must go and talk to Beatriz and her grandfather. Rafael, I suspect you had better go prepare for your wedding before we have an angry bride on our hands."

"I wish there was a way to talk to Catrina," Rafael said. "I should prepare her."

"Make the plans to leave right after the wedding. Then," Reeve said with a smile, "if I were you I would explore the secret passages a little further. I wouldn't be surprised to find one of its little secret doors didn't lead to Catrina's room as well."

Rafael seemed startled and he looked at Rodrigo questioningly.

"I don't know," Rodrigo said to the unasked question. "I have only used Benjamin's and Elana's."

"I wish I had time. I would see the extent they really go," Reeve said. "I know one thing: I think Don Francisco knows about them."

Both men were startled at Reeve's words. "How do you know?"

"I passed his room. It was the only one bolted from inside. He had to know about it to secure it. I don't think he wanted visitors in the middle of the night. I barred Elana's door so he couldn't use it if the inclination struck him. At the time, I didn't know it was you doing the nocturnal wandering. I thought it might be someone who might intend Elana some harm."

"If he knows, then he might already have been doing some wandering," Rafael offered.

"It's a chance we'll have to take. We have no time for anything else," Rodrigo said.

"Rafael, you go along and get ready. Rodrigo, you talk to Beatriz and her grandfather."

"What are you going to do?" Rodrigo asked.

"Somehow I have to talk to Elana. Then I am going to talk to Don Francisco de Vargas. He should be in his room. If he's not, I'm going to check that door, then if possible, I shall barricade it from the passageway. If he does decide to use it, it won't be tonight, and by tomorrow, no one will care."

"You had best be careful, Reeve," Rodrigo said.

"Don't worry, I've too much at stake to get careless now. I'll be careful."

The three rose and left Rodrigo's room together. Rafael returned to his, his mind now on the wedding soon to be performed and the very beautiful bride he would claim. Rodrigo went to Benjamin's room, where he found the old man alone.

Quickly he told Benjamin all their plans. "I will hold you back, my son. I'm afraid you will not be able to travel fast enough to escape if you have me with you."

Rodrigo went to Benjamin's side and knelt by his chair. "You are," he said gently, "a man I respect as I would my own father. You are also a man I admire and one whose life I feel is worth almost any cost. Last and most important, you are the grandfather of the woman I hope to make my wife. That makes you very important to me. I will not go without you and neither, I expect, will Beatriz."

The old man's eyes glistened, and he reached out and rested his hand on Rodrigo's shoulder. "My granddaughter has chosen well. You are a man of pride and honor. You are also very stubborn." The old man chuckled and Rodrigo laughed with him.

"Then you will do as I ask?"

"I shall try. I shall do my best to keep up and not cause you any problems."

"I'm grateful, Beatriz will be pleased."

The door opened and Beatriz came in. Rodrigo rose and the old man could read the warmth and longing in Rodrigo's heart through his eyes.

"Rodrigo," Beatriz said, "what are you doing here? Why aren't you preparing for the ceremony?" She smiled at Rodrigo whose mind was so involved with her beauty he could not think of an answer.

"He has come to share the plans for our escape, my child," Benjamin said softly. Beatriz's eyes fled to Rodrigo. She went to him and put her hand on his arm.

"Rodrigo?"

Unable to help himself, and knowing there was no doubt in Benjamin's mind of his feelings for Beatriz, Rodrigo put his arms about her and drew her close.

"It's not going to be easy for you, Beatriz, but we will be together. I'll be with you to help you if you need me."

Beatriz looked up at Rodrigo and the warmth in her clear, hazel eyes would have melted the soul of any man. "You have always been strong," she said softly. "You have always been here to help me when I needed you. You don't believe I would doubt you now?"

Rodrigo smiled down into her bright eyes. If they had not been in the presence of her grandfather, he would have crushed her in his arms and kissed her hungrily and thoroughly. "I love you, Beatriz," he said gently. "My life has belonged to you for a long time. Soon we will be away from here and safe. Then we will hide no longer."

"I'm not afraid, Rodrigo. I would go with you anywhere."

Her eyes turned to her grandfather. "And I speak for you also, grandfather?"

"Yes, child, you do."

"Then," she said, turning back to Rodrigo, "you must tell us exactly what we must do."

Rodrigo took her hand and led her to a seat beside her grandfather. Once she was seated, he sat opposite her and took her hand in his. Quietly, he began to speak and they did not interrupt until he was finished.

"Do you have any questions?"

They both shook their heads negatively.

"Good. By this time tomorrow, we will be on our way to Reeve's ship . . . and to freedom."

Chapter Thirteen

Reeve moved quickly to his room. He bolted the door behind him and crossed to the window. He knew Elana would have to come back to her room soon to make herself ready. He only hoped she would come alone.

He opened the window slowly, his eyes scanning the area intensely. No one was about so he slipped out and made his way quickly to Elana's room. Once inside he found it still empty.

He checked behind the tapestry in the alcove. The door was still braced closed. If anyone tried to get in they had been unsuccessful. He did not know how long Elana might be, so he took the two sabers in his arms and went through the doors into the passageway. As quietly as he could, he went to the room he now knew was Don Francisco's.

He laid the sabers down quietly and laid his ear against the door to see if there was any sound from the other side. Nothing. Quickly, he set about using the sabers so that the door could not be opened even if it were unbolted from the other side. He wanted Don Francisco to get a surprise should he try to use the passage.

He made his way back to Elana's room. Just as he entered he heard a sound outside her door. Not knowing if she were alone or not, he stood in the doorway of the hidden doorway and pulled the tapestry across it. He could still hear but he could not see.

He heard the door open and close, and the sound of one single person walking across the room. Elana was alone. Relief flooded him and he quietly pushed the tapestry aside.

Elana was laying clothes across her bed that she was planning on wearing to the wedding. Her back was to him and she was so engrossed she did not hear him cross the room.

He came up behind her and spoke her name softly. A quick gasp of shock and she spun about. There was so much fear in her eyes that he immediately regretted what he had meant just to be a surprise. She was shaking all over and her breathing was labored.

"Elana! My God, I'm sorry. I didn't mean to frighten you so."

"Reeve," she sobbed and collapsed against him, clinging to him. It was then he knew that it was not just his surprise that had upset her so badly. He held her away from him and studied her closely. Something had frightened her.

"What is it, Elana? What has frightened you, love?" he said gently.

"I'm so glad you're here, Reeve. I'm not frightened when you are here. It's all right now. You just startled me, that's all."

"Don't lie to me, love. You're still shaking." He drew her against him and bound her to him with iron-hard arms, just to give her the sense of security he felt she needed. "Elana, you've been in the queen's apartment all morning?"

"Yes, then we went to help Catrina dress."

"Something happened."

"No, Reeve, really I—" She lifted her head to look into his eyes and the words died on her lips.

"Tell me, Elana," he said softly. "You might as well, because you're not leaving my arms until you do."

He felt her body draw close to him as if she needed the

174

warmth. His arms tightened about her waist. She spoke in a very quiet voice.

"It's to be announced formally tonight at the wedding celebration."

"What is?"

"Two more weddings in the near future."

"Who?"

"Beatriz. She's to marry Don Esteban, and Diego Sandoval . . . and me."

Now he held her away from him and she was startled again by the blaze of intense anger.

"You were just . . . just told, as if you were so much merchandise to be sold?"

She nodded. "Reeve, you know there is nothing we can do now."

"You're wrong, love, you're so very wrong. You didn't really think I would let it happen, did you? Don't you have any more faith in our love than that? He will touch you over my dead body."

"Don't say that! There is nothing worth your life!"

"You are. But don't worry, it's never going to happen. We've already made plans. I have just come to explain what we're going to do and to tell you that I'm taking you out of here."

"Reeve . . . Rodrigo?"

"We made the plans together."

Her eyes brightened. "My parents?"

"They're safe."

Tears sprang to her eyes and she sagged against him as if all the strength had been drained from her.

"Oh, thank God. Thank God."

They stood together clinging to each other. Gently, Reeve tipped her face up and bent his head to touch her mouth with his. It was a light, sensitive kiss that told her more of his love and understanding than anything else could have done. He held her face between his hands and gently kissed away the tears that slipped from beneath her lashes.

"Elana, don't ever believe, no matter what happens, that I will ever leave you. My sweet, sweet Elana, you belong to me."

He heard her soft murmured yes as again his mouth captured hers in a flame-touched kiss. Their lips blended, their bodies molded to each other's, their arms entwined and they fused as one.

He was hungry for her as he had never been before for anything or anyone, yet he knew this was not the time.

It took the greatest feat of will he had ever possessed to move her away from him. "Elana, our time is short, so I must explain what we are going to do."

"All right."

"Sit down, I'll explain quickly."

Obediently, she sat and Reeve explained their plans and about the secret passageway. She was shocked but said nothing. He made sure she was secure in the knowledge that this would be the last night they would spend in the palace. At the next day's dawning, they would ride away, never to return.

Relieved, her smile soon returned. "I will be all right now, Reeve. I promise. Just to know we will soon be together forever is enough to give me strength to get through."

"Good girl. Remember when they make their announcement tonight that I'll be near. Don't be afraid. He can't touch you."

"I'll remember." She reached up and touched his face and smiled. He knew she was all right and smiled.

"Now I have to bathe and dress. The wedding is less than two hours away."

"Umm." He smiled. "Don't tempt me."

He enjoyed her bright smile and the warmth that leapt into her eyes and again cursed the position they were in. He was resigned that he must wait.

He touched her lips with a feather-light kiss and walked to the window. A silent wave and a quick smile and he was gone.

Catrina stood by the window with her back to the room of chattering people who were preparing her for her wedding. She quickly unfolded the note she had been given. Of course she knew it was from Rafael. She read it quickly, then, as the note instructed, she tore it into as many pieces as she could. She took the pieces, walked across the room, threw them in the remains of a low burning fire, and watched them disintegrate. It was a time they had planned for.

Quickly, she turned to the serving girls. "While the celebration is going on, I want you to pack my clothes. My husband has chosen to go to his home after the celebration and I must be prepared to leave."

"Yes, Senorita."

Catrina stood before her mirror and looked at her reflection. She still could not believe the happiness that flooded her. This was the day that had lived in her dreams for years.

The gown she wore was a miracle of beauty. Although there was not enough time to make the gown she had dreamed of wearing, she was more than pleased with the one she had chosen.

Her dark hair had been coiled elaborately upon her head and a diamond tiara was placed on it. The gown was of pale rose and she had been laced so tightly that the soft rise of her breasts swelled under the thin fabric. She wore voluminous petticoats over which rested the soft silk rose dress. It was Rafael's favorite color and that is why she had chosen it.

She closed her eyes for a moment reliving the precious day they had found each other. Tonight he would be hers forever. She could not recall ever being so happy.

There was a rap on the door and one of Catrina's maids ran to open it. It was to carry the news to her that it was time for the ceremony. The messenger was followed by Catrina's mother and several minutes later, by Don Ricardo. Her parents' eyes glowed with pride and honor. Although her mother wept copiously, she still smiled and hugged her daughter tight and often.

Don Ricardo, suspicious moisture in his eyes, held his daughter close for several moments.

"You are ready, Catrina?"

"Yes, Father." She smiled up at him. This man had raised her, known her, and loved her always. She had gone to him for all problems from skinned knees to unrequited love which had always included Rafael Chavez. He understood her as no one else had, and had loved her in his strong, unswayable way. There had always been room in the safety of his lap when any problem faced her, and there had always been kindness and consideration in his guidance.

"You are lovely, my child."

"Thank you, Father."

"You have carried your name with honor, Catrina. Now you join a family of great pride. You are an Alverez, remember that. If ever you have need, remember, we are here."

Tears of happiness touched her eyes. "I will remember Father, and Father?"

"Yes?"

"I love you."

Again he smiled. "Catrina," her mother said, "we have been told you are leaving late tonight, after the wedding?"

"Yes, Mother, Rafael has chosen to go home immediately."

"But Catrina . . . so soon?"

"Mother, it is Rafael's choice; I shall do as he wants. We will visit his home for a while and then we shall come to see you."

Her mother sighed in resignation. Her rule over her

daughter was gone.

Catrina would have liked to have told her mother the real reason for the trip but too many ears were listening. She did not want to do or say something that might endanger her parents. They would return home within a day or so. By then, Reeve's ship would be safely on its way and none would ever know that Catrina and Rafael had warned them.

Catrina's parents walked with their daughter to the queen's personal chapel where the wedding was to be held, and where Rafael already awaited her. Only a few were to be present at the wedding, although many guests would be at the following celebration.

The king and queen were present with the queen's ladies-in-waiting, with the exception of Beatriz and Elana. A few gentlemen stood near Rafael who waited impatiently for Catrina.

Reeve's eyes were on four others who stood nearby. Don Francisco, Don Esteban, and Salizar, whom he did not know, but whom he had felt an instant distrust of. Beside these three stood another man, a man Reeve did not know.

The man was not overly tall, and dressed in the harsh brown robes of the order of St. Dominic. His tonsured head, with the haloed fringe of hair encircling it and large, rather soulful dark eyes gave him a benign, almost angelic look.

He had a suspicion who it might be, but there was no way to question anyone present. Rodrigo and Rafael stood close to the priest who was to perform the ceremony. The king and queen were seated on two high-backed gilt chairs on a raised dais not far from them. Isabella watched closely to make sure all things were done to her liking.

Reeve was, by now, wondering where Elana and Beatriz were. In only a few moments, they arrived.

The door to the chapel opened and Beatriz and Elana walked in, both flushed and nervous because they were late.

For Reeve, as for Rodrigo, the entire room became brighter. Reeve envisioned the day when Elana would stand with him and say the words that would make her his wife.

Now they waited only for Catrina and her parents. Rafael found his heart was increasing its beat rapidly, and his throat became so dry that he wished fervently he had a glass of cool wine.

Then she came, and Rafael forgot all but the vision of loveliness that appeared before him. He was still in a state of wonder that lady fortune had given him so much.

The mass was performed quietly and the wedding proceeded without a flaw. Reeve watched Elana through most of the ceremony, allowing his mind the freedom of fantasizing. But a few minutes before the ceremony, his eyes went to Don Francisco. He was startled to see Don Francisco's eyes on Elana and filled with heated desire.

He was first shaken by the intensity of Don Francisco's look, then he was filled with anger. This was the man who wanted to take Elana from him. This was the man who had caused so much grief and fear among his friends . . . and this was the man he would defeat if it took the last breath in his body.

Don Francisco turned his head as if he were suddenly aware of someone watching him. His eyes met Reeve's and held for a long moment, then he smiled a slow insolent smile, as if Reeve were already out of the way and Elana was already his. Reeve could have struck the smile from his face, but he controlled the violent anger within him and smiled coldly in return. It was not what Don Francisco expected and his smile faded, then he turned his attention back to the completion of the wedding.

There was a moment of complete silence when the wedding ceremony was finished. Then the royal couple rose, and Isabella beckoned Rafael and Catrina to come to her. They went to her and knelt before her.

"We wish you both a long and happy life together," Isabella

said. "We have chosen to present you with a small gift."

Isabella was handed a small box by one of her guards, and she turned back to the couple kneeling before her and handed it to Rafael.

"Your Majesty does us great honor by attending our wedding and allowing it to be performed here," Rafael said. "We would name a daughter after Your Grace should God grant us one and Your Grace would permit."

"I would be quite pleased, Senor Chavez."

The royal couple swept from the room which promptly was filled with congratulations, hand clasping, and kisses for the delighted young couple.

A dinner was to follow, small and very informal since the royal family would not attend. Then there was to be a large celebration afterwards.

The dinner was enjoyed by all and everyone was in a most relaxed and pleasant condition when the musicians began to play.

As the celebration began, Reeve was the first to notice that Don Francisco and the unknown guest at the wedding were not present yet. Although everyone gave the appearance of enjoying themselves, one could read the tension and tangled nerves beneath the surface.

They had several hours yet before Rafael and Catrina could safely leave. It was more important now to keep up the facade of carefree enjoyment.

For Rafael and Catrina, it was not quite as bad as it was for the others. They would be able to get away. For Elana and Beatriz, it was quite different. They knew of the announcement to be made, and they knew of the long dark hours before they could go. They were frightened of the unknown they would have to face when they rode away from the palace the next day.

Reeve, who could read Elana as well as he could read his own heart, and who knew her fear of both Don Francisco and Diego, kept himself near her, his smile and the warm touch of his eyes keeping her secure. Rodrigo also gave Beatriz as much courage as he could.

They watched and waited and knew nothing about the men who talked together in a room above them.

Juan de Torquemada was one of the most learned, eminent, and respected theologians of his age, an upholder of the dogma of the Immaculate Conception and the most ardent champion since Thomas Aquinas of the doctrine of papal infallibility. Such was the austerity of his character that he never ate meat or used linen in his clothing or on his bed. He observed the rule of poverty completely. He lived in rigid purity and, as Don Francisco knew, he would react with imagination on what he had just told him.

"You are sure of what you have just told me?" he questioned Don Francisco quietly.

"I have been an obedient servant of the church for some time as Salizar will tell you. I wish only to be of use to you. I would not accuse unless I had some proof of my accusations. It is a nest of vipers in the bosom of the church that must be eliminated."

"And you will bring me this proof?"

"Tomorrow, Your Eminence," Don Francisco said smoothly. He needed enough time to frighten Elana into surrender.

"Excellent. I will speak to Her Majesty in the morning. She will, of course, have to set up a tribunal here."

It had been the way of the Inquisition not only to suspect readily, but also to allow suspicion to usurp the place that elsewhere is reserved for proof.

The stern purpose of Torquemada and the severity with which he intended to proceed were plainly revealed in the gaze

182

that met Don Francisco's.

Don Francisco was quite satisfied. After more polite words he excused himself. He wanted to return to the celebration in time to offer Elana a way out of the dilemma in which he had deliberately put her. He smiled knowing he held the best incentive over her head that would make her accept his offer.

No one noticed the reentry of Don Francisco into the room, for attention had been drawn to the tall man who stood beside the queen's chair. He had silenced the guests and announced that they were to listen as he announced a royal proclamation.

Elana, who stood near Reeve, trembled with the knowledge of what the announcement would be. With calm deliberation, Reeve caught her eyes with his and held them, offering her his strength to sustain her.

For Beatriz, it was the same and only Rodrigo knew the terror that went through her when the hard, cold words were spoken.

It was done, as far as the court was concerned, as far as society was concerned, as far as all but a few were concerned: Elana de Santangel and Beatriz de Mendosa were promised in marriage to two of the most eminent members of royal society.

Don Francisco gloated; Diego's smile of smug satisfaction spoke the same emotion. It took every ounce of control Reeve had not to fling it in their faces that Elana was his, would always be his, and that soon he would be taking her out of their grasp.

Diego hovered near Elana the balance of the evening, grating on her nerves until she could have screamed.

When Rafael and Catrina had said their goodbyes to all and had spoken a few quick whispered assurances to Reeve and Rodrigo, they left for what everyone thought was a trip to Rafael's home where they would spend the first few months of their marriage before a return to court.

After the royal couple had left, Reeve and Rodrigo kept a close eye to the safety of Elana and Beatriz. No matter how Diego and Don Esteban tried, they were both unsuccessful in getting them alone.

Finally, they had to escort them to their rooms where they found the safety of maids and servants.

Elana bade Diego a quick and cold good night. She could not ruffle his contentment even with that. He stood close to her.

"Good night, my rose," he said in a smooth voice. "Soon I will have the pleasure of being on the other side of that door when I say good night. I find it most difficult to wait. I shall request that the marriage be held soon."

"Does it not matter to you, Diego, that I find you distasteful, that I dread the very thought of sharing a moment with you?"

He grinned. "All young brides are a little timid. It will be my responsibility to make you more . . . susceptible to my pleasures."

Her eyes glittered dangerously and even Diego backed away, knowing no matter how badly he wanted her, he could not force her to accept him until it was official.

"Good night, my rose, sleep well. I shall be spending more time with you starting tomorrow. You will learn, my rose," he said softly, "and it will be my pleasure to teach you." He had reached out as he spoke to gently caress her cheek. Elana pushed his hand away.

"I am not yours yet, Diego. Don't touch me."

Diego chuckled and shrugged. "A matter of time, my rose, just a matter of time." He turned and walked away. Elana watched his retreating figure. Hatred and fear broiled within her and mixed with a desire to see Reeve, to have him hold her and tell her everything was going to be all right.

Elana sighed deeply and turned to open her door. She knew Reeve was making preparations for the next day. He would have gone to give orders for the horses to be saddled early. But she needed him and tears burned her eyes as she thought of the long hours before they would be able to leave.

Elana entered her room and closed the door behind her. Her eyes fled across the room, and a soft sigh escaped her as they met clear, silver-gray ones whose tender gaze knew and understood exactly what she felt.

"One more word from him, my love," he said with a laugh, "and I was about to come out and commit murder."

"Reeve," she half laughed and half cried as she ran across the room and threw herself into his waiting arms.

His hunger was unleashed now and he made no attempt to disguise it. His mouth caught hers in a flame-touched kiss that enfolded and engulfed her and swept away all thoughts but him.

Chapter Fourteen

His mouth was insistent, demanding and it shattered every thought she had. She was caught in a flow of liquid molten flame that took her breath away and left her clinging to him.

The fire of her need was as great as his, and her kiss told him of that need as no words could have done.

"You're here," she whispered as his mouth released hers.

"Did you doubt I would be?" he replied gently. One arm held her bound to him and the other gently caressed and soothed her shattered nerves. "Did you think I could stand one more minute without you? I've been thinking of nothing but you for hours."

His lips brushed the smooth flesh of her throat and touched lightly the soft rise of her breasts above the neckline of her dress. "Elana," he murmured, "don't be frightened. Tonight is the last night you will be here. In a few weeks we will be on my ship and heading home."

"Oh, Reeve, I have never wanted anything more in my life than to go home with you. The night will be so long."

"Then," he whispered, "let's make it short and memorable." His arms surrounded her again and she willingly raised her lips to meet his. His mouth covered hers and they kissed long, deeply, and lovingly.

Touch by touch they undressed each other, kissing and caressing each other until they stood together flesh touching flesh. With his mouth and hands he stroked her, rousing her until she was heated with a desire for him that turned her to liquid flame.

One slow caressing step at a time they moved toward the beckoning bed. They tumbled to it together. Reeve held her tighter, his lips seeking the softness of flesh. A soft sound escaped as they succeeded.

Elana lost herself completely in the hunger of his kiss and the heat of his seeking body.

Despite his need, Reeve controlled his urgency and sought with infinite patience and tenderness to raise her passion to a level that matched his.

Elana sought the feel of him, the taste and the scent of him, making him an indelible part of herself. Her hands caressed the hardness of his muscled arms, the breadth of his back, then the narrow waist, drawing him closer to her. His pleasure was intensified by the way she sought him as deeply and intensely as he did her.

Reeve pressed warm kisses on her face, ears, and neck. Her body writhed beneath him, touched him and teased him. His mouth lowered to roused, taut nipples and his tongue caressed lightly until they hardened with the flame of need.

Both of them were lost to the flame that engulfed them, caught in a storm more violent than any that nature could provide. Elana surrendered to him with a completeness that was beyond the realm of anything Reeve had ever known before.

Soft thighs parted and surrounded him, accepting him with a violent need. She arched against him as he moved with long, slow strokes. The rhythms increased, the passion increased, and each sought a treasured ecstasy well remembered. It burst upon them like a searing brand.

They tumbled back to reality. Reeve held her still trembling body close to him and rocked her gently. There were no words that could describe what he felt, and when he looked into her wide, warm eyes, he knew no words were necessary, for she shared completely the longing and the love he felt.

"This has been the most rewarding time in my life, my sweet," Reeve said softly. "I came to Spain for a short visit and here I find all my heart, my life has needed for a long time. I'm grateful to the powers that brought me here. I cannot believe I have gone through my life until now without you. I shall never let you get away, Elana. I love you beyond all reason, all thought."

"We will be safe, won't we, Reeve?" Elana asked hopefully. "I want so much to be with you, to share your life, to bear your children. I would rather die, than to be without you."

"Don't speak of dying, love," Reeve replied. "We will be together. We will be safe. Tell me, love," he said, smiling, "will you be happy as the wife of a simple ship's captain? It will be a different life from all you are used to. A small house and my ship are all that I have. Is that enough for you?"

"My heart! Do you not know by now that I would go with you anywhere, live with you anywhere? My happiness is you, not where we live. You are all I need, all I will ever need for happiness."

"Maybe I know, but I like to hear you say it," he said, chuckling.

Elana laughed softly and nestled closer to him. She sighed deeply as she rested her head on his shoulder and her slim arm lay possessively across his chest. Her slender legs were entwined with his. They were content for the moment to hold each other so.

"Reeve, Beatriz's grandfather, has he already gone?"

"Yes, we saw him safely through the passageway to the

189

SYLVIE F. SOMMERFIELD

outside where a guide was there. He is well on his way to the rendezvous where we'll meet him tomorrow. Your brother is a very clever man. That passageway is an intricate bit of maze. What bothers me is where else it leads, how many people know about it, and if anyone but us has been using it lately."

Elana shivered and Reeve's arms tightened about her. He knew she thought of the times someone might have entered her room while she slept.

"I don't want to think of those who might have wandered in it. All I want to think about is that soon we'll be free of it all."

"It's all right, Elana, it's just my stubborn curiosity. We'll forget it."

"How will we be traveling, Reeve? It is a long distance from here to San Sebastián. What will we do for food?"

"Elana, the best that can be done is a caravan of Gypsies. Your brother has made friends in some strange places. Still we will be disguised and they know the land as no one else does. I doubt if Don Francisco or anyone else will think to look for us there. Besides, they'll be heading toward where they think my ship will be. By the time they get there, they will find it gone with Catrina and Rafael aboard. By the time they get around to searching in the right direction, we'll be gone too. On our way home."

"It all sounds so simple."

"It is."

"If it goes as planned."

"Something bothers you, Elana?"

"I don't know, Reeve. I can't put my finger on anything wrong, it's just a feeling. I suppose I'm just hoping it works so badly that I am seeing something that isn't there."

"I know how you feel."

"You sense it, too?"

"A little, but it's just tension. When we're on our way, when you're in the open air and free, you'll be all right."

190

Again, she was silent, and they lay so for a while, then Reeve heard a very welcome sound: Elana's soft laughter.

"What's so amusing?"

"I just thought of a very funny sight."

"What was that?"

"Have you ever seen the Gypsies?"

"No, why?"

"Well, they're dark-eyed, dark-haired, and some are rather dark-skinned."

"I don't see what's funny about that."

"Not them . . . you!"

"Me?"

Elana sat up and looked down into Reeve's inquisitive eyes. She was a vision in the pale glow of candlelight that Reeve woud never forget. A cloud of dark hair fell about her ivory shoulders and her slim body half draped in the sheets caught his breath within him.

"Reeve," she said gently as her hand lightly caressed the mat of golden hair on his broad chest. "I love so much about you. You are so strong and so gentle. I love the way the sun touches your hair and makes it glow like gold. I love the way you look at me with such warmth in your eyes that it makes me tremble with wanting you. But how will you disguise your hair or those fantastic silver eyes? You don't think for a minute you would convince anyone you were a gypsy, would you?"

Reeve smiled, reached out and brushed her hair away from her shoulders so he could devour her beauty completely. Then he caught its mass in his hand and slowly drew her to him to kiss her with a depth that left her dizzy.

"Well, my very smart miss, I have no intention of disguising myself. Rodrigo has told the caravan about me and they certainly know what to expect. They have sworn secrecy, and Rodrigo says they are remarkable about honoring their sworn word. Should an outsider appear, I will hide until they are gone. But you, my love, I can hardly wait to see you as a Gypsy girl."

"You don't think I will fit in?"

"Not exactly." He grinned. "You look too much like a lady. You're not wild enough."

"Not wild enough?" she demanded.

Reeve taunted her further. "I've heard some pretty exciting stories from Rodrigo about the Gypsy women. You just don't fit the mold."

Her eyes began to glow with evil laughter. "Not wild enough to suit you?" she said softly. She leaned toward him until her soft breasts pressed against his chest. Soft parted lips touched his and slowly, sensuously they possessed his senses with a kiss that would have set the surrounding forests on fire.

He groaned softly as his arms surrounded her and bound her to him until she was as breathless as he. Her passion whipped about him like a whirlwind, leaving him gasping in wonder at the demanding flame that surged about him and engulfed him until he lost both breath and control.

Elana put her leg across him and rose above him, a vision of wild abandon. Her hair wild about her and a smile of supreme pleasure in her eyes captured and held Reeve in a world where only Elana was reality. Her golden body blended with his, a twisting, writhing flame of woman, and Reeve was forever lost.

His body lifted beneath hers to meet her more than halfway while his large hands spanned her slender waist. She was woman, magnificent in her possession, the eternal flame of life, and she lifted him beyond anything he had ever known before.

Senses spiraled upward, alive as they had never been, finding the source of all pleasure, of all knowing. Elana trembled like a leaf in a violent storm and called out to him in words of love that were branded on his heart forever more.

Completion exploded upon them with a violence and they

BETRAY NOT MY PASSION

lay gasping and exhausted. Her slim body lay upon his gently
now, and he caressed her slim, sweat-slicked flesh. Reeve was
left breathless, without words and without the ability to say
them if had possessed them.

After a few moments, to restore their breathing and bring
their pounding hearts under control, Reeve turned and gently
laid Elana back upon the bed. He rose on one elbow and looked
down into her eyes. He bent his head to brush the lightest of
kisses on the tears of passion that still touched her cheeks. He
watched with pleasure the glow of her warm eyes.

"I have dreamed dreams in my life," he whispered, "but
never like this . . . never like you. God, I love you, Elana."

"Why do you love me, Reeve? I have only been the cause of
problems for you. If not for me, you would have been gone
from here by now, and you wouldn't have to go through all this
to get people to safety."

Reeve smiled as he reached with gentle fingers to caress her
hair. "I love you because you are the most beautiful, the finest,
the most honest and sensitive thing to come into my life. And
besides," he said, chuckling evilly, "you warm a bed like no
woman before you has ever done."

"Oh!" she said as she laughed and pretended to strike him
which he thwarted by bending her in his arms. They laughed
together while he rocked her in his arms. "Reeve?"

"What?" he said as he kissed her brow, lay back, and drew
her against him.

"Have there been many?"

"Many what?"

"Other women."

"Elana, is that important?"

"Tell me."

"Why?"

"I . . . I just want to know."

"Yes, there have."

193

"A lot?"

"Elana!"

"Tell me!"

"It depends on what you mean by a lot," he said in an attempt to dodge her question artfully.

"Tell me . . . ten, twenty?"

"I really don't remember."

"Was there one special?"

"You're special."

"I mean before me," she insisted.

Reeve turned on his side and looked at her. A small half smile touched his lips. "Are you by any chance jealous, love?"

Elana reached up and took his face between her hands. "Yes," she said softly, "I am. I wish I had known you always. I wish I had been the one you loved always."

"Oh, Elana," he said gently, "don't you understand, my sweet? You are the first woman I have ever loved. And it will be for always so there will be none after you."

He was satisfied with the tremulous smile and the sigh of contentment as she nestled closely against him. "Sleep, love, we have to get a very early start and tomorrow promises to be a very difficult day. We have to make a lot of miles between us and Don Francisco and his element."

Elana's arm came gently about him and her slim form curled close. Reeve drew the blankets over them and after a while, he heard her soft, even breathing that told him she slept.

He lay for a long time, holding her and wondering if she really knew the danger of this trip. To him, she seemed delicate, almost fragile, and he worried about how she would take the trip. His arm tightened about her as the fear lurked within him that she would not be strong enough to handle it. Silently, he vowed to care for her at all cost.

No matter his vows, when he slept nightmares overtook him and some time later, he woke with a start, sweat covering his body. He had dreamed too much and now a great unbearable fear shook him. He held Elana close and it took him a long time to ease himself again into light slumber.

Dawn had not yet touched the sky when Reeve slipped silently from Elana's room to his. He knew they could not take any extra clothing or blankets with them, but he also knew it was necessary to take as much money as he could. He had been prepared for this and had taken quite a bit with him.

He had also made other preparations with Rodrigo's friends to purchase from them a wagon and horses to be part of their caravan. He knew the coins that had exchanged hands gave him the ability to keep Elana with him. It would insure that she would always be within his reach should any unexpected dangers present themselves.

He put the money in a belt that encircled his waist, then he dressed and left his room.

The first rays of the early morning sun had touched the sky now. Reeve walked toward the stable where he had told Rodrigo he would meet him early. He looked back over his shoulder toward Elana's room. He knew she would be waking soon. It would only be an hour or so before the four of them left for their ride.

The stables were large, and the pale glow inside was not quite enough to lighten it. The stalls were dark, shadowed places. Reeve's boots made a sharp sound on the stone floor.

No one else seemed to be in the stable, so he brought out his horse to examine him. He wanted his animal to be in the best condition for the long trip ahead of them. The horse nickered softly and nuzzled his velvet nose against Reeve's jacket, begging for the carrot or other choice treat Reeve usually had for him. Reeve chuckled and brushed his hand down the smooth, arched neck.

SYLVIE F. SOMMERFIELD

"You great ugly beast," he said gently, as he reached inside his jacket to offer the piece of carrot he had there. "We have a long journey, my friend, and this might be the last treat for a long time."

He was pleased with his horse's condition so he took Elana's from the stall and began to examine it. Finding it to his satisfaction, he began to saddle them both, unaware that a shadowed form had stepped from one of the stalls and stood watching him.

Reeve was taken completely by surprise when a soft voice spoke from behind him. He whirled about to face Diego.

"A long journey, my friend . . . with Elana? I doubt it," Diego said softly.

Reeve's mind began to search for a plan. He knew Elana, Rodrigo, and Beatriz would not be far behind him. Once they came and Diego raised an alarm, all would be lost. But nothing could present itself . . . except Diego's death. He wasted no time. Diego was armed with a sword and a knife, and Reeve had no idea how proficient he was with these weapons. He drew his sword from its scabbard and faced Diego with a grim smile on his lips.

"I'm taking Elana with me," he stated firmly.

"She is to be my wife," Diego replied coldly.

"Only if I am dead."

"That can be arranged, my friend," Diego replied as he drew his sword and held it before him.

Elana's life, along with Beatriz and Rodrigo's lay in his hands now, and Reeve knew it. Perspiration touched his brow. If he failed . . . but he wouldn't . . . he couldn't. He smiled at Diego.

"You would take a woman and hold her, knowing she loved another?" he taunted Diego, and was pleased to see the glimmer of emotion in his eyes. Diego shrugged and laughed to hide them.

"I would be a fool to let one as lovely as Elana get away from me. I shall have Elana and all the wealth and power her family possess."

"In my country," Reeve said with a grin, "we have a name for a man who does such things, but we do not call him a man." Now he watched anger light Diego's eyes. He was pleased, for with anger sometimes came carelessness.

Diego sprang, and swords met with a ringing clash. Reeve gave a sudden flick of his blade in quarte. Diego parried and smiled and whipped back a riposte which, though parried in its turn, jarred Reeve's arm from wrist to shoulder.

"Not bad, not bad," Diego said with a chuckle. "You have a good eye . . . how's this?" A feint, a slash as the blade wheeled and came down. Reeve parried but at the cost of extreme effort and tingling muscles.

Suddenly, Reeve's astute eye caught something, a small line, a flaw in Diego's sword. Would it withstand a severe attack?

Diego sprang again. Cut and thrust . . . cut and thrust faster and faster. But this time, Reeve struck again and again at the flaw. Reeve was tired, his arm felt like lead, and his breath was becoming labored.

Then Diego struck again, with his full force. Reeve brought his sword against the flaw again . . . and Diego's sword snapped. Reeve struck again before the shock of what had happened came to him. He drove his sword home and without a sound, Diego fell.

Reeve was panting with the exertion and the sudden flow of emotion. He knew he did not have much time before Rodrigo, Beatriz, Elana . . . or someone else were to arrive. He didn't want Elana to see Diego; her fear now was enough and he did not want it made worse.

He slid his sword back into his scabbard after wiping it free of blood. At the far end of the stable was a small dark area. Reeve dragged Diego within and threw a blanket over him.

He went back to the area in which they had fought. Blood stained the floor and he hastily threw straw about to cover it. He was hardly done when he heard voices and someone approaching.

He quickly bridled both horses and pulled them along behind him. Rodrigo and Beatriz were just about to enter when Reeve came out to meet them. He handed the reins to Rodrigo.

"I'll bring the saddles and the other horses," he said and before Rodrigo could answer, he turned to reenter the stables. Beatriz was too nervous to notice, but Rodrigo sensed immediately something was wrong.

"Beatriz," he said quietly, "stay here and hold the horses. I'll go help Reeve." He went inside to find Reeve with four saddles on the floor and busy bridling two more horses.

"Reeve?"

"What?"

"What's wrong?"

"What makes you think something is wrong?" Reeve said, but his eyes would not meet Rodrigo's questioning ones.

"Reeve," he said gently, "we're friends. I've brought you into this thing. Whatever has happened, I think I've a right to know. I think I've the right to help if I can."

"Rodrigo, what has happened does not involve you yet. If we're caught, you honestly won't know anything about it. I intend to keep it that way."

"And you think I would let that happen. What kind of man do you think I am? I will claim knowledge no matter what they say. You would not let us stand alone. We would not let you stand alone either. We stand or fall together."

"You're a stubborn cuss, aren't you?" Reeve smiled slightly. Rodrigo grinned broadly in return.

"So my mother has always told me."

"I suppose you're too stubborn to convince this is for your own good?"

"Too stubborn," Rodrigo answered.

They stood looking at each other and Reeve knew Rodrigo meant exactly what he had said. In a quiet voice he spoke. "I have just killed Diego Sandoval." Rodrigo's eyes widened in shock. "He is in the back stall. He caught us, and we fought. I killed him."

"*Madre de Dios,*" said Rodrigo said softly. Then his eyes held Reeve's. "Let me help you to saddle the horses, *compadre*. We had best go as quickly as possible."

Reeve nodded and without another word, they saddled the two horses and, carrying the other saddles, they went out to join Beatriz and to saddle the rest of the horses.

The horses were ready, and the three of them looked toward the palace to see Elana walking rapidly in their direction.

Reeve watched her walk toward him, a smile of warm, trusting love on her face. He watched as the sun touched her and made her seem to glow with vitality.

I love you, Elana, he thought, and I'll keep you safe, my love, I swear. If it costs my life, I'll keep you safe.

Chapter Fifteen

For the benefit of any viewers, they rode their horses slowly from the palace grounds. When they reached the edge of the forest, Reeve urged them into a steady ground-eating run. He wanted to put as much distance between them and the possible pursuers before they stopped to rest.

They rode until Reeve could feel his horse falter beneath him. He drew it to a halt. "We'd better rest the horses, Rodrigo, or they won't last."

"You are right, and I think Elana and Beatriz need a little rest, too."

They dismounted. Reeve went to Elana, put his hands about her slim waist and lifted her down to stand beside him. For a moment she gripped him as if it were difficult to stand.

"Tired?" Reeve questioned.

"I'm fine, Reeve," she said, smiling.

"Rest a while."

"We can't rest too long," she said worriedly. "They will discover that we aren't returning and they will look for us."

Reeve knew Elana would not really feel safe until she stood on the deck of his ship and watched the shores of Spain fade.

"We can rest for a little while. There's a little food, I want you to eat."

"I'm not hungry."

Reeve took Elana's shoulders and smiled assuringly into her eyes. "Hungry or not, I want you to eat a little. If you want to make this trip safely, you have to do as I ask. Trust me, Elana, and do as I say . . . please. I want my wife to be well when I get her home." She nodded, and Reeve drew her into his arms to rock her gently against him and to comfort her as much as he could.

They ate what food Rodrigo had managed to bring, although, Reeve noticed, Elana ate slowly and very little.

"Rodrigo," Beatriz questioned, "will we join my grand-father soon?"

"Most likely tomorrow morning."

Elana's eyes grew wider. "We will be sleeping outside?"

"We'll have to make camp tonight. The horses will not bear traveling all night at this pace. There is no one following us just yet. If we make an early start, we will join the caravan in the morning sometime before midday," Rodrigo answered.

Reeve took a cloth from the bundle behind his saddle and wiped the cooling horses dry. He took a small amount of grain and fed them. "We'll let them drink as soon as we get to water," he said. "I think it's best we get on our way."

It was an embarrassing moment for both Beatriz and Elana who needed a few private moments. Reeve wanted to smile at their obvious fluster, but it would only have made the embarrassment worse.

"If you ladies would excuse us for a moment," he said, and a surprised Rodrigo followed him as he motioned him when he passed. Elana was grateful for Reeve's tact, for she knew he had left them alone on purpose.

After a few welcome moments, the women rejoined the men and were helped to their saddles. Then they were again on their way.

If the morning's travel had been hard the afternoon was worse. Reeve pushed them to the limit of their tolerance. By the time they reached the place in which they decided to camp, the women and their mounts were near exhaustion.

When Reeve lifted Elana down, he did not release her but lifted her in his arms and carried her to the soft grass beneath a tree and laid her gently down.

The horses were hobbled for the night, and Rodrigo built a fire. A small amount of food was eaten, and by the time a large full moon rose, they were all prepared for sleep. It had become quite cold and Reeve knew Elana would spend a miserable night with the blanket she had to cover her. He wasn't sure how Rodrigo, her brother, would take it. But Elana's comfort meant more to him now than Rodrigo's pride. He was well aware Rodrigo was watching him. He spread his blanket near the fire and sat on it, then he looked at Elana.

"Elana, it is too cold for you to try and sleep. Bring your blanket and come over here. I want you to lie beside me. It will keep you near the fire and protect you from any animals that might stray."

Elana gazed at her brother for a moment and he returned the look in silence. Then, she rose and walked slowly to Reeve and sat down on the blanket between himself and the fire.

Reeve held Rodrigo's eyes with his as he spoke very softly. "She'll be safe and warmer here, Rodrigo. I mean, she'll be . . . where she belongs."

Rodrigo smiled. "I've no doubt of that, Reeve, my friend. Where she belongs and where she most desires to be. I am right, Elana?"

"Yes," Elana spoke quietly, "I belong here, Rodrigo."

Rodrigo nodded, then he took Beatriz's hand and drew her with him to a blanket on the opposite side of the fire. He looked across the fire and grinned. "I have been racking my mind trying to think of a way to get my sister not to frown on the situation. You have solved my problems."

Elana laughed softly as Rodrigo drew Beatriz down beside

203

him and the blanket over them both. She turned and smiled up at Reeve.

"I am so happy you are near, Reeve. I have never felt safer in my life," she whispered. Reeve lay down and pulled her down beside him where she curled herself against him. He drew the blanket over them both and they lay and watched the flames dim to a bright glow. "Tell me of your country. Tell me of you," she said quietly.

Reeve was quiet for some time, then he spoke gently. "There is not much to tell of me. I have lived a very uneventful life. A ship's captain may sound romantic, but it can also be a lot of hard work."

Elana turned to look up into his eyes. They glowed silver in the light of the fire. "What were you like as a boy?"

"Mischievous."

"As a young man?"

"Wild and unpredictable," he said, laughing.

"And now you are gentle, kind, and . . . just a little mysterious. Why is it I can't quite believe you have lived so quietly and uneventfully? There is something mysterious about you, my love."

"What is the mystery? I am a man who loves you. That is no mystery and that is the only important thing in the world."

He smiled and brushed her lips with a light kiss. "No more talk . . . sleep. In the morning you will be stiff and sore and you will have me dragging you away."

"Away from being the wife of a man like Diego? Away from fear and into a future filled with love . . . filled with you? No, Reeve, I will only feel gratitude."

Reeve could only think that he wished Rodrigo and Beatriz were anyplace else than sleeping across the fire from them. Their eyes touched and held and he could feel her with his mind and his heart. He bent and took her mouth with his in the most gentle of kisses. When he released them, he was warmed by the glow of love in her eyes.

"*Tener hasta nuestra reuniones siempre,*" she said softly.

"I like the sound of that. Now," he said, "what did you say?"

"To hold until we can be together forever," she replied softly.

"Yes. How do you say 'until forever'?"

"*Hasta siempre.*"

"*Hasta siempre*, my love," he whispered, "*hasta siempre.*"

Elana sighed in deep contentment and curled against Reeve's warmth. With satisfaction, she felt his arms enclose her. After a while they both slept.

The fire slowly died, the moon hid her face below the horizon and dim rays of sun began to appear. Before they crested the horizon, Reeve was already awake. He rose quietly not to waken the others. He rebuilt the fire and unwrapped the small amount of food they had left. Then he went to get the horses. He saddled and bridled them and led them back to the fire. The others had stirred awake. In less than an hour, they had eaten and were on their way.

The trail began to wind uphill into a range of low hills. They followed until they crested them and looked down into a valley green and welcoming. From where they sat, they could see the cluster of wagons near the small stream that meandered through the valley.

"My friends are waiting," Rodrigo said.

"Then we had best join them and get moving," Reeve replied. Before anyone could move, riders left the area of the Gypsy camp and rode toward them.

"We've been seen," Reeve added.

"We have probably been being watched for the past two hours. These people don't have a habit of letting anyone surprise them."

They kicked their horses into motion and rode down into the

valley to meet the ones who rode toward them and held their safety in their hands.

They met on a flat plain just a short way outside the ring of wagons and sat facing each other. Reeve watched Rodrigo greet his friends, and as he did, he examined them closely.

"Hola Rodrigo!" the tallest of the two men called. "Welcome! It is good to see you again."

"Pedro, my friend," Rodrigo said, "it is good to see your ugly face again."

Pedro laughed, and his hand clasped Rodrigo's shoulder. Reeve was, at first, taken by surprise at Pedro's immense size: Reeve was tall, well over six feet, but Pedro was larger, and Reeve was sure none of the pounds were fat. Pedro's eyes were such a deep brown they appeared black, and a glow of deep intelligence and awareness was in their depths. His hair was black and thick and he sported a matching thick black full mustache. He wore a reckless devil-may-care air as if it were part of him, but Reeve suspected this man was very quick and very wary.

"Pedro, you know my sister, Elana, and this is Beatriz de Mendosa, my future wife, and Elana's future husband and the man we have to thank for the chance of escape, Captain Reeve Burke. This is my good friend, Pedro Garcia."

Pedro's eyes turned to Reeve after he had greeted both women with a broad smile. Reeve was amused to see Pedro accomplish a flourishing bow to the ladies from horseback.

"Senor Captain Burke," he said. "It is always a pleasure to meet a brave man."

"I think in this situation, you are the brave one, Pedro. I can leave on my ship. All I have to do is run faster than the ones who follow. You have to remain here. We are grateful for your help," Reeve replied.

"De nada, Senor Burke. Por Dios! It is good to cheat the Inquisition of more blood."

"I don't know how far behind us they might be, I'm sure we had a good three quarters of a day's head start. If they didn't travel at night, and I don't see how they could have tracked us in the dark, then we are well ahead of them."

"*Ay de mi!* It does not matter," Pedro said. "From here you will disappear. Some of my men are already erasing any trail you might have made to here. We have our ways, Senor."

"We must get to San Sebastián as quickly as we can. Captain Burke's ship awaits us there," Rodrigo said.

"It is a long, hard journey, *mi amigo*. For the ladies it will be difficult. There are no comforts with my caravan."

"Senor Garcia," Elana said softly, "what comfort is there in the arms of the Inquisition? I would prefer the discomfort of your caravan and the chance for freedom."

Elana had spoken in Spanish and Reeve did not know what she said, but the pride in Rodrigo's face and the warm glow of admiration in Pedro's told him all he needed to know.

Pedro answered in rapid Spanish and Elana smiled. Reeve made a mental note to ask Elana what he had said that brought the light of laughter to Elana's eyes. Before he could speak, Pedro turned to him. "Come, Senor, we must move. There is someone in our caravan who has come a long way to see you again. You are old friends, I am told, and your friend is most anxious to see you."

"Old friend?" Reeve questioned. "I don't remember any old friends except the ones with me. Who is it?"

"I would not spoil the grand surprise." Pedro laughed again, but Reeve was sure he saw a devilish light in his eye. His instinct told him he was not about to like this . . . grand surprise. He couldn't for the life of him think of anyone who would come all the way to a Gypsy caravan to see him. Some sixth sense told him it meant trouble and he was never one to deny his instincts. He was resigned to the inevitable. He was not going to get Pedro to tell him, so he had to go and find out for himself. He was also well aware of Elana's curious gaze.

"Well, let's go see this . . . old friend."

Pedro laughed again as they turned their horses and the group rode back to the caravan.

They dismounted when they reached the center of the camp, and their horses were taken by young boys whose job it was to care for the caravan's herd. They would be brushed, fed, and watered and guarded well.

They had just turned away from their horses when Beatriz's eyes lit with joy. "Grandfather!" she cried. She ran across the small area toward her grandfather and threw herself into his open arms.

The old man held her close to him. "My child . . . my child. We are together. We will be safe. We need not be afraid any longer."

"Was your escape difficult, Grandfather?"

"No, the young woman who saw me safely through the passageway and to this caravan was quite kind and helpful."

"I must thank her when I see her."

"I think you will be meeting her soon," her grandfather said as they rejoined the group and he accepted the grateful wishes of the others.

Pedro motioned to Reeve who walked with him to another wagon, followed by Rodrigo, Elana, and Beatriz and her grandfather. They all stood in expectation as Pedro called out to the person within. "*Hola!* I have brought our guests," Pedro called. The covering of the back of the wagon was pushed aside and Reeve stood in complete shock as she stepped out . . . his mysterious beautiful lady from the ship. There was a moment of complete and utter silence as she came down the two steps to the ground, walked to Reeve and smiled up at him.

At that moment, Reeve wished fervently the ground would open and swallow him. He was aware of many things. Pedro's amusement, Rodrigo's silence . . . and Elana's eyes touching him. It was probably the first time in his life that all words failed him.

"So, Captain Burke," she said softly, "I told you we would meet again soon. I have not forgotten the night aboard your ship."

The words sounded incriminating even to him and he knew how they must sound to Elana. He could have claimed he did not even know her name, but Pedro thwarted that plan by turning to Elana and the others.

"This is Carmen Almedo. She is one of the most excellent workers against the Inquisition in existence. She is very brave and responsible for saving the lives of many."

"We are most pleased to meet you," Elana said softly, "and we are very grateful for your help. I'm sure your assistance has always been deeply appreciated."

If no one else knew her true meaning, Reeve did, and was quite sure he was in for some rather uncomfortable moments. He felt he was about to discover his little kitten had claws.

"We must make you comfortable," Carmen said. "The trip is long and hard. I'm sure we can make it much easier." Her words were meant for all, but her eyes were for Reeve alone. They were dark and sultry and Reeve could not misunderstand their meaning. But neither could Elana.

At the moment all Reeve could think of was that he wanted Elana and Carmen separated until he could find a way to get Elana alone and explain what didn't happen between himself and Carmen, and to get Carmen alone and explain to her what did exist between himself and Elana. It was Rodrigo who came to Reeve's rescue.

"I believe we have a wagon of our own, Pedro. Would you take us to it so Elana and Beatriz can get settled? As you say we must be on our way quickly."

"*Si*, the wagon is there." He gestured toward a wagon that sat across the central fire from where they were. He led the way and Beatriz, Elana, and Carmen followed. Rodrigo fell back to walk with Reeve. He chuckled lightly and the gaze Reeve turned on him was not exactly friendly. Rodrigo managed to look innocent and shrugged. They stopped by the wagon, and Pedro spoke again.

"There is food at the fire. If you would eat quickly, we will leave. By the time we are ready to camp tonight we will have covered much distance."

They agreed. Pedro and Carmen left them temporarily to see to the preparations to leave. Elana remained silent and Reeve did not push the situation. He wanted to get her alone where he would have time to explain completely. He decided to wait until they camped for the night.

The rest of the band was busy with the preparations to leave. They only smiled in passing at the visitors, but each was too busy now to stop and talk. There were over fifteen wagons scattered in the clearing on the bend of the river. Yet there seemed to be no confusion. Each seemed to know exactly what to do.

Finished with their food, Elana and Beatriz chose to ride with Reeve and Rodrigo at least for a while, but her grandfather entered the wagon. The wagon would be a place to rest if needed, or to sleep when the time came.

They rode on each side of the wagons as did many others. The wagons, to Reeve, seemed to move slowly, yet they managed to cover a great deal of distance before Pedro called a halt for the night.

The sun was sinking below the horizon when he did. The wagons were placed in two large circles and a communal fire was built in the center of each. Food was prepared and they all sat about the fire while they ate. Once finished, guitars seemed to suddenly appear.

It was hard for Reeve to believe there was any danger behind them when there was so much laughter and beautiful music here. The sky was bright with a full yellow moon and a million brilliant stars.

Elana sat near, but her eyes had not turned to him since they began to eat. For the first time he became seriously worried about what was going through her mind.

Suddenly there was the sharp sound of castinets and all eyes turned to see Carmen, her arms above her head, poised for the dance. "Viva! Carmen!" came the shouts of encouraging voices.

In the light of the campfire she was amazingly beautiful. Her dark hair fell like a cloud about her. Her slender body was arched and her eyes were half closed as if she were caught in the midst of vibrant passion.

The guitar strummed, the castinets answered and Carmen danced. She danced like a wild and sensuous flame. No one could seem to take their eyes from her. The progress of the dance found her in front of Reeve, and the balance of the dance was an open invitation.

She swayed before him, a fiery beauty that moved with the rhythm of the music as if they were one. Reeve found it almost impossible to keep his eyes from her.

With the final touch of the guitar, Carmen touched Reeve, smiled seductively, and walked away. Reeve's eyes met Elana's across the fire.

They both remained still, trying to reach each other over a sudden chasm that seemed to be separating them. Reeve felt a pain, a sudden sense of loss, and the fear reached to touch him that he could actually lose Elana over a nonexistent thing.

Elana rose slowly and bent to lift the guitar from the hand of the man who sat next to her. She walked around the fire and knelt before Reeve, placing the guitar in her lap, and then she began it softly. In a very gentle voice, her eyes glistening with

211

unshed tears she sang:

> To love, there's no beginning
> there's no end.
> To love, there's no time
> for fear or pain.
> To love, there's no time
> for broken hearts, and lost
> memories so sweet.
> So I hold you in my heart,
> and I keep you in my dreams,
> and I'll belong to you forever
> as I pray that you'll belong to me.
> To love, there's no half
> remembered dreams.
> To love, there's just now
> to build into forever,
> time is all . . . to love.

The song faded softly with the last notes of the guitar, and all that could be heard was the crackle of the fire.

Reeve felt a beautiful emotion swell within him until he could barely breathe. He wanted her at that moment more than he had ever wanted her before. Their eyes held, hers filled with warm understanding, and his with the promise of forever she had just spoken to him.

Elana rose and laid the guitar aside and left the fire, walking toward her wagon. Reeve rose quickly and moved rapidly to catch up with her.

He took her shoulder and turned her to face him. She looked up into his eyes. "Elana, I'm sorry."

"For what?"

"For what you might have thought, for any pain I might have caused you."

"Reeve," Elana said softly. She laid her hand against his chest and felt the solid beat of his heart. "It is your past, and it doesn't concern me. I want your future. I want to share all the days with you. I do not easily give up what I love, want, to another. She can claim your past all she wants to, but I will fight for your future. I will fight anyone or anything that tries to take you from me. I love you, Reeve, and I will do anything to hold you."

"And I love you, Elana."

"Then she must beware," Elana said, her eyes sparkling dangerously, "or she will find it is not so easy to take from a de Santangel." Reeve chuckled.. "And I have sharp claws, Reeve. I will tolerate a past. I will not tolerate a future."

"Come walk with me, my tigress. I have a need to hold you in my arms. Even if it's just for a moment."

Elana smiled and Reeve slid his arms about her waist and they walked from the circle of wagons to the trees that stood by the stream. Both were unaware of Carmen who stood in the shadows and watched.

"For now," she whispered softly, "he is yours . . . for now."

Chapter Sixteen

The soft haunting sound of a lightly strummed guitar followed Reeve and Elana as they walked through the shadows and stood by the river. Without a word, Reeve drew her into his arms and held her close. The thought that she could have been lost to him so easily still made him shake inside.

The stars were bright and the full moon lit her face with a pale glow as she lifted it for his kiss and their lips blended in mutual pleasure.

She slid her arms about his waist and moved against him with an urgent warmth that stirred his blood and heated his loins. He bound her to him and savored the pleasure her slim body gave him.

Reluctantly he lifted his head and looked down into her eyes. He laughed softly. "So, my little tigress, I thought you might resort to violence, but you've got a velvet glove over those claws."

Elana smiled and replied softly, "But I wanted to cut her heart out when I saw you look at her. I . . . I felt . . . lost. Oh, Reeve, if I ever lost you . . . I—"

"Elana," he said gently, "I thought we knew and understood each other more than anyone else could ever understand. You're part of me, Elana, and I could no more leave you than I could stop breathing. Don't you know by now that I love you . . . I love you," he breathed softly as again he took her mouth with his.

Her arms encircled his neck and her warm moist lips parted to accept his questing ones. One arm about her waist bound her to him while his other hand loosened the heavy coil of her hair and let it fall about her. The silken feel of it in his fingers was another pleasure his memory would always hold. He knew as surely as he lived that nothing would ever ease the hunger for her that lived deep within him. If he possessed her a million times it would only leave him with the need to possess her again . . . forever.

Slowly he drew her down beside him. With gentle fingers, he loosened the buttons of her dress and allowed his hands to caress the warm softness inside and listened to her murmuring sound of pleasure. His head lowered to taste a passion-hardened nipple and caressed it with his tongue. Her hands tangled in his thick golden hair and drew him closer and she murmured his name over and over.

The hunger within him grew until it was a raging volcano. Elana's heart hammered wildly in the intoxicating excitement of his touch. For now, they were safe, enclosed within each other, reaching for that rare and beautiful thing they would always share. One touch, one kiss would always be the magic that would join them.

A wild enchantment enfolded them as they sank into the ecstatic pleasure of each other. Hands searched, touched, and clung, taking possession of warm, heated flesh and eliciting a flame of desire that consumed all rational thought.

A silken thigh, soft as velvet beneath his searching hands led to deeper and deeper exploration. His open mouth slanted across hers in a deep wild possession that rocked her world, leaving her gasping in breathless wonder. Naked unleashed hunger consumed them in a violent whirlwind of heated surrender.

Elana arched against him, meeting his deep thrusts with a giving that shattered whatever restraints she might have had. There was nothing held in reserve. They gave all to each other, blending into one like the breeze that touched the trees and the stars that lit the sky above them.

They lay together, entwined and content. She was secure in the safety of his arms, and more at peace than she had ever been before.

The rapid thudding of mingled heartbeats slowed to a peaceful rhythm. Reeve felt, no matter the situation they were in and the difficulties they might face, that he had never been happier in his life than he was at the moment. They may have an ordeal to face, but Elana was here where he could care for her, and freedom and happiness lay at the end of the journey.

"What are you thinking?" Elana questioned softly.

Reeve laughed. "Any man with blood in his veins who could lie with you in his arms and think of anything else but you would be totally insane." He was pleased with her soft answering laugh.

"Elana?"

"What?"

"What did Garcia say to you?"

"Pedro? When?"

"When we first arrived today."

"Oh."

"Well?"

"He made a rather flattering remark about you," she said. He waited for her to continue but she remained silent.

"So you're not going to tell me what he said?"

"I would not," she said innocently, "want to contribute to your conceit. My mother always told me it was wrong to be filled with one's self."

Reeve turned and looked down into her eyes filled with teasing laughter. The combination of the moon's glow and her

217

love for him made her face warm and glowing. "Must I drag it out of you by force?" He laughed as he spoke.

"Force?" she taunted.

He put both arms around her and crushed her to him. She gasped in surprise. Then he began to kiss her fervently and fiercely, his arms tightening more and more. Breathless and unable to move, she wriggled helplessly. Her soft breathless laughter was muffled as he kissed her again and again.

"Tell me," he said, laughing.

"You monster." She giggled. "I'll tell! I'll tell!" He released her only enough to let her catch her breath, but he refused to release her until she told him. "He said," she spoke slowly, "that the golden caballero at my side looked as though he would see to my comfort from now on. He also said that he thought you looked quite capable of doing whatever you decided to do."

"Well, he was right about one thing. I intend to take good care of you. Once we're free of all this, Elana, you won't ever have to be afraid of anything if it's in my power to stop it."

"I know, Reeve, I know." She pressed her lips against his throat and closed her eyes to enjoy the peace of lying close to him and knowing she was safe.

"Reeve?"

"Yes?"

"If your ship is all that you have, will we live on it?"

"Would you like that? We could go just about anyplace you chose."

"But what of children?"

His eyes held hers and he caressed her hair gently. "To have children would be a blessing. If we did, I would build you a house. Maybe a small place near the sea."

"Yes. Oh, Reeve, sometimes I think—"

"What, love?"

"I think this is a dream. Your love is too beautiful to be real

218

and that something somehow is going to come along and separate us."

"Don't think that way, Elana. We're not going to be stopped. We'll get to freedom. We'll get home."

She sighed and stirred in his arms.

"Elana?"

"Umm?"

"There are a lot of missions strung out between here and San Sebastián."

"Yes."

"Tomorrow let's ask Pedro if he will stop at the nearest one."

"A mission . . . why?" She laughed softly. "Do you feel the need of confession?"

"No, just the need of a priest."

"A priest, whatever for?"

"Because," he said gently, "I don't believe you would feel truly married without one."

Elana was silent for a moment, then slowly she sat up and looked down on him.

Moonlight bathed her skin in a soft gold glow and her dark hair formed a cloud about her face.

"Reeve?"

Reeve sat up beside her and reached to touch her cheek lightly. "I know it is not what you expected your marriage to be. But Elana, I love you, and if you will, I want to make you my wife as soon as possible."

"Oh yes, yes. I would love nothing more than to become your wife as soon as possible."

"In a mission in the middle of nowhere?"

"No matter where, no matter how," she said. "I will be joined with you forever. Even if they catch us, I would die knowing I belonged to you and that they could not force me to marry another."

219

With mingling laughter and tears, she found herself again enclosed in iron-hard arms, and they fell again to the soft, warm, grass-covered earth. Her hands clung to him, threaded through his hair, and drew his head to her for a deep, lingering kiss. His lips found her cheeks, her closed eyelids, then burned against her throat and traced their heated path to the soft passion-peaked breasts. Elana felt a flowing, rapturous desire that left her weak and dizzily clinging to him.

As he knew it always would, it filled him, this wild thundering passion that Elana could build within him. One touch, one kiss, would always have the ability to rekindle the flame that burned within him.

The magic was theirs. It sang through their blood like the wild Gypsy music. It blended them together, fusing them into one.

They walked back to the Gypsy camp in the wee hours of the morning. Reeve and Rodrigo were to sleep under the wagon, and it was very reluctantly that Reeve watched Elana blow him a silent kiss and enter the wagon. Already his arms felt empty and the blankets in which he rolled for the night were much colder than he ever remembered.

The camp was stirring early and Reeve was one of the first, mainly because he wanted to speak to Pedro before they started on the day's trek.

He walked across the circle of open ground, past the now dead fire, to Pedro's wagon. He gave a sharp rap on the wooden platform outside Pedro's door.

It was only a few minutes before Pedro opened his door, stepped out on the platform and jumped down to stand by Reeve.

"*Ay Maria,*" he exclaimed happily. "It is going to be a glorious day. We should make many miles today."

"Pedro, I have to speak to you about something."

"Speak up. What is it you need, my friend?"

"How far is the closest mission?"

"Mission?" Pedro's brow wrinkled as he tried to follow what Reeve was talking about.

"Yes, a mission."

"Well, let me see. Two more days will take us to the mission of San Martin. But why would you want to go there? It's out of our way and there's nothing to see."

"I need the services of a priest."

Pedro stopped walking and turned to look at Reeve. Then his face creased in a delighted smile.

"There is," he cried delightedly, "about to be a wedding if I am not mistaken."

"You're not mistaken, my friend. Elana and I would like to be married as soon as possible." Pedro extended his hand to Reeve who accepted it in a firm grip.

"You are a lucky man, my friend. That is a lovely lady you are getting. May you have a good and happy life together."

"Then," Reeve said grinning, "I invite you to my wedding and we will have a grand party afterwards. It is time Elana had something to smile about."

"Good. Let us get on our way. The idea of a party sets well with me as I'm sure it will be with all the others. They look only for an excuse to laugh and to dance and in the past few years, there's not been much of that."

"Well, we'll give them a cause for celebrating." Reeve laughed as he clapped Pedro on the shoulder. "Now, I have to go tell Elana."

Pedro watched Reeve walk across the clearing toward the wagon in which Elana still slept. He stood outside the wagon and called to her. "Elana!"

It was only seconds until Elana appeared, her face pale and her eyes wide with fright. Beatriz, just as frightened appeared behind her with her grandfather.

"Reeve! Have they found us?" Elana cried. "Have they

221

come for us?"

Reeve immediately regretted his excitement. It was obvious he had frightened them all nearly to death.

"Elana, my God, I'm sorry. I didn't mean to frighten you . . . all of you. It's just," he said, smiling up at her, "that I had something to tell you and I found it hard to wait."

He could see the relief clearly written on all their faces. Rodrigo had appeared from under the wagon, and now they all waited for whatever it was that Reeve had come to tell them.

"Elana, we're stopping at the mission in San Martin . . . day after tomorrow. Do you all think we can get ready for a wedding by then?"

Beatriz's and Rodrigo's faces beamed with delight, and a soft sound of pleasure from Elana was muffled as Reeve lifted her from the wagon, and she was caught in an embrace from which she never wanted to leave.

To Reeve and Elana the wagons seemed to crawl. They rode together, riding ahead to find a secluded place where they could stop. They laughed and talked together, putting all the dark thoughts aside. This was their time and they did not intend to let anything spoil it.

Reeve had a way of reaching within Elana, and consequently she found herself talking more and he listening more. Slowly, he learned everything there was to know about the woman he loved. It was some time before a contented Elana realized that, though he knew her completely, she did not know much more about his past than she did the day they had first met. He would artfully turn the conversation to other things or make love to her until her head swam with pleasure, and she forgot any questions she might have asked. She also knew that whatever his past contained, it did not matter to her.

Their happiness in each other so complete, neither of them

were aware of Carmen's watchful gaze or her intense jealousy that was rapidly blossoming into hatred . . . hatred for Elana.

Bright sun heralded the day they would be married. Pedro told them they would reach the mission before night fell. He also laughingly told them the entire tribe planned on a large celebration to congratulate the newlyweds.

There was not a woman in the caravan who did not contribute something to Elana to wear for her wedding. She was brought to tears by their open generosity, and although her family had at one time possessed great wealth, she had never felt richer in her life.

Reeve and Pedro rode ahead of the caravan that afternoon to reach the mission first and talk to the priest there about the wedding. Beatriz rode with Elana, and the conversation they had was to startle Elana and change Beatriz's life.

They had ridden just a little ahead of the wagons and were quite alone. Elana was aware that Beatriz had been quiet for some time and suddenly realized Beatriz seemed to be both nervous and searching for words to talk to Elana.

"Elana?"

"Yes?"

"Are . . . you frightened?"

"Frightened . . . about what?"

"Being married . . . being . . . with a man?"

"Any other man I might be, but with Reeve . . . I . . . I . . . belong to him, and he is so strong, so gentle. No, I would never be afraid of Reeve."

"I mean . . ." Beatriz hesitated, her cheeks flaming, "I mean to . . . to be with him."

Elana's gaze grew more astute and she realized instantly. It was Beatriz who was afraid. "Beatriz . . . you and Rodrigo . . . he has never . . . I mean, you have never?"

Tears formed in Beatriz's eyes and she caught her lower lip between her teeth and averted her head. "I know you think I'm

223

a silly child. No, I have always been afraid, and Rodrigo is too much a man to force me to do anything. Oh, how I have always wanted to give myself to him . . . to belong to him completely. But . . . always, I am afraid."

"Beatriz," Elana said gently, "of what are you afraid? Rodrigo or yourself?"

Beatriz remained silent for a moment, then she turned her eyes to meet Elana's questioning ones. "You are so wise, my sister to be." She smiled. "I am an idiot, but . . . it is myself of which I am afraid."

"Why?"

"Oh, Elana! Rodrigo has known many women of the court and elsewhere. How could I ever expect to please him? You do not notice your brother, but he weakens the heart of most of the women, many more beautiful and more experienced than I. What could I ever hope to give him? How could I ever hope to please him? I am afraid he will be so disappointed in me he will turn away. Oh, Elana, I could not bear it should he take a mistress. I love him so much."

Elana drew her horse to a halt as did Beatriz. Then she reached over and touched Beatriz's hand gently. "Beatriz, you have something to offer that no other woman has. You love him. Don't you think he knows the difference between the love you have for him alone and the . . . if you want to call it love . . . that those other women have for any handsome caballero who rides along? If he didn't love you, want only you, he could have looked elsewhere. But his eyes have always been just for you. My brother is a very clever man. He knows quality and real love when he sees it. He'll wait until you are ready. And he will never turn to another woman once he has found the truth of your love. Don't you be afraid, Beatriz. Do what your heart tells you to do. You'll be happy. I know my brother as none other does, and I know he is honorable and faithful. If he says he loves you, if he says he wants only you, then you can believe him."

Beatriz smiled and Elana smiled warmly in return. "Thank you, Elana," Beatriz said softly. "Thank you, dear sister. I will try to always make him happy."

"We all are insecure, Beatriz. You and Rodrigo are not alone. Reeve and I are frightened, too, of the future and of the past. But we will be together, and for me, that is enough to take one day . . . no, one precious moment at a time."

A shout interrupted them and they turned to see Reeve and Pedro riding toward them. Beatriz watched as Elana's eyes lit with pleasure and her cheeks grew flushed.

Elana felt the renewed pleasure course through her at the sight of Reeve's riding toward her. The setting sun glistened in his golden hair, and he seemed to fill her horizon with the breadth of his shoulders and the ease with which he controlled the huge black stallion he rode.

In a few minutes he was at her side, his silver-gray eyes smiling warmly into hers, causing her heart to flutter within and leaving her breathless.

"*Hola!*" Pedro called. "We have made all the arrangements. Soon, my little one, you will be a very beautiful bride. We must dance tonight and have a grand celebration. It is not every day Pedro Garcia gets to give away such a lovely lady in marriage. I am honored, Lady de Santangel."

"And I am honored to have a man as brave as yourself to stand for me. I will make sure that the second dance is for you. The first," she said, smiling at Reeve, "will be for *mi esposa* . . . my husband."

Both Beatriz and Pedro were warmed by the look of warm, intense love that passed between Elana and Reeve. It was as if they were the only two people in the world.

They rode back to the wagons and less than two hours later, they were making camp less than a half mile from the mission.

There was a great deal of confusion and happy laughter in

Elana's wagon as Beatriz and some of the young women helped with her dress.

Pedro would bring the women, so Reeve and Rodrigo went on ahead where they would await them.

The mission was a small stone building and obviously quite poor. Its walls were a rough brown adobe. Inside, rough-hewn pews sat in uneven rows. The altar was the thing that caught Reeve's eye. It was a huge slab of rough-cut marble and behind it hung a large crucifix of weathered wood. An abundance of candles Reeve had paid handsomely for lit the usually shadowed interior. It was, in its rough way, very beautiful.

The priest was a man whose age Reeve could not guess. He was small and slim and his skin was weathered and brown, yet he had large, quite intelligent eyes. He also had a smile that lit his face and made him seem to grow younger. He spoke good English marked only by a heavy accent.

"The bride comes soon, Senor Burke?"

"Yes, Padre, she is coming now," Reeve replied.

Without any one's knowledge he had given the priest more money than he had seen for a long time. Reeve knew it would soon trickle from the priest's fingers to the poor families who attended mass here.

The group of women entered with Elana before them and followed by the balance of the tribe. Reeve's eyes were for Elana alone and he never missed Carmen.

She walked down the candle lit aisle toward him, creating a vision he would never forget. It was the first time in Reeve's life that he could ever remember trembling with an emotion he could not control. He felt as if some force was restricting his breathing, and his hands felt wet and were shaking, he hoped not visibly. Elana stood beside him in the quiet little church. She raised her eyes to his and he could read, as he always would, the warm, giving love.

He knew he went through the entire ceremony, barely

226

hearing the words the priest said. He was aware, with every sense he possessed, of the slim woman who stood beside him and softly repeated the words that would join them together for the rest of their lives.

True to his word, Pedro began a celebration that would last the remainder of the night. Those were his plans, but Reeve's were completely different. At the first opportunity, when the men were drunk enough not to notice, and the women were happily avoiding their amorous intentions, Reeve and Elana escaped in the darkness to a quiet place Reeve had planned on hours before.

Beatriz stood and watched Reeve take Elana's hand and draw her with him out of the circle of the campfire light. She had spent the evening thinking of the words Elana had spoken, and she realized she wanted the kind of love that Elana and Reeve shared.

She looked across the campfire at Rodrigo. He held a drink in his hand and was laughing at something someone had said. How magnificent he is, she thought, so handsome.

She had been watching him for some time and he suddenly became aware. He looked up and their eyes met. Rodrigo was struck so hard with the look he read on her face that he sat immobile, stunned, and disbelieving.

Beatriz rose slowly and walked around the campfire with Rodrigo watching each move. She stood beside him and slowly he rose.

He looked down into warm eyes and felt uncertainty sweep over him. That he wanted her more than he had ever wanted a woman in his life he knew, but did she want him? Was it promise he read in her eyes? Did he dare reach for her love? Could, he pray, that—

"Rodrigo," she said softly, "I would speak to you."

"Of course, Beatriz. Would you sit beside me?"

"No. I . . . I would speak with you alone."

"Alone?" he breathed softly. Then he reached to take her arm. "Come with me, we will find a quiet place to talk."

Beatriz walked beside him. He felt her presence, inhaled the soft scent of her perfume, and fought the desire to grab her up in his arms and take her into the surrounding dark and ravage her.

They were a long distance from the others, standing beneath a large tree. Rodrigo turned to her. "What's the matter, Beatriz?"

She stepped close to him, so close their bodies touched. Then she reached up a hesitant hand to touch his face. "I love you, Rodrigo," she said softly, "and if there are no more tomorrows . . . I would have now . . . I would . . . I would be with you tonight."

Chapter Seventeen

Of all the things Rodrigo had heard or faced in his life, nothing had shaken him more than this. Taken completely unprepared, he sucked in his breath and couldn't find words to say. A very uncertain Beatriz became even more so. He heard a soft choking sob and felt her quiver and begin to move away from him. It was only then that he regained his senses. He reached for her and tenderly drew her trembling body close to him.

"Beatriz, my love, my sweet," he whispered as he held her, knowing the uncertainty and fear she felt, yet overjoyed that she had come to him. Beatriz, his goddess, the woman he worshipped and had never dared to touch before, knew and understood what he felt, had felt the same intense desire for him. It was difficult for him to believe his good fortune. He did not intend to let her slip away from him.

With gentle fingers, he lifted her chin until their eyes met. His heart leapt with the sheer joy of what he read in her eyes. "I love you, Beatriz, you know that, and I want you beyond all reason . . . are you sure . . . very sure?"

"I am such a coward, and such a fool," Beatriz replied softly. "I have always wanted you and always been afraid of my own emotions. I am no longer afraid, Rodrigo, and I am sure of one thing. I am where I belong, where I have always wanted to be, and I will never leave your arms unless you turn me away."

"My God, woman, I am not a complete idiot. I am only stunned. Turn you away! I would have to be completely insane. After needing you and wanting you for so long, I find it impossible to believe that the powers above have answered all my prayers."

Rodrigo turned to her and bound her to him and the deep hunger for her exploded within him as his mouth swept down to take possession of her. A deep and passionate kiss stirred their senses and they clung breathlessly to one another.

Rodrigo cursed the place in which they stood. It was certainly the most inconvenient one. Then it occurred to him that they were not far from the church's stable and, he hoped, a hayloft filled with hay. Without a word, he led her, holding her hand tightly with his as if afraid she might be gone should he loosen his hold.

The stable was devoid of all animal life, and there was a wide and open area as if the building had been used more as a storage barn than as a stable. Pale moonlight touched the room, making visibility difficult but not impossible. His first instincts had been right as he looked up and saw that the loft was indeed secluded, clean, and filled with new hay. He turned to Beatriz as if looking for reassurance in her eyes. He saw many things, fear, softened by love, and tension coupled with need.

He took her in his arms again and brushed her lips lightly with his. "I should take you back to the caravan," he whispered, "and if I didn't need you more than my life's blood, I would. Beatriz—"

"No," Beatriz replied, "do not ask me again if I am sure. I am frightened . . . but I am sure."

"I don't want you frightened of me," he replied.

"But I'm not."

"But you just said—"

"I am frightened, but more of me than of you. I would never

be afraid of you."

"Of yourself? I don't understand."

"Oh, Rodrigo," she said softly as she buried her face against his chest and her slim arms held him, "I am so stupid, so inexperienced. What if I displease you? What if I am such a child I cannot make you happy? I would die should I see the love in your eyes die."

Again, Rodrigo was silenced by the profound emotion that overwhelmed him.

"You have made me happier than any man has a right to be, just by saying you feel for me the way I feel for you. Don't you understand that you could make me unhappy only by leaving me? You please me with every breath you take, every move you make, every word you say, and when you say I love you, Rodrigo, it is all to me."

Her mouth was soft and moist as his lips sought hers again. They parted under his searching mouth, and she surrendered to the passion that flowed from the center of her being. It left her weak and she clung to him, her body molded to his, and her arms drew him closer.

He lifted his head and their eyes smiled into each other's. Beatriz felt any fear she might have had flow out of her to be replaced by a stir of vibrant emotion, both new and exciting.

Rodrigo stepped back from her and held out his hand, and without any doubts, Beatriz put hers in his. They walked to the short ladderlike steps that led to the loft. Rodrigo aided her and they climbed to the semi-dark loft. He drew her into his arms and down beside him.

Rodrigo could feel her trembling inexperience, yet his senses soared with the pleasure of her tentative reaching for him. He did not want this to turn into something frightening for her so he controlled his need as he sought to raise hers. Tenderly and with infinite care, his lips possessed hers with soft, lingering kisses. Slowly he felt her respond until she was

clinging to him and returning his kisses with a vibrant warmth
of her own. Gently, his hands sought the velvet touch of her
skin, loosening, with expertise, the restricting clothes that
held her from him. He heard her soft muffled gasp as his hands
found her cool slim body, yet he thrilled to the fact that she
drew closer, seeking his warmth and more of the magic his
touch created within her. And it was magic, the flame that
licked to life within her. Her heart was pounding furiously,
matching the wild throbbing of his.

She had no knowledge of his expert ability to disrobe
without interrupting their mutual pleasure, and her senses
reeled under the wild intense pleasure when their bodies met
breast to breast, thigh to thigh. His hands caressed in heated,
searching touches and his lips traced flaming paths over her
sensitive skin until she cried out with the ecstatic pleasure.

Caught in a flame that dissolved all rational thought but
Rodrigo, she called to him in soft murmured words of love that
filled his heart to overflowing joy. Need touched need and the
wonder of it filled them, until they lost all touch on reality and
dissolved into the mutual blending that caught their senses and
suspended them in a cauldron of flame.

His knee expertly separated her slim thighs and he lifted her
to meet him, knowing it would be painful at first, and he tried
to make it as easy as he could. Nature had endowed Rodrigo
quite generously and the last thing he wanted was to hurt her,
or worse, frighten her from any future encounters.

Beatriz was caught in the flowing molten lava that moved
through her veins and urged her to find the fulfillment of the
need that consumed her.

The sudden pain startled her and she cried out involuntarily, causing Rodrigo almost as much pain as it did her.
Then he filled her and a spreading warmth coursed through
her, and she clung to him, lifting to meet him, letting the
sensual pleasure fill her being. She had never known such a

feeling of sharing as she did now, and she wanted to draw him closer, keep him within to hold for all time.

Rodrigo had possessed many women before, but nothing had prepared him for the glory of the soft and gentle woman he held. He knew without doubt all past and present and future were Beatriz and only Beatriz.

They moved together now, one thought, one flame, one need, lifting beyond now, beyond reality to the flaming world of mutual surrender in which lovers dwelled. She was his and he hers with a completeness that both fulfilled them beyond a feeling of everlasting need for the love only they possessed. He held her quivering body close to him as they tumbled from the stars back to reality. He heard her rasping breathing, felt the trembling in her slim body and the way she clung to him, wondering in fear if he had possessed his rose only to lose her.

He lifted his head and looked down into her eyes and saw there all he would ever need to know. At that moment, he could have wept with the joy of knowing he had not lost his dearest possession but had only made it more sweet and more complete.

He did not want to leave the sanctuary of her slim body, and he bent to lightly touch her mouth again to taste the sweetness that would live within him as long as there was a breath in his body.

"My heart," he whispered, "my love, you're my life. You're all I need to fill my world and make it whole." His lips touched and tasted the salt of her tears that lay on her cheeks. Then he lay on his back and drew her close to his side. Her head resting on his chest and her legs entwined with his, he caressed her until he felt the trembling cease. "You are no longer afraid?" he questioned hopefully and waited tensely for her answer.

Beatriz sighed deeply and her arm that lay across his waist tightened possessively.

"No," she whispered, "I am no longer afraid of anything as

233

long as you hold me and want me forever. I have wanted you and never known what I wanted. Now I want you more. My heart is filled with you and only you."

"*Amada mia*," he said, chuckling softly and brushed a kiss against her soft hair. "You have said the words to make everything complete."

"Rodrigo?"

"Yes?"

"For us it will always be like this . . . so beautiful, so complete?"

"For us it will be better. We will find each other in many ways before our long life together is complete. Each time will be better; each time we will share more for we will know each other more."

Beatriz laughed softly.

"Why do you laugh, my rose? Don't you believe me?"

"I do," she sighed. "I think I should just die with the pleasure of it should it be like you say."

He chuckled now and tightened his arm about her. "Then," he said agreeably, "I shall just have to spend much time proving it to you." He enjoyed her answering laughter.

The night was a complete joy for all who rode with the Gypsy caravan. The fires dwindled and all became quiet. The lovers shared their pleasure of each other and never knew of the lone rider who rode away from the camp in the wee hours of the morning.

Carmen had watched Elana and Reeve the hours before the wedding and her hatred grew, but it was aimed not at Reeve but at Elana. Jealousy twisted within until all she could see was that Reeve could have been hers if Elana were out of the way.

She stood between the wagons and watched the festivities, watched Reeve steal Elana away, watched Beatriz and Rodrigo leave and knew they would be sharing the night together. Grim determination filled her and a plan to rid herself of Elana filled her mind.

She circled the camp, keeping to the dark shadows for she did not want anyone to see her leave. When she reached the area where the horses were, she bridled and saddled one in silence. She mounted and walked the horse away from the camp so no one would hear. She knew where all the guards were and adroitly circled them also. Once away from the camp, she kicked her horse into a rapid run. She wanted to be at her destination and back before dawn; that way no one would suspect her of betrayal. It was over an hour and a half of riding before she reached her destination which was a cluster of small adobe houses. They were for the most part dark and the people within slept. One sat at a short distance from the others and from the window shown a glow of dim yellow light. It was in front of it that Carmen drew her horse to a halt and dismounted.

She walked rapidly to the door and knocked. The door was opened by a tall dark-eyed man. Recognition and pleasure sparkled in his eyes at the same time.

"Carmen," he said, holding the door open. "Come in, Chiquita. It has been a long time since you have been here."

Carmen stepped inside and the man closed and bolted the door behind them. It was just over an hour until the door opened and Carmen left. She mounted and rode away, and the man stood on the low porch and watched her receding figure until the night swallowed it up. Then he left the house and walked to a low stable and mounted a horse himself. He rode into the night. After a while, he circled and passed the sleeping caravan and continued on in the direction from which they had come.

Reeve lay on his side, braced on one elbow, and smiled down into Elana's eyes. Elana had lost much of her original shyness, and she had surrendered to his desire to enjoy her beauty by letting him undress her. She lay in the glow of the fire, her body gleaming ivory and gold. He bent his head and leisurely caught her mouth with his in a deep and satisfactory kiss. Slowly he let his lips drift to her slender throat and the pulse that beat there.

One hand lay possessively on her hip and it stirred to caress first the flat plane of her belly then up to the soft curve of her breasts. She sighed deeply as his mouth caught a sensitive nipple and suckled enough to send a vibrant shiver throughout her body. She murmured soft Spanish words for which he needed no translation.

Again, he lifted his head and their eyes met. Her eyes sparkled with teasing pleasure, but this was one night he intended to enjoy to the fullest. He had no intention of hurrying.

He lay beside her and they looked up at the millions of gleaming silver stars. One arm about her, he drew her against him. Slim legs twined with his, and he closed his eyes to feel more fully the soft breasts that pressed against him and the velvet feel of her skin.

"I was thinking," Elana said softly.

"What, love?"

"Of all the changes in my life in such a short time. I would never have believed this would have happened a few weeks ago."

"Do you regret any of it?"

"Only, I suppose, in disappointing Her Majesty. She had always been so good to me."

"Good to you? Does that include trying to make you marry a man like Diego even when she knew you didn't want to?"

"She felt what she was doing was best for me, I suppose."

"No, Elana, I don't think it was her at all. I think there's more behind it than your queen wanting you to marry some wealthy grandee. Don Francisco had something to gain from all this."

"I had felt that, too, but what could he gain by having Beatriz marry Don Francisco or me marrying his nephew? They would control all we owned."

"And," Reeve said gently, "he would control them. Tell me about your family, Elana. Your brother said your parents were safely away and that was all that held you here."

Elana explained her family's unique and very powerful position in Spain, and Reeve knew he had done well to snatch Elana from under Don Francisco's nose. Once Elana and Beatriz were safely married to Don Francisco's choice, their families' days would have been numbered. It also made him more certain Don Francisco would do his best to keep them from leaving the country. He worried if Rafael and Catrina had safely reached his ship and if it would be waiting for them at San Sebastián. He began to sweat at the thought of what might happen if Rafael and Catrina were caught, and if they were convinced to tell just how and where he and Elana were to be found.

He had been quiet for some time, absently caressing Elana's smooth skin. She was well aware that his mind was elsewhere, and that he was not exactly happy with where it wandered.

She sat up and Reeve's attention was held by the vision before him. Bright moonlight and the glow of the fire cast her half in light and half in shadow.

One creamy shoulder, one soft rounded breast, one slim hip, amber in the fire while the other was pale ivory by the touch of the moon. He could not see her eyes, but felt their warmth as she reached out and ran her hand up over his lean ribs to rest on his broad chest.

"Husband," she whispered, "have you forgotten me?" She felt the rumble of soft laughter deep in his chest and was as pleased with the sound as she was the gentle touch of his hand as it slid up to her slim waist, then to capture a passion-ripened breast to caress gently.

Her breath caught as his two hands spanned her waist and drew her down across him. His open mouth caught hers and his hands slid down from her waist to softer, rounder parts to draw her tightly to him.

With wild, almost abandoned passion, she responded, laughing to herself at the passing vision of Lady Elana of Queen Isabella's court, in the deserted plains of Spain, making mad passionate love with a man of which she knew little and cared deeply.

His lips touched her with fire, nibbling gently on her skin, and his hands were hard and demanding as they sought to explore every inch of her.

She gasped at the ecstatic flame as his mouth caught a passion-hardened nipple and his hand found the other. She cried out as he teased them with a heated splendor that neared pain. Then suddenly he turned and drew her beneath him.

His eyes glowed like silver flames with the depth of his passion. He lay half upon her but eased his weight so that she was not supporting him. Then he began a conquest so intense and so wild that she thought she would surely die of it.

He lowered his head to brush her lips with his, then let them begin a fiery journey that sent quivers through her being as if she were touched with the jagged lightning she had often watched nature explode with. The fiery pulse that beat at her throat . . . down to sensitive breasts until she cried out in search of him . . . down to the flat smooth plane of her belly, the soft flesh of her thigh. She moaned and tried to free herself from this ecstatic pain-pleasure, but he held her bound with iron-hard hands, and found the center of her need and explored it until she was gasping, moaning, calling to him in a need so deep she could no longer bear it. Then she felt him as he filled her with a need that matched her own. Hard and throbbing she could feel him within and she twined herself about him as if she could make them one.

At first he tormented her with slow rhythmic strokes that drove her frantic, and her body arched to meet him, demanding more. Then he could no longer control his desire. He gripped her body with hard, urgent hands to meet his demands more fully. She clung to him as he drove to the depths of her with stronger and stronger force.

She was lost, mindless, abandoned, and consumed by the flame that engulfed them. She heard his breathing harsh and rasping in her ears. She also heard her own voice crying out to him. Her hands felt the rippling strengths of the muscle across his back as she held him. There was no other thing in existence but the blinding, heated need that possessed them, molded them forever into one being, one heart, one need.

She panted in soft ragged gasps as they clung weakly to each other, overcome with an emotional and physical experience such as they had never known before.

Sweat bathed them and their worlds reached for reality, yet they could not separate. Still keeping his full weight from her, he gathered her tightly into his arms and rocked her against him.

Her eyes closed and she wordlessly clung to him, feeling their thudding hearts begin to slow to steadier matching beats. After a moment, he drew the blankets over them.

"So," he said softly, "did I convince you that there is no way in this world I could ever forget you?"

"Oh, Reeve," she sighed softly as she nestled close to him, "I have never felt so before. It was as if your soul touched mine and you were within me, knowing me more completely than I know myself."

"I do," he whispered softly. "I will always be part of you as you are of me. I say I love you, Elana, but those words are only a part of what I feel. There is so much more and I want to be able to tell you, my dear beloved wife, every day for the rest of our lives."

"Yes," she whispered, "Always."

"Always . . . how do you say that in Spanish?"

"Siempre."

"Siempre, my love . . . siempre."

She sighed in the deepest contentment she had ever felt. Her body, warmed by his, soon became exhausted and her heavy eyes closed in sleep.

Reeve held her, unable to sleep. He had just shared an experience that to him was almost beyond comprehending. Now he was overcome with the fear that had lain in the back of his mind. Would they make it to freedom? And if they did not, what could happen to Elana?

He held her slim body close to him, knowing a part of him would die should he ever lose her. He remembered the original reason for his journey and the good-natured fun in which he had started it. Now, many lives depended upon him, and the one he loved most in the world was first among them.

He finally slept, but only after he had solidified his determination to get Elana and the others away safely.

They had no more time to share alone than the one night. Reeve hated that, but Elana laughed it away as they prepared to return to the caravan late the next morning.

"We promised each other always," she said, "and always begins today."

He laughed and drew her into his arms for a long, leisurely kiss. "I love you, Elana."

"I know." She smiled up into his eyes. "Now, we must go out of this country so we can begin our always together."

They rode back to the caravan, filled with their love, their promise of tomorrow. But there were to be many tests of their tomorrows that would begin sooner than they bargained for.

Chapter Eighteen

There was no time to spend to leisurely enjoy each other. All involved knew the race meant their lives. Pedro had the caravan prepared early the next morning. Even though they were reluctant to end the precious moments they shared, both Reeve and Elana knew their future depended upon it.

Carmen had returned to the caravan before dawn and no one ever knew she had been gone. She rode with Elana and Beatriz, making herself as pleasant as she possibly could. Everyone was convinced any problems that might have existed between Reeve and Carmen were gone . . . everyone but Pedro. He knew Carmen too well.

She seemed entirely too friendly and open. He knew Carmen as a woman whose emotions ran high, and as one who rarely gave up on anything she really wanted, and he suspected she wanted Captain Reeve Burke. He wondered just what had happened between Carmen and Reeve. Pedro watched and admired Elana. He thought of her as a rare and beautiful lady. Reeve was fortunate, he thought, to have a woman who understood past indiscretions. His woman, he knew, would have wielded a sharp stiletto and still been shouting her anger. Elana was pleasant to Carmen, but he was well aware she kept Reeve in sight and rode with him. She was no one's fool, he thought. She had and would hold Reeve, no matter what they faced.

Pedro decided to keep a much closer eye on Carmen himself. He had a strange feeling he had not seen the last of Carmen's anger.

Reeve may not have shown the thoughts in his mind, but he also was not quite sure he had seen the last of Carmen either. He also knew women too well. Hell, he knew, had no fury like a woman scorned . . . yet he had no idea hell would burst upon them as it was to do.

Pedro rode at the head of his caravan always while they traveled. Just before the midday stop, Reeve rode up to ride beside him. Pedro knew he had something on his mind so he waited patiently for Reeve to speak.

"Pedro?"

"*Si.*"

"How long has Carmen been with your caravan?"

"Ah, Carmen," Pedro said quietly. "Carmen comes and Carmen goes. It's been almost two years she's been doing so. Carmen takes good care of Carmen."

"What do you know about her past?"

"Nothing. I never asked, and I've no intention of doing so. She has saved many lives, that I know . . . as well as I know she has things in her past she doesn't want known. She knows people . . . all kinds . . . from all places."

"Who does she work for?"

"Carmen?" Pedro laughed.

"That's what I thought," Reeve said, a dark scowl on his face.

"My friend, what worries you?"

"I'm pretty sure you already know."

"*Si.* I suppose if I were you, I would be worried, too. Carmen is a woman, *aiee*, what a woman. She is also one who sets her mind on a thing and gets it . . . one way or another. She has her eyes on you, my friend, and I think the presence of your woman has upset her and roused the evil touch of jealousy. Yes, I would worry, too, if I were you . . . or if I were your woman."

"Elana," Reeve said softly. "Pedro, if she spoke to the wrong people, it could cost Elana and Rodrigo their lives."

"The wrong people aren't here."

"I know, but I still have this strange feeling something is wrong."

"Let us hope it is only a feeling. There is no way we can say anything to her. She has done nothing to let us believe we're in more danger than what you are running from. I would suggest you keep a close eye on your woman and your friends . . . and Carmen."

"Don't worry, Pedro, I intend to. How far do we have to go?"

"We reach Palencia by tomorrow this time. From there, it's two days to the coast. We will camp on the coast and then ride to the harbor where I hope we find your ship."

"My ship will be there. Ralph is a man who can be trusted to carry out orders. We don't intend to go too near Palencia, do we?"

"Cities are places we make a point to stay away from," Pedro said with a laugh. "We will circle it and camp on the other side."

"Two days from there," Reeve mused, "and we'll be safe."

"Maybe we should have a small celebration?"

"When we get past Palencia," Reeve replied.

"Good." Pedro grinned. "Maybe Carmen will dance for you again."

"Good God," Reeve said. "I hope not. That last dance was almost my last!"

Pedro laughed heartily. Reeve turned and looked back along the line of the caravan. The smile on his face faded as he saw Elana and Carmen riding together, in avid conversation.

Elana had been riding slowly alongside the wagon that

Beatriz's grandfather rode in. Her eyes were on the broad-shouldered golden man who rode beside Pedro at the head of the caravan. A half smile touched her lips as her mind drifted to memories sweet and warm.

She could feel the possessive touch of him and she trembled at the warmth that filled her. Reeve was here, and the pleasure of knowing it filled her world with a glow that brightened everything she saw. The days seemed brighter, the nights warmer, and the world a better place than she had ever known.

Elana was so engrossed in watching Reeve that she did not realize Carmen rode beside her until she spoke.

"What?" Elana said as she turned startled eyes to Carmen. "I'm afraid I was daydreaming."

Carmen laughed softly as her eyes lingered on Reeve. "Yes, I can see what you were daydreaming about. He is quite handsome, your man. Golden hair is rare to see in this country."

"Yes," Elana agreed. She found herself uncertain. Carmen had been friendly, yet she could not shake the feeling that something in the friendliness was wrong or different . . . something cold.

"We are not too far from your destination. Soon you and your husband will be boarding his ship and heading for England and safety." Carmen laughed. "I would not be surprised if Pedro would choose to have a celebration. Once we have passed Palencia, it will be no time until we reach the coast."

"Yes," Elana said softly, "*if* we reach the coast." When she had said it, she didn't know why she had said it. It was a feeling from deep inside her.

"If they have not caught up with us by now, what makes you think they will? We are far enough ahead of them to stay so until we are safe."

"I suppose you are right, but I will not really feel safe until I see the coast of Spain disappear."

"Are you frightened?" Carmen said softly.

Elana turned to look at her, but could read nothing in her face. "Yes, yes . . . I suppose I am."

"Frightened of what? Not being able to hold your man?"

Again the question struck a vulnerable spot in Elana. She held herself under rigid control and kept a tight rein on her temper. She was sure Carmen was trying to bait her. Her eyes were clear and controlled as she looked at Carmen again, clearly seeing the challenge in Carmen's eyes. She smiled. "No, Carmen, I am not afraid of holding Reeve. We are part of each other, my husband and I. One does not cling to or strangle one you love. He knows in his heart I belong to him . . . and I know . . . I know, he will always belong to me, no matter what any outside influence may try to do."

Carmen laughed softly, recognizing the answering challenge. "Of course you do. Well, we will all be happy soon, within days we will end this journey. Then, each of us, I hope, will get exactly what they want."

Carmen kicked her horse and it surged ahead before Elana could reply. Elana watched her ride away and again felt the light and unnamable touch of fear.

Reeve turned his horse about and rode back to Elana's side. For a moment he allowed himself the pleasure of drowning in emerald eyes and the warmth of her promising smile.

Elana wore only a cotton peasant skirt and a white blouse that hung loosely about her neck. A wide red scarf circled her slim waist and her feet were clad in leather slippers that laced about her slim ankles. Her dark hair, parted in the middle, hung in two thick braids. The sun had begun to kiss her skin to a golden glow. He felt her amazing beauty reach out and hold him as it always would. He reached out and lightly touched her cheek.

"What a beautiful Gypsy you really are." He smiled.

"I am no longer Lady de Santangel," she said quietly.

"You are always Lady de Santangel, but you are always my Gypsy woman. I love you both and I don't know which one I love the most. Just about the time I decide on one, the other taps me on the shoulder." Elana laughed and he was pleased with the sound of it. "It won't be long, Elana. A few more days and this will be all over. Although I will admit there have been some pleasant memories of the nights I spent with a Gypsy girl."

"I have memories, too, my husband, and we will carry them with us as long as we live."

"After we pass Palencia it will be a short time to the coast. Ralph will be waiting with the *Golden Eagle*. Everything will be all right." Elana looked at him quickly; knowing him as well as she did now, she sensed that he felt the same as she: something was wrong. Her eyes grew wide and she gazed at him in silence, but before she could speak, he said, "Elana, Rafael, and Catrina must already be talking to Ralph. It will take no time for him to bring the *Golden Eagle*. Our lives are in good hands, so we won't worry. A few days, love, just a few days."

"Yes, Reeve, just a few days."

Don Diego Chavez sat in the carriage opposite Rafael and Catrina. He could not understand why his son had chosen to rush home so quickly. It was impossible since everything had to be done so quickly. Since Rafael knew most conversations were overheard, he had to explain to his father what they were doing. Now that they were safely on their way, he planned to tell his father immediately for they had to make all speed and pass their hacienda to reach Reeve's ship. Don Diego would not question his son in Catrina's presence, yet Rafael knew he desired to.

"Father," Rafael said, "I think it's time I explained to you what the reasons are that we are in such a hurry."

"I know," Don Diego replied, "that it must be serious, just as I know at the palace, the walls have ears. Has it to do with Reeve and the ones he came to help?"

"Yes," Rafael replied. Quickly he went on to tell his father why they had to get to Cadiz and get Reeve's ship safely on its way. "Once they are gone, we can return home and none will be the wiser. No one will ever know we were the ones that warned Reeve's ship. By the time they find out how well they've been fooled, it will be too late to find Reeve and the others."

"And where will Reeve be taking the others?"

"To the coast near San Sebastián."

"The opposite direction completely."

"Yes, that way was the least suspicious. No one would think they would run any other direction than Reeve's ship. It should be gone by the time they figure out what happened."

"Some quick thinking, my son."

"Most of which is Rodrigo's plan."

"There is still the chance of a great deal of danger both to you and to them. What if Don Francisco is not fooled? What if he thinks to spread in two directions, to trace Reeve and the others? He is not a stupid man, even though he is an evil one. Maybe it would be best to send Catrina to friends where they won't think to look for her if worse comes to worse."

"No!" Catrina said firmly. "I go where Rafael goes, no matter what happens."

"Catrina, maybe Father is right. It's so dangerous."

"Rafael," Catrina said quietly but firmly, "you are my husband. We have just vowed before God to share the rest of our lives together, for better or for worse. Now you want me to desert you at the first sign of danger? I will not go, and I will not hear you speak of it again, neither of you." Her eyes flashed defiance at both men.

"I was afraid you might say that," Rafael said with a grin. "I would have told my father you are certainly much too determined a woman to let anything stand in your way. We'll go on together, my love."

Catrina smiled and slid her arm through Rafael's. "We might just spend some time in Cadiz together after we have warned the ship. It would be nice visiting the shops there, and having you to myself for a while before we have to return home."

Don Diego's eyes grew warm as he watched his son and Catrina together. That they loved each other deeply was obvious. He remembered well the love he had felt for Rafael's mother. It would be a pleasure to have the two sharing his home until their own was built. The idea of their bringing the brightness of love back in his home filled him with joy. Maybe, he thought, there would one day be children. Children he could watch grow as he had Rafael.

"We will be home soon," Diego said. "From there it would be best if you two went on by horseback. You could travel faster and return home faster."

"Excellent idea, Father."

"Yes, excellent," Catrina agreed.

"Well, it will be nightfall before we reach home. Much too late to travel by horseback anywhere. We will start just before dawn. Of course, we will have to stop again at the inn, but if we begin early the next day, we will reach Cadiz before dark."

They agreed to this also. The balance of the trip was spent in conversation about the plans for the future. As Rafael had said, it was nearing midnight before they arrived at the Chavez hacienda.

Catrina's head lay on Rafael's shoulder. His arm about her held her close while she slept.

When the carriage drew up before the door, Don Diego stepped down without disturbing Catrina. Gently, Rafael lifted Catrina in his arms and carried her to the door which his father

248

held open for him. With a quiet good night to his father, Rafael carried Catrina to his room.

Once inside, he pushed the door shut as quietly as he could. He walked across a room, and, though dark, he knew it like he knew himself. Gently he laid Catrina on his bed.

As quietly as he could, he opened the window to the cool night air. He lit one candle at the far end of the room so the light would not disturb Catrina. He wanted her and laughed at himself as he fought the urge to waken her. She was exhausted from the long trip, and he didn't want to disturb her. What he wondered was how he could undress her without waking her. He took off his jacket, hung it on the back of the chair, slipped out of his boots, then walked to the bed and looked down on his sleeping wife. Gently he reached to touch her cheek. Her skin was smooth beneath his fingers and his heart quickened.

How beautiful she is, he thought, and the need for her was almost a pain. His breath caught as her eyes slowly opened. Catrina looked up at the man who stood by the bed. Even though he stood in shadows, she could feel the intensity of his mental reaching for her.

Catrina reached toward him and he took her hand in his. She drew him down and he sat on the edge of the bed. Gently he lifted her hand to his lips and kissed her fingers, then he bent forward and took her mouth with his.

Rafael could feel the sweetness of Catrina through every nerve and sense in his body. When he released her lips, he heard the words he desired most.

"Oh, Rafael," she whispered, "I want you so." It was the only incentive Rafael needed. He drew her into his arms and felt the warmth of her slim arms enfold him. They kissed deeply and passionately.

Rafael stood and drew her up to stand close to him. The pale light of the candle's glow bathed her in gold and shadows. Their eyes held as he reached to release the hooks of her gown. It fell in a rustling heap to the floor. With gentle fingers he slowly removed the rest of her clothes. She stood before him, aware of the warmth of his gaze that devoured her.

Catrina moved into his arms and he closed them about her. Molded against him, she could feel the thundering beat of his heart. Their lips met and blended again in a deep, lingering kiss.

It took Rafael only moments to rid himself of the remains of his clothes. He closed his eyes in an agony of pleasure as he drew her slim, cool body against his. Passion-hardened nipples teased his senses as they pressed against him. His hands slid to her slim hips, drawing her tightly to him.

They tumbled to the bed, aware now of only the taste and touch of each other and the flame of mutual desire that possessed them. Slowly, expertly, Rafael began pressing tiny kisses over face, throat, and breasts. His hands began a tormenting caressing of her hips and thighs, stroking them lightly with gentle fingers until her sensitive skin heated, and he felt her stir to frantic life.

Wave after wave of exquisite sensations drove her to near madness, and she cried out softly. Her lips covered his face with delicious nibbling kisses and she laughed softly as she felt him tighten his arms about her, and a half-smothered moan of pleasure seemed drawn from him.

Suddenly he turned and drew her beneath him. She welcomed the surge of his hard body as he thrust deeply within her. Her eyes closed and she allowed the rhythm of his desire to fill her. Letting go her hold on all reality she surrendered to this all consuming need.

She welcomed the pressure of his heavily muscled body as he drove to the depths of her. Her hands caressed the rigid muscle of his back and waist to the hard, thrusting hips. She trembled as if in the midst of a violent storm. She was whirled away beyond all knowing, beyond all reality except the blending of her body and his. She moved beneath him, searching and finding all as his powerful body possessed hers to the very depths of her soul.

She quivered in his arms like a wild creature unable to control the fiery desire as his kisses scalded her skin. She felt a delicious mixture of ecstasy and pain and could not understand the soft crying sound she heard, unable to realize they came from her.

A shudder tore through him and she clung to him. They surged together in a passionate joyous violence. He held her for another moment, then rolled on his back, drawing her close to him. He was breathing raggedly but he chuckled weakly.

"God, woman, you are more than any man could pray for in his wildest dreams."

Catrina curled closer, nipping his ear lightly with her teeth. He enjoyed her soft, pleased laughter. "I love you, Rafael. I want to please you more than anything else in the world. Am I to understand you are pleased with me?"

"Pleased?" He laughed. "If I were any more pleased, I should die of it!" They laughed together and he rocked her in his arms, grateful again that she belonged to him. She had become the center of his life and the entire hope for his future. "We'll be leaving early in the morning, Catrina," he said. "Maybe it would be best if you waited here for me."

Abruptly she sat up beside him and looked down with her eyes aglow. "Stay here! Rafael Chavez, I shall be riding beside you tomorrow. Did you think you were going to ride off leaving me twiddling my thumbs and waiting? No, I shall go with you." She bent to kiss him firmly and lingeringly. "I want to be with you, Rafael . . . always."

He reached up to twine his hand in her hair. "If something went wrong . . . if something should ever happen to you, Catrina . . . I . . . don't think I could live with that. Why don't you stay where I know you're safe?"

"And I should worry and be filled with fear for you. No, I would be with you, Rafael. Whatever is to happen to us, let it happen when we are together, when I can feel you, then I will be happy."

"Stubborn wench," he said softly as he drew her down to rest against his chest. He caressed her lightly and heard her sigh contentedly. "We will go together. I guess I wouldn't choose to be separated from you either."

They talked in quiet whispers for some time, about future plans for the life they would share together. Reluctantly, Rafael kissed her and said quietly, "I suppose you are very tired. You must get some sleep, little one. We do have to start very early."

He could feel the cool touch of her hand on his cheek, then it slid through his hair, drawing his head to hers.

"Truly, husband," she whispered as their lips met, "there are things that interest me more than my need for sleep."

Her throaty laughter was muffled by a hard insistent mouth that took immediate and very effective possession of hers.

Chapter Nineteen

The sun had not risen, but a pale glow of half light touched the horizon as Rafael and Catrina stood in the kitchen and sipped hot chocolate. Both were dressed for riding.

"We'd best get started, Catrina," Rafael said quietly. She nodded and they left the kitchen and walked across the grounds to the stables. Once there, Rafael saddled two horses and within minutes, they were on their way.

From Rafael's home, which was centrally located between Toledo and Cordoba, they rode at a slow and steady ground-covering speed. They stopped at midday to sit beneath a tree and eat the small amount of food and drink the bottle of wine Rafael had carried along.

They had rested only a short time, and Rafael was forced to start them on their way again. Catrina made no complaint.

"We'll spend the night at the inn in Cordoba. Tomorrow we'll get an early start again and we should make Cadiz by late tomorrow night."

"I cannot say I will not be happy to find a soft bed tonight. I feel like I'm attached to this saddle, and I swear I smell like a horse." Catrina laughed.

Rafael stood and reached down to help Catrina to her feet. "Come along, woman. I'd like to spend the rest of the day

253

under this tree with you, but I'm afraid we have to move along."

He pulled her up beside him and kissed her quickly, then helped her mount. Again, they were on their way.

When Cordoba came into view, both of them were tired enough to appreciate it.

The inn was an even more welcome sight. They were taken to their room and Rafael ordered a tub of water to be brought and some food. It cost him a considerable amount of money, but Catrina looked so tired he felt it was well worth it.

Catrina slid into the warm water with a deep sigh. She lay back and closed her eyes only to open them in surprise as Rafael stepped into the tub and sat down close to her.

"Sorry, love," he said, grinning, "it looked too comfortable. "I'll wash your back . . . and any other places you might not be able to reach." She laughed softly and all tiredness seemed to disappear. He rubbed the soap between his hands and began to caress her firmly yet gently. Again she closed her eyes to savor his touch. He bent his head to taste her lips, nibbling gently and tracing its soft firmness with his tongue. She forgot being tired; she forgot the tub of water and everything that surrounded them. His hands moved over her, exploring sensitive breasts that seemed to stir beneath his hands as the nipples hardened to passion. Down the curve of her waist to slender hips and soft thighs. His hands found softer sensitive places that sent a current through her.

Rafael rose and lifted her dripping from the water and they tumbled laughing to the bed. His lips began their own possessive journey turning her sighs to moans as they slid from slender throat to hardened nipples, from there to slender waist and flat belly, down to the center of her need that almost made her cry out with pleasure.

She reached for him, allowing her hands to roam his hard body until she gripped his hardness and guided him to her.

They joined in a splendor of agonizing need.

He moved within her hard and deep until they were consumed by the magic that touched them . . . and they slept in each other's arms, unwilling even in sleep to part.

The next morning she woke before dawn to find the bed empty. She sat up startled, fear written plainly in her eyes. At the same time, the door opened and Rafael came in. The relief of seeing him brought tears to her eyes. He came quickly to her side.

"Catrina! I never meant to frighten you. I thought I would get the horses saddled quickly and let you get the last few minutes of sleep. Today will be difficult for you."

"It's all right." She smiled through the tears. "You are here."

"Yes," he said. "I will always be here. Come, little one, on your feet. I'm afraid we have to go. Although, I would much rather crawl back into that bed with you."

Catrina rose from the bed and Rafael grew silent at the golden perfection of her. He watched her dress, memorizing every inch of her slim body. "I'm ready," she said.

Rafael laughed. "I'm afraid I am, too, but we've got to go anyway." Catrina laughed with him and they left the room in which they had shared so much.

As they left Cordoba, Catrina began to notice that Rafael looked back over his shoulder more often than usual. What she did not know that in the moments that Rafael was saddling his horses, he noticed three men who seemed only to be lounging about. But some familiar thing caught his attention and triggered an alarm within. Were they following him? If they were, when would they close the trap?

Now they rode slowly and he kept looking to see if the three men were truly following them, or if it was his imagination.

"Rafael?"

"What?"

255

"What are you looking for?"

"Looking?"

"Don't play with me, Rafael," she said seriously. "Are we being followed?"

He knew it was no use to keep secrets from her; she was too attuned to him. "I'm not sure, Catrina. I don't see anyone now." He went on to explain about the three men at the inn.

"Maybe it is just my imagination; I'm seeing things that aren't there." Catrina didn't believe this for a moment, but she said nothing. They rode on, stopping only to rest the horses and nibble at some food. Neither of them seemed to be hungry.

The afternoon grew hot and oppressive and they rode now in silence. As the sun began to lower toward the horizon, gray clouds began to form. After a while, they obliterated what sun was left, and the wind began to rise. There was no doubt in Rafael's mind they were in for a storm. He only hoped they would reach Cadiz before it broke. They reached the outskirts of Cadiz just as the rain began to fall. By the time they reached the inn, they were both completely soaked.

Rafael found them a room quickly. Once inside, he told Catrina to take off her clothes. He wrapped her in a blanket from the bed.

"I want you to climb into that bed," he said.

"Rafael, you're not going—"

"I'm going to the ship. We've got to get that message to the ship. Once it's done, we'll be able to relax."

"Don't leave me, Rafael! Let me go with you."

"It's not far, Catrina. I'll only be gone an hour or so." He bent over the bed and kissed her. "Keep the bed warm, I'll be back before you have a chance to miss me."

Catrina tried her best to hide the fear that touched her. She sat in the center of the bed and watched as Rafael dried his hair and tried to brush off most of the moisture. He took a blanket to carry with him as he rode to the docks, then he returned to the bed and sat down beside her. He lifted and kissed her hand, then her wrist.

"I'll be right back," he said softly. "Close your eyes and stay warm . . . stay warm and wait for me."

"Yes," she answered quietly, "I'll wait."

"You are an angel, my love, and I love you more than the breath in my body. When I come back we will go home, and I will have you all to myself. We'll start our lives together. I love you, my dear wife. I love you."

"And, I love you," she whispered.

He rose and walked to the door where he turned to look at her. She was a vision, her slim gold body in the harsh dark blanket. Her wide eyes watched him and he saw the world in them. It was a vision he would long remember.

He closed the door behind him and walked down the long hall and the steps; then he was outside. He put the blanket around him and went to the stables and saddled his horse.

It took him less than a half hour to reach the dock. There he saw the *Golden Eagle* rocking gently in the harbor. He walked to the gangplank and called out to the man who stood watch.

"*Hola!* Aboard the *Golden Eagle*!"

The man looked over to see who called out to him. "Aye, what can I do for you?"

"I have to talk to Ralph. I have a message from Captain Burke."

"Come aboard."

Rafael walked up the gangplank and stepped on the deck of the *Golden Eagle*.

"Come with me," the sailor told him. He followed the man below decks where they stopped in front of a door. He knocked and in a few minutes, the door was opened.

"Yes, Tucker, what is it?"

"This here gentleman wants to talk to you. He says he has a message from the Captain."

Ralph's eyes switched to Rafael who gazed back at him.

Whatever he read must have pleased him, for he smiled. "Come in."

He stepped aside and Rafael entered.

"It's all right, Tucker."

"Aye sir," Tucker replied, then he turned and left Ralph and closed the door behind him.

"You have a message from Captain Burke for me?"

"Yes, I have."

"Sit down, I'll pour you a drink."

Rafael sat. Ralph poured a glass of rum and handed it to Rafael. Then, he sat opposite him. For the next twenty minutes, Rafael explained all that had happened and what Reeve wanted him to do. He pointed out the spot on the map where the *Golden Eagle* was to pick up its captain.

"I'll weigh anchor and be gone before morning," Ralph said. "It should get us there at about the right time. Can I get you another drink . . . to warm you up for the cold?"

"No," Rafael replied. "I'm going back to the inn. I'll be warm, don't worry."

"Well, goodbye. Thanks for delivering the message, and for the story. I hope everything goes well for you."

"*Gracias*," Rafael replied. He shook hands with Ralph and left the ship. With a light heart, he rode back to the inn. He climbed the stairs two at a time and opened the door of his room. The smile on his face died and his heart leapt in fear. The room was a shambles. Catrina was gone and a tall dark man sat in a chair in the center of the debris with his arms folded and a smug smile on his face.

"Come in, Senor Chavez. We have a great deal to talk about. Come in please." Rafael felt rage broil within. He controlled it with the grimmest effort. His first need was to find Catrina. He stepped inside and closed the door.

*   *   *

Catrina had watched the door close behind Rafael and felt a feeling of utter desolation. She felt his absence immediately.

"Only an hour," she whispered softly to encourage herself. She knew it would be nearly impossible for her to sleep until he returned. She rose and walked to the fire Rafael had built before he left. Her clothes, hanging before it, were very nearly dry. She began to dress. She donned her shift and petticoats, then her stockings and shoes. She left her dress hanging to finish drying and sat before the fireplace, and brushing her hair.

A deep reverie stole upon her and she let herself sink into a deep daydream. Her mind held only visions of Rafael and the magic he had wakened within her. At the very thought of him, her body grew taut and warm.

She closed her eyes and savored the feelings that stirred within her. Soon it would be over and she and Rafael would go to his home. Their whole lifetime lay ahead of them and she smiled to herself at the thought of the days and nights they would spend together.

Caught in her reverie, Catrina was not aware of the stealthy steps in the hall that stopped in front of her door. She did not hear the soft whispers as the intruders prepared to enter. She was jolted from her dreamlike state as the door burst open and the three men entered.

She leapt to her feet, a muffled cry on her lips. Catrina, though unprepared for the attack, was not a coward. She stood and glared at the three, creating a vision that stirred their blood. "Who are you? What do you want? You had best depart or I shall scream and rouse the entire inn."

One of the men laughed as he began to move toward her. "Scream, my little dove. Do you think anyone will interfere with the arm of the Inquisition? No one will come to your aid, so you had best surrender easily. I would not want to use force on one as beautiful as you."

Her heart thudded heavily as she realized the truth of his statement. She knew quite well few had the courage to defy the Inquisition. No one would help her. Her mouth firmed and her shoulders straightened. She would not surrender easily. She began to back away from them and with a soft chuckle, the man began to stalk her as if it were an amusing game.

"Ah," he said softly, his eyes raking over her, "a sweet flower with thorns. Come little flower, there is no use to fight us. We will take you from here to be questioned."

"Questioned? About what? Why do you want to question me? What interest could the Inquisition have in me?"

"So innocent." He laughed. "With such beauty, one could almost believe you . . . almost, but not quite. Your man has information we want. I am sure he would be much more willing to talk if we suggest to him that you would be . . . ah . . . upset if he did not."

"I don't know what you are talking about, and I'm sure Rafael does not either. We are on our wedding trip."

"A nice masquerade, but we are cleverer than you. You will tell us what we want to know." His voice became hard. "Believe me, you will tell us."

Fear such as she had never known before drained her and she shook with the terror that filled her mind. One of the men waited by the door to block her escape and the other two began to move toward her. She thought of the window and dashed toward it, only to have her way blocked. The man reached to grab her and caught the strap of her shift. The fragile cloth tore and the three men were treated to a sight of her soft vulnerable curves. It roused their blood and they pressed the attack.

Catrina ran toward the bed, rolled across it and came up on the other side, making wildly for the opposite window. Before she could reach it, a hard arm came about her waist and lifted her from her feet. She fought wildly but her strength was no match for his. She kicked out at the second man who approached her, catching him in the groin and sending him cursing to his knees. The man who held her chuckled as if he were enjoying the fight. Catrina was naked to the waist and he was enjoying the view. She kicked and fought but the third man caught her legs and held her.

"Tie her ankles," the man who held her said. In moments, her ankles were bound. "Go and get the horses," the first man commanded. With sneering, knowing faces, the two men obeyed.

Catrina panted with the exertion and the terror that filled her. Pressed against the man behind her, she could not move. Her arms bound firmly, she quivered in fear as she heard his hoarse rasping breath in her ear. Tears spilled on her cheeks as she realized she was powerless to stop whatever he intended to do. She could feel the hardness of his manhood press against her buttocks. She moaned softly as she felt his lips touch her ear, then move slowly down her slim throat to her shoulder. She heard his heavy, rasping breathing as he firmly gripped her wrists and bound them together behind her. She was powerless to move. He stepped around her to face her and his eyes burned against her skin.

She closed her eyes in agony as he reached to caress her, sliding his hands over her skin and squeezing her breasts. He bent his head and began to nibble and suck at her sensitive nipples, first one, then the other. She knew his intentions and the pain of helplessness made her dizzy with its intensity. She felt his hands fumble with her petticoats, lifting them to run his hands over her flesh. Then the door was again thrown open and another man stood framed in the doorway. He was tall and broad shouldered. Catrina would have claimed him handsome had she not been so frightened. The man close to her came instantly alert.

261

"Garcia! You filthy bastard! Take your hands off of her. You were sent to bring her to me, not to rape her. I ought to castrate you."

"Don Carlos," Garcia stammered. His face grew gray as the blood drained from it. Catrina watched fear replace the lust in his eyes. "I was not going to hurt her. She was a tigress, I had to subdue her."

"Subdue!" Don Carlos spat. "Good God, man, does it take three men to subdue one woman, especially one the size of her? Get below, I'll bring her."

"Yes, sir," Garcia said. He rapidly moved away from Catrina. He left and closed the door behind him.

Don Carlos walked toward Catrina, taking a cloak from his broad shoulders as he did. When he reached her side, he knelt and unbound her ankles, then her wrists. His dark eyes gave no sign of his awareness of her as he did. Then he put the cloak about her shoulders. "I am sorry for that animal," he said. "You were not meant to be hurt."

Catrina could barely find her voice and she still was shaking from the encounter. Don Carlos walked to a table and picked up a bottle of wine. He poured her a glass and handed it to her. "Drink this. It will calm your nerves."

Catrina took the glass with trembling hands and lifted it to drink. As she did, she studied his face. Deeply masculine and vividly dark and handsome. He had eyes so dark they were nearly black. His nose straight and his mouth wide and firm. Dark winged brows matched his thick, dark hair. His eyes caught hers and he smiled a reassuring smile.

"Again I am sorry for what you have just been through." His smile faded. "Where," he said softly, "has your husband gone?"

"I . . . I don't know," Catrina replied.

"Come now, my dear, a man in his right mind does not leave

his new bride on a night like this unless it is very serious. I repeat . . . where has your husband gone?"

"Who are you?" Catrina whispered. "What do you want with me?"

"I am Don Carlos Manrique, and I have just told you what I want from you, at the moment. I want to know just where your husband has carried his message."

Catrina's eyes widened. How did this man know Rafael and she were carrying messages?

"We," he said softly, "must know where the others are hiding."

"Others? I don't understand you."

Don Carlos walked to her, the half smile still on his face. Casually he reached out and struck her. She gasped at the shock of it. "You are very beautiful, my dear, but don't take me for a fool. Before another night is over, I will know all I need to know, and you or your very foolish husband will tell me."

This man was more deadly and dangerous than anything she had ever faced before. His smile was gentle, but his eyes were knowing and cold, and she was sure they missed nothing. "I will tell you nothing," she said softly. "And Rafael will tell you nothing also. We are on our wedding trip, nothing more. If you are to bring us for questioning, you must have a charge to put against us. Rafael Chavez is not a name to be taken lightly. This will get you nowhere."

Again he chuckled softly. He reached out and cupped her chin in his hand lightly, lifting her face so he could read her eyes more clearly. "Tonight you and your husband will be taken to a place I own. A quiet place where no one will disturb us. By the time I bring charges against the Chavez family, you and he will be most willing to confess to whatever I decide to accuse you of."

"Never!" she grated angrily.

"Do not say never, my sweet. You have no idea what you are talking about."

"If you are going to torture us, why did you stop Garcia from raping me? Why did you not just let him have his way with me? It would have made no difference."

"When I give a command, I expect it to be obeyed. Garcia will find that I mean every word I say as you and your husband will. I want you as you are." He moved closer to her and she could smell the strong masculine scent of him. He was like a magnificent male animal and she was startled that his nearness disturbed her so. "I do not want other hands to touch you. What will one day be mine, I will not allow to be soiled by an animal such as Garcia."

Her breath caught in her throat as she lifted her eyes to his dark piercing ones. She saw the truth and felt a deeper terror than she had ever known before.

His hand caressed her hair lightly. "You are afraid," he whispered, "because you know I can stir you to passion, and I will. It will be in my time, when I am ready to take you, and Rafael Chavez will know. Oh yes, he will know, and it will destroy him. I will tell him how I possessed you, how you cried out and writhed beneath me. I will tell him of the sweetness he will never possess again. I will tell him how you wept and begged me to take you . . . and then . . . maybe one night, before I kill him, I will show him."

"No!" Catrina cried. "Rafael would never believe that. He will know I would never give myself to anyone but him. He loves me and I love him. He will believe in me . . . he will believe in me!"

"Shall we test that love?" He laughed again. "Shall we show him how I can master you if I want? Will he believe in you then when you beg me to take you and he is forced to watch?"

"I would kill myself first," Catrina said raggedly. "I would rather die than come to you."

"We shall see . . . we shall see."

He took her arm in a grip that felt like iron and guided her to the door. They went down the stairs and out to waiting horses. He mounted, then drew her up before him. Then he turned to Garcia. "Wait in their room for her husband. When he comes, tell him we have his wife and if he does not come to me, I will see to it that he never sees her again."

"Yes, sir," Garcia replied.

Carlos kicked the horse into motion. He held Catrina close against him, one iron-hard arm possessively about her waist. Catrina thought about the words he had said, and it seemed to her that there was more to this than just getting information. The echo of his words in her mind sounded like hatred . . . hatred for Rafael. Was it a personal vendetta? Was he going to use this cause to take revenge on Rafael for something about which she knew nothing?

"Don Carlos," she whispered, "why are you doing this to me? I have not harmed you. Why do you want to destroy my life? Who has ordered you to do this?"

His arm tightened at the word order. "No one orders me, they request my aid. In this case it is not aid; it is a pleasure."

"I was right, you hate Rafael. Why?"

"In time . . . in time. The truth lies between your husband and me."

"And I stand in the middle."

"Be silent!"

"I am the one to be punished."

"I said be silent!"

"I cannot!" she cried.

He pulled his horse to a halt and in the half light, his dark eyes burned down into hers. He gripped her chin and his mouth descended to take command of hers in a fierce and violent kiss. When he lifted his head, she felt beaten and ravaged. "One more word, and I shall take you here, in the

265

mud, like a slut. Do you understand?"

"Yes," she whispered in a choked voice.

They rode on, but Catrina's mind held to one spider web of hope. During the kiss, his mouth had softened and his body had responded. Was there a weakness? Could she find it in time to save both herself and Rafael?

Chapter Twenty

Rafael gazed across the room at the man who sat so calmly amid all the evidence of what had taken place in this room.

"Where is Catrina? Where is my wife?" he demanded.

"Do not demand here, Rafael Chavez," Garcia said with a laugh. "Listen and be quiet. If you want to see your wife again . . . ah . . . in reasonable condition, you will come with me."

Rafael's face turned to granite as he tried to contain the boiling anger and fear within him. "Where is she?"

"In a safe place."

"I want to see her."

"Oh, you will, you will."

"I want to see her now!"

"That's not possible. It will take us some time to get there. He has taken her on ahead."

"He? Who? Who has taken her?"

"Why," Garcia said softly as he held Rafael's eyes, "Don Carlos Manrique."

Rafael's face turned pale despite his efforts at control. He was well aware of Garcia's self-satisfied smile. "What does Carlos have to do with this?"

"He was asked if he would . . . ah . . . detain you and ask you a few simple questions."

"Catrina had nothing to do with this. Why did he not come to me?"

Garcia laughed. "He has known your stubborn nature for too long. He needed to do something to get your undivided attention. I believe he has succeeded. You will come with me now, won't you, Senor Chavez?"

"You know I will," Rafael said. "What are you called?"

"Garcia."

"Garcia," Rafael said in a soft, cold voice, "if anything happens to my wife, I will find it a personal pleasure to kill you in the slowest and most painful way possible."

Garcia's face lost its smile. He knew that Rafael meant what he said and for a minute the cold look of death in his eyes reached out to touch him. "Don Carlos will be waiting for you. We had best go." Without another word, they left the inn and rode toward a fateful meeting. The rain had stopped quite some time before, and they rode by the light of the moon through the muddy trails.

Rafael's mind was in a violent turmoil. He was worried about Catrina, and he knew his adversary, although he had no idea how he got involved in this particular affair. By now he also knew his destination. It took almost an hour and a half of rugged travel until they came to the huge hacienda. It sat in a secluded valley, and Rafael was sure it was well guarded.

They rode down into the valley through the huge elaborately scrolled gates and up the gravel drive. They both dismounted and Garcia tied their horses. He would care for them after he had delivered Rafael.

They walked to the door that Garcia opened. The house inside was magnificent and spoke of exquisite taste and a great deal of money. Garcia led Rafael to a closed door upon which he knocked. The voice that told them to enter was a voice Rafael knew . . . too well. "Go in, Senor Chavez. I will care for the horses."

Garcia turned and left Rafael gazing after him with the desire to commit murder obvious in his dark eyes. Then he turned, opened the door, stepped inside, and closed it behind him.

Carlos stood behind a huge mahogany desk. Their eyes met across the room and Carlos smiled. "Welcome, Rafael. It has been a long time since we have met."

"Not long enough, Carlos."

"How unfriendly." Carlos's smile grew broader. "I welcome you to my home and you are obstinate."

"Stop the pretenses, Carlos, where is Catrina? I want my wife."

"Ah, the lovely creature, Catrina. I must compliment you on your taste, Rafael; she is exquisite."

"What have you done with her, Carlos? Damn you! If you have hurt her, I'll—"

"You will do nothing, Rafael," Carlos said coldly. "You will sit down and listen to me, for if you do not, your wife will pay the price of your stubbornness."

Rafael sat slowly down in a chair across the desk from Carlos and waited.

"Very good. You have gained some wisdom over the years. As a younger man, you were much more hot-headed and foolish."

"Now?" Rafael questioned.

"Now, you will answer some questions my friends have asked me to ask you. After that . . ." He shrugged. "Maybe you can take your wife and go home."

"What questions?"

"Where are the de Santangels and their friends?"

"I have no idea. The last time I saw them was at my wedding."

"Oh, Rafael," Carlos said in a sympathetic voice, "how foolish of you. Shall I go and ask your wife the same questions? Maybe I can . . . convince her to answer me."

"We left the palace immediately after the wedding. How could Catrina or I know what has become of people we left behind?"

"I shall have to give you some time to think about your stupidity. I have someone in the rooms below this one that you should talk to."

"Catrina?" Rafael asked hopefully.

"No. But come, you will see." Carlos walked to the door and opened it. He motioned to Rafael with a grim smile on his face. Without a word, Rafael passed through the open door. They walked down a flight of steps that was long and very narrow. This passed into an even longer hallway that seemed to be hewn from solid stone. On each side of the hall were doors each about eight feet apart. They stopped at the last door, and Carlos took a key from his pocket and unlocked it. He pushed it slowly open. "Enter and discuss your position with one who shares it."

Rafael bent to enter the rather short door. It was promptly closed behind him and he again heard the key turn in the lock. His eyes slowly became accustomed to the dark, and he saw and recognized the man who stood across the room from him. "Father," he said quietly. Don Diego walked across the room to his son. Pain was written clearly on his face. "He has Catrina," Rafael said softly.

"Dear God," Don Diego said, "surely he cannot be so cruel to use her. It is hatred for us that is responsible for this. She is innocent."

"Do you think that matters to him? He wants something from me, Father: the information about where Reeve has taken Elana and Beatriz. Once he has it, we're expendable . . . but once he has it . . . what will he do with Catrina?"

"This is an impossible situation. Of course he does not believe you that you know nothing about it. Did you tell him you left right after the wedding and that they were still at the

270

palace then?"

"He's not a fool, Father. Of course he knows more than we imagine. I would give my soul to see Catrina. She must be frightened to death."

"What will you do?"

"What choices do I have?" Rafael said, laughing harshly. "If I tell him what he wants to know, Reeve and all the others will probably die. If I don't tell him . . . you and Catrina will be his victims."

"Rafael," his father said firmly, "we must keep silent until that ship has time to arrive. We must hold him off a few days. Then it will not matter. I am sure he will begin with me. He will keep you unsure about Catrina until the last minute. We must play for time. Catrina will be safe as long as we can hold out."

"He is demented. You know that and I know that. We cannot guess what he might do to her."

"No, he knows if he hurts her you will never speak. He will keep her away from you. He will lie to you and claim things, but you must have faith in her and know what he claims is not so. It is the only shield Catrina has. He will try to tear you apart as he will try with Catrina to get her to speak. Your love for each other and your faith in each other will be given a test such as no two people have ever known."

"He is a monster that never should have existed. I should have killed him when I had the chance," Rafael said bitterly. "One day I will . . . if he hurts Catrina. I will see him die slowly. I will hear him beg for mercy."

"Don't become the beast he is," his father said gently. "It would give him pleasure to know he has put you to this. Keep your mind about you, my son, or Catrina will be lost."

Don Diego could see the anguish on Rafael's face. He reached out and rested his hand firmly on Rafael's shoulder. "You have to be strong for her sake. No matter what is done to us, you must remain quiet until that ship has reached its destination. You must close your ears to his lies and the pain they will cause. You must also be prepared for the both of us to suffer. Rafael, my son, we must not let him win . . . we cannot lose Catrina."

"Of course I know you are right, Father, but I need to see Catrina even if it is just for a moment. I need to know she is all right. I need to let her know I am here and that I love her."

"Maybe, somehow, we can talk him into one meeting. You can doubt that she is alive, tell him he must prove it to you. Maybe he will let you see her."

"I will try."

Rafael sagged to the narrow cot which, besides one chair, was the only furniture the room held. "How in God's name did he ever get involved in this? How did he know about everything? What is his part in all this? I don't understand."

"Since the last time you and Carlos crossed swords, he has made some powerful and influential friends. They are evil ones, but he serves them well. Don Francisco de Vargas is among them, and Carlos has been made the arm of the Inquisition here in Cadiz. He carries much power now and it has helped to unsettle his already unstable mind."

"Don Francisco de Vargas," Rafael snarled, "they are two of a kind, both poisonous vipers. Both should be killed for the good of society." Don Diego sat down in the chair opposite Rafael, and in silence, they both waited for the inevitable.

Catrina gazed about her at the spacious and very beautiful room in which she had been placed. If it had not been for the iron bars on the windows, she would have believed herself back in the royal palace in Madrid. She had already tried the windows and found the bars solid. She had also tried the door, knowing before she did it would be locked.

She walked to the bed and sat down to wait. She knew,

without doubt, Carlos would be back. She also knew that if he was not now, soon, Rafael would be a prisoner here as well as she. Something within her trembled in fear and she gripped herself firmly. She would not let him terrorize her. Until she knew just what she must face, she would try to keep control. She refused to let her mind touch Carlos. There was something about him that was vaguely familiar, and she could not understand what that something was.

Rafael must be beside himself with worry about her, she thought. Surely she would be allowed to see him even if it were just for a moment. This was all she needed: to know he was alive and well, to feel his arms about her just once more. If she begged, she wondered, would Carlos let her share a moment with Rafael? If she had to, she knew without doubt, she would beg.

She heard the lock turn in the door and slowly rose to her feet, not knowing what to expect. Two men entered carrying a huge wooden tub of water. Behind them came two more, one carrying a small table, the other a tray that was covered but from which emanated the tantalizing odors of hot food. A young woman brought up the rear. Over her arm she carried a gown of pale rose silk. She laid it over the back of the chair. Then she came to Catrina and smiled at her.

"Don Carlos," she spoke in rapid Spanish, "has ordered a bath and clean gown for you, Madam. Then he said to tell you he will join you later for supper."

"He's coming here?"

"Yes, Madam, within an hour. He said to tell you to be ready to receive him."

Now Catrina was truly frightened, but determination helped her to control her trembling. She had to see Rafael. She would make herself all Carlos wanted her to be but would never willingly surrender to him. If he meant to injure Rafael by using her, he was to be disappointed. He had not reckoned with several things: her pride, her love for Rafael, and her silent but firm determination not to dishonor the Chavez name by allowing herself to be seduced either by fear or deceit.

After the men had gone and closed the door behind them, she disrobed and climbed into the scented water. It was deliciously warm. The scented soap was soft as she lathered her skin. When she rose from the tub the young maid held a large towel for her. Even the young maid gazed in wonder at Catrina's pale gold beauty. She is the loveliest creature Don Carlos has ever brought here, she thought.

Catrina dressed in the gown the maid had brought. It was tight about her slim waist and was cut so low that Catrina was distressed. In front of the mirror, she gazed at herself as the maid brushed her long dark hair until it sparkled like ebony. It hung about her like a night-filled cloud. To her own eyes, she looked like a temptress prepared to receive a lover.

A new emotion blended with her fear. If he meant to have her it would have to be rape for in no way would she surrender to this cold and fearful man. "Rafael," she murmured softly. "Oh, Rafael, I love you. I love you."

Tears hung on her long dark lashes as the maid left closing the door softly behind her. Catrina stood alone, afraid, and after some time she heard the solid approach of footsteps. She turned to face the door as Carlos entered.

He stood with his back against the door and let his eyes slowly roam over her. She could feel the heat of them touch her skin lingering on the soft rise of her breasts above the soft material of the gown he had chosen. She saw naked alive hunger in his eyes. Her eyes widened and she backed away from him a step. This was not what he wanted, just yet. There would be time for her fear later. For now, he wanted to find if he could get answers from her. He walked to the table and uncovered the food.

"Ah, it smells delicious. Come, join me for supper."

"I am not hungry."

"You will sit opposite me and eat," he said firmly. She gave a negative shake of her head then gasped as in a few steps he was beside her. His eyes burned down into hers. "Take your choice, my flower, sit and eat with me, or join me in that bed. You have one minute to decide." He turned and walked back to the table knowing quite well she would follow obediently.

She sat opposite him and watched as he put food on her plate and set it in front of her. Then he poured a glass of wine for both of them. She watched him closely as he did and that same tingle of familiarity touched her. There was something about him that she knew.

They ate in silence. He ate with a rousing appetite while she choked down a few bites. Finished, he lifted his glass of wine and sat back in his chair to study her again. "What a lovely creature you are," he said softly. "I congratulated your husband for acquiring such beauty."

"Rafael! He's here!" Carlos saw the joy leap into her eyes. Her cheeks grew pinker and she smiled for the first time since he had seen her. He was aware of a strange tightness within him but refused to see it for what it was.

"Yes, he is here."

"Please, Don Carlos, let me see him for a moment. He must be frantic with worry. Please let me see him." She bent toward him, her face intent, her eyes pleading. Carlos rose and walked behind her. He put his hands gently on her bare shoulders, feeling her start beneath his hands. She refused to turn and look up at what she knew she would see. "Please," she repeated softly, "let me see him."

"Oh no, my sweet," he said quietly, "I don't want him to see you. I don't want him to hold you. He is a very stubborn man. I must break that stubbornness." His hands began to lightly caress her smooth skin. Catrina rose abruptly to her feet and turned to face him.

"Don't touch me! I would rather be imprisoned than to be forced to submit."

"Forced." He laughed. "No, my love, I will not force you. You will come to me of your own free will."

"Never!"

"Even for the life of your husband?" Catrina's face paled and she could have wept. He knew. He knew her love for Rafael would bring her to him, and worse, he read her well. He knew that she knew it, too.

He walked to her and stood so close she had to tip her face up. She did, obstinately. Again, he chuckled. With one finger, he traced the line of her jaw from chin to ear. Then he let his finger run lightly down her throat to the pulse that throbbed in panic. Rafael had wakened her body and it waywardly responded to Carlos's expert gentle touch. She wanted to scream out in anger. Instead she gazed mutely at him.

"You would like to see him?" Her eyes lifted hopefully and wordlessly she pleaded for the moments he could give. "I might consider that," he mused. "I just might consider it."

"Don't play with me!" she demanded.

"I have no intention of playing with you," he said softly. "I said I was considering it. You did not let me finish. There are conditions to your seeing him."

"What conditions?"

"For tonight, since I have other plans, one willing kiss will do. I would taste what I intend to possess when the time is right." She gazed into his taunting eyes and knew he meant what he said. Her need to see Rafael filled her and she ached with the touch of it. With salty tears brimming her eyes, she lifted her mouth. But he stood immobile. "I did not say I would kiss you," he said with a smile. "I said you were to kiss me . . . with sincere passion."

She knew he was bending her pride and she knew he meant to do exactly that. He meant to use Rafael to bring her first to her knees and then to his bed. She was Catrina Chavez! She would go to her knees for no man. She would not let him break her pride or her spirit. She would survive!

Using all the expertise Rafael had taught her, she kissed him. Putting her arms about him, molding her slim body to his. Her mouth parted and her tongue traced his lips with light flicks until she felt his soften, part, and begin to search hers.

His arms surrounded her like iron hands, and his mouth first became insistent then demanding. She chose that moment to pull away from him. Their eyes met.

"So," he said softly, "you win the first encounter, but, my sweet, I will win the war."

"I want to see my husband."

"Come with me," he said. Catrina followed him to the door. They left the room and walked to the steps that led below ground. Down the steps, down the long hall. Carlos unlocked the door and held it open. "Go inside. I will bring him to you. You will have ten minutes." Was he lying? Was this another form of trial for her? She had to take the chance, for beyond anything else was her need to touch Rafael. She stepped inside the cold dark room and heard the door slam shut behind her. She waited what seemed to her to be a long time. Then she heard the footsteps. She watched the door with her heart in her eyes.

The door opened and Rafael appeared. With a cry, she flew across the room and into his arms. "Rafael!" she cried and then all words ceased as his lips found hers in a deep throbbing kiss. He crushed her in his arms until she could barely breathe but she didn't care. She could feel his heart pounding against her.

Carlos leaned against the door, watching them. Behind him stood a man of immense size and limited intelligence who existed to do the work Carlos demanded of him, which covered a great deal.

277

Rafael caught Catrina's face between his hands and studied her face, searching for what he was afraid he might see. What was evident was her deep love and need for him. "Catrina, are you all right? He hasn't—"

"I'm all right, Rafael, I'm fine." She sobbed. "Oh Rafael, I'm so frightened. I thought I would never see you again."

"It will be all right," he whispered as his lips again touched hers. He held her in his arms until her trembling ceased. Then he held her a little away from him and turned to look at Carlos. "Can we not have a moment alone?"

Carlos chuckled. "As I told your wife, you have ten minutes. Make the most of them, Rafael. I am an impatient man."

The suggestive words twisted within Rafael. He would have liked nothing better than to leap on him and smash him. Carlos read the emotion. He laughed again and drew the door shut. Rafael turned back to Catrina. This time the kiss was deep, gentle, and fulfilling.

"Catrina," he whispered as he held her close, "are you really all right? No one has hurt you?"

"No one has hurt me, Rafael, but you, what about you? I don't understand all this. I have a feeling . . ."

"What?"

"I don't know. It's strange. It's as if I know him somehow. I've never met him, yet I know . . . I don't understand."

"*Querida*, it's not important. What is important is that you are all right. Don't let him frighten you, my heart."

"He wants to know where Elana and Beatriz are, doesn't he? You did get the message to the ship, didn't you?"

"Yes, it is well on its way by now."

"How long?" she said softly.

"A few days."

"Then we must remain silent for a few days."

"Catrina, my father is here, too."

"Don Diego, why?"

"Both of you are to be used against me. He wants the information, but he wants me, too. We have an old debt to settle."

"You knew him before this?"

"Yes, I did." He did not elaborate on his answer, and she knew it was a painful situation he did not want to explain yet.

"Rafael," she said softly, "I love you. More than the breath in my body. There is nothing I would do to hurt you, you know that."

"*Querida*." He was startled. "Did you really think I would believe a word he said? We won't let him touch our love, Catrina, no matter what he does or says, he'll never really touch us. Do you understand, *Querida*? You are part of my heart, part of my body, we will not let him touch any of our love. Have faith that one day we will find a way out of this. Keep believing in my love as I in yours."

"I do believe, Rafael, I do. Oh, Rafael, what will he do to you . . . to your father . . . to me?"

"It won't be long until he makes his demands known. He will question me first, then my father."

"And me?"

Rafael didn't want to answer.

"And me?" she questioned softly.

"Catrina, he wants to use you as a tool to break me. He will try to bend your will to his, and he will try to master you. Oh, he will not force you, rape is not his way. But he will try every way his devious mind knows to break your pride. *Querida*, I'm sorry. I wish I had never brought you. I should have made you wait."

"No, Rafael," she cried as she tightened her arms about him. "No matter what happens to us, I want to be with you. Hold me, Rafael, hold me!"

Willingly, he bound her close to him and again took her soft pouting mouth with a kiss that warmed both her spirit and her body.

Again the door opened and Carlos entered. "Your time is up, Rafael. I'm afraid you will have to relinquish your bride."

He reached out and took Catrina's arm, drawing her away from Rafael.

"Carlos, let her be. Let her stay with me."

"Oh no, my dear Rafael. I enjoy her company much too well. Besides, I have some plans for you right now that do not include this lovely creature."

"No!" Catrina cried.

"Tonio," Carlos ordered, "take her back to her room." Tonio drew a struggling Catrina from the room and closed the doors. Rafael and Carlos stood looking at each other.

"Don't do anything to hurt her, Carlos," Rafael said softly, "or as sure as there is a God in heaven, I will find a way to kill you this time."

"Rafael, Rafael, I have no intention of hurting her. I have possessed many women and none has ever complained that I have hurt her."

"You are a bastard, Carlos, in more ways than one."

Carlos's smile faded and his mouth twitched in anger. "When I take her, Rafael," he said, "I shall break her. I shall bend her to my will until she crawls to me. And when I finally own her soul, I shall make sure you are there to see."

"You don't know Catrina. She is not like the other whores you have lain with. She is a woman of a kind you have never known."

"I know of one thing. She is a woman in love, and for that love, she would give anything . . . anything. I will be sure to keep you informed about my progress." His taunting laughter was back again as he watched Rafael's face gray with anger and helplessness.

Rafael was taken back to his cell. He tried to explain to his father what had happened, but his words were choked with both anger and fear. Both he and his father knew that soon the game would truly begin.

Catrina was thrust into her room by Tonio, who left and locked the door behind him. She threw herself on the bed and wept, the first tears she had allowed herself. She heard the key turn in the lock, heard the door open and close.

He walked across the floor and stood by the bed. She knew he was there and it took all the courage she had to sit up and meet his eyes with hers.

"It is about time, my sweet," he said softly, "that your lessons are to begin. Soon I will prove to you that what I want, I always get. Stand up and come with me. I have something to show you that might change your mind about being obedient." Catrina slowly rose and followed Carlos from the room.

Chapter Twenty-One

Palencia lay before them. By nightfall they would be past it and on the last leg of the journey. It was enough to fill everyone with happiness. Pedro had claimed they would have a celebration once they were camped for the night.

Reeve rode up beside Elana who smiled warmly at him. The days had been oppressively warm and Elana had braided her long dark hair. Her cheeks were pink and her skin glazed golden by the sun. She was well aware that she was happier now than she had ever been in her life, and the tall golden man who rode beside her was the cause of it.

In fact, there seemed to be a note of gaiety that pervaded the entire caravan. Rodrigo and Beatriz, Reeve and Elana, lovers so obviously bound to each other, created the atmosphere of warmth that seemed to touch everyone.

If the days were beautiful, the nights were glorious. Elana grew more wildly in love with her husband every day and every night. Their lovemaking was an exquisite thing that filled her world. They had become so attuned to each other that they often could share just a glance and know what the other was thinking. It was so now, when he reined in his horse to ride next to her. His eyes roamed over her with a warm look that brought the sparkle of devilment to her eyes and a blush to her cheeks.

"Reeve," she said with a laugh, "don't look at me like that. Everyone will think you intend to ravage me right here."

"Happily, love." He chuckled. "Happily." He enjoyed her soft laughter. Soon they would pass Palencia. It would not be long then until they reached the coast. He was secure in the knowledge that Ralph would have the *Golden Eagle* to meet him. Rafael and Catrina should have had no trouble getting the message to him.

He intended, one day, to have Rafael and Catrina visit him and Elana. When all the trouble was over. He was pleased with the thought that at least Rafael and Catrina were safely away from all of this and in all probability, enjoying their happiness with each other at Rafael's hacienda.

"Oh, Reeve, just think, we will camp on the other side of Palencia tonight. In a few more days we will be on the coast and safe."

"I'm glad you're keeping that thought in your mind. It makes you smile more often, and, my love, when you smile the whole world is brighter."

"The whole world?"

"Well, at least my part of it." They laughed together. Reeve reached out and lightly touched her cheek as if, after all the time they had shared, he could still not quite believe she was really his. Her smile became warmer as her eyes held his.

"We'll be free, Reeve. All this running will be over."

"Yes love, free to build a life of our own. Will you miss your past, Elana? Will you miss the glitter of the court?"

"I may miss some of my friends for a time, and my parents, if they can't join us soon. But all those things are not as important as you. You've made my life a whole new thing, Reeve. Since you have come, I have never felt the fear that used to live with me every day. Both Rodrigo and I will be grateful to you the rest of our lives."

"Rodrigo can be grateful," Reeve said, "but, it's certainly not what I want you to feel."

"You are a wicked-minded man, Reeve Burke." Elana laughed.

"I, Madam?" Reeve said innocently. "Wicked-minded? My thoughts are pure, Madam, I assure you. You malign me."

"Well," Elana said casually, "there is a stand of trees in the distance. It should be shady and cool. I have it in mind to go there and enjoy it for a few moments while the others eat their midday meal. Since you are so innocent-minded and pure at heart, I don't suppose you would care to join me."

"You jest, Madam." Reeve grinned. "Just try and keep me away." Again, Elana laughed. Then she suddenly kicked her horse and it leapt ahead.

"Race you!" she shouted over her shoulder.

"Hey! That's unfair!" he cried, but her horse was already several lengths ahead of his. He kicked his horse and it leapt ahead. He could hear her laughter as he raced to catch up with her. They were almost at the stand of shady trees when he drew abreast of her. Together they entered the shady area and drew their horses to a halt. Reeve dismounted and went to Elana's side. He put his hands about her slim waist and lifted her down to stand beside him, but he did not release her.

They both knew they had a very short time before the caravan began to move again, but every precious moment they could share was important to them. He touched her upraised lips with his in a tender kiss, savoring their soft, moist giving. Slowly the kiss warmed them. Her arms slid up about his neck and her soft rounded curves molded themselves to his large hard frame.

They were both completely intoxicated with the kiss, but well aware this was not the time or place to let it go to the conclusion they both desired. When he released her lips, he held her close, and she rested her head against his broad chest.

"Only a matter of days, love," he whispered. "Days and we'll be able to forget all the pain of the past. I can't wait to get you to my country. I want to share so much with you. I want to show you so much. Oh, Elana, I love you so much, so very much. I begin to wonder how I lived my life before you. It seems now to have been so empty. You have filled every dark corner of my heart."

She closed her eyes, sighing contentedly as his hands caressed her gently. "I would always stay in your arms, my husband," she said gently. "I would share your life and give you children. It is all I ask, all I want, and all I need."

He tipped her chin up to look deeply into her eyes and smiled at the reflection of his own love he saw in their depths. "You know you are more than I had ever hoped to find?"

Her laughter sparkled. "Then I expect you to show your appreciation completely . . . and often." He bound her against him until she could barely breathe and this time the kiss was so deep and so demanding that she grew dizzy and clung to his stability. They were both shaken by the flame that seemed to lick to life each time they touched.

The caravan was in sight by now and the rumbling sound of voices interrupted their pleasant solitude.

"I suppose we must go," he said.

"I'm afraid so. It's probably for the best. I don't think I could have stood much more."

Reluctantly, they walked to their waiting horses. He lifted her into the saddle, mounted himself, and they rode back to the caravan. They were greeted by Beatriz and Rodrigo, who had been riding together.

"Elana," Rodrigo called, "come and ride with us."

Both Elana and Reeve brought their horses abreast of Rodrigo's and Beatriz's. The four rode along slowly together. "Pedro has told us he has planned a celebration tonight. Once we are past Palencia," Beatriz said.

"It is a thing to celebrate," Rodrigo said. "We are very nearly at the coast. We have succeeded, Reeve, and we are grateful to you for making it possible. We owe you much, my friend. It is a debt nearly impossible to repay."

Reeve smiled at Elana. "Rodrigo, I have been repaid with more than I had ever hoped for."

"Reeve, my friend, I must ask you a question."

"Yes?"

"There is no doubt in your mind about our rendezvous with your ship?"

"No, by now, Rafael and Catrina have had more than enough time to have gotten to Ralph and told him our plans. He is most likely on his way by now."

"We will have to let Rafael and Catrina know of our gratitude. They took a very large chance to do what they did."

"Once we're safely home, we'll send them a message."

"Then," Rodrigo said quietly, "for all intents and purposes it's all over. It's hard to believe after all the fear we've been through. I can really hardly believe it." He turned to Beatriz. "We have left a lot behind, but we have so much to look forward to."

The magnitude of their escape held them all silent for a while. They rode very close to the head of the caravan. Several wagons behind them, Carmen's dark eyes watched the four as they rode together.

She pushed the others from her mind and let her hungry eyes dwell on Reeve. He rode tall and broad shouldered, his golden hair brilliant in the sunlight. This was the first time in Carmen's life she could ever remember wanting a man so desperately, and the first time that any man had not been easy for her to conquer. Reeve smiled at her, yet looked past her vibrant beauty to the green-eyed girl who rode laughing beside him. It was as if Carmen did not exist. She smiled to herself. Soon the obstacle of Elana would be gone. There would be no way for Reeve to save her. They would all be gone, all but

Reeve, and she would be there to console him for his loss. By tomorrow, she thought, all that stood between her and Reeve would be eliminated. Tonight they would celebrate, and tomorrow . . . he would be hers.

They circled the town of Palencia carefully. It took them all afternoon and much of the evening. The sun set on the horizon when Pedro finally called a halt. He looked back over his shoulder at the town in the distance.

"We make camp here," he ordered. Quick to obey his commands, the wagons were drawn into two circles and the fires for the evening meal were started.

There was laughter and friendly camaraderie while the evening meal was eaten. Reeve and Elana had become some kind of symbol to the Gypsy caravan. They had gone to a great deal of trouble and tempted disaster in helping them to escape. The success of their venture put them in a state of euphoria.

The food was enjoyed by all and as the fires blazed, the guitars brought dancers to life. The dances were lively and exciting, and they were accompanied by the clapping of hands and cries of enthusiasm from the onlookers.

Pedro had opened many bottles of wine. In the enthusiasm, Elana drank enough to release what inhibitions she had. Reeve drank quite a bit more than she. He was not drunk but was mildly intoxicated. Intoxicated with the wine, the music, and a lovely Gypsy girl named Elana. She was lighthearted and her laughter sparkled. Elana was experiencing a freedom such as she had never known.

She found herself tapping her feet and clapping her hands to the music. Rodrigo and she were both excellent dancers and Reeve urged them both into a performance. He watched her slim body sway to the music. The dance began slowly, then built higher and higher in intensity. They moved with abandon and Reeve was held spellbound.

There were so many facets to Elana and it seemed every day he was discovering a new one. Elana, the cool and elegant beauty of the court; Elana the wild Gypsy girl, Elana the temptress, the lover, Elana . . . his for now and forever.

The dance whirled to a stop and she stood before him. Her breasts rose and fell rapidly and her eyes were bright as the stars above them.

The guitar strummed a soft melody and she moved with graceful ease into Reeve's arms. Even though they were inches apart it seemed to Reeve as if she melted within him, taking possession of him completely. He could smell the soft, tantalizing scent; he could feel the magic of her heat, his blood. Passion darkened her green eyes and he knew, with the increasing beat of his heart, that she wanted him as much as he wanted her. He watched, as his hands held her waist and they swayed to the music, the half parted vulnerable lips, the shadowed eyes, and the slim arms that reached for him.

The dance over, they slid their arms about each other and walked slowly into the shadows. They left the music and gaiety behind them to seek a quiet moment.

They walked beneath the trees near the camp. With the moon high and full and the sounds of soft music, it was a night filled with magic. It was a night for lovers. They turned and looked at each other and no words needed to be spoken. Each knew what the other was feeling.

He gently brushed wayward strands of hair from her cheek, letting his hand caress her soft, silky hair. With infinite tenderness, he cupped her face between his hands and bent his head to softly brush her lips with a kiss so deeply sensitive that she could have wept with the sheer joy of it.

She closed her eyes and surrendered to the ecstasy. She felt his hands gently begin a warm journey, gently caressing her trembling breasts, her slim waist and curved hips. Then slowly he drew her close to blend against him. She was breathless with the flood of urgent desire that filled her. She began to tremble with the joy of just feeling. Her skin was alive with his touch.

Slowly he bore her down with him to the soft grass. She felt the bold urgency of his hard body against hers, setting her aflame until molten waves flooded her with a pleasure nearly unbearable. His greedy mouth captured hers now in a searing kiss, warm and devouring. His hands began an exploration of the sweet treasure he desired so deeply, and she opened to him, softly murmuring her pleasure at his wandering caresses.

He set her afire with the flame of his need, urgent and almost unbearable. Whispered words of love encouraged him. She heard answered words of love whispered hoarsely and the wild beating of his heart against her.

Then he was within her, immersed in the depths of her love. Her hands caressed hard muscles as they tensed and flexed to seek the deepest need that consumed them both in a volcanic explosion that lifted them both to a swelling ecstatic rapture.

Soft murmuring guitars and the warm breeze ruffling the trees were the only sounds that reached the lovers as they lay in deep contentment, holding each other in quiet peacefulness.

"I wonder," Elana said softly, "if I have not loved you always. In my heart I have searched for you. Now we are together. We will be together always, won't we, Reeve? You will never leave me?"

"Leave you." Reeve chuckled softly. "I could not leave so much of myself. I could not exist elsewhere as half a man, always needing the other half to make me whole."

"The other half," she said softly as she looked up into his silver eyes, "that is what we are, is it not, Reeve, my husband? Two halves that join to make one complete person."

"Yes. I love you, Elana. I need you like I need the air to breathe or the food to nourish me." His lips tasted hers softly. "Why is it that I've tasted and touched and possessed you, and each time I do it only creates a need for you deeper and deeper? I believe you are practicing some kind of witchcraft, my love."

"I am." She laughed softly as she let her fingers twine into his thick golden hair. "I have cast a spell over you and you will never be free of me forever. You are my prisoner forever, husband, and I am a jailor. I shall never set you free."

"Such a terrible thought." He chuckled softly. "To be imprisoned by you the rest of my life. I shall try to bear up under the strain." Their happiness sounded in low murmuring laughter. It was a rare and beautiful night.

The happiness of this warm magical night seemed to have touched everyone in the caravan. It seemed to be covered by an aura of contentment. For Beatriz and Rodrigo, it was also a special time. Awakened to each other, they had begun to explore, to learn. Beatriz was fascinated and well pleased to learn, for Rodrigo seemed to have an ability to arouse her emotions and her senses to a level beyond her understanding. And Rodrigo was the most willing teacher. If it was new for Beatriz it was just as new for Rodrigo for, in all his experience, he had not felt about any woman the way he felt about Beatriz. He had taken his first woman at the young age of fifteen. Thoroughly enjoying the situation he sought more. With his tall hard body and rugged good looks, he found it easy. Each time gave him some new facet to explore, and explore he did. Now he was glad that he did. Nothing pleased him more than to know he gave Beatriz pleasure. He was amazed at times at his own emotions. He had seen some women as beautiful as she; he had possessed some women with more experience than himself; yet this delicate beauty could lift him beyond any experience he had ever had. He loved her so deeply that at times it overcame him. The fear struck him that if they were to lose this struggle, if she were taken from him, that the best part of him would die.

She slept in his arms now, and he held her close, wondering why, despite Reeve's assurances that all would be well, he felt this nagging worry. His arms tightened about her as the fear

291

that always attacked in the middle of the night began. The anxiety created a spasmodic reaction and as if he actually could feel her being drawn away from him, he gripped her firmly, binding her to him.

Beatriz's eyes fluttered open as she felt him tighten his grip. She knew without speaking what he was thinking and feeling for his emotions matched hers. She had been frightened for too long. She had wanted freedom and Rodrigo too long to believe her good fortune would stay. At any minute she expected the hand of fate to reach out and snatch her happiness from her. She sighed deeply and smiled to herself. She was happy, happier than she had ever been in her life.

Her head had been resting on Rodrigo's shoulder so she pressed herself closer to him and kissed the side of his throat.

"Rodrigo, what is wrong?" she whispered.

"Wrong? Nothing, why? What makes you think something is wrong?"

"Don't you think I can feel your worry? You hold me as if you were afraid I might vanish, as I want to hold you when I feel the fear inside me that I cannot put into words."

"You feel such a fear, Beatriz?"

"Sometimes. It's as if I can't quite believe all this, that we're free. That we can love each other and spend our lives together without a dark shadow hanging over us. I keep thinking that at the last moment something will snatch you away from me. I could bear anything else but losing you."

"Reeve seems to be so sure. He has faith that his ship will be waiting. Pedro also seems sure we're well ahead of any that follow."

"Still you think they are near?"

"I don't know what I think. Pedro's scouts say there is no one near. If we're that far ahead, there should be no problems."

"No problems," she repeated softly. "I pray so, Rodrigo. If they should catch us—"

"Don't say that! Don't ever think it!"

"But if they should, it would mean . . . what . . . what do you think they would do?"

For several minutes Rodrigo was silent, then he spoke softly. "You and I both know what would happen. You would be quickly married. As for Elana and Reeve, they have committed the worst they could have done. They have married. For Reeve, it would mean death. Elana must be free to marry whomever Don Francisco chooses."

"Diego."

"No."

"No, but I thought—"

"Beatriz . . . when we left the palace . . . before we reached the stables, Reeve was already there."

"Yes, why?"

"He was found there by Diego. Diego threatened to expose us. They fought, Reeve killed him."

"Mother of God," Beatriz breathed softly. "Don Francisco would be in a rage. Reeve must escape. They will kill him in the most horrible way their evil minds can think of."

"Yes. Both Reeve and I would be eliminated quickly. We are a barrier to what they want."

"No, Rodrigo they would not kill you," she cried. "We are not married. Surely they would not have a reason to kill you. I would do whatever they wanted! They cannot kill you!"

"Beatriz," Rodrigo said softly. He tipped her chin up so that their eyes met. "Do you really believe, after all we have shared, that I could let another man touch you? You know, and they know, that I would have to die before I would let them have you. You are mine, my love, and I will not let you go."

Tears touched her eyes and he could feel the chill of fear touch her slim body. He held her close. "Damn," he groaned. "Why do we talk like this. We are safe. Don't be afraid, Beatriz. We will reach the coast in a little over two days. The ship will be waiting and we will be free. We must not surrender to this stupid feeling."

"Hold me, Rodrigo, love me. I feel safe when you are in my arms. Tell me it will be all right and I will believe . . . I will believe."

He kissed her deeply and hungrily, pressing her close to him, feeling her grow warm with the need of assurance. With gentleness, he reached within her and calmed her fears, and seeking to reassure her that they would share this magic forever.

Pedro, too, lay awake in his wagon, wondering why he could not find sleep. He rolled over with a groan and put his arm across his sleeping wife. He had eaten and drunk to the limit of his capacity which was a great deal. He had made love to his woman, a woman he had loved singularly for ten years. He should sleep . . . but he couldn't.

Why did he feel this eerie thing, as if some tragedy was to occur and he could not stop it? He wanted the fleeing couples to reach the coast safely. He wanted their freedom as a blow to the Inquisition whose brutality, inhumanity, and terror he knew well . . . too well. He sighed deeply and pulled his blanket tighter about him. After what seemed to be a long time, he drifted off to sleep.

The very depths of night. When the moon was nearing the horizon and the stars began to disappear. The blackness touched the caravan, campfires died . . . everyone slept. Everyone but one.

Carmen left her wagon quietly. She moved with the quickness and stealth of a predatory animal. She left the encircling wagons and walked some distance. Beneath the even darker shadows of the trees, a man stood. She knew he waited and she went directly to him. Few words were exchanged before they parted, but they were words that would have a profound effect on all who slept not too far away.

Chapter Twenty-Two

Unaware, unprepared, the caravan slept, uneasily. The deep sense of some imminent disaster might have been the thing that brought them to startled wakefulness when the caravan was struck.

Guards, taken by surprise, had been silently attacked, bound, and left helpless to warn the others, yet it seemed that each of the men leapt to their feet grasping for their weapons at the first sound of running horses, but it was already too late.

Pedro, his heart pounding with the knowledge that his senses had been trying to warn him, was out of his wagon, sword and pistol in hand to greet the attackers. Reeve and Rodrigo reacted the same, but all their efforts met with more numbers than any of them could have hoped to defeat.

Carmen watched carefully, her eyes on Reeve. Her heart sang with the thought that he would one day be hers.

Elana and Beatriz were dragged from the wagons screaming and fighting wildly against their captors. Wood was thrown on the almost dead campfires, bringing them to sudden brilliant life. With Pedro and his wife held at pistol point, the remains of the camp immediately became docile. They loved and respected their leader too much to let one overt action on their part cause his death.

The leader of the attacking group dismounted and walked to

Pedro's side. It did not take Reeve or Rodrigo long to realize the two knew each other. He was tall and slender. Very dark of skin with hair and eyes of nearly the same color. He could have been nearing forty, but Reeve could not tell his age for certain. What was to follow was to change all the plans Carmen had made. The first tingle of her own deception came when the leader of the attack spoke quietly to Pedro.

Reeve and Rodrigo stood near, their hands bound firmly behind them. Across the fire from them was Elana and she was just as helpless as they. Elana's eyes sought Reeve's across the fire, and he tried to give her comfort and hope in his gaze.

Carmen watched Reeve. She knew he would be freed soon, but it would be too late to save Elana. She would already be gone . . . gone from his life for good. Carmen knew quite well the efficiency with which the Inquisition worked. Once Elana and Reeve were separated they would never see each other again.

She had made her plans well and had bargained away the lives of Elana and Beatriz. Once they were taken, Pedro and the caravan would be free to go . . . and Reeve would be left for her to console once Elana was gone. There was no possible way Reeve could get Elana free. She had made her plans and her bargain, but she was unprepared for the traitorous defeat of all her plans.

The leader of the band of attackers smiled at Pedro. His eyes were cold and hard even though the smile was broad. "So, Pedro, my friend, did I not warn you that you were on the wrong side? Did I not tell you that one day you would be caught? Too bad, my friend, you should have listened to me."

Pedro, too, smiled, but the smile would have chilled the heart of most people. It caused the smile on his tormentor's face to weaken. Then, casually he spat, the spittle landing on the toe of his aggressor's very shiny boot. Now the smile became a grimace of anger. "So, Juan . . . you have crawled out from under your rock again to prey on the innocent? What reward have you been promised for this bit of treachery?"

"Keep your mouth closed, Pedro, before you anger me enough to kill you."

"You will not kill me," Pedro taunted. "I am facing you. You kill from behind and I would not turn my back to you. Why are you here? If you harm me or my people you will be looking over your shoulder the rest of your life, and sleep will be impossible for you to find."

Though Juan tried his best to control it, a touch of fear crossed his face. He knew Pedro as a man who did not threaten lightly and did not forget a threat once he uttered it.

"I don't intend to harm you or your people. There are travelers with your caravan." His eyes turned to the figures of Elana and Beatriz. "They are of interest to me. We have been searching for quite some time for them. There is a large reward for their return to face the tribunal."

"The money is filthy, Juan. In the end it will cost you more than it is worth. They are innocent."

"That is not for us to decide."

"Juan," Pedro said softly, "leave them here. Go and forget you have even seen us. This is not justice, it is tragedy. Don't be a part of it. They are like rabid dogs and one day they will turn on you."

"I cannot do that. Word has already been sent."

"You are a fool. There is still time. Let them go, say you were mistaken."

Juan laughed harshly. "They will believe that? They will not question me further? You are the fool, Pedro. The money jingles in my pocket, not yours. I am going to let you go. That is all I can do."

Juan dismounted slowly and walked to Reeve. They stood face to face while Juan studied Reeve's face. Steel-gray eyes returned his gaze. There was no fear here for himself. Reeve's face was cold and angry.

"So," Juan said softly, "you are the Englishman who has caused so much trouble? Did you think we would allow you to just walk into our country and take what pleases you without a struggle or a word? You have caused me much trouble, my friend. My men and I have been searching for you for many days. It seems we were searching in all the wrong directions."

"If you were searching in the wrong directions," Reeve answered coldly, "how did you find us?"

"Ah!" Juan grinned. "I have my friends also, Senor."

"Someone has informed on us," Reeve said firmly. His eyes turned to Pedro whose expression had slowly changed as he digested Reeve's words.

"Yes," he said softly. His eyes went slowly from person to person. All among his caravan met his piercing gaze levelly, even Carmen, who could feel the chill of fear touch her even though she remained outwardly calm. Not for a minute did Pedro suspect she was the one who had.

"I will find out one day, my friend Reeve," Pedro said firmly, loud enough so his voice carried well among all. "I would advise the one who is guilty to dig his own grave, but he can leave the filling to me."

"Pedro, don't worry. When we get back to Madrid, I shall send for the English ambassador. He will see that this force is brought to light. They cannot hold us for long."

Juan pretended amazement. "Why Senor Burke, we have no intention of holding you, or causing you any harm. In fact, you can go your way as soon as we are gone. We have the three we sought."

Elana nearly fell to her knees with the relief she felt. They would not take Reeve. He would be safe and free. It was all she had been able to think of since the moment they had been dragged from their beds. She shook violently with the pain she felt. No matter what she must suffer, they would do no harm to

Reeve. She tried to catch Reeve's eyes, but he was glaring coldly at Juan.

"These are my friends," he stated. "They have asked me to take them safely to my country. One way or another, I intend to do that if I have to follow you to the ends of the earth to do it."

"Don't be foolish, my friend. Take your freedom and go before you find yourself in a situation that might prove very costly."

Elana's heart nearly ceased beating. The informant must not have told Juan about her marriage to Reeve. She knew Reeve would be in serious danger should Juan find out. The last thing she wanted now was for Reeve to claim her as his wife. His fate would be sealed. Before she could speak, Juan turned from Reeve and snapped orders. "Leave him tied until we leave. Take the two women and de Santangel."

"No!" Reeve said. It was so commanding that Juan turned to look at him in surprise. "Surely," he said with a smile, "you don't believe you would be able to stop us?"

"I will go with you," Reeve said.

"I have no use for you."

"You will when I tell you—"

"No," Elana cried. "No, Reeve, don't condemn yourself!"

Reeve turned to Elana, the hard steel of his eyes fading to tender warmth. "I should let you face this alone, Elana?" he said softly. "Only a few days ago didn't I make a solemn vow never to do that? You are now the wife of an Englishman. I believe my country would be very upset at my death or if any harm should come to my wife."

"Wife," Juan said, his frown deepening. This was a situation he had not bargained for. Carmen had not bargained for it either. She gazed in amazement at a man who seemed to be casually sacrificing his life for the woman he loved. She watched Elana's face soften with pain and love for the man who

299

faced her across the fire. There was not a person in the camp
who could not feel the current that flowed between the two.

"I do not believe you," Juan shouted.

"But I have proof," Reeve replied. Juan's eyes grew shrewd.
"Just what and where is this proof?"

Both Reeve and Pedro chuckled softly at this. "Do you take
me for a fool? No one knows but me, not even my wife."

Juan turned to Elana. "You are married to this Englishman?" If her mind wanted to lie, it would have been impossible
for Juan read her eyes too well. Before Elana could answer,
Juan snapped rapid orders. "Take the Englishman with us. We
will let Don Francisco decide what to do with him. Hurry, let us
go before any new problems arrive."

Carmen had slipped away from the group and run to her
horse tethered beneath the trees. While Juan and his men were
forcing their four prisoners onto their horses, she rode to a
spot safely away from camp where she could meet Juan.

Helplessly, Pedro watched Elana and the others as they
slowly rode from his camp. He knew too well the fate they
could possibly face. In his mind, he was certain Don Francisco
would rid himself of the obstacle of Reeve and Rodrigo as soon
as possible. He wondered if Reeve did have proof of his and
Elana's marriage. It was a barrier Don Francisco would have to
eliminate. Elana was a lady of the court. If she had married and
there was proof, then Don Francisco could not force her into
another. Without doubt, once thwarted, Don Francisco would
not hesitate to kill Reeve. A widow was just as good for his
purposes.

Pedro began to think of what was best for him to do. Despite
the dangers, he could not bear the thought of the deaths of
Reeve and Rodrigo, or the fate of Elana and Beatriz. His people
waited in silence, and it was then that he noticed the absence of
one of them . . . Carmen.

Carmen had ridden rapidly and was well ahead of Juan and

the others. She sat on her horse in a stand of trees and waited. When she sighted Reeve's golden head among the others, she remounted and rode toward them. Juan was surprised to see her coming, and he kept up the pretense of not knowing her until he discovered her purpose.

The four prisoners also watched her ride toward them. Puzzled as to why she came, not one of them once gave a thought to the fact that this was their betrayer. It was Reeve's sixth sense that told him something was wrong.

Juan brought them to a halt and Carmen halted her horse less than six feet from them. "What do you want, woman?" Juan demanded.

"I must talk to you," Carmen demanded.

"I have nothing to say to you, Gypsy girl. Go back to your caravan before I decide to take you along with me. It is several nights before we reach Madrid and my bed is very cold."

A low murmur of appreciative laughter rippled through the mounted soldiers. Carmen smiled. "I must talk to you . . . alone." Again, the sound of laughter from men who would have loved nothing more than to share Carmen's favors with Juan.

With an arrogant self-assured grin Juan turned to his men. "Wait here, I will see what she wants." He motioned Carmen to ride with him, and they moved toward the stand of trees in which Carmen had waited. It would be secluded enough for Juan. For several years he had tried to get Carmen to his bed unsuccessfully. Now, maybe he had the opportunity he needed. He knew quite well he had something Carmen wanted . . . Reeve . . . and he knew also that he could do nothing about it. He knew it but Carmen didn't.

Beneath the shade of the trees they dismounted, tied their horses, and faced each other.

*   *   *

Reeve twisted a little on his horse so he could see Elana who rode beside him. With his hands bound behind him it was difficult.

Elana's face was white with fear, yet he didn't know it was more fear for him than it was for herself. She had to face an unwanted marriage; he had to face death.

"Have faith, Elana, it is not over yet. I have some protection, and I don't think Don Francisco is fool enough to just murder me. It would be too difficult to explain. We'll get out of this. Just don't give up."

"Oh, Reeve, why did you do it? Don't you understand it might cost your life? You do not know him like I do. Reeve, he will find a way to . . . to . . ."

"Elana," Reeve said firmly, "I don't care what or who he is. He can be beaten and we will do it. There wouldn't be much of a life if I had to leave this country and leave the most important part of me behind. You are my life, Elana, and together we will find a way out of this . . . or together we will face whatever we must. But it will be together."

Tears brimmed her eyes and escaped to roll down her cheeks, yet her eyes looked at him with an intense love he could almost physically feel. Her hands had also been bound behind her, yet they seemed somehow to touch each other. It was a long and precious moment, yet it seemed to give her strength. He watched her shoulders straighten. He smiled and tremulously she returned it.

They now waited in silence, wondering what Carmen and Juan could be talking about, or why Carmen had come at all. Again, the premonition tingled through Reeve. Was Carmen the informer? Surely she was not. Why would she accept the danger of helping them to freedom only to betray them, yet it was there, the sensation that his thoughts walked the right path.

*   *   *

Juan and Carmen dismounted and tied their horses under the darker shadows of the trees. They knew they could not be seen by the others. Carmen turned to Juan, her face dark with anger. "Liar!" she spat. "You made a bargain. Is this the way you keep your word?"

"Now, Carmen, calm yourself. What could I do? Once he said they were married, I had no choice. Don Francisco would have skinned me alive if I had told him."

"You didn't have to tell him! She would not have told them. I should take my knife to you."

Juan laughed. "Well there is nothing I can do about it now."

"Bastard! You had best do something, or I swear you will not live to be a year older. I or one of my friends will find you and slip a knife between your ribs."

"What would you have me do?"

"Set him free."

Juan grinned. "And why should I take such a chance for you? What good would it do me?"

Carmen had no difficulty in reading Juan well. She knew his price for Reeve's life. They stood facing each other, she with her eyes ablaze with fury; and he assured, now that he held all the cards, wore a pleasant, expectant half smile.

"If I am going to jeopardize my life, don't you think I should be rewarded in some way for the sacrifice?"

"I'll pay you."

"Really? How much?"

"How much?" Carmen repeated. "You tell me."

"Carmen," Juan said softly as he walked close enough to almost touch her. His hand reached slowly to touch her hair. "I do have a price. The only question is . . . are you willing to pay it?"

"And I am supposed to trust you, after you have betrayed me once already?"

"Do you have any choice? I am the one who has what you want. I am selling. Are you buying?"

"You'll set him free now?"

Juan laughed again. "You don't really take me for a fool do you, Carmen? I release him now and you will disappear like a shadow. No, I will set him free the day before we arrive in Madrid. Until then, you will travel with us."

"I can't do that."

"And why not?"

"He will know. He will know it was me."

"We'll find a way around that."

"How?"

"I will simply take you with us by force for them to see. I will drag you away. They will most likely feel very sympathetic toward you and very understanding. It is quite simple."

Carmen gazed at Juan, knowing that she wanted Reeve free, knowing she would pay the price of his freedom, yet understanding for the first time that love such as Reeve and Elana knew was not like this: It was a sweeter and more giving thing. This was lust and for the first time she began to know and understand the difference. Somewhere within she tried to justify it all. Reeve would one day be hers, and she could blot all this from her mind. They would be happy together, and she would taste and know the beautiful and gentle thing that existed between Reeve and Elana.

"Well?" Juan said softly. "Do we have an agreement or do I take him to his death?"

The word death vibrated through Carmen's entire being. She could vision Reeve, tall, golden and handsome, being tortured to death. Tortures of the Inquisition were well known to her. "Yes," she said softly, "I agree."

"Very intelligent. You have just bought your friend's life. And now, we will seal our bargain."

Carmen closed her eyes and tried to hold a vision of Reeve in her mind as Juan pulled her roughly into his arms and kissed her. His kiss was nearly brutal, hungry with a violent greed.

Roughly and carelessly his hands caressed her, and a cold hard knot of fury and resistance formed within her. Once she was sure Reeve was free, she would repay Juan for this violence.

"Tonight," he rasped hoarsely, "tonight when we camp you will be with me."

"What will we do now?"

"We will go back to them. Then we will have an argument and I shall become angry and drag you along by force. That way no one will be suspicious."

Carmen moved out of Juan's reach. Then she walked to her horse and mounted. She sat and watched Juan as he moved to his horse and mounted. Within her began to grow a deep and very black hatred.

They rode back to the waiting group. Carmen refused to meet Reeve's searching gaze.

"What was so important that she had to talk to you alone, Juan?" one of his companions questioned.

Juan laughed. "The foolish woman was begging for the lives of these people. She even went so far as to threaten my life. Promised me a knife in my ribs if I didn't let them go."

The men laughed heartily. "And did you tame her a little, Juan?" one of his companions called out. Carmen's eyes flashed angrily.

"Carrion!" Carmen cried. "They are innocent of any crime. All you have to do is say you did not find them. Are you men or animals?"

"She is a tigress, Juan. Maybe you should teach her to be more careful of her words."

"Yes, maybe I should. Maybe," Juan said as he gave Carmen a sly knowledgeable grin and winked at his men, "I should take the tigress along."

Reeve had been watching Carmen closely, and despite her seemingly indignant rage, he still had the feeling something did not read exactly true.

305

SYLVIE F. SOMMERFIELD

"You will take me nowhere, you filthy animals. Why don't you go and leave us all alone. These people have done you no harm and you have nothing to lose if you set them free."

Juan was very close to Carmen, who was completely unprepared for what he did next. With one violent move, he struck so hard that she was knocked from her saddle to the dusty ground. She looked up at Juan in shocked amazement.

"Tie her and bring her with us," Juan commanded. Carmen fought wildly, but the two men who caught her bound her securely and put her back on her horse. Within a few minutes they were again on their way. Now Elana and Carmen rode on each side of Reeve, while Beatriz and Rodrigo rode just behind them with half of Juan's men bringing up the rear and Juan and the others rode ahead.

Pedro was deep in thought. He was as sure as he could be that Carmen was the one who had betrayed Reeve and the others, just as he was sure that she had already gone to join their captors. Now he searched desperately for what he should do next to try and get them free. He knew he was completely outnumbered and out-armed by Juan's men. His wife gazed silently at him, knowing he was blaming himself for not being more careful.

"What are you going to do, Pedro?" she questioned.

"The only thing I can do. I am not able to set them free myself. I shall go on to the coast and find the ship. Once I tell them and they inform the ambassador, Don Francisco will be forced to set Reeve free."

"Will there be time?"

"I don't know. I only know I have to do something. I cannot just sit here and let those young people face him alone. I will send a rider to find Rafael Chavez. Maybe together we can find a way to get them free."

"Pedro?"

"What?"

"Do you think it was Carmen?"

Pedro turned to look at his wife. There was a deep sadness in his eyes. The two of them had a deep admiration and respect for the Carmen who had endangered her life to save so many. It was hard now for either of them to face the idea that she had betrayed helpless people and possibly sent one or all to their deaths. He sighed raggedly. "Yes," he said quietly, "I do."

Tears touched her eyes and her lips trembled. "There must be more to this. Carmen is not a betrayer. She has had her pain, too. I cannot believe she would turn to the ones who hurt her so badly."

"We will not condemn her until we know," Pedro said, "but what reason does she have to vanish except to join them? Come, we must get the caravan started and get to Reeve's ship as soon as we can."

They moved slowly, both weary and frightened. Frightened that what they thought about Carmen might be true, and frightened that they might not be able to reach help in time to get Reeve, Elana, and their friends free of the fate they both were sure was in store for them. By the time night fell, they were well on their way to the coast.

The campfire glowed brightly and Carmen sat beside it. Juan sat possessively close. They had finished a very late meal, and Carmen knew the time was close to pay her debt for Reeve's freedom. Her eyes sought Reeve who sat with Elana at a nearby fire. They had been unbound long enough to eat.

Anguish filled her as she watched Reeve's gentleness with Elana. The night had grown chilled despite the fire, and both Reeve and Rodrigo had removed their heavier jackets to place on the women's shoulders. Reeve held Elana close to him, her head resting on his shoulder.

Juan made a great production of forcing Carmen to sit at his fire and eat with him. For the benefit of Reeve and the others, he had even struck her, knocking her to the ground, to prove his command. She had seen the glow of pleasure in his eyes and knew he had enjoyed it.

Some deep longing grew within her to know the gentleness she saw in Reeve's eyes when he looked at Elana. She wanted to share that unnameable thing she could only feel but could not describe. She closed her eyes as Juan's arm slid about her, and he drew her forcefully against him. Elana would be gone. Reeve would be set free and unable to save her. He would need someone and she would be there. It would all be over and Reeve could help her forget as she would help him.

Now Juan had risen to his feet and violently jerked her to hers. It drew everyone's attention. Though she struggled, he drew her with him to the shadows. Laughter and many ribald remarks followed them, and Reeve and Rodrigo, though they had leapt to their feet, had been held helpless at rifle point.

Once in the depths of the shadows, Juan pushed her roughly to the ground and was quickly upon her. There was no warmth, no gentleness, no kindness in his touch. He wanted her and he intended to enjoy her no matter what she felt or wanted.

Two hours later he left her. Alone, bruised, and exhausted. He had done things to her she hadn't known were possible. She bent her head and wept for the pain and the humiliation she had experienced. She determinedly held at bay the knowledge that love was not as brutal as this. One day she would repay Juan for this. For now, her mind and heart held only one thought: Reeve must be free. It was the only thing that held her together.

Chapter Twenty-Three

Carmen had returned to the camp long after everyone, with the exception of the guards, slept. Juan had rolled in his blanket near the fire and slept, not caring where or how she would sleep.

She walked to the half-dead fire where Reeve and the others slept. Even in sleep she could see Reeve's care for Elana. He held her close to him with his blanket about her. Her eyes sought Rodrigo and Beatriz who lay opposite them. They, too, seemed to be content to hold and warm each other.

Why, she demanded to herself, why, when she so desperately needed someone to reach for her, to care for her, did she find this emptiness, this loneliness that left her world dark and her soul searching for a thing she had never known before?

Quietly she lay down and drew her blanket about her. She gazed with unseeing eyes at the burning embers. After a while Reeve stirred and she knew he was wakening. She closed her eyes to slits so that she would appear asleep yet could still watch him.

Reeve moved gently away from Elana, tucking the blanket about her. He sat by the fire and picked up a stick to stir it to new life. Reeve remained silent for some time. Then he spoke in a very quiet voice.

"Carmen, I know you're not asleep. I want to talk to you."

Reluctantly, she opened her eyes. Their gaze met across the fire and held for what seemed like hours. Then she sat up and drew the blanket close about her.

Reeve studied her face, seeing the darkened eyes and bruised mouth. "Are you all right, Carmen?" he asked gently.

"Yes . . . yes," she said softly, "I'm all right."

Reeve gazed about him, marking in his mind where the guards were placed, then he turned again to Carmen. "Carmen, you know this area well?"

"Yes."

"Come closer," he said.

She moved to sit close to him, the pleasure of being with him taking all other thoughts from her mind.

"Take this," he said as he handed her the slim stick with which he had been prodding the fire. She gazed at him in questioning surprise. "Draw a map in the dirt," he whispered. "I want to know the best route to escape if the opportunity should come."

Her mind whirled as she bent forward to do what he asked. If they should escape he would take Elana with him and she would have no other opportunity to separate them again.

"It is impossible," she whispered. "You would need food and water. Where would you get them? Juan would hunt you down. This time he would kill you and Rodrigo and make the women's lives a living hell until, or if, they should reach Madrid."

"Surely you must know safe places to stop along the way?"

"Don't be a fool! These people do not cross the Inquisition. They value their homes and their lives too much. There is no escape. But you . . . you do not need to worry. You can go back to your own country. It is the others he wants. You will soon be free."

Reeve's eyes fled quickly to Elana. "Free," he said softly. "I can only be free if Elana is free. I could not leave this country without her."

"But it means your life!"

Reeve smiled into Carmen's questioning gaze. "She is my life," he replied gently. "It would be worth very little to me should I lose her."

"I don't understand you," Carmen said in wonder. "You would sacrifice your life for hers?"

"What can be logically understood in love, Carmen? It is just that way. We are part of each other, two halves that make a whole. I cannot tell you any reason for it. I can only say that it exists. If anything happens to her, part of me dies. I must find a way to get her free."

Despair, deep and vibrant, washed through Carmen. "There is no way," she said bleakly. "You know her fate as well as you know your own." She could have wept for the final knowledge was forcing its way into her mind and her heart. She did not want to face it.

"I will never surrender to that. Someway, somehow, I will get her free of this. There has to be a way and I will find it even if I die trying."

"No! Do not speak of dying," Carmen cried softly. "Oh, Reeve," she moaned in desperate agony, "why can you not see? You must give her up. It was a doomed love from the start. Her fate is a court marriage. Can you not accept that and know that there is another who loves you just as deeply as she? Can you not see what you can and cannot have?"

Their eyes held, and his were touched with pity and sadness, two emotions she did not want. Yet she knew with finality that he would never reach for her, that his heart and soul were Elana's forever. All she had sacrificed had been in vain. She had lain with that animal for Reeve. She had let him use her with violence for Reeve. And all Reeve could say was that he loved Elana. Jealous anger filled her until she could have cried

out with the pain of it. She had to strike back. She had to hurt
him as much as he had hurt her.

"It is too late for you both," she snarled softly. "You will be
set free before we reach Madrid, but the others will be taken to
Don Francisco. He will have her and there is nothing you can
do about it. Nothing!"

"So," Reeve said softly, "it was you. I felt it was so, but I had
to find out for sure. What do you mean I will be set free?"

She flung the words at him, telling him of her betrayal and
her bargain. "I have bought your life!" she cried. "Don't ever
forget that. I have paid for your life by giving myself to him.
And you speak to me of love for her! She is not going to be with
you! Not ever! He will have her and he will use her for
whatever he wants and there is no way you can stop it."

"If I am free, I shall take my proof of our marriage to the
queen. There is no way they can force her to do anything."

Carmen laughed harshly. "You are a fool if you believe that.
Don Francisco is not stupid. You will never get your proof to
the queen. If you do, they will claim it forgery. Who do you
think the queen will listen to? You or Don Francisco? Can't
you see it's useless? You are beaten. She is lost to you."
Carmen fell to her knees before Reeve. "Look at me," she
whispered. "I love you, Reeve. I have given everything to get
you free. I could please you, I could make you happy. Stop
trying to get something you cannot have. All you have to do is
take your freedom. We will go away. I can make you forget she
ever existed."

"Carmen," Reeve said gently, "it cannot be. I love Elana
completely. I cannot leave her. I'm sorry."

"I don't need your pity."

"Carmen, listen to me. You cannot truly believe Juan will
set me free. He is no fool, either. Don Francisco would kill him.
He is using you, but when the time comes, he will not set me
free."

312

"No, Juan and I have worked together before. He will keep his bargain."

"Not this time. His own life is at stake."

"You will not take your freedom and me?" she questioned softly.

"I wouldn't if I could. But I know he would never offer it."

Carmen stood up and looked down at Reeve. Her eyes were cold and dark. "Then die for her," she said. Carmen turned and walked to another fire where she lay down and curled the blanket tightly about her.

Reeve watched her without knowing that Elana had wakened sometime before and had lain listening to them. After a while, Reeve returned to her side, drew her against him, and lay in silence, yet she knew it was sometime before he slept.

Carmen held fast to the belief that Juan would set Reeve free, and somewhere deep inside she felt once he was free and Elana was gone, Reeve would turn to her for consolation. She was certain if she were given enough time, she could make him love her despite what he had said. She kept that belief until two days before they reached Madrid.

Their nights had been the same. Juan had taken advantage to possess her as often as he chose, even taking some small pleasure in her humiliation. He grunted in pleasure as he thrust himself brutally within her. She cried out as his rough hands explored her. He had thrown her to the ground like a wild animal in heat and now, satisfied, he rolled off of her and lay panting at her side. Carmen sat up, but Juan grasped her hair and jerked her back down beside him. He fondled her with harsh hands, hearing her muffled exclamations of pain.

"I am not finished with you yet," he said with a laugh as he rolled to face her. He enjoyed seeing her naked beauty beside him and had taken great pleasure in forcing her to strip slowly while he watched.

He reached out and cupped one soft breast in his hand and massaged it roughly, rolling the nipple between thumb and finger and watching her face as she tried to control the pain. He bent his head and took her bruised lips in a kiss that ravaged her mouth and left her gasping.

"You enjoy being mounted by a man who knows how to service a woman, don't you?" He laughed. "And I enjoy you. You are the softest and sweetest I've ever had. These nights have been very good. I have a notion to keep you, you pleasure me quite well."

She wanted to spit in his face and thrust a knife between his ribs, but Reeve's freedom hung close before her eyes. She smiled instead.

"Yes, Juan, you are the kind of a man I have never had before." The double meaning was not caught by Juan who was too involved in handling her.

Carless of her feelings he roused himself to passion, then proceeded to brutally use her again. When he rolled from her this time, she felt broken and empty. He stood up, breathing heavily and, without looking at her, began to dress.

"Juan, we are two days away from Madrid. You must keep your bargain and release Reeve."

"Tomorrow night," he said sharply.

"When we camp?"

"No." He grinned down at her. "After I have had you one last time. I always wanted to lie between those soft thighs. I am going to enjoy every moment. My men envy me. They would like to share my good fortune."

"You told—"

"How good you are?" He grunted another laugh. "They enjoyed the stories almost as much as they would enjoy you if I gave them a chance."

Carmen gasped at his open brutality, yet she refused to speak the words in her mind. All she could think of was that Juan meant Reeve's freedom, and that soon she would be rid of him forever.

Juan left her, not worrying about whether she would follow or not. He knew quite well she would. He had the power to force her to do what he wanted.

Carmen watched him walk away, and the only thing at that moment that stood between himself and death was Reeve. Her hand went to the long slim hidden stiletto she carried, her fingers twitching with the desire to fling it. From experience, she handled a knife well and could have killed him without a sound.

Slowly she stood up and dressed. Then wrapping her shawl about her, she walked back to the campfire.

She stood just outside the rim of light and watched the two couples who sat together. They were engrossed in their conversation and had no thought of her presence.

"Are you tired, Elana?" Reeve questioned.

"I'm fine, Reeve," she replied, but the dark shadows beneath her eyes spoke more eloquently than her words.

"Come over here. Sit close to me," Reeve said.

Reeve was sitting on a broken log and Elana sat down on the ground beside him and rested her head on his lap. With gentle hands, he massaged the base of her neck and shoulders. Gently he brushed her hair aside and caressed her until she sighed deeply and closed her eyes.

"Oh, Reeve," she said quietly, "I am so sorry to have brought you to this. I—"

"Don't, Elana, don't say that. No matter what we have to face, I would rather be with you than anywhere else."

"It is as much my fault as anyone else's," Rodrigo said. "I am the one who planned and plotted all this. I thought, since Lord Bragham had cared enough to send a ship, the rest would have been easier."

"We are certainly far from being defeated," Reeve added.

"Reeve, how can you say that?" Beatriz said. "We are lost, there is no way to escape now."

"Beatriz," Reeve said gently, "we are still alive. As long as I am alive and I have faith and hope, we can find a way to get free of this. We must keep both our heads and our courage. Don Francisco . . . yes, even the Inquisition can be beaten, and we will do it."

Elana lifted her head and gazed up at Reeve. At that moment she felt closer to him and more protected by him than she had since they had first found each other.

Carmen watched their eyes meet and hold. Reeve smiled and reached to touch Elana's cheek with a gentle caress.

"You're tired, my beloved. Come, lie with me and sleep."

Reeve rose and stretched. Then he took his blanket and spread it on the ground. Elana lay down beside him and he drew her close, pulling her blanket over them both.

Rodrigo did the same. A strange type of peace seemed to touch them. Reeve's strength seemed to have soothed some of their fears. After a while the fire began to die and those about it slept.

The day's travel began early. It would be the hardest day of travel for Juan intended to reach Madrid by the following morning. He pressed them hard, and by the time they stopped for the midday meal, they were stiff, sore, and tired.

"We will rest here only an hour," Juan said. "Eat and rest as much as you can. I want to reach the city by tomorrow morning. I have already sent a rider on ahead to tell Don Francisco that we are bringing the prisoners back." He smiled coldly at Reeve and Elana. "I'm sure he will be very pleased. He may even send out someone to welcome us." Juan laughed, enjoying his taunting of people he thought were helpless.

They ate dry crusts of bread and meat washed down with tepid water from skin containers. Reeve noticed quickly that Elana ate very little. He stood close to her and drew her against him. They did not speak for a while; there was no need to. She rested her head against his broad chest and closed her eyes, listening to the stability of his firm, steady heartbeat.

Too quickly they were ordered back onto their saddles. Reeve lifted Elana, and his astute gaze saw the trembling of her hands as she lifted the reins. He felt the exhaustion in her body as his hands spanned her slim waist. She had not complained for a moment, yet he knew that his presence was the only thing that kept her going. His silent promise was renewed within that he would remain her strength forever.

They rode, long and hard, stopping only to drink and rest the horses. Juan had told them they would not camp until it was too dark to travel any further. The next day would bring them to Madrid.

Juan seemed to take even greater pleasure in taking Carmen that night. He was demanding and brutal, and her mind was numbed and left with only one thought: the next day she and Reeve would be free.

Dawn, pale and gray, saw the camp stir to life. They moved like dark shadows as small amounts of food were eaten and the horses were fed and saddled.

Carmen moved to the small fire where Reeve and the others sat. She wanted to be near him when Juan informed him that he would be going no further.

Two men accompanied Juan who walked toward the prisoners. All five of them stood. Carmen was completely unprepared for what happened next. Firmly and none too gently, she found herself grasped and pulled away from the group. She began to fight and to protest but there was no escape from their hold.

Reeve, Elana, Rodrigo, and Beatriz were pushed roughly

317

toward their horses and ordered to mount quickly. It was then that Carmen knew she faced the final betrayal. Now she began to fight fiercely, like an untamed animal. As she did, she screamed at Juan who stood not too far from her and smiled a malicious smile. He listened to her anger as if it amused him.

"Pig! Carrion! Lying bastard! You never meant to keep your word. I will see you dead for this!"

"I think not, Carmen." Juan laughed. "I will leave you here with my two friends who have been lucky enough to have won you with the dice. When they have finished having their pleasure with you, they will make sure you do not follow us."

Carmen gasped, momentarily silenced by what Juan had said. She gazed quickly at the two grinning men who held her. Then her eyes fled to Reeve. She could see clearly that both he and Rodrigo would help her if they could, but guns brushing their chest kept them immobile.

"For the love of God," Elana cried, "let her come with us! Don't hurt her."

Carmen gazed at Elana. This was the woman she had betrayed, whose whole life might be forfeited because of her, yet she begged for Carmen's life.

"She is a bitch," Juan snarled at Elana. "She is the one who betrayed you. Why do you beg for her life?"

Reeve realized then that Elana had known all along what Carmen felt for him.

"What she did," Elana said softly, "she did for love." Her eyes turned to Reeve. "We can understand that completely, can we not, my husband?"

His pride in her left Reeve momentarily speechless. If his arms had not been bound, he would have crushed her to him. He smiled and let his eyes tell her just how he felt. And he knew she read him well.

"Too bad," Juan snapped. "I have no reason or time to drag her along."

Carmen's head was bowed for a moment as tears of regret and anguish touched her eyes. Then her eyes lifted and even Juan was startled with the intense hatred that seemed to physically touch him.

Eternally superstitious, Juan's face paled under Carmen's gaze. He felt something reach out to touch him. At that moment he was glad he had told the men who held her that after they had enjoyed her, they were to kill her. By the end of the day she would be dead, and he knew he would never feel at ease until then.

He ordered them all to their horses. Elana and Reeve had to be forced for Carmen's dark eyes lingered in their minds. Beatriz was in tears and Rodrigo's eyes were moist.

Once mounted, the group began to ride toward Madrid. Elana and Reeve both turned in their saddles to look back. Carmen stood quietly between the two men. She seemed to have lost all strength and will. She seemed small and broken between the two tall men. Her head was bowed and her dark hair fell about her, hiding her face.

Elana's eyes blurred with tears as they crested a hill. Carmen faded from sight and they rode on toward Madrid and what fate had planned for them.

319

Chapter Twenty-Four

Madrid lay before them, a city of beauty that belied the danger that lay waiting for them. The entire group was exhausted, but Juan would not permit them to rest. He urged his horse ahead and they rode down the hill upon which they had stopped, across an open plain and through the large gates of the city.

Reeve was praying silently that he and Elana would be kept together. He knew she was very frightened and yet he had to admire her courage. It had kept her going under tremendous pressure.

The horses came to a halt at the side gate of the palace. The four prisoners were forced to walk through the gates, then were stopped in front of a large wooden door where several men waited for them.

The man in obvious command spoke to Juan. "Don Francisco is very pleased. I will take the prisoners to their cells. He would like to speak to you, perhaps to reward you."

Juan smiled, very pleased with the possibility of a large reward. He nodded and left. The man who had spoken first turned and spoke to three of the men with him. "Take the women to the cells. I will personally take care of the men. In a short time Don Francisco will speak with them all. One at a time."

Reeve and Rodrigo both protested violently, but several blows and threats with guns forced them to move through the wooden door which had been thrown open.

Once inside the doors, they were pushed ahead of their guards down a dimly lit hall. At the end of the hall another door led to a flight of stone steps. Down . . . down . . . down until the walls began to seep water and the stench of dungeons came to them.

They found they were not even to be locked in the same cell. They were in cells across the hallway from each other. There was a small square opening in both doors through which they could see and speak to each other.

"Good God," Rodrigo rasped, "I hope they don't lock Beatriz in a place like this."

"I don't think they will," Reeve replied, but deep within he wasn't so sure. "I think they will be taken back to their own rooms and locked in. Rodrigo, they plan to use us against them."

"To use us?"

"What do you think Beatriz would agree to do to protect you? I'm afraid, knowing Elana as I do, that she would do whatever they chose if she thought it would mean safety for me."

"Damn!" Rodrigo groaned. "What can we do?"

"Nothing, only pray that they are strong enough not to believe any lies they are told."

"Yes," Rodrigo replied softly. "Reeve, I don't think there's any hope for the three of us. But, for you there's a chance. Maybe you can get out of this yet. They never found Beatriz's grandfather. It almost seemed as if they were not looking for him. If you get free, will you find him? Assure him that we tried our best and that even getting one of us free was not in vain?"

"You sound as if you are already defeated," Reeve said

angrily. "There is no way I will leave this country without Elana."

"Don't be a fool. You can get free. Elana and me . . . we have no chance."

"I'm the only chance Elana has, and I won't let her go so easily. We are married, by a priest, in a church. I'll shout it from the rooftops at the first opportunity."

"Do you really have written proof?"

"Yes, I'm glad I had the papers made out, witnessed and signed."

"But you have it hidden?"

"That I do. I wanted to make sure we were free. They want that paper, so they'll keep us alive until they find it. It will at least give us time. Maybe we can find a way yet to get out of this."

Rodrigo was silent for a moment. He did not share Reeve's optimism. He knew the trickery of the Inquisition too well.

"I hope they keep Elana and Beatriz together. They will at least be able to support each other. Beatriz . . . she's so fine and delicate. I don't know how she will stand if they should question her."

Reeve, too, hoped they would be together. He walked to the pile of straw in the corner of his cell that supplied the only place to rest. He sat down. There was an ache deep within him that needed only Elana. His mind conjured up a picture of her and held it. What would she have to face? Was she thinking of him, holding onto the strength of their love as he was? What would happen next?

They were left alone for what seemed to Reeve and Rodrigo to be many hours. There had been one candle in each cell, and Reeve watched it burn and grow smaller. It was less than an inch high and the flame was growing feeble when he heard the sound of approaching footsteps. Both Reeve and Rodrigo were at the door immediately. The guards opened the doors, pushing them back roughly. Their hands were tied together before them. All this was done in silence. They were pushed into the hallway where two men stood waiting for them.

"Where are you taking us?" Reeve demanded.

"Keep silent, prisoner," one man said as he pushed Reeve roughly. Reeve smiled at the man beside him who seemed to be a little more aware than the others.

"I have a gold coin for the answer to my question," he said softly. He saw the man's eyes flicker in response. He had struck greed and it made him elated. Enough gold coins might buy him some information.

"Maybe," he said gently, "there are more gold coins with that one."

"What do you want to know?" the man whispered.

"Where are Elana and Beatriz?"

"Where are your coins?" the man replied.

Reeve twisted until he could reach within his shirt and loosen three coins. He let them jingle lightly in his hands then passed them to the guard. "Where are Elana and Beatriz?" he repeated.

"Don Francisco holds them in a room next to his."

"Together?"

"Yes."

"Where are we going now?"

The man grinned. "You have more coins? I might just tell you."

Again, Reeve handed him two more coins. The man realized Reeve had many, but he did not want to face Don Francisco's anger. He was not sure just where Reeve stood, and stealing from him might cost him more than he was willing to pay.

"Well?" Reeve said.

"Don Francisco would speak with you. We are taking you to him."

Reeve remained silent. To the guard's disappointment he

offered no more coins and asked no more questions. As far as Reeve was concerned, he was going exactly where he wanted to go: to see Don Francisco. There was no more conversation, and the only sound to be heard was the sharp click of their boots on the cold stone floor.

Elana watched Reeve being forced away from her. She felt the emptiness almost immediately. She and Beatriz were forced along the marble-floored passageway. Soon it became obvious where they were going: to Don Francisco's apartments. Both of them had already tried insisting that they should be taken to the queen. Absolute silence met their words and they knew it was useless.

They entered Don Francisco's apartments. In the anteroom, they waited in silence until the door to Don Francisco's office was opened. Elana and Beatriz were pushed inside and the door was pulled closed behind them. They were alone.

"Oh, Elana, I'm so frightened," Beatriz said in a soft, broken voice. Elana went to her and put her arm about Beatriz's shoulder.

"We must keep our courage, Beatriz. As Reeve said, we are alive, and as long as we are, we shall have hope. We cannot allow Don Francisco to believe that we will give up so easily."

"I know, I know," Beatriz replied, but Elana could feel the fear vibrate through her.

"Beatriz?"

"What?"

"If Don Francisco does not say anything about our marriage, then we must say nothing. We can hope that Juan forgot to tell him. It might mean Reeve's freedom, and if he is free, we know he will do all in his power to free us."

"I will say nothing, Elana."

"Thank you," Elana replied softly. She gave Beatriz's

shoulders a reassuring squeeze, then their attention was drawn to the door as it opened and Don Francisco, accompanied by two other men, strangers to both women, walked into the room. They watched him silently as he walked close to them. Then he smiled a tight, malicious smile.

"Welcome back to court." He chuckled. "Did you enjoy your little journey? I hope so, for it will prove to be a very expensive little trip."

"Why did you drag us back here, Don Francisco?" Elana said. "Why did you not let us go? What do you want from us? I will not marry Diego, no matter what you do to me. And if the queen hears of your treatment of us, she will give us our freedom."

Again, Don Francisco laughed. "I'm afraid, my dear, it is useless to go to the queen. In fact, she cannot give you an audience. She made her rules a long time ago. You have been put into my hands. You," he added softly, "have much to lose, so tread carefully, if you value your life, think before you make your decisions."

"Decisions?"

"Yes. Your first one will be the day of your marriage to Diego. The second will be," he said smiling broadly at both women, "just how long the lives of your brother and his stupid friend will be."

Elana held Don Francisco's gaze and he could not help the leap of desire in his veins and the admiration that filled him.

"I," she said softly but firmly, "will die before I marry anyone not of my own choosing, and especially Diego. He is an animal. As far as the lives of Rodrigo and Reeve," she said lifting her head proudly, "they are both too much men to take their freedom at our expense."

"Oh my dear, you are so foolish. I am going to have you taken to the dungeons where others are being . . . questioned. You will see just what I have planned for your brother and his friend. After that, we will talk again. I think then your choice will be very different."

He turned to the two men who had accompanied him. "Take them," he commanded. Elana and Beatriz were grasped roughly and dragged from the room and down the long corridors to the steps that eventually led down to the torture chambers. Soon the sounds of people in agony came to their unwilling and frightened senses. The foul odors were enough to nauseate them, but the scene that greeted their eyes when they entered the main torture chamber brought a cry of anguish from both of them. They stared horrified and disbelieving.

In the very center of the room, a man, if he could still be called a man, hung in chains. Slowly, he was being skinned alive. Surrounding them were more forms of torture that brought anguished cries to their ears. The man who hung in the center held Elana's gaze. No matter how hard she tried not to look, she could see Reeve.

She wanted desperately to blot the scene from her sight but she could not. Reeve, her beloved Reeve; could she see him like this? No, her heart demanded. She knew then that Don Francisco had succeeded. She would do anything he demanded to keep Reeve from this.

She closed her eyes, weaving on her feet, and felt herself being led from the room. Taken again to the room in which they had first been held, they sat in mute agony until they had to face Don Francisco again.

Reeve and Rodrigo stood before Don Francisco. Slowly he sipped from a goblet of cool wine while he regarded them intently.

"So," he said gently, "you thought you were very clever. Did you really believe I would let you escape me? I would have gone to the ends of the earth to find you, just to prove you could not beat me. Now," he added, "you are in my hands, and I will reward you . . . believe me, I will reward you well."

"I want to speak to my country's ambassador," Reeve demanded.

Don Francisco laughed. He rose from his seat and walked to stand close to Reeve. "By the time your ambassador or anyone else hears of this, you will be," he said and shrugged, "regrettably very, very dead. I am afraid I must be forced to apologize to your country for a very regrettable mistake, one I can do nothing about."

Reeve knew Don Francisco meant what he said, but his main worry was the whereabouts of Elana.

"I want to see Elana."

"No, not possible. I have plans for Lady Elana, and they do not include you."

"Where is she? What have you done with her?"

"She is receiving a small lesson in obedience. After a few hours, she will be quite willing to do as I say."

"What do you think you will get from all of this?"

"A very convenient marriage, for both of them. Once I have what I want, I will dispose of you. All the problems will be gone."

"Hardly," Reeve replied.

"What do you mean?"

"Elana can't marry anyone else. She is already married."

Don Francisco's face turned white with anger. "Impossible!"

"No! She is married to me. In church, with a priest. A thing the queen would hardly overlook. If anything happens to me, the proof of our marriage will go directly to the queen. Then all your efforts will have been in vain. Besides, since Diego is dead, just who did you plan on having her marry?"

"I am afraid you are very wrong, my friend," a soft voice

328

came from behind them. Both men were stunned with the familiarity of the voice. They turned to stand face to face with a man they had thought was dead . . . Diego. "I hate to disappoint you," Diego said with a smile. "You should have been more careful than to leave without checking to see if I were really dead." His smile faded and his eyes began to glow with a deep and violent hatred. "Too bad, my friend. That is a mistake you will soon be sorry for."

Reeve had no doubts that Diego spoke for both himself and Don Francisco.

"I shall enjoy her very much, more since I know how much she means to you. It will give me great pleasure to teach her all I want her to know."

Reeve spun around to gaze at Don Francisco. "I'll remind you," he said, "the proof of our marriage will go directly to the queen. She will want to ask Elana questions. Can you keep her from doing that? I don't think so."

"You will tell me where that proof is," Don Francisco said coldly.

"Never."

"You will tell me."

"Let Elana and Beatriz go to the queen. Let me see that they are safe. Then you will have the proof. Until then, no matter what you do, I will never tell you."

Don Francisco was silent for a moment, then slowly he seemed to relax. "I will think about what you have said."

"No!" Diego cried. "He must die now. I want her and I will have her now!"

"Shut up, Diego," Don Francisco snapped. "Send for the guards to take them back to their cells."

Reluctantly, Diego did as he was told. When Reeve and Rodrigo had gone, he turned to Don Francisco. "Why did you let him get away with that?"

"Silence, Diego. Use your head. The noble young man

thinks he is protecting her. He will die under torture before he tells us where that proof is. But, maybe there is someone he will tell."

"Who?"

"Why," Don Francisco said and smiled, "his beloved wife, Elana."

Diego was silent again then they both began to laugh softly. "Of course, you are right." Diego laughed. "He would tell her. And you are going to send her to find out."

"I am."

"And then?"

"And then they will die; she will be yours and we will have the power of the de Santangel and Mendosa names. Now, go and bring her to me."

Elana sat, pale and shaken, but she was jarred back to reality when the door opened and Diego walked in. She summoned what reserve of strength she had and rose to her feet, coldly watching him approach her.

"Leave me alone, Diego," she said with all the courage she could manage to muster under the circumstances. Still Diego crossed the room and walked closer, and slowly Elana began to back away.

He stopped just a few inches from her and, though his lips smiled, his eyes were cold and hungry. "No, Elana, I will never leave you alone, again. How very clever you thought you were. After our betrothal was announced you made a fool of me by running away with another man. It was also stupid of you to believe me dead. Did he boast to you that he had beaten me with the sword and left me for dead? Did it please you, Elana?"

"Fought . . . swords . . . I . . . I don't know what you are talking about. Please, Diego, leave me alone."

He reached out and grasped her arm in a painful hold and jerked her close to him. "No, I will not leave you alone, and don't pretend innocence with me. Of course your lover told you he tried to kill me. He left me for dead in a dirty stall like some kind of animal."

"Diego, you're hurting me," she cried as his grip ruthlessly twisted her arm. At the helpless cry, he smiled, but released his hold.

"No matter. Nothing has changed. Soon you will belong to me, and soon this will all be forgotten."

"I will never forget Reeve . . . never."

"But you will have no choice, my dear."

"Why?" she said fearfully. "What do you mean?"

"I am afraid Don Francisco would like to explain that to you. Come with me."

For the first time Elana went with him without a struggle. She wanted to understand just what Diego was talking about and what threat it was to Reeve.

They walked along the marble hall together to Don Francisco's room. Once inside, she faced again the man who had brought so much pain to her life. They looked at each other across a room, Elana trying hard to control her fear, and Don Francisco debating to himself just how he was going to take advantage of it.

"Sit down, Elana," he said. "We have something of great importance to discuss."

"What do we have to talk about?"

"The life of Reeve Burke and your brother?" he questioned softly.

Slowly, Elana sank into the chair. Her legs had suddenly become too weak to hold her. "What do you want?" she whispered.

"Now you are talking sensibly. I take it your little . . . visit to the dungeons has enlightened you as to what could happen to your," he said and shrugged, "lover, and your brother."

Her wide eyes saw no mercy in his. She knew that unless she did what he wanted, Reeve and Rodrigo would pay the price.

331

But she didn't know what he wanted. "What do you want of me?"

"It seems," Don Francisco replied in a silken voice, "that you have been foolish enough to marry our wayward captain."

Elana's face paled. Reeve had told him. She knew a real terror, for she knew that in the telling he had signed both his and possibly Rodrigo's death warrants as well. "I still don't understand. What do you want of me?"

"You want to keep your captain alive? Do you want him to suffer the fate of that wretched man below us?"

"No . . . please—" Elana replied.

"It seems your captain has hidden some proof of your marriage."

"Proof?"

"Does he have a marriage document?"

"Yes. The priest gave it to him."

"Where is it?"

"I . . . I don't know. Reeve took it, and at the time, I felt it was safe with him, so I did not ask. After a time I forgot about it."

"He is the only one who knows where it is?"

"Yes . . . yes, he is."

"I want that proof," Don Francisco said quietly.

Elana gazed at him for several minutes. "And after you have it," she replied, "you will kill him."

"Not necessarily."

"Don't take me for a fool, Don Francisco. Once you have that proof in your hands, you will destroy it. Then you will destroy Reeve. I can't let that happen."

"We can . . . ah . . . come to some mutual agreement. That way you can protect their lives."

"And Beatriz and I?"

Don Francisco shrugged. "You will not be harmed, but there are things that must occur, things I must have. Once I do, you

332

will be free to do as you choose."

Elana smiled slightly and Don Francisco knew she did not trust him for a moment. "I do not care about me," she said softly, "but I want Reeve, Rodrigo, and Beatriz to be free. Tell me what arrangements you have in mind, and I shall consider what you suggest."

"You are a very brave woman."

"No, not brave. But I love." Her eyes turned scornfully from Don Francisco to Diego. "It is an emotion I hardly believe either of you would understand, and Reeve loves me. For that and his life, I would do what you ask. If I can have proof of their freedom."

"Agreed. What proof do you want?"

"I want Reeve and the others to be taken either to the queen or to the English ambassador. When they are, then—"

"Don't think I am a fool either," Don Francisco said with a laugh. "If I deliver them to either party, then I will have no leverage. No, my dear, we must think of something better than that."

"What?"

"Suppose," Don Francisco said thoughtfully, "we find a mutual party . . . one you can trust, and he or she will get the proof that your lover and your brother are free. Then you will turn over to me both yourself and the proof of your marriage."

"Who would this person be? There are few at court that I would trust and even fewer who are not already in your power and would do whatever you ask them to do."

"What would you say to . . . Rafael Chavez?"

"Rafael," Elana exclaimed happily. "Of course I would trust him."

"I will send for him. He will see that Reeve and the others are free. Then he will come to you. After he does, you will give him this proof."

"I agree."

SYLVIE F. SOMMERFIELD

"Excellent. I will send for Chavez immediately."

Elana was sure there was no way Rafael would not tell her the truth.

"You will be sent to your . . . husband. Find out where the proof is. Within days, Chavez will be here."

Elana nodded and Don Francisco told Diego to take her back to the room she shared with Beatriz.

When Diego returned he was furious for Elana had again resisted his advances. "How can you agree to this? They are all in our power. This Chavez will get them free."

"Ah, Diego, still the unbeliever. I," he added softly, "will bring Chavez here, but another of my . . . friends . . . will hold his wife."

Diego smiled and then joined Don Francisco in laughter. Soon, all their plans would be completed. Soon, all they wanted would finally be in their power.

Chapter Twenty-Five

Reeve lay on the foul-smelling straw. It had been some time since he and Rodrigo had been returned to their cells. From the time they had been returned to their cells all was silent . . . entirely too silent to suit Reeve. Don Francisco had them all right where he wanted them. Why didn't he do something? Reeve expected at least some form of torture to try to get the proof of his marriage.

He was grateful for the instinct that had made him hide the marriage contract. It had been a sudden feeling, but Reeve usually followed such things. In fact, he remembered quite well the instincts that had brought him where he was. He regretted much . . . but not Elana.

Where was she, he wondered. How was she? He could close his eyes and draw a vision of her in his mind. He could feel the silk of her hair and taste the sweetness of her lips. His body ached with the remembrance of her slim, cool body close to his. He would have given anything in the world to be able to hold her, even for a moment.

"Reeve," Rodrigo called softly. Reeve stood up and walked to look out the small barred window in his door.

"What?"

"I don't undersand this. Why doesn't he do something? What's he waiting for?"

335

"He's letting us think, making us worry and wonder just what he's planning on doing next."

"Well, he's succeeding quite well. I'm worrying all right, but not about me. What has he done with Beatriz and Elana?"

"I wish I knew," Reeve replied quietly.

"Reeve, I know he needs Elana and Beatriz for his plans, but why in God's name is he keeping us alive?"

"Well, Rodrigo, he wants something from me."

"What?"

"Rodrigo . . . when Elana and I were married, I took the marriage certificate and I hid it . . . well. It's some small hold I have. If he kills us the certificate will go to the queen and my country's ambassador. If that happens, he will lose Elana and he knows it."

"Holy Mother," Rodrigo breathed. "Reeve, he'll torture you until you tell him where it is."

"Will you believe me, Rodrigo, when I tell you that it is one secret that will go to the grave with me. No matter what he does."

"Reeve—"

"No matter what. Do you understand that?"

"Yes," Rodrigo replied softly, "you are much more man than I. The thought of the tortures that man's mind can conjure up would terrify me."

"I didn't say I wasn't frightened to death. But Elana's and Beatriz's lives depend on it, too. I will never speak, and he knows it."

"He is such a devious-minded man, Reeve. He will try to devise a plan to get you to tell him."

"It won't matter. This time he's beaten."

"I hope you are right." Before Reeve could answer again, the sound of footsteps came to them. After a few moments guards approached. They stopped in front of Reeve's door.

"Stand back," one of them ordered Reeve, who obediently

moved back away from the door. He was curious as to whether this was the moment he would be tortured or the moment Don Francisco would set them free.

The guard unlocked Reeve's door. Both came in. Reeve's hands were bound before him and he was pushed out through the open door of his cell. For a moment he paused in front of Rodrigo's cell. Their eyes met in mutual understanding.

"*Vaya con Dios*, my friend," Rodrigo said softly.

"Thank you . . . until we meet again." Reeve answered quietly. Rodrigo watched until the two guards and Reeve disappeared.

Reeve walked between the two men, up from the dungeons into the marble halls of the palace. He thought he was being taken again to Don Francisco and was mildly surprised when they stopped in front of another door.

"Where is this?" he asked.

"Don't question. Go inside and wait. In time you will know." They untied his hands. Reeve moved through the open door and immediately it was closed behind him. He stood and gazed about him. It was one of the most beautiful rooms he had ever been in. What surprised him was that a tub of hot water sat nearby and clean clothes lay across a huge and very comfortable-looking bed. He wasn't quite sure if all this was for him, and if it was . . . why?

He stood so only for a few minutes when another door opened at the far end of the room and his breath nearly stopped when he saw the person who entered from the other side.

"Elana," he whispered in disbelief. He was afraid that his need to see her was forcing him to see a vision that was not there. She was so very beautiful, her dark hair loose about her and her slim body enclosed in a shimmering gold gown. Then she was moving toward him and he could think of nothing else. He moved rapidly and they met in the center of the room.

"Reeve," she cried. "Oh, Reeve, my beloved." He lifted her

and felt her slim arms about his neck and her soft curved body molded to his. In heated, vibrant, and explosive need, his mouth caught hers in a kiss so deep and so filled with his desperate passion that she was filled to overflowing with his magical touch.

He could not seem to get enough of her. Hungrily, his lips devoured her while his hands sought to convince his senses this dream was real.

"Elana, I can't believe this is real. I've been praying and dreaming and hoping and I can't believe it."

"Reeve," she sighed as she rested her head against his chest and felt his strong arms rock her against him.

Reeve held her away from himself, and his gaze examined her closely. "Are you all right?"

"I'm fine, Reeve, I'm fine. But you, you look—"

"Don Francisco's dungeons are not the nicest places in the world. Elana," he added gently, "why are we here? I can't believe in Don Francisco's humanity. What's his motive?"

The last thing Elana could say was the truth. She had to find where Reeve had hidden the proof of their wedding to save his life, which meant more to her than anything else in the world. Added to that was the life of her brother and Beatriz. The three of them free were worth any sacrifice she could make now or in the future.

"We have two days to share, Reeve. I have begged Don Francisco for that much. After that the trials are to be held. We have two days to share, Reeve. We must make it a lifetime."

"You begged!" he exclaimed angrily. "Begged that . . . that . . ."

"Reeve, no matter what he is, we cannot escape our destiny any longer. He has given me two days with you. I love you, Reeve. Don't be angry with me," she added softly. "Give me these two days, please."

"Angry with you," he whispered against her hair as he drew her back into his arms. "Elana, I have held you in my mind so

338

long, I can't believe I'm holding you. It's just that I can't stand the thought of you begging him for anything."

"It doesn't matter anymore, Reeve. We have each other and we have now. We must carry these two days with us forever."

"No, Elana, no! We must not think that way. Yes, we have these two days, but we must reach for tomorrow, too. We must believe we will survive. We will survive!" he said positively.

Their eyes held and she felt the intense magnetism he had always possessed slowly flow through her. She felt his strength, his love, and his need lift her and fill her. Maybe, her heart whispered, maybe there would be a miracle, a way to be together. Her heart wanted her to believe as he did, but her mind told her it was only a dream . . . only a dream she did not dare believe. When Rafael was brought to her, she would tell him where the proof was. After that, Reeve and her brother and Beatriz would be set free from all of this. He would be safe, and for her, that was all that mattered.

"Elana, look at me," he said softly, "I love you so very much, and even though I don't believe Don Francisco is a giver of gifts, I'm grateful just to see you and hold you even if it is only for a little while."

"Reeve, I want to be with you. I can bear whatever the future may bring." Tears slipped down her cheeks. "But only if I have these hours to hold. Love me, Reeve, for today, love me and let us share what time we have." Reeve's magnetic silver eyes held hers for a long time, reading clearly her need. Then she sighed deeply.

"All right, Elana. For us the world outside just doesn't exist. We'll take today and tomorrow and hold it forever."

"Yes," she said softly as his lips touched hers. "Yes, my love . . . yes." The kiss was long, lingering, and very gentle. She could feel her very soul weep with the intensity of her love for him.

*   *   *

Reeve sank into the hot water, relieved to wash the filth of the dungeons from him and ease the tense muscles. Elana sat cross-legged on the bed and smiled at his pleasure. She took the time to admire again the near perfect symmetry of his bronzed muscular body and the striking contrast of his burnished gold hair and silver eyes. She wanted to frame him in her mind for she knew once he was gone from her life, he would not be able to reenter it. He would be lost to her.

"Why don't you join me?" he suggested. She wrinkled her nose at him and laughed.

"I shall wait here. Maybe it will give you some reason to hurry."

He gazed at her, this creature who possessed every ounce of his being, and he could not help but smile in return. She was still tan and still had the startling look of soft innocence.

Her eyes sparkled with mischief as she watched him make short use of his bath. He rose from the water, toweled himself dry, and walked to her, bouncing down on the bed beside her and drawing her into his arms to kiss her slowly and leisurely.

His hair, still damp from a rapid washing, lay in thick curls at his neck. She reached to tangle her hands in it, and pull his head to hers to taste again the welcome warmth of his kiss, a warmth she knew she would lose too soon.

Reeve was so attuned to Elana that he could feel the tension in her body. He sensed there was much more to this than he knew, and he felt again the old sense of alarm, yet he could not put his finger on the cause. He wondered what Don Francisco had planned for them to face when these two days were over.

But all other rational thought was lost to him as Elana's cool, slim body touched his and her warm, insistent mouth made thinking of anything else but her a complete impossibility.

"Elana," he whispered against the soft velvet skin of her throat. He heard the muted sigh of pleasure as his hands and lips sought softer, more vulnerable pleasure.

He pressed his lips against the soft breasts and could taste the texture of her skin and feel the rapid beating of her heart. He knew that Elana could always waken this vibrant desire within him. If he possessed her forever it would never die.

The knowledge that after these hours she would never share the magic of his love again filled Elana with an urgency to draw him within the depths of herself. She desired, more than any other thing, to accept his seed and quicken with his child. After he was gone, it could be the link that would help her survive the shame and pain of belonging to Diego.

Reeve felt her need and knew again that there was something different. Again, the strange intuitive voice told him there was something wrong, yet he was enfolded in Elana's flame so deeply he could not force himself to think of anything else.

They lost themselves completely in each other and heard only their ecstatic calling to each other as they reached the height of their mutual consummation in a blinding moment of ecstasy.

They lay together, holding each other, silenced by the brilliance of their love. Candlelight touched the room with shadows, creating a haven that, for the moment, allowed them to believe they were cut away from the violent world that hovered outside their door.

The shadows lengthened as the night grew deeper and a pale gold moon rose. Elana slept in the safety of his arms but Reeve could not. Gently, without disturbing her sleep, he eased from the bed. The room was chilled so he stirred the dying embers of the fire to life. He went to the window and looked out at the peaceful scene. One would not believe that any danger lingered here. Reeve turned to gaze at a sleeping Elana. She lay on her side facing him. Her body, slender and softly curved beneath the sheets, wakened a gentle memory within him. Her lips, slightly parted, were rosy and warmly inviting. Her dark hair could almost be felt in his hands. This slim, gentle girl could awaken in him a violent need that could sometimes startle him. Again he wondered why he felt the same strange, warning feeling.

His gaze roamed toward the door. Quickly he crossed the room, but even as he reached for the handle, he knew it was locked. At that moment another thought entered his mind. In anger at himself he wondered why he had not thought of it before: the secret passageways! Was there one in this room, and could it possibly lead to freedom?

Slowly, he began a search. Methodically, he began to examine every inch of the paneled walls . . . nothing. Inch by inch, sensitive fingers searched and he found nothing. He was startled when Elana's quiet voice spoke from the bed.

"Reeve, what are you doing?"

He turned to face her, smiling broadly and a look of new hope in his eyes. "Something I should have had enough sense to do a long time ago," Reeve said and laughed.

"I don't know what you are talking about," Elana replied, her eyes wide and questioning.

"Elana, the passageways . . . like the one that led to your room. There might be one here. If we can only find it. Wouldn't it come as some surprise to them if they returned to find us gone?"

"Reeve," she breathed softly as the light of new hope touched her eyes.

"Come on, Elana, help me search."

Quickly, she left the bed, and at any other time, her absolute beauty would have distracted him completely. Now their lives depended upon their finding the hidden door . . . if there was one.

Slowly, methodically, they traced all the edges of doorways, windows, corners, moldings, anywhere that a hidden spring could be found. To be rewarded with nothing. No sign of a hidden doorway, yet both of them felt the same. If there had been a hidden passage in most of the other rooms, why not this one? They both felt they were overlooking some obvious thing that might be their key to freedom.

"They are as good at hiding things as you are, Reeve." Elana said.

"What?"

"Well, you must admit, they are as frustrated as we are. We want to find the hidden passageway, and they want to find out where you have hidden our marriage papers."

Reeve laughed. "Well, they'll never find them. They will be frustrated for a long time."

"Nor will I, should I ever need them," Elana said quietly. She waited in breathless silence for Reeve's answer.

"I hadn't thought of that," he said quickly. She could have wept, knowing he trusted her so completely. "I should tell you where they are in case I am not here. You will need them to prove to the queen we are married."

"Yes, Reeve," she said quietly. "Tell me where they are and I will not use them unless I feel it is absolutely necessary."

He went to her and put his arms about her. She lifted her chin to return his warm open gaze. This information would save his life and that of her brother and Beatriz, and that was all that mattered.

"They are in a place I hardly think Don Francisco would look. You see, when we were captured, I did have them with me. I knew I had to put them in a safe place."

"Where?" she breathed.

"In the cell where they held me. There is a loose rock in the far left corner. The packet of letters is under that. When this is over, I shall return and retrieve them. I want the world to know you are my wife, that I am lucky enough to have the most beautiful woman in the world at my side for the rest of my life."

"You hid them in your cell!" she exclaimed. "Right under

Don Francisco's nose?"

Reeve laughed. "I hope he's on a merry goose chase trying to find out where I put them. He'll have a devil of a time finding Pedro again, should he think they are with him, and I'm sure he has no idea where we were married, so he cannot harm the Padre. Only we know where they are, love, and that will put an effective stop to his plans.

"Reeve, you laugh, but . . . he could . . . torture you or . . ." She could hardly speak.

"No, love, we can bluff this out. If he harms, or even thinks of harming any of us, I shall announce to the world we are married. He doesn't want word of that to get to the queen or she will take us out of his control. He will try, but we must remain strong. We will win, love. Believe me."

"Yes, my love, I know that. This is nearly over. We must do what is necessary."

"I knew you would understand." He kissed her gently. "Now, it's getting light. Let's find that door. It's got to be here."

Again, they began their search, but it seemed as if they were wrong. The sun rose and the bright new day lit the room, but still no sign of a door presented itself.

Both had dressed quickly, but Elana had assured Reeve that no one was to disturb them. Again she did not account for the deceitfulness of Don Francisco. They heard the key turn in the lock and the door was swung open. In the doorway stood four armed guards.

"No," Elana said softly. "No! You were to leave us alone today! He promised."

"You should have known. He could not be trusted," Reeve said angrily.

"Stand away from her," one of the guards ordered Reeve. Reeve and Elana exchanged a painful look. "Move!" the man demanded. Reluctantly, Reeve moved away from Elana.

Two guards gripped Elana's arms and began to drag her from the room. Reeve, held at pistol point, could only watch.

"Don't be frightened, Elana," he tried to reassure her. "He does not have the proof, remember."

The door closed between Reeve and the guards and he was left alone.

Elana was dragged, fighting, to Don Francisco's room. There, she faced him, anger flashing in her eyes. He surveyed her with a calm smile.

"So, you have found what I want to know?" he asked.

"Why?" she demanded. "You promised me today!"

"Why, my dear," he said in a velvet-smooth voice, "I would think one night in your arms would loosen any man's tongue."

"You are—" she began.

"Now, my dear," he said with a chuckle, "let us not call names. Did he or did he not tell you where the papers are?"

"Yes, he did."

"Excellent."

"Rafael is here?"

"No, but I have sent for him. He will be here soon."

"Then," she said softly, "I do not want to see you again until he is here. Then, when Rafael tells me that Reeve, my brother, and Beatriz are safely with the English ambassador, and only then will I tell him what you want to know."

"You are an obstinate female," he said gently. "When you are married to my nephew, we will have to teach you to be a little more obedient."

"You may have me in your power, but Reeve and the others will be safe. I will do all that is necessary to keep him and the others out of your ungodly power. Do as you will with me," she announced proudly, "but I will always know you were beaten and they are safe."

Don Francisco's face reddened with his suppressed anger which gave Elana a great deal of satisfaction. She vowed that she would remind him and Diego often about their defeat. It would be one of the few things she would have to carry her through the long days and nights. That, and the sweet memory of Reeve's love.

"You are a bitch," he snarled. "It will give me great pleasure to tame you."

"I am no longer afraid of you." She smiled. "You would not dare hurt me after Diego and I are married. The queen would forbid it. Reeve and the others will be beyond your reach. And I," she added softly, "I will pray daily that I carry Reeve's child, for he will be the heir that will have all of both my wealth and Diego's, and again, you will have been defeated."

Don Francisco felt a white-hot rage, yet he contained it well. The time would come when he had Elana at his mercy, when he could tell her that her beloved Reeve was dead as would be her brother, and Beatriz would be safely in his power. Then he would make her suffer for the words she spoke so carelessly now.

He struggled to regain his composure and adjust his cold smile. Soon, he thought, he would make her beg for his mercy. The thought of his future possession of her fragile beauty nearly inflamed him. In the back of his mind, he could conjure up pictures of what he planned to do.

"Take her to her room! Lock her in. She is to have no servants, no visitors. She is to be fed once a day at sundown. Until then, she is to speak to no one. Is that understood?"

"Yes, Don Francisco," the head guard answered. Two guards took Elana from the room. When the door closed after her, the other two waited for further orders.

"I want you to go to the Englishman," Don Francisco said slowly and coldly.

"Yes, Don Francisco. And what should we do with him?"

"You will take him," Don Francisco said calmly, "to the very depths of the dungeons. There you will begin the torture.

Go to any lengths, use any method you feel necessary." His cold eyes held them as he added softly, "But I want him to be broken . . . utterly and completely broken. She will have him alive but maybe both she and her captain will wish he were not."

The two men turned and left the room. Don Francisco allowed his rage to overtake him for a moment. His hatred for Reeve was so intense that he could taste it. He would see Reeve a broken, spiritless man, then he would give him to Elana, make him a dog to be whipped before Elana's eyes. Would she then be so defiant? Would she then want to give herself to the broken shell of a man Reeve would become? He allowed the pleasure of his thoughts only for a few minutes when a knock sounded on his door. At his command, the door was opened and he was surprised to see the same two guards returned.

"Why have you returned? Did you carry out my orders?"

"We cannot, sir."

"Why?"

"The prisoner, Don Francisco," one answered fearfully, "he's . . . he's gone."

Chapter Twenty-Six

Reeve gazed at the closed door as violent anger overwhelmed him. He took the few steps to the door and in the uncontrollable moment, he struck it with his fist several times as if he could batter it down. Three inches of solid oak were not about to be moved by his futile anger.

He knew it would only be a matter of time until Don Francisco sent someone either to kill him or return him to his cell. Both ideas were to spell doom if carried out.

He gazed around the room in desperation. He knew that somewhere there was a door, but where . . . where? Again, he began to examine the room, but again, there was no sign. He sagged to a chair and gazed at the huge bed in which he and Elana had so recently shared so much.

He must have been looking at it several moments before the realization struck him . . . the bed! It was the only area in which they had not searched. It was a large four poster that sat on a raised dais. He moved rapidly to the bed. First, he examined very carefully the wood paneling behind the bed, but there was no sign of any door. He walked to the foot of the bed and grasped the thick post, intending to push the bed aside to examine the walls more closely.

It was a shock when his pressure caused the bed to slide sideways and more of a shock when it revealed a stone stairwell leading downward into . . . He did not know what, but at this moment, he did not care. It was a passageway that led from this room and the only opportunity to escape.

It was a dark hole and he knew he could not travel without light. He took a candle from the candelabra on the table. He went down several steps, then set the candle in drippings of the wax so it would remain upright and lit while he searched for a way to slide the bed back into place.

A ring embedded in the stone wall proved to be what he searched for. He grasped it and pulled and with satisfaction, watched the bed slide back into place. He picked up the candle and as silently as he could move, he began to work his way down the cold, narrow stairwell.

The steps went down nearly fifteen steps before he found himself on a landing. From the landing three passageways led away into a black void. He had to choose quickly which one he would take.

He chose the one directly ahead of him and moved down it several steps to find himself at the top of another flight of steps. Again, he walked down fifteen or so steps to be faced with two passages.

He had no idea where he was in relation to the castle. All he knew was he would continue to explore until he was either found or found a way out.

Again, he walked the passage a short distance and found another flight of steps. He moved downward again. This time, the steps did not end at fifteen, but continued to descend . . . and he continued to follow.

The walls became damp and the cold chill was very familiar. He knew he was deep in the bowels of the castle. He hoped now that what he followed might be leading to the dungeon. If so, he might be able to find Rodrigo.

Down, down, and further down he walked, then the steps ended in a square area that had a door on all three walls. He was not sure of what he might find on the other side of any of the doors, should he open them. He again braced the candle so it would remain upright, then he chose a door. He went to it and pressed his ear against it to see if he could hear any sound from the other side. Nothing. He placed both hands against the door and applied a small amount of pressure. If it moved, he did not want it to move far. He closed his eyes and prayed silently that it would not alert anyone who might be on the other side.

A crack less than an inch appeared and a light came through. Reeve immediately turned, grasped the candle and extinguished it. He returned to the door and looked out. His heart leapt with pleasure as he gazed at the area of cells in which he and Rodrigo had been held. Rodrigo was close. Now he had to find a way to get to him.

There was a large open area between himself and the cells. He was about to push the door completely open when a guard walked into his line of vision. He froze while he watched to see if there were any others.

He scanned the area, but it was soon obvious that there was only one man on guard. Now he wondered if he could get to him before he could sound an alarm. It was a chance he would have to take.

The guard had his back to him, but six feet of distance lay between himself and the guard. Very, very slowly, he pushed the door open. It was soundless and he was grateful to the powers that seemed to be watching over him. Now he had to reach the guard before he could turn and discover him. Reeve was weaponless and if the guard should turn, it would mean sure death.

One step . . . two . . . three . . . four. He was a few inches away when some instinct alarmed the guard. He spun about, surprise on his face, which was soon changed as Reeve's fist, with all his strength behind it, caught him with a smashing blow that dropped him in his tracks.

Quickly, Reeve bound and gagged him and dragged him to an empty cell. He placed him on the straw within and closed the door on him. Now he moved slowly down the stone corridor to Rodrigo's door.

Rodrigo lay on the straw of his cell, and if the guard had been surprised, Rodrigo was even more so when Reeve's whispered call came from his cell door. Rodrigo leapt to his feet and moved quickly to the door. Absolute shock registered on his face when he saw who stood on the other side of the door, smiling at him.

"Ah, Reeve! How in the name of saints did you get here?"

"Don't ask questions now, Rodrigo, there's no time. I've got to find a way to get you out of here."

"That guard brought my meal. I take it he is not among the conscious at the moment?" Rodrigo grinned and Reeve smiled back. "There should be a ring of keys on his belt."

"Wait, I'll go get it."

"Do I have a choice?" Rodrigo smiled. Reeve had to laugh as he quickly made his way back to the still unconscious guard. A quick search revealed the keys. He took them and locked the guard in, then he returned to Rodrigo's cell. In a few minutes, Rodrigo joined him in the corridor.

"Now, how did you get down here?" Rodrigo said.

Quickly Reeve explained.

"So, you found our hidden passageways. It has been the way we have always helped victims of the Inquisition escape," Rodrigo replied.

"You have done it often?"

"As often as we could."

"Does Don Francisco know about these passages?"

"No. If he did, we would have been caught long ago."

"You know your way about them?"

"Like the palm of my hand."

"We've got to find where Don Francisco has put Elana

and Beatriz."

"Then we go to his rooms first."

"Good," Reeve said as he retrieved another lighted candle. Then he turned to lead the way back through the hidden passage. Rodrigo followed and carefully closed the door after them.

Once within the walls, Reeve motioned Rodrigo to lead the way. Rodrigo took the candle and began a rapid ascent of the steps, Reeve very happily following him.

•

"What do you mean he is gone!" Don Francisco exclaimed. "He cannot be gone unless you fools left the door unbolted."

"No, Don Francisco," one guard protested, "we did not. We had to unlock the door to get in. When we did, he was gone."

"And you checked the windows?"

"Bolted, sir."

Don Francisco glared at them. "Then," he said softly, "there has to be another way out of that room. I suggest you search for it before I devise some punishment for your negligence."

"Yes sir," they both said as they backed away from Don Francisco's rage and closed the door.

An avid search of the room brought no results and fearfully the guards reported this to Don Francisco.

"Get out!" Don Francisco shouted, but before they could reach the door he spoke again. "Wait!" They turned to face him. "Go and bring Elana de Santangel to me."

"Yes sir," they said in relief and left quickly . In less than half an hour a surprised Elana was again brought before Don Francisco.

"Did you think I was not miserable enough that you had to bring me into your presence again?" Elana said.

"Do not push your fortune too far, my sweet. I have taken

all from you that I intend to take. Then the next clever words that are not answers to my questions will be met with punishment."

"I have no answers to your questions, Don Francisco, and I would not give you any if I did."

"It seems there are ways in and out of this castle about which I know nothing."

Elana gazed at him. She had no idea at the moment what he was talking about or what he was leading to. She knew all the secret passages, for she and Rodrigo had discovered the already ancient passages when they were children and had been brought to court on visits. What she didn't know was what he had discovered, for some of them were dead-end passages that led to nothing but blank walls. Only a few led to rooms.

"It has just occurred to me," he said smoothly, "that I had overlooked the idea that many, such as Senor Mendosa, have come and gone without anyone's knowledge. That leads to the thought that there must be ways of coming and going without anyone's knowledge."

Her heart leapt. He had not discovered them, she thought. He had just surmised their existence. Now he wanted her to tell him where they were and where they led.

"I am afraid," she replied in a voice as cool as his, "that I have no idea what you are talking about." She watched the fury leap into his eyes.

"I have come to the end of my patience with you. Sit down," he commanded.

Elana sat in the chair he had pointed to, trying to force her mind to the puzzle of what he had left unsaid. Why, when other things had seemed so important to him, when he had seemed so assured and so in control of the situation, did he have a sudden interest in hidden passages?

"Your companion, Senorita Mendosa, seems to know nothing about them either."

"Why should she? We were brought here to attend the

queen. Why should the queen's ladies be scurrying around secret passages like rodents?"

"You, I think," he said smiling, "are a woman of great inner strength. I doubt if you would tell me what I want to know should I even try to force you."

Elana did not answer and tried to keep her face expressionless. The idea of torture in the castle dungeons terrified her, but the last thing in the world she wanted was for Don Francisco to know it.

"What good would it do you?" she said. "I do not have the answers you want."

"I wonder," he said, "if you would be so stubborn if I decided to . . . question your friend, Senorita Mendosa? She seems more susceptible to the futility of keeping her lips sealed. Of course, I would have you there to watch. Maybe you would take pity on her agony and decide to tell me what I want to know."

Now the fear leapt unbidden into her eyes, and he smiled at the sight as she rose to her feet.

"Ah, I have finally gotten your undivided attention."

Don Francisco walked to Elana's side. He reached out a hand and pulled the heavy combs from her hair, letting the hair fall about her. He slid his hands in the thick mass of it. Elana gritted her teeth and glared at him. With the two guards outside the door and Don Francisco's superior strength, there was little she could do, but she did not intend to let him intimidate her. She would not retreat an inch from his threat, nor would she let him know the terror that washed through her.

Don Francisco moved around behind her and gripped her shoulders with both hands and drew her back against him. He enjoyed the silken touch of her hair and the soft fragrance. "Such a lovely creature you are," he said softly. "I should hate to see you . . . damaged. Better that I let you watch your friend being questioned. Then you will understand and be a little more obedient. I have wanted you for a long time."

Elana trembled both in fear and in the absolute disgust his touch brought. "Beatriz is innocent. We do not have the answers to your questions, Don Francisco. Why do you not let us go in peace? I will kill myself before I belong to Diego, or to you."

"Diego." Don Francisco laughed. "He will not be pleased to hear your intentions. Diego will do as he is told. At the right time, he will wed you, but do not doubt for a moment just who you will belong to. The Mendosa wealth and the de Santangel name with their combined powers will be mine."

Elana moved away from him and turned to face him. "You are a vile man," she said angrily. "Do you think I would ever suffer your touch, be your possession? There are many ways for one to die and I would find them. Unless you keep your word to release Beatriz and my brother and let them and Reeve go free. I am sure Beatriz would feel the same as I. Neither of us would choose to live with what you demand."

A flash of anger and Don Francisco struck her across the face. The force of it knocked her to her knees. With strong hands, he gripped her and jerked her to her feet.

"Where are those secret passages?" he demanded. "And where are the papers your lover has so foolishly hidden?" He shook her violently and she cried out at the brutal grip. "You will tell me," he said in a deadly voice. "You will tell me."

Don Francisco gripped her arm in a viselike grip and dragged her to the door. It slammed behind them and for several minutes the room they had left was very quiet. Then slowly a small panel in the wall slid open and a lone figure stepped out. A slender dark shrouded figure who gazed at the closed door in a gaze so filled with hatred that, had anyone else been in the room, they would have been able to feel it.

*　　*　　*

Reeve and Rodrigo reached the landing where the two passageways branched off. Rodrigo made an abrupt turn into the left and moved along the long narrow passage. Reeve followed, hoping they could find a way to reach Elana and Beatriz. It would be quite another matter to get them safely out of the castle. But he was determined to face one problem at a time. For now just to find Elana and know she was safe would be enough. He was sure Rodrigo was feeling the same as he, wanting only to find Beatriz.

He stopped abruptly, nearly colliding with Rodrigo who had come to a halt. He faced the blank wall, and silently motioned Reeve to come beside him. There was a small crack in the wood through which they could survey the room. Rodrigo motioned him to come up beside him and cautioned him to silence.

Reeve gazed through the small hole and into a small bedroom. Beatriz was seated in a chair, her face white with tension. By the door stood a well-armed guard.

Rodrigo drew Reeve with him, well away from where any chance of their whispers could find their way through the wall. "That guard will sound an alarm before we can get three steps into the room," he said.

"Yes," Reeve replied. "I have a suggestion you may not care for, but I think it's our best chance at the moment."

"What?"

"Let's find Elana so that we know where both of them are. There might be a chance she's alone. If so, we can get her, come back here, and at least if an alarm is raised, we can make a run for it through these passages. At least we will all be together."

"God, I hate to leave her there alone," Rodrigo replied. "If she only knew I was this close maybe she wouldn't feel alone or so frightened."

"There's no way unless we enter that room. Once we do, the alarm would be sounded. We would never find Elana then." Reeve knew how very dear Rodrigo held his sister. In the dim light he could read his face.

"All right. But . . . I would look again. I must see her again."

"Of course you must," Reeve replied, understanding the same emotions he would have felt had it been Elana on the other side of the wall. Rodrigo went to the wall and gazed through. Suddenly he reached out and gripped Reeve's arm, dragging him to the wall. He motioned for Reeve to look through the crack.

Inside the door had burst open. Beatriz gasped in fear as she rose to her feet. Two guards and Don Francisco entered, dragging Elana with them. "Bring her with us," Don Francisco ordered and pointed to Beatriz.

"Where?" Beatriz cried in fear. "Where are you taking us?"

"I need answers to my questions," Don Francisco snarled. "And it seems the both of you need more incentive to tell me what I want to know." He turned to the guards. "Take her. We will see how a few questions asked in the torture chambers might loosen their tongues."

Beatriz cried out as the guards grasped her roughly and dragged her from the room. Don Francisco and a shaken Elana followed.

"Can we get to the torture chambers by these passages?" Reeve questioned softly.

"Yes."

"Let's go. We must get there quickly, and we must find a way to help them."

They ran down the passageway, Rodrigo in the lead and Reeve following as quickly as he could. Both were praying silently they would be in time, and that they would be able to help when they did arrive.

Juan Ortega was satisfied. He looked about the room Don Francisco had given him. He remembered Don Francisco's praise for what he had done and his promise for better things in Juan's future.

He gazed at the young maid on the bed. She cried softly after his brutal use of her, but he did not care. There would be much money and many more women for him to enjoy.

He had forgotten Carmen completely and was less than interested in the fate of Elana and Beatriz, Reeve and Rodrigo now that he had turned them over to Don Francisco. The only nagging worry that lingered like a shadow in the back of his mind was the possible vengeance of Pedro. This was a man he would fear if they ever again came face to face.

He felt a little safer here in the castle in Madrid and did not harbor any plans for departing the city in the near future. No, he thought, he would spend the rest of his days here in the service of Don Francisco. It would give him all he had ever wanted: money, drink, and women. He walked to the bed and gripped the trembling young girl by the arm and dragged her from the bed.

Of course, she had been given to him by Don Francisco as part of his reward. She had been a pleasure to master and to use, and he knew he was going to find much more pleasure in her before he tossed her aside for another.

She was still weeping, and dark bruises had begun to appear on her soft, sensitive skin. She was quite young, no more than fifteen, and had been a virgin, which had pleased him even more.

Holding her with one hand, he slapped her sharply across the face. "Cease your tears as I will give you more to cry about. Do not bother to dress, but go into the next room and get me some wine."

He watched her slim figure move across the room. Her dark hair fell tangled about her and he could still feel the softness of her beneath him. He would enjoy her again soon for he could always feel the heat in his loins at the sight of such helpless beauty. It seemed as if her helplessness made him stronger.

She walked slowly into the next room and he could hear her moving about. The soft tinkle of glass and the liquid sound of pouring wine.

He sat in a chair, propped his feet up before him, and closed his eyes for a minute. He could hear the girl moving about the room but kept his eyes closed. He would renew his strength, then he would take her again. The thought pleased him and he smiled.

She set the tray down on the table beside him, then he could hear her move about, picking up the clothes he had brutally torn from her. He must have dozed for several minutes when something solid settled itself in his lap; at the same time something sharp pricked the skin of his cheek. He opened his eyes and the smile on his lips faded as he looked into the grim eyes of death.

"You! No! No!" But they were the last words he was ever to speak. The sharp blade sliced the jugular neatly and in moments, his wide, sightless eyes stared at eternity before him.

She moved about, doing to Juan what she had promised herself would be done. Then she crossed into the outer room and looked at the girl Juan had abused so badly.

The girl stared in shocked silence at the dark, veiled form. She had seen what had been done to the man who had raped her and had not been sorry. She was only shocked at the strange woman's brutality and the soft easy smile that was now on her face.

Jenette had been a young maid in the castle for two years and had not known Don Francisco's eyes had been upon her. She had been forced to go with Juan and had been terrorized into submission. Now she watched the strange dark woman as she handed her a bag of coins.

"Go and dress. Then report the death of this one. Then take this money and leave the castle. Go to your home and make a new life for yourself, but unless Don Francisco is dead, never return."

"Yes . . . oh, thank you. May the good Lord bless and forgive you."

"I no longer care. I did what he justly deserved," the woman's voice said quietly. "Now go, for I have more revenge to seek."

The girl nodded, ran to gather her clothes, dressed, and left the room. The woman turned to gaze for a moment at Juan. She had done much to him and hoped those who saw would remember.

Quietly, she crossed the room, pressed her hand against a well-hidden spring, and the silent panel slid open. A moment later, it closed behind her soft laughter.

The girl had called the guards and told them that she had been sent to clean the room and had found Juan dead.

Their faces paled at the sight that sat before them. Later they were to spread the story.

He had sat in the chair and someone had cut his throat, but that was not all. He had been ruthlessly castrated, and the word revenge had been carved across his chest.

All of them wondered what crime he could have committed against anyone that would bring down such revenge upon him. No one but the dark, shrouded form that walked the secret passageways knew the answer, and she was too intent on her plans to give the death of Juan another thought.

Later that night, the young maid slipped from the castle and disappeared so that if any further questions about the death of Juan Ortega were to be asked, there would be no one around to answer them.

Chapter Twenty-Seven

Catrina gazed about her in absolute horror. The cell-like room with its cold stone walls had an aura of death. She turned to face Don Carlos, her chin in the air and pride in her eyes.

"If you mean to frighten me, it will do you good. And if you mean to torture me into submission, you are wasting your time. No matter what you do, my love for Rafael will remain. He knows and understands that and he will have faith in that, no matter what."

Don Carlos laughed. With a very gentle hand, he reached to caress her. She pushed his hand away. "Torture you?" He chuckled. "No, my sweet, I have no intention of torturing you. You will, as I have told you before, come to me of your own free will. I do not want you damaged in any way. To mar that beautiful skin would be unthinkable. No, when your husband witnesses your surrender, I want you to be beautiful and unflawed. I want to enjoy you and I want him to again see the beauty he will never have."

"I will never betray Rafael, he knows that. He knows what you are trying to do and he will not let you succeed."

Don Carlos chuckled. "So . . . he knows. Just what, my beauty, does he think he knows?"

"That you want to break his will through me. You will not succeed, Don Carlos. Rafael knows my heart as I do. He knows my love, and he knows no matter what you say, that I will never betray him."

"What do you understand of betrayal? Rafael knows, as I do, that to everything there is a price. I will find out what the price of your betrayal is. Then," he replied in a cold voice, "I will pay that price and destroy him utterly as he tried to destroy—"

"You," she said softly, her eyes wide and searching. "I don't believe you. Rafael is a strong and honest man. He could have done nothing to deserve this."

Don Carlos's eyes held no sign of any emotion. They were ebony eyes, without feeling, without tenderness or care. She could not read them and so did not know or understand the turbulent emotions that seethed within him. His eyes held hers, denying her any entrance into his mind, and for a long breathless moment, they fought a silent battle. It only ceased when a door on the opposite side of the room opened.

Two men dragging another entered the room from the far end. They dragged the helpless man to the center of the room. As they grew nearer, Catrina had to gasp in shock at his physical condition.

Quick orders from Don Carlos and the man was bound by two ropes that hung from the ceiling, his arms stretched tautly over his head. His head hung listlessly forward, and Catrina could hear a groan from his swollen, cracked lips.

Catrina resisted, but Don Carlos drew her relentlessly forward until she stood inches from the man. He had been dreadfully and methodically tortured. Welts and burns covered much of his nearly naked body. He had been beaten unmercifully.

Catrina spun about and faced Don Carlos, her eyes filled with rage. "This is unbelievable! What has he done to merit such treatment?"

Don Carlos smiled as if he were being patient with a wayward child. "He has tried to remain silent when I needed answers to questions. He has finally seen fit to answer me now. And I shall reward him by not letting him die. You see," he added softly, "his life is in my hands as is yours, and your obstinate husband and his father. Tell me," he tormented, "shall I have him punished a little more so that you can see?"

"No!" she gasped raggedly. She covered her face with her hands and turned away. She did not see Don Carlos silently motion for the man to be taken away. Tears fell, streaking her cheeks. Rafael had told her they must remain silent until the ship had time to rescue Reeve, but could she? If Rafael or her father-in-law were tortured in front of her eyes, could she keep silent?

Don Carlos gazed at her, an open hunger on his face he was not aware of. A thought touched his mind that startled him. He wanted her and he did not want her for a night. He wanted her to stay with him. Despite his control, the jealousy he had always felt for Rafael bubbled inside. Always Rafael had been able to possess what he wanted . . . the thought twisted within. How? How could he keep this one and have her willing? Once the thought entered his mind, he began to search for plans to fulfill his desires.

Don Carlos knew he was more than an expert with the seduction of women. Could he subdue her? Could he make her surrender to him? He enjoyed the thought of the challenge. He would not use brute force on her, but he would bring her to her knees and through her, he would do Rafael the most harm possible. He would make his beloved wife turn from him and leave him empty and alone as Don Carlos had been so long ago.

He reached out to gently slide his hand down the length of her silken hair. She seemed lost in her pain and fear and unaware of his touch until she felt his hand on the curve of her waist drawing her close to him. She stiffened and turned to face him.

She was a vision of distressed beauty, and the hunger for her swelled to a tidal wave within him.

"Come with me," he said firmly. "There is a story you should know. Maybe then you will realize your husband is not the paragon you might think. He, too, has had his vicious, yes, even animalistic times. You then might be a little more understanding of the agony others have felt. Come." He took hold of her arm and guided her back to the door through which they had come and back to the room that was her prison. There she turned to face him again and he prepared to attack her fortress of strength with all the resources he had.

Rafael and his father had been silent for some time, each contemplating the situation and what they could possibly do or say to find a way out of it. The most important thing in Rafael's mind was Catrina and her well-being. Who but he knew the devious twisted mind of the man who held them prisoner? Who but he knew just how effective Don Carlos could be? And who but he knew the answers to the questions that would be in Catrina's mind once Don Carlos was finished with her?

He knew Catrina's sheltered innocence and he knew the finesse in which Don Carlos could take the sharpest mind and twist it until it knew only what he wanted it to know.

"Rafael?"

Rafael was startled back to the moment by the soft question. "Yes, Father?"

"I think I know what you are thinking."

Rafael sighed deeply, rose, and walked to the iron bars that held them prisoner. "I'm sorry, Father, but I cannot help my thoughts." He turned to face him. "There is so much hatred between us. I have tried to stay away from him and have succeeded for so many years. Why did his evil head have to rise up now? Why at such a time when we had so many problems to begin with?"

His father rose and walked to him. For a moment, he gazed at Rafael's broad back, then he reached to place a consoling hand on his son's shoulder. "I am sorry, Rafael, truly sorry for all the pain you have been through. I am sorry, also, that we have drawn Catrina into this. We must fight our battle here. At least we have one consolation. Reeve and the others will be boarding that ship in another day or so. They will be safe. Maybe if you then answer his questions, he will let us go."

Rafael laughed harshly and turned to face his father. "Do you actually believe that?"

"No . . . no, I suppose I don't."

"Father," Rafael said softly, "for the first time in my life, I'm afraid . . . I'm truly afraid. It . . . it's not for me. I know him, you know him . . . but Catrina does not. Yes, Reeve and the others will be safe. You and I can face whatever he might do . . . but . . . I don't think Catrina can."

"Why in God's name would he harm her?"

"To punish me."

"He is only threatening her to make you afraid. He would not truly harm her. It is a bluff."

"God, I wish I could believe that," Rafael replied softly. "But you and I . . . we remember too well, don't we, Father?"

Don Diego remained silent as he slowly returned to his seat and lowered himself into it as if he were suddenly very, very weary. "Yes, Rafael, we know him too well."

"And in our hearts, we know what he will do. Slowly . . . slowly, she will not know it, he will twist her thoughts until she does not know what to believe. And he will not let me near her again to tell her what is true and what is not."

"Do you doubt her love?"

"No, not for a moment."

"Then, she will not believe him no matter what he says. She will be stronger than he believes. I believe that she will win this battle, and I believe so because I have seen the love she has for you. It is a wall against which all his gentle battering will not be able to see a crack. He will fail, and it will be a defeat that will forever put him from your life."

"And all I can do," Rafael said, "is to stand here and pray you are right. All I can do is send my love to her in my thoughts and hope that is enough to keep her safe."

"All his evil cannot touch the love she has for you. It is a force such as he has never met before. It is a force, my son, against which he has no defense."

Rafael turned to gaze at his father. "I hope you're right, Father. I hope you are right, for my life depends on it. Catrina is my life. If I were to lose her, there would be no use to anything . . . anything at all."

"What is it that you have to tell me?" Catrina demanded of Don Carlos.

"There is much I have to tell you. Much you do not know."

"About Rafael? Then I do not want to hear your stories. I know my husband as you and no others know him, and I will not believe anything you have to say against him."

"Will you not?" he said softly. "Let me ask you, do you think you have the ability to open your mind and face a truth honestly or will you blind yourself and deny it, even if it is before you?"

"I know the truth of Rafael. It is in his love for me."

"I would ask you to come with me."

"Where?"

"To another room not far from here. There is something I would like you to see." He held the door open and gazed at her with dark eyes that held challenge. Without a word, she walked from the room, and he pulled the door closed behind them. Then he walked down a long hall with Catrina walking silently at his side.

At the far end of the hall, he stopped in front of another door which he opened. He waited for her to follow him inside.

Once inside, she surveyed the room which was lit only by the glow of a fire in a large fireplace. Don Carlos lit candles without a word, then turned to watch her face as the room was bathed in light.

It was a warm, masculine, and very attractive room, but that was not what held Catrina's stunned attention. It was a huge portrait that hung over the fireplace and the two smaller ones that hung on either side of it.

She turned her shocked gaze to Don Carlos who was also looking at the portrait. It was of a very beautiful woman, in fact, one of the most beautiful she had ever seen. It was when she realized the identities of the two smaller portraits that she questioned him.

"It's . . . one of them is Rafael."

"Yes, you are right."

"And . . . the other is you."

"Again, you are right. Of course, the portraits are almost ten years old. We were both much younger then."

"But the woman."

Don Carlos's eyes focused on the picture of the woman, and again Catrina could not read any sign of emotion in their ebony depths. He spoke softly, almost as if she were not present in the room.

"She . . . is our mother."

"Your . . . Rafael and you . . . she is . . ."

"She is our mother. You see, Rafael and I are brothers. Now, will you listen to the story your husband neglected to tell you? Will you listen and understand?"

Slowly, Catrina sank into a chair. Her legs were so weak they could no longer hold her erect. "Yes," she whispered softly, for in her heart she knew the words he had just spoken were true. Now she knew why Don Carlos had looked so familiar to her. The three portraits were obviously of a very beautiful mother and her two sons. "You . . . you do not have the same name," she said helplessly.

"No, we do not. He is a Chavez," Don Carlos replied coldly. "The great Chavez family, the untouchable, the brilliant, the—"

"But I don't understand. How can you hate your own brother so. It . . . it is unnatural."

"In most circumstances it would be. Not this one. I shall tell you and you can judge for yourself. All people are made up of many facets. You should know them all before you hate or love them."

"Don Carlos, I will never change my love for Rafael. I have loved him always, and I always shall. The only thing you could provide would be my understanding how you feel. But no matter what injustices have been done to you, you are wrong in trying to punish your own brother. What does it make of you?"

"Rafael and I have crossed swords before," Don Carlos said gently. "We fought over another woman. A woman like you who did not know. This time I would explain to you why we must one day, one of us must destroy the other."

"Another woman?"

"Your husband has been very . . . casual with the women he has loved and discarded."

"I don't believe you."

"Even the woman who bore his child," Don Carlos replied in a soft, even voice.

Catrina was stunned. She sat gazing at Don Carlos. Her face had gone pale and her wide eyes dominated it. "I . . . I don't believe you."

"No, of course you don't. You would not understand why I

have done what I have done, but I have proof to show you. Now, I will tell you a story. Then you will see that I have cause to do what I am doing and to feel the way I feel."

"Don Carlos, what are you going to do to us?"

"I have been asked by Don Francisco to return you to him."

"Both of us?"

He smiled. "I have been asked for both of you, but I'm sure he would not mind if your husband were . . . unable to go."

Now that she observed him more closely, she could see why the familiarity had touched her so. He did look much like Rafael. He was very handsome, yet there was something she could not put her finger on. Some subtle difference between them that was more than appearance. A harder more angry look about the eyes, a tightness in the mouth that she knew was a part of Don Carlos but not in Rafael.

"Do you know what he has planned? He will give us to the Inquisition. He will confiscate all of Rafael's possessions."

"I would wipe the Chavez name from society for all time. As for you," he said with a shrug, "I stand between you and any harm at the moment. Maybe I shall continue to do so."

"You do not really believe I would let you do to Rafael what you plan to do, then choose to stay with you? I have told you, Don Carlos, there is nothing you can say that will change in any way my faith in my husband. I love him, and he loves me. Of that I am always sure."

"Then sit down, my dear, while I tell you things you should know."

Catrina sat slowly down. From where she sat she could clearly see the portraits above her and Don Carlos who stood nearby. It gave her a strange feeling to know there were things dark and secret in Rafael's family . . . things he had chosen not to tell her.

"I would tell you of a woman named Consuelo. She was very

371

beautiful, so beautiful that she attracted the eye of many handsome men. But her father had his eye on a man of consequence, a man with a great deal of money and position.

"Consuelo fell in love with another man. She loved him completely and they tried to run away together when they found she had been promised to another. But they were caught. Consuelo was taken back to her family to carry out her duties and the man who loved her so desperately was beaten and left to find his own way home. He very nearly died doing so.

"Consuelo was married to the man of her family's choice, and she was miserably unhappy. The man who really loved her was watched carefully that he did not approach her again. But their love was a thing that neither could destroy. Eventually, they found a way to meet. Oh, their love was a beautiful thing. But they were careless. Consuelo found she was carrying her lover's child. She knew her husband would send her away in disgrace and most likely kill the man she loved. So she deliberately seduced him, allowing him to believe he was the father of her child.

"The child was born, and he would have been heir to . . . to all. But it was not to be. He was five when disaster struck. Consuelo was again pregnant, this time with her husband's child. When Consuelo and her lover exchanged letters, they were found.

"Her husband faced her with the truth and he forced her to reveal that the first son was another's. Despite all he threatened, she stood fast to the claim that she had not seen her lover for a long time and that the child she was carrying was truly his. The man loved her and believed her. But from that day forward he could not even look at the first son again. He turned from him and left him abandoned, cold and alone. The second son was born and became the child of the man's heart.

He was given everything and was loved.

"Then when the first son, neglected and filled with despair, tried to find his place in the family by claiming his rights, he was forced to leave the only home he had known. He was returned to the father he had never known, and who did not want him because he resembled so closely the woman he loved and could never have.

"It was a life of grief and deep despair. It seemed no one wanted him, no one, and he searched in desperation for love— love in any form.

"The two half-brothers would see each other occasionally, but their worlds were far apart. The second one knew he had all the world had to offer, and he became arrogant and proud, and he made his position clear to the son who could never find a place of security in his world.

"The eldest was twenty-five and the younger, twenty when the second tragedy struck them."

"You and Rafael," Catrina whispered.

"Yes, me . . . and Rafael."

"You spoke of tragedy."

"Yes, the tragedy was the arrival into our lives of Maria Cordova. She was to ignite the flame of love and desire in the breasts of both men.

"Rafael was well used to getting anything he could desire to have, while I . . . I suppose I could never quite believe that Maria loved me. I was not used to love. I did not understand it, no, I did not believe it.

"We were both young, wild, and hot-headed and prepared to fight for what we wanted. Especially me, who had never known love at all.

"We both courted her, and begged her to decide which of us she wanted. Rafael could not believe she chose me. He would not give up. He felt, if he possessed her, she would change her

373

choice so he deliberately seduced her. He came to her later in the night when he knew her parents were away. With wine, sweet words, and lies upon lies, he seduced her. Then he left her. He was well pleased. He had possessed the only woman who had ever refused him and he had beaten me again.

"She came to me, confessing in tears of anguish for she had found herself with child."

Don Carlos could hear the soft muffled sound from Catrina, both of disbelief and of fear and pain. "When I told her I would marry her anyway, she was filled with shame. She could not do what my own mother had done. She could not face bearing a child who belonged to another man. One night, one very beautiful star-touched night, she took her life." Don Carlos's voice died to an anguished whisper, and for several moments silence reigned.

The atmosphere had been deliberately set by Don Carlos. The story had been told by a master storyteller. The effect was nearly cataclysmic.

Catrina fought any thought of believing what this man said. "Rafael is not the kind of man you are trying to make me believe. He would not do the things you say he has done."

"No? Well then, look at these." Don Carlos went to a small chest that sat on a nearby table. From it he took a packet. These he handed to Catrina. Then he sat in a chair near the fire and remained silent.

Catrina looked at the packet of papers, and for one terrified moment she was afraid to open them. Then, as if it were some denial of Rafael to be so afraid, she lifted the packet. It contained several legal documents and at least ten letters. She opened the first letter and began to read.

Time moved slowly by and still no sound could be heard. Don Carlos sat gazing at the low burning fire as if he were alone in the room. He did not even look at Catrina.

Catrina sat deathly still. Her face was pale and tears streaked her face. Then, after over an hour, she folded the last paper and laid it in her lap. Then she lifted her gaze to Don Carlos.

Rafael paced the floor like a caged animal. His father sat in silence and watched his son's wordless anguish.

For Rafael, it was very nearly unbearable. All the thoughts in his mind centered on Catrina. Where was she? What was she doing? Had he harmed her in any way? What did he plan to do to her? Would he be able to see her, talk to her, hold her again? It was a raging battle that tormented him.

"My son, you are doing exactly what he wants you to do. You must control yourself until you know what is happening."

"If he were just man enough to face me!" Rafael said angrily. "I would fight him again as I have fought him before."

"He is not that kind of man and you know it."

"Catrina," Rafael said softly. "Catrina."

"She is here in spirit, Rafael. You two fight the greatest battle you have ever known, but you will both prevail."

"Damn him to hell! If I ever have the opportunity again, I will not be soft and merciful as I was before. If he has harmed her in any way, I will find some way to kill him if I have to do it with my bare hands."

"Control yourself, Rafael. No matter what the situation, he will come here again just to gloat over us. You know that he will not force her. That is no triumph over you. He will try to sway her will, and I for one do not think he will succeed."

"Catrina is so gentle, so innocent. She has never faced a man such as he. Father, she does not know such evil, how can she fight it?"

"She will fight it with just such weapons. Innocence, gentleness, and her love for you. If she has never met such evil, he has never met such goodness and faith. That faith will defeat him."

Rafael remained silent now. All his thoughts were on Catrina. It was as if he felt he could somehow transfer all his strength and will to her.

Neither could sleep as the night grew longer, and they were still awake and waiting when the first gray light of dawn touched the sky. For Rafael it was severe agony as he wondered just how Catrina had been forced to spend the night.

Chapter Twenty-Eight

Catrina laid the papers in her lap and contemplated the man who sat gazing at the fire. Carlos was well aware of her gaze and consummate actor that he was, assumed a look of pain and grief.

The packet had contained several letters between Consuelo and Manuel. In them Consuelo had told Manuel that she was carrying his child. In them she also said that she would go with him should he return to claim his son.

Besides the letters, there was the marriage certificate for Consuelo and Diego and with these certificates of the birth of two sons, Carlos and Rafael. On the birth certificate for Carlos, the last name, Chavez, had been crossed out, as if someone had done it in anger and the name Manrique had been added.

The most damaging thing in the entire package was a note, obviously written by a woman in deep distress. If what Carlos said was true, it was written by Maria after Rafael had seduced then abandoned her . . . *if* what Carlos said was true. The note was not long but it was filled with pain.

My dear love:
I call you my dear love, but I have no right to do so. I know you have asked me to be your wife and for your precious love and forgiveness I am grateful. But I cannot

377

come to you soiled with such a sin. You are too good to be held to such a thing.

I would set you free, my heart, free to find a woman worthy of your love as I am not.

I will leave this life and take with me all evidence of the terrible thing we have done to you.

Please, only remember me with love . . . for a time, then let that time pass away and find a life and a love that can fill your world as it deserves.

Good by my love.

Maria

It was the last thing that Catrina read and she could feel the agony within it. Maria, so Carlos said, had taken her life along with the child that would have been Rafael's. Catrina thought back over the years since she had met Rafael. She had been about nine and Rafael was already fourteen. They had been inseparable from the moment Rafael had taken pity on her loneliness, since they had just arrived in the area, and he began to teach her to first ride, then to cope with her world. She had begun to love him at nine and her devotion had grown from that day.

But, she had not known what his life was like before she was nine or for the years he had gone away to school. There were also years of which he had never spoken, and she had never asked. She could not believe what Carlos said. She would not believe, yet she wanted desperately the solace of Rafael's arms and the assurance that he loved her and all of Carlos's stories were lies.

If they were brothers and he had been coldly pushed from the love of a family, then some of his story must be the truth. The three portraits spoke eloquently, for no one seeing them would deny they were all three of one blood.

But just how far did the thread of truth go in his words? How much was fact and how much the fantasy of a twisted mind?

Catrina knew of one thing with all the certainty of her life: She would not succumb to the influence of what he said, but she would seek the answers from him if only for her own peace of mind and justification of her faith.

Carlos suddenly seemed to remember just where he was. He turned from the fire and rose from his chair.

Catrina handed the packet of papers to him but he shook his head negatively. "No, take them with you. Think about what I have said. Maybe," he said gently, "I have been too harsh in my search for revenge, but you may understand a little of the reason for my attitude."

"Even if I said I understood your pain at the treatment you . . . might have had as a child, I cannot believe what you say about Rafael." Her eyes held his proudly. "I love him . . . I shall always love him, and, if the worst were to happen, if you have told me the truth, I will still love him and I will forgive him."

Carlos watched her and he knew that somewhere deep within, Catrina was shaken. He was satisfied for the moment. He would develop his plans and work against her stubborn reserve of strength. In the end, he thought, he would change her. He would seduce her, and when he was finished with her, he would make sure that Rafael would know exactly what he had done. He already knew Rafael would know why he had done it.

"Come," he said. "You will return to your room. Take the letters with you. You may want to read them again." He was even more pleased with his subtle campaign when she did keep the packet. Without a word, she walked ahead of him to the room in which she had first been locked. She stepped inside and he said a soft "good night" and left her alone before she could answer. She stood quietly and heard the key turn in the lock.

Absently, she held the packet of papers close to her heart. "It's not true, Rafael . . . it's not true. I shall never believe. I love you, Rafael. I love you."

Tears she had refused to let Carlos see fell unnoticed now. Catrina went to the bed and lay down on it with her eyes closed. Still the damnable papers were in her hand.

Carlos returned to his room quite satisfied. He had planted the seed of doubt, and he intended to build upon it until he had destroyed her will and her love for Rafael.

A light rap sounded on his door and at his command, a man entered.

"Yes?"

"There is a messenger here, Don Carlos. He says he has ridden long and hard with an urgent message from Don Francisco."

"Send him to me."

"Yes, Don Carlos."

The man left quickly and in less than twenty minutes he returned, accompanied by a man who was dirty and looked completely exhausted.

"You have a message for me?"

"Yes, Don Carlos, Don Francisco has asked that you send the prisoners to him. It is very urgent that he have Rafael Chavez at once. He said it is of the utmost importance that Chavez is needed to induce another to answer his questions."

Don Carlos frowned deeply. He did not care if Rafael were to be returned, but he had no intention of letting Catrina go quite so easily. She was the kind of challenge he enjoyed, sweet and innocent, with a will of iron. He wanted to break her almost as badly as he wanted to see Rafael die.

"Thank you. Go and get some food and rest. I will take care of everything." The man nodded. He was exhausted and would enjoy some food and rest. It did not occur to him that Carlos had no intention of sending both Catrina and Rafael. He turned and left the room and for some time, Carlos remained quietly thinking. Then he rose.

Taking two guards with him, he walked down to the cell in which Rafael and his father were held.

Sleep was a complete impossibility. Rafael could not close his eyes, for if he did, visions appeared that left him trembling and sweating. He had no words left that would give voice to the misery he felt. He would have given his soul just to see Catrina, just to hear her say his name and to know that she was all right.

His father slept from exhaustion. Rafael had insisted he lie down. The stress of the situation had been almost more than the elder Chavez could bear. For some time he had tried to sleep, but had again risen from the hard stone slab that served as a bed to quietly pace the floor and to pray.

He heard the sound of footsteps and turned to face the door as it was unlocked and pushed open. Don Carlos and the two guards entered. The two, Rafael and Carlos, gazed at each other for several minutes in silence, then Carlos smiled.

"So," he said softly, "you find it difficult to sleep. That is a shame. Your woman does not. I have just left her and she is sleeping like a . . . a satisfied woman should sleep."

Rage filled Rafael at Carlos's blatant remarks. "If you think for a moment that I believe a word you say then you are a fool. I above all know you for the liar you are."

"Well," Don Carlos said with a laugh, "I will not waste my time here arguing with you when I prefer to be with her. Besides, you are leaving us."

"Leaving? Where? Why?" For a second Rafael was terrified. "I am not leaving here without Catrina."

Don Carlos laughed. "Do you think you have been asked for

your choice? Don Francisco requested that I send you to him immediately. I intend to do just that. Besides," he said, his smile viciously triumphant, "I do not need either of you at the moment. I am enjoying all the Chavez family I need. When you are returned to me . . . well, I will be here to show you just how it feels to be betrayed."

"Betrayed!" Rafael said. "You of all people can stand there and speak of betrayal to me?"

"But of course I can," Carlos said softly. "After all, I have just spent several hours speaking of betrayal to your wife. She is a very understanding person. She believed everything I said . . . everything."

Rafael's face grew pale and he gazed at Carlos in complete disbelief. "You . . . you told her the truth?"

"Well . . . with a few minor changes."

"What are you talking about, Carlos? For once in your miserable life, tell me the truth!"

"But Rafael, I told her the entire story. I showed her the portrait of a woman and her two sons. I told her of love, of hatred, of betrayal. Oh, the only liberty I did take," he said, chuckling, "was to change the names about. Your name and mine. It was a terrible blow to her to find out your true nature and to learn about what you did to Maria."

"Maria," Rafael said softly. "You made her believe that—"

"That you were responsible? Oh yes . . . yes. I gave her all the proof she needs. Even the last letter Maria wrote."

"Before she killed herself and your baby! Your baby, you bastard! I would have married her, but she felt she was not good enough, that she would dishonor the Chavez name. The only dishonor to the Chavez name was what you brought to it. Father was right in letting you go when you wanted to return to your own father. Why did you even come back?"

"Because I lost all his wealth and because he turned ugly and mean. We had the same mother and yet your father refused me."

"You refused him first. He would have shared everything with the two of us, but you, you wanted everything. You wanted to be a Manrique! You are one. You are not a Chavez. It was your choice!"

"Well," Carlos said softly, "now your wife believes it was you that was responsible for Maria's death. But don't worry, Rafael, I will console her while Don Francisco helps me to regain all I lost. You see, once you and your father are gone, I am the only heir to the Chavez wealth. I will have that and I will let your wife pay the price for all you have done to me."

Rafael, pressed beyond any normal thought, leapt at Don Carlos. He knew he meant to kill him. But he did not succeed. The guards pulled him away. He was panting and fighting the men who held him.

The sudden stir wakened Don Diego, who rose only to find a pistol leveled at his son's heart. But it only took him a moment to put the pieces of the puzzle together. He knew Carlos too well.

"What evil are you doing, Carlos?" he asked wearily.

"Sending you back to Madrid. Back to the waiting arms of Don Francisco." Carlos turned to the guards. "Bind them and take them to Madrid. Turn them over to Don Francisco, no one else. We would prefer if no one else knew of this transaction. Go carefully and make sure they do not escape. If they should try to, kill them."

Rafael and his father were quickly bound and dragged from their cells to the stable where they were put upon horses. Rafael could only gaze helplessly at the receding hacienda as they rode away.

* * *

383

The day dawned bright and clear. Catrina rose from the bed feeling weary and emotionally drained. She walked to the window and drew aside the heavy drapes to be met by iron-barred windows. Before she could do anything else, the door was unlocked, Two men entered carrying a tub of water. Behind them appeared a woman a little above middle age. Over her arm she carried a gown. It was white with small violet flowers. Laying it across the bed, she locked the door after the two men and turned back to Catrina.

"Don Carlos would like you to bathe and dress. I will dress your hair and he will join you here for breakfast in an hour."

Catrina knew it be to no avail to resist, and she felt the need of a bath and clean clothes. She was determined to face Don Carlos on his own ground. She meant to fight both for Rafael's honor and for her own sake, for she had cleared her thoughts and had faced what she thought Don Carlos had planned for her.

She discarded her clothes and stepped into the tub. Despite her situation, she enjoyed the steaming, scented water. She was surprised that the dress fit her as if it had been made for her.

Sitting at a low table, she remained still while the woman brushed out her hair and braided it in a thick long braid and wrapped it about her head in a shining coronet.

"La Senorita is very beautiful," the woman said.

"Thank you."

"Is there anything else I can get for you?"

"My freedom," Catrina said softly.

"That is not in my power, Senorita."

"I know." Catrina smiled. "I'm sorry. You have been very kind. Thank you very much."

The woman bowed slightly and went to the door. She unlocked it, left, and Catrina once again heard the click of the key of her comfortable prison.

Again she rose and went to the window. She stood looking at the sky. A sharp click, the closing of the door, and she did not have to turn around to know Don Carlos was there.

"How very lovely you are," he spoke softly. Catrina turned to face him. He stood holding a large tray which he placed on a table. "Come, you must share breakfast with me. I detest eating alone. The food is quite good."

He motioned her to sit opposite him. For now, she would do as he said for above all, she wanted some word of Rafael. Where and how he was.

He filled a plate and set it before her, then filled one for himself. "Did you sleep well?"

"Did you expect me to? After all of the terrible things you told me, did you really expect me to just go to bed and sleep as if nothing had happened? You have done much to destroy my life."

"No, not to destroy your life. Just to let you know the truth about the man you married. He has lied to you. He is not what you think he is."

"Let me go, Carlos," she said softly. Their eyes met and again she found it impossible to read them. It was then that another truth came clear to her, and it was then she realized what she would believe for all time. Rafael's eyes had always been unshuttered, clear, and open to her. No, her heart said, Don Carlos had lied, and now she wanted to find out what that lie really was.

"No, my dear, I cannot do that. Despite how much charm you hold for me, I must do something to undo the terrible wrong your husband has done. He has cheated me of my life. There must be some repayment."

"Then, please Carlos, let me see Rafael. Let him at least defend himself. Does he not have a right to that?"

"No, he does not. He never gave that right to me nor did he give it to Maria. He caused her death as surely as if he had killed

385

her with his own two hands."

"I don't believe Rafael is capable of that."

"You read the letters."

"Yes."

"And still you don't believe?"

"No, I do not. I do not think I ever shall unless Rafael were to say it to me himself."

Carlos admired her for her defiance of all that seemed so clearly true. Some long dead thing stirred to life within him. Catrina watched with wide eyes as he slowly rose from the chair and walked around the table toward her.

The guards pushed Rafael and his father relentlessly, and by the time they stopped, both men were exhausted. Having their hands bound and tied to the pommels of their saddles made them even more uncomfortable. Rafael could not think of his own discomfort, for his mind was filled with thoughts of Catrina. She stood alone against Carlos . . . alone. He closed his eyes and nearly groaned with the visions the thought brought. Catrina . . . gentle and sensitive Catrina. Could she withstand the expert maneuvering of a man as clever and convincing as Don Carlos? He desperately needed to find a way to escape his captors and get back to Catrina. But it was not that easy. The guards, knowing the severity of Don Carlos's rage, were extremely careful not to leave themselves open to the escape of their prisoners.

A sleepless night, another day of anguished travel. Another night, another day and Rafael's desperation grew and grew until he could hardly bear it.

It was their fifth day of travel and Rafael knew they were not too far from Madrid and whatever fate awaited them there. They camped again and as they sat at the campfire one of the guards spoke to Rafael.

"We will reach Madrid tomorrow."

"I know well just where we are and what we face," Rafael replied coldly.

The guard had felt some touch of pity for a man who had to face the threat of Don Francisco. "Senor Chavez," he said quietly, "I regret having to be a part of taking men such as you and your father to such a fate. If it were possible to do anything else, I would do it."

"I'm sorry. I did not mean to speak so."

"I can understand how you feel," the guard said.

"No, you cannot understand." Rafael laughed harshly. "We have a long night ahead of us and since I cannot sleep, maybe you would not mind listening to a story."

"Yes, I would."

Rafael told him the entire story from the illegitimate birth of Carlos to Rafael's and Catrina's capture. He told of the situation with Reeve and Elana.

"I am sorry for your friends and for your woman. But I have no choice. If I do not take you to Madrid, it would be my life that would be forfeited."

Before Rafael could answer, a muffled sound came from the darkened area where the second guard had been keeping the first watch. The sound of a scuffle then a solid thud.

The guard next to Rafael began to rise to his feet. Again a soft swish of sound and another thud and the second guard stared at the knife that had struck him. Then slowly he sagged to the ground, dead at Rafael's feet.

Rafael and his father gazed in shock as a form stepped out of the darkness into the light of the fire.

Chapter Twenty-Nine

The door to the torture chamber was pushed open. Beatriz and Elana were dragged within by the guards, followed by Don Francisco.

The torture chamber was a large square room that looked as if it had been hewn from solid rock. Within the room were many instruments of torture. Terrible instruments devised by twisted minds to inflict more pain and punishment than the human body or mind could stand.

Two short stone pillars stood near one wall. They were about two and a half feet high, and on the flat top of each was embedded a huge iron ring. From the ring two short lengths of chain ended in larger rings.

Elana and Beatriz were each taken to one of the pillars. The rings at the ends of the chains were fastened to their wrists. They were very effectively bound to the stone pillars and there was no hope that they would be able to free themselves from the heavy chains, no matter how they struggled to do so.

Both women were utterly terrified, for stories of the terrible things done within these walls had been coming to their ears for many years. Both of them had long since heard stories of strong men whose wills had been broken here. Yet neither woman wept or begged for mercy. Elana turned defiant eyes toward Don Francisco.

"You may do to me what you will, kill me if you choose, but I do not have the answers you seek."

Again Don Francisco chuckled as he walked to her. He stood close and it was impossible for her to stop him from doing anything he chose to do. They both knew the truth of this. She watched him come, trying to control the terror that rose up within her.

Don Francisco stopped so close that the others could barely hear the words he spoke. He reached out to caress the nape of her neck, drawing his hand slowly forward. Gentle fingers caressed the soft skin above the neck of her gown. His dark eyes burned hungrily down into hers.

"I told you before, I have no intention of marring that lovely skin of yours. But, you will tell me what I want to know. You have a great love for your friend Beatriz. Shall we test it? Shall we see just how much you will allow her to bear?"

"How can you be so monstrous?" she cried. She was very near to tears and knew as well as he that she would not be able to bear watching Beatriz suffer.

"I am not the one being monstrous," he replied with an innocent shrug of his shoulders. "You are the one forcing me to do this. You need only speak and I shall return you both to your rooms."

"And then what will you do?" she questioned, sarcasm heavy in her voice. "Auction Beatriz off to the highest bidder and turn me over to Diego? Do you consider that a choice? I would rather be dead. If I cannot share the rest of my life with Reeve, then I would choose not to speak and you can do what you will."

It was a bluff and Don Francisco could read the fear in her eyes. He smiled, then the smile faded as he reached out and slid both hands into the mass of her dark hair. Relentlessly, he held her head between his hands as he bent his head and ravaged her soft mouth with his.

She could not move because of the chains about her wrists and the hold he had on her body. She was completely helpless and he knew it. The soft appreciative chuckles from Don Francisco's two guards made her shame even greater.

When he released her the rage within her overpowered her. Angrily, she spat in his face, then stars sparkled before her eyes as he struck her. The power of the blow forced her to her knees and she could taste blood in her mouth. She heard Beatriz cry her name as Don Francisco reached down and dragged her to her feet.

"I shall have many wonderful hours taming you." He laughed. "You are a challenge that will become my greatest pleasure." Don Francisco turned to the two guards. "Prepare her!" he ordered as he pointed to Beatriz who gave a low moan as absolute terror seemed to be forced from her. The two guards unlocked her chains and dragged her to face a blank wall. Above her head two more rings were embedded in the wall. Her arms were raised and fastened to these. Beatriz was trembling so badly that she would have fallen had she not been chained to the wall.

Elana watched with horrified eyes, then she turned to Don Francisco. "Let her go . . . please . . . let her go," she whispered.

"No, my dear. I shall give her a small taste of the whip." He grinned. "You must be made to understand. Maybe if you receive a good lesson, you will become aware that I mean exactly what I say."

He nodded to one of the guards. The guard turned back to Beatriz. With one hand he grasped the neckline at the back of her dress and ripped it apart. None too gentle hands stripped the dress from her until it hung about her slender hips. Her long hair fell below her waist, shielding her body.

"Move her hair away," Don Francisco ordered. "I do not want Lady Elana to miss the view. The touch of the whip to such

391

soft tender skin is an interesting sight."

One of the men went to Beatriz who was shivering as if she were caught in a high cold wind and crying softly in despair. She felt there was no hope for her. He separated her hair and pushed it over her shoulders before her. Her slim body was brought clearly into view.

The guard backed away while the second guard picked up a wicked-looking whip from a nearby table. The handle was thick and braided. Five long tails extended from its length by three feet. He stood less than three feet from Beatriz and looked at Don Francisco.

"Two," Don Francisco said softly as his eyes held Elana's. "To begin with," he added.

The guard drew his arm back, prepared to strike.

Reeve and Rodrigo raced down the passageway. The candle had long been forgotten and their eyes were slowly becoming accustomed to the dark. Still Reeve was grateful that Rodrigo knew his way about the passageway for he wasn't too sure of himself.

They did not waste their breath talking to each other. Rodrigo flew and Reeve followed.

They nearly tumbled down the stairs in their haste. Before too long, they were within the walls of the dungeon.

Since the dungeons were divided into separate rooms, to make sure that they were at the right one, Rodrigo placed his eye against the crack that had long ago been cut through the wall. The sight he saw brought a groan of anguish involuntarily from his lips.

Elana, chained to a short pillar with Don Francisco beside her. His beloved Beatriz stripped before the hungry gaze of others. But the worst was the sight of the man who held the whip. His sister and the woman he loved more than his own life were about to be punished for the deeds for which he felt responsible. Guilt and rage filled him. He threw himself at the secret door. Reeve, who sensed what was happening, without seeing, joined him. But both were to be shattered by the shock when the hidden door refused to open. Again and again Rodrigo pressed the spot that was to release the spring. Again and again their combined forces pushed against the door. To no avail. The door absolutely refused to budge an inch.

Reeve and Rodrigo were baffled by the failure of the door to open. "Come on, follow me!" Rodrigo said. He moved from the door and ran further down the passage. Without questions, Reeve was behind him.

The passage ran completely about the dungeon room and Rodrigo knew there was another door. He turned the corner and raced down to the center of the wall. There he again threw himself against the hidden door, and again, the door failed to open.

None of the noise they made with their forced attempt at entry could be heard within the dungeon room, for the very thing that made entry impossible was the reinforcements Don Francisco had made that would make the rooms soundproof. They had blocked the mechanisms of the doors so that they could not move.

"I don't understand," Rodrigo cried. "It has not been many years since Elana and I were here. These doors worked then."

"Maybe something is blocking them," Reeve offered.

"It must be. Reeve! We have to get in there. He is about to whip Beatriz. God! She must be in despair thinking there is no one to help her. We have to get in there!"

"We only have one chance," Reeve said.

"Anything! Anything!"

"We have to go out into the palace and use the hallways. It is the only way down. We will have to be careful, but we can do it."

393

There was no question in Rodrigo's mind. At that moment he would have raced into the fires of hell to reach Beatriz. "Let's go," he exclaimed.

Without another word, they turned to retrace their steps.

The guard's arm rose high and descended rapidly. The whip hissed through the air and fell across Beatriz's back. A scream of pain was torn from her lips as the touch of flame seemed to sear her body. Elana jerked at the scream and tears welled hot in her eyes, blurring her vision as the whip was again lifted high. It descended again with a whistling crack and again Beatriz screamed as hot agony cut through her.

The guard turned to Don Francisco to see if the order to continue would come. He was a sadistic animal of a man, well chosen by Don Francisco for the job he was to perform.

Strips of red welts crossed Beatriz's back; from these little droplets of blood had begun to form and traced red lines down her white skin.

Don Francisco turned his gaze from her to a pain-stricken Elana, whose eyes were frozen on Beatriz. "So, my dear?" he said smugly. "Shall we continue to see how long it takes before she becomes unconscious? I have seen it take hours if the whip is applied properly. I assure you, my sweet, my man is excellent at his job. He knows just how to make someone suffer for a long, long time."

Elana turned stricken eyes to him. She was defeated and he knew it. She could stand whatever he planned to do to her, but she could not bear to see Beatriz suffer so. He smiled in satisfaction and a hatred welled up in Elana so deep and so black that she sobbed with the agony of it.

"What kind of an animal are you?" she gasped raggedly.

"I am a man who gets whatever he desires," Don Francisco answered. "I tried to warn you before, but you are too

394

stubborn. Now, your answer," he demanded coldly.

"I . . . I will do whatever you ask, only let her go. Please, let her go."

"That is very wise, my dear," Don Francisco began. "But I do believe one little lesson is still in order, in case you should decide to change your mind."

"I don't understand," she replied, but fear had already begun to fill her eyes.

"I believe one taste of the whip yourself would make you understand more fully the extent of my power."

"No," Elana breathed softly. But she knew no matter how she felt, he intended to do it; no matter how terrified she felt, she refused to beg him.

"Still too proud, I see," he said. Don Francisco turned and beckoned the man with the whip to approach. "She will have one taste of the whip," he said. Then he turned back to Elana. Their eyes met and held as his hands slowly raised to the neck of her dress. She refused to make a sound as he tore the dress open, slowly and deliberately, his hot, hungry gaze devouring her. The dress was ripped to the waist. His hands caressed her soft skin for a moment, challenging her will, asking her to beg him for mercy. She stood, shame tinging her cheeks, but pride filled her gaze as the men surrounding her gazed upon her with black, naked hunger. Still his hands caressed her, cupping her breast in his hands.

"Oh, I shall enjoy you completely, my sweet. Once I have bent your will to mine, once you understand I am your master, I shall enjoy you," he whispered.

Elana wanted to cry out, but her pride held her. With grim determination, she put her mind on Reeve and the love they had shared.

Don Francisco nodded to the man who stood behind her. She heard the movement, then the hissing sound of the whip, then red violent pain struck. She gasped and arched her body under the agony, and Don Francisco caught her in his arms as she arched against him.

Rodrigo and Reeve had made their way to the palace. Slipping down the halls, they moved quickly but carefully. It was not too long before they came to the last open area that led to the steps down to the dungeons below. They had only to cross it and descend and they would be able to take Don Francisco and the two guards by surprise. They knew with the element of surprise on their side they could defeat the three. Then they would take Elana and Beatriz into the secret passageways and to safety. It was a good plan, but fate did not mean to make it that easy.

Both men drew their swords, swords Reeve had supplied when he had come to rescue Rodrigo. Now they began to move cautiously across the eight feet of room, toward the stairs. They were halfway across when a cool, amused voice stopped them in their tracks.

"You seem to have the nine lives of a cat, Captain Burke. I had thought you dead by now."

They both spun around to be faced by a smiling Diego. There was death in his eyes and a glittering sword in his hand. The door to the stairs was behind them. Reeve never took his eyes from Diego but he spoke quickly to Rodrigo.

"Go quickly. I can hold him here. Get them out if you can."

"Reeve, I cannot leave you."

"Rodrigo, dammit man! Get out of here. If you do not get Elana and Beatriz, they may die under that man's hands. Get to them, get them free."

"But you . . . Reeve, he is an expert with a sword."

"I know," Reeve replied softly. "Go and get Elana free, Rodrigo. That is all I ask."

Rodrigo knew Reeve was choosing to lay down his life for

Elana. He gazed at Reeve with deep respect, then he replied softly. "I shall get her free."

"You will die down there," Diego said with a laugh. "After I have finished with this one we will come to make sure of that."

"Go, Rodrigo," Reeve said quietly. His gaze had never left Diego.

Rodrigo clapped him on the shoulder, a silent word of respect and admiration. Then he spun about and passed through the door to the stairs that led to the dungeon.

Diego and Reeve stood in silence, Diego's eyes filled with challenging amusement and Reeve's filled with wariness. He knew Diego's prowess with a sword and respected it.

Slowly he raised his sword before him and laughed softly. Diego raised his. They touched lightly. The gauntlet was thrown. The battle was begun as they slowly began to circle each other.

Don Francisco held Elana against him, enjoying the promise of what he would enjoy more fully. She quivered in his arms from the force of the blow, then she drew herself away from him and stood erect. Her eyes were filled with the pain of the whip, but they were also filled with several other emotions: anger, disgust, and disdain. For a moment they shook him. But not enough to change his thoughts or his pleasure.

He motioned for one of the men to release Beatriz and the other to unlock the chains that still held Elana.

Rodrigo at that moment reached the bottom of the steps. The huge wooden door that led to the dungeon stood slightly ajar. He knew there would be more than one guard. If he could remember well enough from his quick look, there would be two with Don Francisco. Three men to one. He thought of it but did not allow it to stop him. His fear for Beatriz was too great.

He and Reeve had found a small chamber on their way and

397

confiscated a pistol they had found there. Rodrigo was glad at the moment he had shoved it in his belt. It would be the only thing that would free them.

He drew the pistol from his belt and with a quick, sharp move, he booted the door open. Everyone within was taken completely by surprise. No one more than Don Francisco.

Beatriz and Elana turned hopeful eyes toward the interruption. "Rodrigo!" Beatriz cried.

Don Francisco had drawn his sword from its sheath, but he and both guards knew the pistol was more than an even match. He tried to bluff.

"You can only kill one of us with that pistol, my friend. After that you have only your sword."

"More than enough," Rodrigo replied with a smile. "No matter what happens," he added softly, "It is you I will shoot first. It will give me great pleasure to kill you."

Don Francisco's smile faded as he realized Rodrigo meant what he said. Rodrigo kept the pistol pointed at Don Francisco but he cast a quick look at Beatriz. Then he gave a quick look at Elana.

"Unlock the chains," he snapped at the guards who moved rapidly to do what he ordered. Beatriz seemed to momentarily lose the strength she had, for when the chains were unlocked she sagged to her knees.

When Elana's chains were unlocked she immediately ran to Beatriz's side and helped her. Both women covered themselves as best they could with the remnants of their dresses, but still the white-hot rage could be seen in Rodrigo's eyes at the sight of them.

He wanted to go to Beatriz, take her in his arms and shelter her from any more harm. He could clearly see the blood on her back and the stains as the drops touched her clothes. Beatriz struggled to her feet and, with Elana's help, she moved to Rodrigo's side.

"Oh, Rodrigo," she murmured as she laid her head against his chest. He could feel the heat of her tears against his skin. Don Francisco at that moment saw death as closely as he ever would. It should have been so; Rodrigo should have fired; because he did not, he lost the opportunity because a harsh voice came from behind him.

"Do not move," came the command. Rodrigo froze and his heart almost stopped.

Don Francisco smiled again. He walked toward Rodrigo and took the pistol from his hand. "Too bad, my friend. You should never have left your back to the door."

"Not with you or your people around," Rodrigo said. "From the back is always where you seem to strike."

Rodrigo supported Beatriz who clung to him. Elana was holding on to his arm now as if she could not believe that escape, which had been so close, now was being snatched from them.

"How did you get free from your cell?" Don Francisco questioned.

"I would imagine you would like to know that," Rodrigo said. "Was that why you were whipping these women?"

"Do not get clever with me, my friend. You are very close to death."

"I have been close before."

"There is a passageway throughout this castle. You must have known it for some time, you and your sister. You have made a fool of me. It was you who smuggled Antonio Flores from here, was it not?"

"It was," Rodrigo said proudly. "And the Menendes family, the Castilan brothers, and all the rest you have found missing from your hole of Hell."

"You have a debt to me that I intend to collect."

"By killing me?" Rodrigo said. "The secret will go with me. I am the only one who knows. Elana and Beatriz have no knowledge of where the passageway is. Only I and a few I trust, and I will never tell you."

"Then you also know just where Captain Burke is?"

Rodrigo smiled. "I do, and I expect he will take what proofs he has now to the queen. What will you say then? How will you explain what you have been doing?"

"No, he will not go to the queen," Don Francisco replied. "He will come to see about the safety of his women first. In fact, I would wager that he might not be far behind." Don Francisco threw back his head and laughed when he saw the expression on Rodrigo's face. He knew he was right. Reeve was coming and he would be here, prepared for him.

"This time," Diego said, "I shall make you pay. I shall leave you dead in this passage. Then I will make sure your women know what I have done."

"At least you are right about one thing, Diego." Reeve grinned. "Elana is *my* woman, and she will always be. She would spit on you before she would be with you."

What Reeve wanted at the moment was Diego's anger. There was no flaw in the sword Diego held before him this time. It was strong and Reeve knew quite well the very excellent reputation he had for being able to kill with it.

"How does it feel, Diego," Reeve said with a laugh, "to have someone purchase your women for you? And how does it feel to know the woman you want would rather die than be with you?"

Diego, in a flash of hot anger, attacked. Swords clashed. Again Reeve strived to keep himself calm. Each thrust parried, each slash was stopped. The two men came together like a colossus of war.

Perspiration covered their brows and wet their skin until their shirts clung to them. Neither would let their guard down long enough for the other to take advantage.

Reeve continued to strike verbally, edging Diego's anger on and on. It was the only hope he had. His arms felt like lead; he was breathing with difficulty. It seemed as if Diego would never tire.

But then it happened. A moment, a speck of a second when Diego's blade was not quite fast enough, when his guard was not quite high enough.

The sword pierced Diego's heart, and this time there was no doubt in Reeve's mind that when he collapsed, he was dead. Reeve stepped over Diego's body after making sure he was dead. He went down the stairs rapidly, but when he reached the door of the dungeon, it stood partly open.

Instinctively he felt the same warning touch of alarm. Something was wrong. Slowly, he moved to the dark shadows of the wall. He was about to move toward the open door when a hand reached from the shadows and jerked him into a small alcove.

He was prepared to fight again, when a soft, familiar voice spoke to him. "Put down your sword, Reeve. We must save your woman and your friends."

Reeve stared in absolute amazement at the person who stood in the depths of the shadows, for he knew the voice, and he knew it well.

Chapter Thirty

"How in the name of God did you get here? I thought you were—"

"Dead?" came the amused voice. "Yes, I suppose many thought I was dead. But I do not die so easily. I have already begun to repay those responsible."

"Juan?"

"Someone cut his throat . . . a shame. He was such a . . . man."

"You?"

"Yes, who else? Are you the one to tell me he didn't deserve it?"

"No, there are many here who deserve it. I must go in there. He has Elana, Beatriz, and maybe Rodrigo."

"Yes, he has them. But he expects you. He will lock them up and wait for you to come for them. Then he will kill you."

"I have to go after them."

"Yes, we will free them. But there is another way. A way he least expects. I have others with me and this time we will make our escape easier by making sure he will not follow."

"I . . . I cannot just walk away and leave them with him. They will think I have deserted them."

"Reeve, you must do as I say. If you do not, Don Francisco will eventually succeed in killing you."

"How do you know what happened in there?"

"I have been watching, but it happened too suddenly and there were too many. I was alone or we would have done something. Reeve, if he succeeds at nothing else, he wants to kill you. He knows you will come for them."

"Then he'll be prepared for anything we do."

"He will lock your friends up and guard them. He will watch for you to step into the trap. He cannot afford for you to escape."

"What must I do?"

"Come with me for awhile. We will join the friends I brought with me. Then we will give Don Francisco a few surprises."

A sharp sound interrupted their words, and they drew back into the shadows. Don Francisco came out of the dungeon. He held Elana by the arm with a pistol at her side. The two guards came out with Rodrigo and Beatriz, followed by the last man.

Rodrigo was surprised that Reeve was nowhere about. The thought entered his head that Diego had killed him, but if he had, Rodrigo knew, Diego would have been there to brag about it.

They were returned to the large room in which Elana had first been held. When the door was locked behind them, Elana sagged wearily to the bed, and Rodrigo took Beatriz gently into his arms. She clung to him without a word. Their only source of solace was to hold each other.

"Beatriz, my love, I'm so sorry," he whispered against her soft hair, "I'm sorry."

"Oh, Rodrigo." She wept softly. "You are here. That is all that matters. Hold me. I'm so frightened."

His arm went about her and she cried out softly as the rough fabric of his coat brushed her back. In his need to hold her, he had forgotten about her back. Now he turned her around and drew the ragged dress away from her back. He gritted his teeth as the anger flowed through him. At that moment he would have gladly strangled Don Francisco and the men with him. The welts had bled little but they were red and sore.

Angrily, Rodrigo went to the door. He pounded furiously on it until a very startled guard opened it.

"I need some warm water and ointment for her back," Rodrigo demanded.

The guard closed the door and in less than twenty minutes it reopened, a young maid appearing with a basin of water and cloths. She also had two dresses over her arm. It was obvious to Rodrigo that Don Francisco had been informed of their needs.

Elana remained quiet while Rodrigo gently bathed Beatriz's back and applied the ointment. His touch was gentle and Beatriz made no complaint. When he was finished with Beatriz, he turned his attention to his sister.

Once both women were dressed they sat together to discuss their situation. It was then that Elana asked, "Rodrigo, how did you escape your cell, and . . . Reeve . . . is he all right? They didn't—"

"No, Elana, they didn't, although they intended to. He found the passageway after they took you. He came down to rescue me." He went on to explain all that happened and watched Elana brighten.

"Then Reeve is safe! He's free!"

Rodrigo told of the meeting with Diego and what he thought might have occurred. "If he killed Diego or . . . I don't know what happened. It was why I was caught by surprise. I expected Reeve. Elana, if you think Reeve would just take his freedom and go, you're mistaken. Wherever you are, you won't find Reeve far away. You and I know how far these passages extend. He's somewhere and I don't think it will take him too long to find us and get us out of here. If he's not here soon, we will try to make a run for it."

"Don Francisco will be waiting for us to do just that. I

wouldn't be surprised if we are being watched right now. If we use the passageways they will catch us and find them. If Reeve comes . . . oh, Rodrigo, they will trap him. We have to do something."

"You have just named our problem, dear sister. We can do nothing . . . but wait. We can't go wandering about trying to find each other. Right now, all we can do is wait."

Reeve moved slowly and carefully toward the cell in which he had first been held. He wanted the papers he had hidden. Once inside the cell, he went to the corner, dislodged the stones and dirt he had placed over them and was relieved to find the packet of papers safely within. He retrieved them and put them in his pocket. Then came the task of getting back into the passageways without being found. He breathed a sigh of relief when the passageway door slid safely closed behind him.

He made his way rapidly to a small room at the very top of the castle. It had not been used for years. No one came near it, so Reeve felt reasonably safe there until the plans he was making were complete.

The room was damp, cold, and dirty. With the light of one candle, Reeve sat down to wait for the others he expected to join him soon.

The door opened again and he turned to see two men . . . and Carmen. He was still amazed at seeing Carmen again, alive. He remembered well the amazing stories she had told him.

Carmen had stood between the two men and watched Reeve and the others ride away. A deep and violent anger broiled within her. He had used her and discarded her like a whore, and she burned with a silent need for revenge. It would be a revenge that would destroy him.

Her thoughts were interrupted by a rough jerk on her arm. Her quick mind searched for a way out. Carmen was clever, much too clever for the rather dimwitted men who had been left to kill her.

When the first man jerked her toward him, she let herself relax against him. He was taken completely by surprise when she smiled up at him with the most seductive look she could manage, considering the emotions that flowed through her.

She knew these two and had seen their lecherous looks before. "Why are you so rough, Miguel?" she asked. "I cannot run away. I am smart enough to know that if I cannot fight you I—" She laughed again softly. "I might as well enjoy it as much as you."

He gazed at her in open lust, taken completely by the invitation in her eyes. "Carmen . . ." he began.

"Now, Miguel," she said smiling up at him, "you aren't going to disappoint me, are you?"

"No." He laughed and drew her roughly into his arms.

Carmen drew a little away from him as she turned toward the second man. "And you, Tomaz," she said, "are you interested in sharing a little time with me?"

"Of course, Carmen." The man laughed.

"I only ask one thing," she said.

"What?"

"I . . . could we have some privacy?" She looked at Miguel. "We could go behind those rocks. Then, when it is Tomaz's turn, you can leave us alone for a while."

The two men exchanged glances. They knew, no matter what she said, when they finished enjoying her physically they were going to kill her as Juan had ordered. But the idea of enjoying her without a fight appealed to both of them.

Tomaz nodded at Miguel who took Carmen's arm and began to drag her behind the rocks. She smiled again at Tomaz and

407

then leaned against Miguel and walked with him. There were several feet between them and the rocks, and she suffered his mauling with a frozen smile on her face.

Behind the rocks was a grassy area. Miguel pushed Carmen to the ground and was upon her, his mouth brutally attacking hers. With rough hands he pushed her skirts up and began to caress her with rough, seeking hands.

He did not care for her feelings, nor did he notice when her hands ceased to caress him. He was so intent on his rape of her that he never saw her hands maneuver the thin stiletto from its hiding place. With one hand she drew his head down to her. Her mouth pressed against his, she lunged, driving the knife through his heart.

The look of absolute shock registered for a moment. Then he collapsed upon her. With all her strength she pushed his body from her. She gazed at him with disgust, then she rose to her feet. In a fit of uncontrolled anger, she drew back her foot and kicked him as hard as she could. "Bastard," she hissed, "rot in Hell."

Quickly, she bent and retrieved her knife. Then she went to the rocks and slowly looked around. A pleased smile crossed her face when she saw that Tomaz was seated with his back to her.

Carmen had been an expert with a knife since she was eleven, and she was not afraid to use it on anyone or anything that threatened her life.

His back was broad, and Carmen never missed. Slowly and silently she stood. She took her time, aimed carefully, drew her arm back and threw.

Tomaz leapt as the knife drove deep into his back. He spun around with wide, disbelieving eyes, clawing at the knife in his back. He staggered toward her. One step . . . two . . . then he fell into the dirt. Carmen stood and gazed at him a look of loathing on her face.

Carmen had been part of a traveling Gypsy caravan most of her life. She was not at a loss being alone where she was. She knew not only where she was, but she knew how to get to friends. With a look of cold fury in her eyes, she went to the horses, took one, and began to ride.

Methodically she traveled, mile by angry mile. The only thing in her mind was to find a way to get to Juan . . . and a way to repay the debt that tore at her heart. She had to get Reeve and the others free.

She knew now of love. She had heard Elana's words and they had struck her heart. After what she had done, Elana and Reeve had chosen to forgive. For the first time, she could really see the emotion and share it. She vowed one solemn vow. She would do two things if it took the balance of her life: She would kill Juan. And somehow she would set Reeve and Elana free to share the rest of their lives together.

Within two days she was exhausted, but she found a small camp. There she rested for a day, borrowed a horse and headed for the castle. She was well used to the hidden passages, for it was she who had aided Benjamin Mendosa in his escape through them.

She found her way inside and made her way about, listening for information. One of the first things she heard was who held Rafael and why.

Friends from within were found and a message sent to Pedro and his friends. A way had to be found to get Rafael and Catrina free.

Then she turned her attention to Juan. She found him, and Reeve was shaken by the calm way she told him what she had done to him. After Juan, she set her mind on a way to free the others. It was only luck that let her find Reeve alone.

"Carmen," Reeve said, "Have you found any information?"

"Don Francisco is keeping all word from the queen. Men watch closely the corridors that lead to her apartments. The secret passages do not go to her apartment either, so there is no way for us to reach her. Another thing . . ."

"What?"

"Torquemada and Don Francisco have filed a case against Elana, Rodrigo, and Beatriz. They will have to stand trial before the inquisitors. Believe me, Reeve, they stand absolutely no chance, unless the queen knows."

"Carmen," Reeve said softly, "I've got to get to her. I've got to."

"I know Reeve, I know. But we have got to wait until Rafael and Catrina can get to the queen."

"I know you are right, but God, it is hard to know she is so close and I cannot go to her."

"Maybe we could let her know you are here. It is a dreadful chance, but if you want to take it . . ."

"What?"

"There are two guards at her door. I can slip out into the hall and attract them. While I do so, you can come through the passageway. You will only have a matter of minutes, but it will be enough to give them courage."

"You speak of courage," he said gently. "I am listening to a great deal of courage now."

"I have a great debt to pay, Reeve. I am sorry for what I have done to you and to Elana. I must do something to redeem my soul."

Reeve rose and went to her. He smiled down into her eyes. "As far as I'm concerned, you are forgiven. I'm sure I can speak for Elana, too. She has a gentle, loving, and very forgiving heart. If we get out of this alive, come to England with us. You won't be safe here."

"Thank you," she said softly.

"Will you come?"

"We will see."

"When do we try?"

"When the night is deep. When the guards are very tired." Reeve nodded and Carmen turned to the men who had come with her.

"Was there any news from Pedro yet?"

"No, Carmen," one man replied.

"Reeve, as soon as we get word that Rafael and Catrina are free, we will have the escape route planned."

"Until then, all we can do is wait."

"You know, of course, that Don Francisco found Diego's body. He knows who killed him. He knows you are here somewhere. If he finds you this time, Reeve, there will be no chances left for any of us. We will all die very quickly. All but Elana, and she will be left to pay for a long, long time."

"You've no need to remind me. I only wish I could get him alone on my own ground. It would give me a great deal of pleasure to cross swords with him. I would hate to leave here and let him go unpunished."

"I know how you feel, but there is no way, so do not harbor any gallant ideas. Take your woman and go when you have the chance. You may never get another."

"I'll not be foolish, Carmen," Reeve said. "But you must admit it is a good thought."

Carmen laughed and nodded, but Reeve could not read the intense look in her eyes when he turned away. Maybe Don Francisco would not be left unpunished.

The night lengthened. Rodrigo had been brought the news that the case had been filed before the Inquisition. No matter which way they looked, the future seemed dark. The only ray of light he had was that Reeve was free somewhere in the castle. Rodrigo only wondered where and how he was. Had Diego wounded him? Was he lying somewhere within the passages alone, bleeding his life away?

Rodrigo had forced Beatriz to the bed to try to rest. She was both emotionally and physically spent. Elana was exhausted, too but worry would not let her close her eyes. She wanted Reeve, needed him to give her the strength she knew was waning.

When Rodrigo had told her all, she could only vision Reeve hurt, maybe dead. It sent a shiver of pure terror through her.

"Elana, why do you not try to sleep?" Rodrigo questioned gently.

Elana smiled. "And why do you not?"

Rodrigo sighed. She worried over Reeve. At least he had Beatriz beside him, if it were any consolation they were together.

The guards opened the doors and checked the room at random. If Reeve were to appear, there was no way he could escape. Elana rose and walked to the window. Through the barred windows she could see the moon-touched lawn.

"My brother," she whispered, "we have taken so many to safety and never drawn any others into danger. Now, the one time that we do, it is the one I love. What have we done to him, Rodrigo? Have we cost him his life?"

Rodrigo rose and walked to stand behind Elana. He placed his hands gently on her shoulders. "Elana, you must stop this. You cannot condemn yourself, nor can I. Reeve made his own choices and I am sure in my heart he does not regret it. He loves you. You have shared a very beautiful moment in your life." He turned her to face him. "Do you remember Reeve saying so often, 'We are alive, Elana, and as long as we are, we must have hope'?"

She nodded, the tears in her eyes and the tightness in her throat preventing any words.

"Well, we are alive, Elana, and as long as we are, we will have hope. For us, and for him. Will we not, Elana?" he added softly.

"I'm sorry," she said weakly as she brushed the tears from her cheeks. "I have not always been such a foolish crybaby."

"No." He chuckled. "You have not. I remember the little beauty who once tried to take my own sword to me when she was angry."

They laughed together.

"Yes, I remember."

"The worst of it is that you nearly beheaded me before I could get it off of you."

Elana laughed, then suddenly the laughter broke and turned to wracking sobs. Rodrigo held her while she clung to him and wept as she had when they were children and she had been hurt.

Rodrigo had known her pain, and he knew she needed to cry now if she was going to have enough strength to get her through what he felt was coming. He knew Don Francisco would force them before the inquisitors, and he knew what their fates would be.

Elana cried until there were no more tears left. She still clung to him.

"My dear sister, you have soaked my shirt completely." He laughed, then he grew serious. "Are you all right, Elana?"

She lifted her head to smile up at her brother. "Yes, now I am all right."

"We've not given up hope?"

"No, Rodrigo, we have not given up hope."

"Good, now, why don't you get some sleep?"

"Why don't you? Go and share a moment with Beatriz. You have shared your strength with me, brother, now I am fine. Now go to her. She needs you now more than I do."

"Are you sure you are all right?"

"Yes, I'm fine. I just want to . . . to pray."

He nodded, kissed both of her cheeks and held her close to him for a moment. Then he left her side and went to the bed.

413

He lay down beside Beatriz and drew her gently into his arms. After awhile they slept.

Elana went to the candle and blew it out. She returned to the window where the light of the moon touched her face. Silently she prayed, but her prayers were no longer for her freedom or for the freedom of her brother and Beatriz. They were for Reeve. Even if it meant that Reeve was lost to her forever, she wanted him to be safe and free.

"Keep him safe, Father. Take him from this land and give him a good rich life he so richly deserves. He would have given his life for us. Since that can no longer be, then give him his freedom. Please, dear God, do not let him die. Do not let him die."

She heard a soft-whispered sound but thought it was the couple on the bed. Wearily, as she had been before, she pressed her head against the cool metal of the bars and closed her eyes. With her eyes closed she could bring the vision of Reeve and the memory of his love closer to her. She felt a gentle touch on her hair, heard the soft whisper of her name. Agony struck. Could she have dreamed him so hard that she could actually feel his presence? But the soft repeat of her name told her this was no longer a dream. She spun about.

Moonlight touched him, turning his silver-gray eyes to deeper gray. Tall, strong, and handsome he stood before her. A low moan of joyous pain was drawn from her as she threw herself into his reaching arms. Their lips met in a searing, blinding kiss. For that one rapturous moment all was forgotten but their love for each other.

She was breathless with the iron-hard arms that crushed her against him. She could feel the strength flow from him to her. His mouth sought hers in a kiss that told her of shared agony and blinding need. He kissed her cheeks, her eyes, her slender throat, then again, sought her lips as if he could draw from her all the beauty and love the world had to offer.

414

She clung to him, knowing only that he was here, he was holding her, and he was alive.

"Reeve, Reeve, my beloved, my heart." She sobbed. "I thought you were hurt or lost to me."

"My dear wife," he whispered against her hair. "I once told you the best part of me is here. I cannot live without you, nor would I want to. Do not be afraid any longer."

"With your arms to hold me, I no longer have any fear. You are alive. You are well. My prayers have been answered."

"You were praying for me?"

"I was praying for my life, because my life is you. Oh, Reeve," she murmured as their lips met again.

This time the kiss was a gentle, searching thing. Each sought to give and each took in return. A magic blinding kiss that sealed the treasure of their love forever. After a moment, he held her away from him. He took hold of her shoulders and gazed intently into her eyes.

"Elana, I do not have much time. I am going to explain some things to you, then I must go. I want you to know we are not defeated. One day I will leave Spain, and you, my dear love, will be at my side. You, and all the others who have given so much. One day soon, Elana, we will be free. Now, listen carefully."

Chapter Thirty-one

Rafael was momentarily stunned when the guard who held him and his father was killed so suddenly, and by the appearance of a man he did not know.

The strange man moved swiftly toward them and knelt to sever their bonds. He smiled up at Rafael. "I know you have many questions, Senor Chavez, and I will be most willing to answer them as we ride. It is a long story and I am sure you are most anxious to return and find your woman."

Rafael stood up quickly and helped his father to his feet. "Yes, I am anxious to have the answers. You are the answer to a prayer. I don't know who you are or who sent you, but you are a blessing and you will have my undying gratitude for as long as I live."

"Come, Senor Chavez, let us ride. It is a long way to Don Carlos's home."

"You know Don Carlos?"

"*Sí*, I know much about him."

Several more men were joining them, one leading Rafael's and his father's horses. "Who are you? Who sent you? How did any one know where to find us? Was it Reeve and Rodrigo?"

"My name is Pedro, Senor. I am master of the caravan that was to help your friends to reach the coast. We failed, and they were captured again."

"Failed . . . how? What happened?"

417

"That, too, is a long story, Senor. We had best ride as we talk."

Rafael nodded and they all mounted. Rafael knew it would take less time to return. He would press their travel as rapidly as he could.

As they rode, Pedro explained all that had happened from the day of Rafael's marriage. Rafael was enraged at Carmen's betrayal, but Pedro turned an angry face to him.

"Do not be so quick to condemn, my friend. It is because of Carmen that I am here to help you, and it is Carmen who will ultimately help your friends to freedom."

"I don't understand, why would she first help them, then betray them, then help them again?"

Quietly, Pedtro explained Carmen's heart. He spoke of her gently and with pity. A pity Rafael soon shared. Having found the love of Catrina, he could understand the emotions Carmen had been feeling.

Pedro went on to explain the situation as it stood now. "Carmen knows that you and Catrina would be welcomed back to court. If you arrive with much ceremony, there is no way Don Francisco can stop her. He has no way of knowing of your escape until it is too late. You and your wife will have access to the queen, and Don Francisco cannot stop you. I have a packet of papers, a letter from Rodrigo, and one from Beatriz and Elana, begging the queen's mercy. We must get your woman free, then return to Madrid as soon as possible. The trial will be held soon and it will be held in a city close to Madrid. The queen will never know of it until it is over and they are condemned. They may even be burned at the stake. Even before she can sign an order to give them their freedom."

"My God," Rafael said, "will we have time to reach them?"

"Yes, Don Francisco will hold them for some time yet. You see, Reeve slipped through his fingers. He has joined Carmen. Don Francisco wants to trap him and kill him before the trial begins. He feels Reeve and his proof of the marriage is the only thing that stands between himself and success."

"Reeve is a very resourceful man. He will not make the mistake of falling into Don Francisco's hands again. But while he is free, I will wager Don Francisco is sweating a bit."

Pedro laughed. "Yes, I'll wager he is, too. There is a silent, massive search for Reeve and the secret passages, but so far neither of them have been found. Now Senor Chavez," Pedro continued, "suppose you tell me just what happened from the time you and your wife married and left Madrid?"

Rafael nodded. For the next half hour he spoke softly, telling Pedro all the circumstances that befell him and Catrina. "Did the ship arrive safely?" he questioned Pedro.

"Our scouts tell us that it did, and is waiting patiently for its master and those he brings with him."

"It is the first time in a long time I have seen a bright ray of hope, Pedro. I will only have peace and be able to concentrate on reaching the queen when Catrina is safe."

"You will kill this one, this Don Carlos Manrique?"

For a time Rafael remained silent, then in a voice heavy and filled with pain, he replied, "Yes, this time I will kill him. May God forgive me."

"After what he has done, don't you think he deserves to die?"

"Yes, he well deserves it, not only for this, but for so many other crimes he has committed."

"Then why do you sound so . . . so reluctant?"

Rafael sighed deeply. "Pedro," he said quietly, "it is not an easy thing, even being what he is, for a man to kill his own brother."

"Brother?" Pedro said in a shocked voice.

"Half-brother. We had the same mother and different fathers. It is a terrible affair." Rafael went on to explain the past and why Don Carlos had chosen this moment to strike. "When Don Francisco sent a message to Don Carlos asking him to find us and prevent us from reaching Reeve's ship, Don

SYLVIE F. SOMMERFIELD

Carlos felt it was the perfect time to get revenge on me," Rafael
explained. He told about Maria. "She would have married me
until he seduced her and left her with child. I loved her even
then, for I knew him for what he was. But she could not stand
the shame. She took her life."

"What a terrible tragedy," Pedro replied. "You should seek
his life. He is an animal that deserves to die."

"He has a vicious sadistic mind. There is no telling what he
has told Catrina. He is like a velvet-covered claw, and if her
faith in our love is not strong, strong enough to protect our
love, he will rip out her heart. I love her more than my own life.
I pray every moment that it is enough to keep her from him, to
shield her heart from his lies, and to keep her faith strong
enough to protect her until I can return."

"I will join my prayers to yours, Senor Chavez. Let us make
all the haste we can. I would only tell you one thing if it will be
of any consequence: A woman, one who truly loves, as I feel
your wife must, is a much stronger foe than Don Carlos can
imagine. Maybe one who will be his ultimate defeat."

"I hope you are right, Pedro," Rafael replied. "I hope you
are right."

Their horses covered much ground until they were tired.
Pedro called a short halt to let them rest, then again they
pushed on. What had taken Rafael and his captors four days
took them only two to return. Rafael was tired. Bearded and
red-eyed from lack of sleep, he gazed down at Don Carlos's
home, then rode down into the valley toward it.

Pedro and his men were very adept at outwitting and eluding
guards who had been set around the house.

Diego had remained behind. His age and extreme exhaustion
made it too difficult to ride with them. Quietly, slowly, and
with deadly intent, Rafael, Pedro, and his men approached the
silent and nearly dark hacienda.

*　　*　　*

Catrina watched Don Carlos approach. Catrina had always been a quiet and very gentle woman. But she possessed an inner strength few would have attributed to her very feminine exterior.

If Don Carlos meant to intimidate her or to frighten her, he did not succeed. She looked at him through eyes that had begun to see him much more clearly than he had ever imagined she could.

Carlos was well used to women who were subservient and easily mastered. He felt self-assured and in his element. He would depend on her gullibility, her pity, and what he thought he could widen: a narrow breach in her faith in Rafael.

Don Carlos would not resort to rape. He enjoyed the challenge of bringing a woman to submission. Especially one as innocently sweet as Catrina appeared to be. He wanted her to be broken, unsure, afraid, and wondering whether what he was saying had any truth to it.

"You have read the letters," he said as he walked to stand behind her. "But you have not seen all the truth."

Catrina was well aware of him when he stopped close behind her chair. Gently, he let his fingers touch the soft skin at the nape of the neck. Rafael had wakened her body to sensual pleasure and no one knew better than he how to use it.

Catrina stood up abruptly and moved away from his disturbing touch. She turned to face him. "What are you talking about?" she said.

"I have some letters you should read."

"What kind of letters?"

"Letters from your husband . . . to Maria."

Catrina remained still, and even though her face paled, she looked at him defiantly. "I do not believe you."

"No?"

"No, I do not."

"Then . . . would you like to read them?"

"No, I would not."

He chuckled softly. "Do you think by not reading them you will make them any less real or any less true?"

"I have told you before, Carlos, and I shall tell you again. Say what you will, do what you will, you will never change what I feel for Rafael. He is my husband, and I know his heart. I will believe in him and trust in him until I die."

"Ah, Catrina," Carlos said sadly, "it is a very rare thing to see such devotion. It is a shame that your husband did not show so much love and consideration for you."

"Now what game do you play with me?" she demanded.

"I play no game, Catrina. I told you what kind of man he is. He deserted Maria in her hour of darkest need. He has done the same with you."

Catrina closed her eyes for a moment, feeling the battering of his will against hers. "Rafael would never leave me."

"Would he not. I went to him last night. I wanted revenge on him for what he had done to Maria. I told him I meant to kill him. It was then that he asked me just what I would take in return for his life."

"That is a lie!"

"You are a woman as sweet and trusting as Maria was. I knew what he meant and I wanted to spare you that. I asked him what he would offer. He offered you."

"Damn you for the liar that you are!" Catrina cried.

"I told him that you were not something to be traded away. I also told him that I thought you were beautiful and, truthfully, I desired you very much. He said that if I desired you, all I had to do was release him and his father. They would go and leave you here. He laughed and told me that if I was very careful and clever, you would fall easily into my arms. He also said it had been easy for him and now there was no challenge left and he was tired of your marriage."

"No, that is not true!"

"He is gone, Catrina. I let him go, for I felt someone as pure and good as you did not deserve to be treated so. I would care for you so that the grief over his betrayal did not lead you to the same fate as Maria."

"I want to see Rafael," Catrina demanded.

Carlos walked to the door and held it open for her. "You may search the entire house. You may question the servants. They will also tell you that your husband and his father rode away from here quite alive and well."

Catrina stared at him for a moment, then she ran from the room. Slowly, Don Carlos followed. Each room proved empty, even the rooms in the deep areas of the basement. In the entire hacienda there was no sign of Rafael or his father. In the huge and very beautiful center of the hacienda Catrina faced Carlos again.

She was panting from the wild exertion, and tears stained her face. "You have killed him!"

"Catrina," he demanded, "look at me!" Their eyes held. This was the first time Carlos spoke the absolute truth and it registered on his face and in his eyes. "I swear by all I possess that I did not kill Rafael. Despite all he has done, he is my half-brother. I did not kill him, nor did I touch his father. When they left this hacienda they were alive and well."

Why did she believe him! Her mind screamed. Rafael would not betray her! He could not! Their love had been too perfect.

Don Carlos felt a surge of satisfaction. The breach had widened. Now, all he had to do to break it completely was to let her read the letters he had so artfully changed by substituting Rafael's name in place of his. He took them from his pocket and laid them on the table. "Read these," he said quietly. "Then you will know the truth." He walked from the room, priding himself on a performance well done.

Catrina stared at the letters for a long time, then she picked them up and sat slowly down in a chair. There were four letters. One by one she opened them and read. The first three made her weep, but the last was the worst.

Maria, I cannot return to marry a woman I do not love. The bride I choose will have to be a woman above reproach, not one who sleeps with any man who pleases her fancy.

There is no way for me to know if the child you carry is truly mine. It could belong to anyone. I will not give my name to another man's bastard. Go and find the lover responsible and force him to acknowledge his deed.

Of course you can always go to my half-brother who has always been foolish enough to love you. Maybe he will take pity on you. But if he does, he is a fool. A woman who does such a thing once will not hesitate to repeat it.

Please do not write to me again or try to see me.

R.

Catrina laid the letters aside. Slowly, she rose and walked back to her room. She sat by the window and remained deathly quiet.

Food was brought to her by a silent-footed maid, but the tray remained untouched. The sun began to lower and still she remained, gazing out the window.

She remained so during the night. It was as if her mind withdrew to a safe place where it could examine all she had been told.

The night faded into dawn and a new day. Again, food was brought and again it remained untouched. Alternately she paced the floor, then sat at the window.

Carlos kept track of what she was doing by questioning the young maid. That Catrina had not eaten pleased him, too, for a weakened body often weakened resistance.

Deliberately, he stayed away from her until he felt she was distraught enough to be more receptive.

Catrina ate very little for the next few days. By the time

Carlos came to her he felt she was weak enough that he could control her.

He walked to her room and entered without knocking. Again she sat by the window. The evening sun touched her skin, making it glow warm and golden. He felt the leap of possessive desire, accompanied by the feeling that, at last, he had beaten her into submission, at last, she would bend to his will, and at last, he would have his revenge on Rafael. When he took her, when he had mastered her, maybe then he would tell her the truth. With that he knew she would break.

Catrina rose slowly to face him.

The moon had just begun to rise when Pedro and Rafael slipped to the shadows toward the main house. There was a light in only one window, and it was toward this one they moved.

It was on the second floor so Pedro had sent one of his men back to their horses for rope. Rafael waited impatiently, his eyes intent on the lighted window. Was Catrina there or somewhere in the depths of the darkened house?

There was a balcony outside the lighted window, and it was only ten feet from the ground. Pedro bent and cupped his hand, and Rafael placed his foot in it. Pedro lifted and Rafael's fingers grasped the edge of the balcony.

With sheer determination, he pulled himself up. Then he tied the rope he had carried firmly to the balcony and let it drape so the others could climb. While they did so, he turned to look into the window.

It was a large study and the fire in the fireplace burned crisply, but the room was empty. Then his gaze caught the three portraits that hung above the fireplace. Old memories filled him with bitter anger, for the woman in the portrait was the cause of the split between the two sons whose portraits hung on either side.

Rafael tested the door and found it unlocked. The others

joined him on the balcony, and very quietly they entered the room. They moved slowly across the room, careful not to make a noise that might draw attention to their presence.

Very slowly, Rafael opened the door a crack to look down the long hall. They were in a room at the far end of the hall. There were at least seven other rooms that lined the hall, and he had no idea which one might be the one in which Catrina was held.

He motioned the others and they quietly left the room and began to work their way down the hall, stopping in front of each door to listen for any sounds from within.

Self-assured, Carlos gazed across the room at Catrina. "So," he said softly, "now you believe. Now you understand what kind of a man you have married? You know how he has used so many?"

"Yes, I understand Rafael completely," she answered, and Carlos smiled in satisfaction. He started to walk across the room toward her but stopped at her next words.

"I have thought of Rafael and all I know of him. He is a gentle, kind, and loving man. He is strong and has deep integrity. His honor has been given to him from his father, as your dishonor must have been given to you. I believe in what was done, I just do not believe Rafael is responsible. If he had been responsible for the child Maria carried, he would have given it his name. His pride would not let him do any less, for that is the kind of man he is. No, I will trust in him. I will believe in Rafael for as long as I live and nothing you can do or say will change what I feel. I recognize you for what you are." She straightened her shoulders. "And I will never surrender. If you desire my shame or my pride, both will have to be by force, for never, as long as I breathe, will I betray Rafael."

This was not what Carlos had planned. He had envisioned a woman on her knees, her strength of will shaken. Instead he saw iron resolve and a pride such as he had not encountered before. A touch of admiration touched his eyes. This was the kind of woman he would thoroughly enjoy. He had tried to break her and failed. Now he meant to have her. He moved toward her slowly. Then she spoke again.

"So, I was right," she said softly. "Until you took that step I was unsure. Now I know I was right. Rafael said once you would try to break my will. He did not know you as well as he thought for he said rape was not your way. I do not think that there is anything that is not your way if you want something."

Her disdain and the look of disgust in her eyes again stopped him for a moment, but only for a moment, for now his anger filled him with grim determination. He had to defeat her. In some way he had to defeat her.

He reached her side quickly as she tried to back away and gripped her arm, pulled her toward him. He was more than twice her size, yet she would not surrender without a fight. And fight she did. With small doubled fists, she struck out at him. She did not scream for she felt no help would come.

Her fingers curved, she scratched long scarlet lines down his cheek, stimulating his rage. Deliberately he struck her, knocking her to her knees.

For a moment she was blinded by the force of the blow. Carlos reached down and gripped her hair, then he slapped her again. This time, she cried out, knowing her strength was slipping.

Satisfied that he had driven away her strength to fight, he reached down and jerked her to feet. "Now," he said hoarsely, "now I will teach you to defy me. Now I will make you beg for mercy."

The door was to his back and he did not hear it swing open until a soft voice spoke. "I think not, Carlos. This time I think it is you who will beg for mercy. But do not expect it."

Carlos watched Catrina's eyes widen and fill with joy, and he knew who stood behind him. He spun about, absolute surprise on his face. "You! How—"

"How did I get free of your assassins, brother? With the help of friends. It is a thing you would not understand."

Rafael's sword was held slightly toward Carlos, and Carlos could read well Rafael's mind. "I am unarmed." He smiled. "Do you commit murder . . . brother?" Carlos retained a hold on Catrina's arm. She had softly called out Rafael's name then had remained silent, but her eyes were filled with Rafael and her heart was clearly visible for Rafael to see.

With one motion, Rafael reached out and slid Pedro's sword from its scabbard. In the same motion, he threw it to Carlos.

"It is more of a chance than you have ever given. I should kill you like the cur you are. Catrina," Rafael's voice softened, "move away from him."

Catrina's heart nearly stopped its beat. Had Rafael escaped everything to find his death of his own brother's sword? "Rafael . . ." she began, and he knew her thoughts.

"No, Catrina, do not ask me to turn my back to him again. We have crossed swords before. I should have killed him then. I will not make that mistake again. Move away from him, my love."

Obediently, Catrina broke Carlos's hold on her arm. She moved to Rafael's side and he drew her close to him to brush one soft kiss against her lips. Then he pushed her toward Pedro, and his eyes turned to Carlos.

"When Maria took her life, I should have killed you. When you turned on the only family you had known I should have killed you. I forgave you many things, my brother, but not Catrina and what you tried to do to her, never Catrina."

Rafael leapt forward and their swords met. Carlos at first smiled with assurance, but the smile faded and turned to a frown. Then the first real taste of fear touched him. He had counted on Rafael's own honor to keep him from killing his own brother. He realized too late that Catrina had been the thing to push Rafael over the edge. He realized as death reached out to claim him.

Chapter Thirty-Two

For one brief moment Rafael stood over Carlos's body in silence. He fought a battle within. Both Catrina and Pedro understood his emotions well. No matter the hatred between them, the man had been of his own blood.

"Rafael," Pedro said, "we must leave here quickly. Other lives depend on you. You must get back to Madrid and to the queen before any word of this can reach Don Francisco."

Pedro's words effectively drew Rafael's attention from Carlos. Rafael moved swiftly to Catrina's side and put his arms about her, drawing her close. "Catrina, are you all right?"

"Yes, Rafael, I am fine."

"You can talk later," Pedro said. "Now we must get out of here."

"Yes," Rafael said softly as he gazed down into Catrina's warm eyes. "We must talk. There is much I need to explain . . . and much for which I have to ask forgiveness."

They moved quickly to the balcony. One after another, Pedro and his men climbed down the rope. Rafael swung his legs over the balcony, sitting on the edge. He turned to help Catrina up beside him. He could tell she was a little shaken by the height. He put his arms about her and drew her close. "Put your arms about my neck, Catrina, and close your eyes. We will be down in a minute."

Catrina did as he said without question. Rafael silently thanked God for the faith she seemed to have in him. He knew of it for he had overheard her last words to Carlos. He also knew it was a thing they had to discuss. He had to prove to her that her faith in him was justified, and he had to tell her just how grateful he was for it.

He gripped the rope and swung free. He heard Catrina gasp audibly and tremble as her arms tightened about him. In a few moments they reached the ground and made their way back to the horses. In less than an hour the hacienda was being lost in the darkness as they rode away.

They rode for a long time, wanting to put as much distance between them and any that might follow.

Rafael hoped Carlos's body would not be found until morning. By that time, they would have joined his father and the others and be well on their way.

Beneath the horses' hooves the ground melted away. Mile followed mile. Catrina, seated behind Rafael, clung to him, resting her head against his broad back and savoring the strength of his lean body. She did not complain of the discomfort, for she knew she would rather be here with Rafael, riding to safety, than any place on earth.

It was in a state of near exhaustion and nearing dawn that found them joining Diego and the others. There was no doubt in anyone's mind that horses and travelers could barely go any further.

"We must rest," Pedro said, "but it cannot be for long. Only until the horses are ready to travel again." There was no word from men who lay in whatever spot that they could find some comfort. One or two of them tied the horses.

Rafael took that moment to take Catrina's hand and drew her beneath the shadow of the trees. No matter how badly Rafael needed rest, he felt he needed Catrina's understanding even more.

The moon was still in the pre-dawn sky and they could see each other well. They were far enough away from the others so that they could not be overheard.

In a moment they were in each other's arms, holding each other silently and preciously close.

"Catrina, my love," he whispered. For one sweet moment their eyes met in mutual need. Then he bent his head and took her sweet soft mouth with his. It melted to the depths of him, melting the hard core that had kept him going and softening the pain, letting it flow from him.

He felt her slim body mold to his and her arms cling, drawing him even closer. When he released her, he found the reward he sought when he looked into the depths of her eyes.

"Catrina, I must tell you—"

Her fingers gently touched his mouth, stopping his words. "Shhh, love, we do not have to use words with each other. There is no need for you to explain anything to me."

"You must know that what Carlos said was mostly lies. But, I did not tell you or any other of Maria. I do not care for any others but you. You must know, you must forgive me."

"Rafael Chavez," Catrina said firmly. "I will say this once and only once, then I do not wish to hear of it again. Carlos told me all, favoring himself. But he did not understand love, my dear husband. He did not know or understand faith and trust . . . not as we do. Do you think I have not felt your love, shared your love not to know you? I know your heart, Rafael, and that is why I did not believe him. What pain there is in your past, Rafael, belongs there, not with us. I want to share your future. We will not let the past touch us. Do not ask me for forgiveness, my love. Talk to me only of your love, for it has been the only strength I have had to hold me these few days."

Rafael could have wept with the pain of his joy. It choked away any words that might have come. "Catrina," he rasped hoarsely, "was there ever a woman as good and loving as you or

431

a man as fortunate as I? Somewhere, sometime in my life, I must have done something good to have God reward me with your love."

"Oh, Rafael, you are so tired, come rest with me." Catrina sat beneath the tree, and Rafael sank gratefully down beside her. She reached to draw him close to her. Her arms about him, he rested his head against the softness of her breasts. She caressed his cheek and heard his sigh of peace. In the contented comfort of each other's arms, they sought the rest they needed.

It was less than two hours later, not enough rest for any of them, yet there was no complaint for all knew that other lives depended upon them.

They rode all the following day until the sun was nearing the horizon, stopping only to feed, water, and rest the horses. When they made camp the second night, Rafael made sure his sleeping area was well away from all others. It had been a lifetime since he had held Catrina, and he had vowed tonight that he would have her in his arms, that she would be where he could hold her till he told her again the depth of his love.

The camp settled into sleep for the night. Rafael and Catrina had taken a walk together to ease the stiffness of their bodies from the hours of riding.

After they had walked for a few minutes, Rafael knew utter contentment and peace. They walked with their arms about each other and talked softly of their future days and nights together.

"Once we have taken the papers to the queen and told her everything, she will have to free the others. Reeve is an Englishman, Elana is his wife, that we can prove. Don Francisco will have such a difficult time once the queen knows what he has been doing that he will certainly be forced to withdraw the charges against Rodrigo and Beatriz. If I were he, I would even absent myself from the court for a while. I would not want to face the queen's rage when she finds out what he has done and why he has done it."

"I would not want to face the queen's rage," Catrina agreed with a laugh. "But if I were Don Francisco, I would not want to face Reeve's rage either." To this Rafael was quick to agree. Rafael stopped walking beneath the sheltering trees. He turned to Catrina.

Without a word, she seemed to melt into his arms, raising her lips to his. All tiredness seemed to flow from him while the sweet, giving love of Catrina filled him with a new warmth. He had forgotten how slim and fragile she had always felt in his arms. He bound her close to him, sensing a newness, a growth in their love, and wondering who had changed the most.

He seemed to be more relaxed and aware of her now than he had ever been before. He had always wanted her with deep desire, but now even that seemed to be different. It was a desire that had been forged in the fire of despair and pain. It had flowed from the knowledge that in many ways he could have lost her, by Carlos's threat and by his own stupidity. The very thought of it now still had the ability to fill him with terror.

"Catrina," he said softly, "I could have lost you. I could bear anything in my life, but I do not think I could bear that. I have not told you so many things you should have known. If I told you, you may not have had to face such a trial. You should curse me for my foolishness. You should deny me your love and still you give so completely, fill my empty arms and heart so completely. It is a wondrous thing for me. I shall never hurt you again, my love, I swear."

"Rafael, my love is yours forever. It has no restrictions. I cannot say I will love him if he does that or I will hate him if he does that. I can say nothing but I love, forever, no matter what small hurts we might come across in each other's future. There is no one else who exists in my heart but you. All others are voices. If they speak against you, I do not hear, and I will not

433

hear. I have loved you always, my beloved husband, and I shall love you until I die."

Rafael was brought to wondering silence as he gazed down into her upturned gaze. It was open and clear and he could read the truth of what she had just said.

Gently, he cupped her face between his hands. With infinite tenderness he kissed her forehead, her eyes, and her cheeks. Then his seeking lips found her moist, parted mouth, and he claimed it in a gentle and heart-rending kiss that spoke to her all the words he could not find to say.

"Will you come to me now, Catrina? Will you let me tell you of my love for you? Will you share this night with me again as before and fill the cup of our love as only you can?"

"My heart," she whispered softly, "I have waited for you to reach for me. I am here, my love, and I am more than willing to belong to you again. I have missed you so terribly."

He took her hand and they walked to the dark, quiet place that he had prepared. They lay together on the blanket. They seemed to be reaching for each other long before they touched. Catrina melted against him and his world seemed to suddenly be filled with her. The pleasure was pure and ecstatic. Their world tilted and spun beyond control.

Warm, sensitive hands removed her clothes with almost worshipped gentleness. She aided him as he tossed aside his clothes, and in moments they were again in each other's arms.

Hungry mouths blended, causing a white heat to ripple beneath their skin. She knew again the flush of sexual desire she had not felt for so long. His touch was divine ecstasy. A moan of pain-pleasured ecstasy filled her and flowed through her like molten lava.

Attuned to her, loving her so intensely, needing her so much, he sensed the awakening of the flames within her. All thoughts were shattered to fragments as his hungry mouth continued a frenzied searching of her sensitive body. The hot tide of exquisite passion lifted them both to a level where they knew nothing but the need of each other.

To the white-hot need within him she felt soft and cool, and he could not seem to get enough of her. He searched her cool body for the answer to this and found it in her depths. There would never be enough. She was the part of him that was alive.

They moved together now in a blending rhythm that would always be their own magic to share. A moan of ecstasy was torn from her as her body arched beneath him, filled with liquid fire, a flooding uncontrollable joy filled her as he freed in her a volcanic burst of sensuous pleasure. They were both hurtled to a place of wild abandon, and it culminated in a burst of turbulent passion that left them gasping for breath and clinging to one another, both unable to speak or move from the sanctuary of each other's arms.

Their bodies still throbbed with almost violent renewal of their passion. Sweat-slicked and exhausted they held each other. Then Rafael rose up on one elbow. He gently brushed the beads of perspiration and dampened hair from her forehead. He bent his head and gently pressed a kiss on her forehead.

She sighed in deep contentment as he drew her closer and drew the blanket over them both. Her head nestled comfortably in the hollow between his shoulder and his throat. Her arm rested across his chest and, their legs entwined, they rested for a short time.

"Rafael?" Catrina questioned softly.

"Yes?" he replied as he pressed a kiss against her hair.

"What will we do now?"

"By dawn we must ride again as rapidly as possible. We will reach our home. From there I will use an unmarked carriage so that no one will know who I am. They will not be prepared to stop us. Catrina, we have to reach the queen."

"It is terrifying to think of what will happen if Don

Francisco finds out. He will have people waiting for us. Rafael, he will—"

He stopped her words with a gentle kiss. "Shhh, little one, don't think of it."

"How can I not think of it? We must be so careful. We must—"

Again, Rafael stopped her speech, but this time by sitting up abruptly.

"Rafael, what is wrong?"

"Catrina, once before I listened to you and took you with me. I took you into a danger you did not have to face, a danger that might have cost your life. A danger that might also have cost me your love. Do not think that I am foolish enough to do that again."

"What are you talking about?" she questioned as she sat up beside him.

"I'm talking about the time I foolishly decided not to leave you in a safe place while I took a message to Reeve's ship. I am taking you to my home where you will stay with my father until I get these papers safely to Reeve."

"Rafael, you wouldn't . . ."

"Wouldn't what?"

"Leave me again."

"Catrina, it is for your own good."

"That was what you said last time. I am no safer alone, so I would rather be with you."

"It is impossible, the danger—"

Catrina bent forward and draped her arm over Rafael's shoulder. Her eyes gazed up into his. Soft breasts brushed his chest, and her dark hair flowed about her ivory skin. Her nearness was enough to unsettle him, but the intent gaze on her face shook him.

"Catrina," he said wearily, "no, you be sensible and listen to me."

Catrina moved closer. Slowly, seductively, she pressed gentle kisses on the corners of his mouth, trailing them to his cheek and firm jaw.

"Catrina, now listen . . ."

Her arms encircled his neck and her warm slim body pressed close to him. Her parted lips caressed his as her tongue flicked lightly to trace the line of his mouth.

Rapidly, he was losing ground and he knew it. He had been determined that she would be left safe, but something was drastically interfering with his determination. His arms were about her and, with a groan of almost despair, he lay back and drew her body across him.

"You are a wicked, seductive witch," he murmured against her lips. "But I will not change my mind. I went through agony when I thought Carlos would take out his vengeance on me through you. I could not bear to go through that again."

"Carlos is dead."

"But Don Francisco is alive and even more dangerous."

"Rafael, I shall be more frightened if I am away from you. I will only be thinking and worrying about you. If you are safe, or if Don Francisco has ended your life . . . I would prefer to face any danger with you than to face being alone. Oh, Rafael, take me with you, please."

"Catrina, I cannot," he replied, and a new anguish filled him when he could see the tears in her eyes. The moon touched her face and he saw the crystal sparkle of them and watched them trace lines down her face and drop in a small warm droplet on his skin. He drew her to him and tasted the salty taste of them. Resistance grew weaker, but still he battled. He did not know in their young love that this was a battle he stood no chance of winning.

"Rafael, I will not be in danger. I will go to the Ramerez home. They are friends. Don Francisco would not dare to touch me. I am an Alverez, and I am married to the son of

437

Don Diego Chavez. There is nothing they can do to me. I will be safe. There is no reason Don Francisco can use to touch me."

"You do not know him, Catrina."

"Rafael, even if others fail, I can get to the queen. There is no way he can stop me. We are of royal blood. He cannot stop me! Don't you see, Rafael, I can help. I can help."

"Catrina, others of royal blood have often mysteriously died. Somewhere between Don Francisco's home and the queen's apartments you would meet with a tragic accident. No, Catrina, that is one thought you must put from your mind."

"I will let that thought go, my husband," she said softly, "but not the thought of staying beside you . . . that I will not forget."

"Catrina, we will not speak of this again," he said firmly.

Catrina rose to her knees beside him, then sat back on her heels. The moon touched her skin, washing it in pale light. It was a vision that left Rafael momentarily speechless. Her hair fell about her like a tangled lion's mane.

She reached with one hand to lightly trace her fingers down his chest, then possessively, her hand rested on his hip. He was well aware of his body's reaction to her touch.

"I love you, Rafael, with my entire being. If anything were to happen to you, I would choose the same time to die. I have taken vows to you, vows I cherish deeply, and I will remain at your side unless you tell me you longer want me there."

"Do you think I am a fool?" he answered softly. "What man in his right mind could say he does not want you? It is only for your protection that I ask you to remain behind."

The word ask had replaced his demand, and Catrina smiled. Her hand caressed his lean ribs as she bent toward him. Warm lips followed slim fingers, and Rafael felt the flame brand him. He groaned softly as he reached for her.

"I would think of long nights without you, husband," she whispered as she slowly continued her gentle seduction.

"Nights when you sleep alone and cannot share what we have now. Nights when we can only send our thoughts to each other and not the joy we feel. Oh, Rafael, let us share always whatever life might offer. Let us not allow them to cheat us of one moment that we can share."

Rafael was assaulted on all sides. His senses were inflamed not only with the beauty he held in his arms but with the agony the truth of her words brought him. If he was caught and could not return, this might be the last time he held her so.

A combination of clever maneuvering by Catrina breached his fortress of resolve and left him very nearly defenseless. Her tears, the gentle touch of her hands, the warm willing body that curled close to his were enough to prove his undoing.

His arms reached to draw her against him and his hard mouth found hers in a kiss that was a combination of helpless anger and defeat. And Catrina knew it.

There were no words, neither wanted to speak at the moment. They wanted only to possess each other, and in fiery passion they gave to each other the complete depths their love would go. Both won and lost, both captured and surrendered, and both were victors in the battle of love.

He held her quietly now, thinking of ways he could keep her safe. "Catrina, if ever I need a defense in the courts, I would surely have you, for I believe you could convince the Devil to surrender Hell."

She laughed softly as she nestled close to him. "I would not oppose you in anything else but our separation, my husband."

"Thank God." Rafael laughed and was pleased with Catrina's responding laughter. "I must admit," he said, "I don't even know exactly where I went wrong. One minute I was decisive and the next, I was thinking of how we would manage it. Somewhere along the line I was completely out-maneuvered. I shall have to keep a close eye on you in the future."

"It was only logic, my love. You were right in changing your mind."

Now he laughed heartily. "Good God, woman, I never had a thought to changing my mind. In fact," he said and kissed her, "after that first kiss I don't think I had another logical thought at all." Their laughter was muffled and very happy as they held each other. After a while, they slept contentedly in each other's arms.

Early morning found them again on their way and traveling as rapidly as they possibly could. They traveled as long as days would permit, and at night Rafael and Catrina found a constant renewal of their pleasure in each other.

When they arrived at the Chavez hacienda, Rafael began the first stage of his plans.

A dark carriage was found and the Chavez crest was removed from its doors to make it unrecognizable. The livery that identified the Chavez family was left behind, and new clothes were found that would again leave them unidentified.

The retinue left and Diego Chavez watched as the carriage rolled out of sight. All his prayers followed the young couple that rode within.

Rafael and Catrina made the journey toward Madrid with only their courage supporting each other. In his pocket, Rafael had the papers sent from Carmen through Pedro that proved Reeve and Elana's marriage, plus signed proof of what Don Francisco had been trying to do. To this, Diego, who was held in great honor by Queen Isabella, had added a long and very informative letter of his own.

Three days later, they crested the last hill that led to the palace. They looked at each other, clasped their hands together and rode toward it.

Chapter Thirty-Three

Reeve and Elana stood together in the shadows. Their time was short, for the guard might free himself of Carmen's intervention and look into the room. He held her close to him, so close she could feel the solid beating of his heart.

"Reeve, just to hold you," she whispered softly, "just to know you are safe. It's enough for me. Go . . . please go. Leave this castle, leave this country. Don't, for the love of God, let Don Francisco find you. He will kill you."

"No, Elana. I have asked you to listen. Now will you put all other thoughts aside and listen to what I have to say."

"I don't understand how you can believe we still have a chance. I don't even understand how you got here, but to believe there is a chance to escape . . . no, Reeve. No, I do not dare. All I can pray for is that you are safe. Go to your ship, Reeve, go and be safe."

"Those are words I cannot hear, Elana. We will leave together." Reeve continued to hold her close. Quietly, he told her about Carmen. He told her of Carmen's escape and the death of the two men who had planned to kill her.

"I'm glad," Elana said vehemently. "They were monsters. What they would have done to her justifies their deaths."

Reeve agreed. Then he told her of how Carmen had found her way back with revenge in her heart. He spoke in a gentle

441

voice as he told her of what Carmen had done to Juan.

"She has great courage, Reeve."

"Yes, she does."

"I wonder if I could have done the same," she said. "It takes much to be able to kill."

"Elana, Carmen has taken our papers," Reeve began. "There is no way for you or me to get them to the queen."

"The passageways?"

"They don't lead to any part of the queen's apartment."

"Then? . . ."

Reeve went on to explain what Carmen had overheard.

"To kill Rafael and Catrina?"

He nodded. "I can't tell you much about how and why Rafael and Catrina were being held. I only know it was at Don Francisco's orders. Carmen went immediately to friends who could contact Pedro. He, in turn, took some friends to aid Rafael in their escape." Reeve looked across the nearly dark room but there was no sign of disturbance at the door. Rodrigo and Beatriz slept soundly. "Elana, it is only a matter of time. Rafael will bring the proof before the queen. All we have to do is keep our courage up and wait. Even though they drag the three of you into court, they will fail. When the queen is given the proof she will come to see what is happening. The queen will not be fooled by Don Francisco. She will ask many questions, and I will be there to answer them."

Elana was strangely silent, and Reeve turned her so that what little light the moon cast touched her face. Tears spilled helplessly and she was trying to stop them. Reeve drew her into his arms, rocking her against him. He would have given his life to be able to erase all the pain and fear she had been living with. He knew the strain had been more than anyone could be expected to bear.

"Elana, my love," he whispered against her hair. He felt her slim arms circle his waist, felt her press close to him as if he were the only source of warmth in a very cold world. "Don't cry. It will be over soon. You have been through so much, and I hate the thought that you have to face any more. I can only promise you that it will be over soon, and I will do my best to make the rest of your life happy. I love you, Elana. We need to have courage now."

"I will do whatever you ask, Reeve. I am frightened, but I will try. It . . . it is just . . . not being with you. I'm so alone when you are gone. I feel so empty."

"It is no easier for me to leave you, Elana. The room I am hiding in is empty and lonely. But we must hold the thought in our hearts that soon we will defeat Don Francisco, and that we will be free . . . free," he added softly.

Gently, he tipped her chin up and bent to touch her moist lips. It was a sensitive, gentle kiss that told her all he felt. He bound her against him, hating the fact that he would have to release her, that he would have to leave her.

Reluctantly, he lifted his lips from hers and they stood together in silence. They found, in their desperation, they could not part so easily. With a small muffled sob, she threw herself into his welcoming arms, and he crushed her against him.

Their lips met, burning, seeking a way to drive the fear away. It was a passionate, hungry kiss that they both thought would have to suffice over the other long dark hours of separation that still faced them.

"Elana," he said half in anger and half in desperation, "I must go."

"I know. Kiss me again, Reeve, give me the strength to let you go."

He blended their lips and bodies in mutual surrender. Elana kept her eyes closed, even when she felt Reeve leave her arms. After a while she knew the room was empty. In agony she buried her face in her hands and wept.

*   *   *

The small wooden door on a secluded side of the castle creaked on rusty hinges that had not been used in many years. There was no one near to hear the sound except the heavily cloaked figure that exited and closed the door.

The figure made its way across the dark gardens to the outer protective wall. Another well-hidden door, hidden behind climbing vines, was found. The vines were pulled aside and the figure pressed against the door. It was reluctant to open after being closed for so many years, but it finally opened enough for the figure to slip out.

The dark figure made its way rapidly toward the darkened streets. There was no hesitation, so it would have been clear to any onlooker that the figure knew well its destination and the route to follow.

From dark shadows to dark shadows the figure moved carefully. The cobbled streets were damp and the figure was careful that the footsteps were as quiet as possible.

There was no interruption on the route, for the figure carefully dodged any late night wanderers that might interfere in its mission.

The final destination was a huge mansion, obviously the residence of someone very important and very wealthy. Without hesitation, the figure moved to the front door and rapped, then waited awhile and rapped again.

The door was finally opened by a sleepy-eyed and not too pleased butler whose expression changed immediately. "Miss Carmen, come in please. Is something wrong?"

Carmen moved rapidly inside and closed the door quickly behind her with a sigh of relief. "Carl, is Mr. St. James asleep?"

"No, Miss, you know he always keeps late hours. He's only recently returned home. He's in his study now. Shall I tell him you would like to see him?"

"No." She smiled. "I'll surprise him."

"It will be a welcome surprise, Miss. It's been a long time since you've paid us a visit."

Carmen smiled and patted his arm affectionately as she passed him. She moved down the dimly lit hall easily, as one who knows her way well. She stopped outside a door and, without knocking, silently opened it.

The room was lit only by two or three candles and the light of a low burning fire before which sat a man deeply engrossed in a book.

He was a man a little over forty. Tall and evenly proportioned. He was not handsome in the classical sense, yet he had a charismatic aura about him. His hair was thick and dark with touches of gray. His skin was tanned and his eyes, had he been looking at her, would have been startlingly green. His nose was rather hawklike and his mouth was generously wide.

Carmen smiled fondly at him and approached on tiptoe until she stood not far from his side. "Is the book interesting, Joseph?" she asked softly.

Momentarily startled, he closed the book quickly and spun about in his chair. The look of surprise changed quickly to one of warm welcome. He rose from the chair quickly and moved toward her, his hands outstretched to clasp hers, and a pleased smile on his face. He took both her hands in his, gripping them firmly, and bent to kiss her cheek.

"Carmen, my dear. It is so good to see you again. It has been entirely too long. I have missed you."

"Thank you, Joseph, I have missed you, too."

"Come sit by the fire with me. Tell me where you have been wandering to now and why you have forgotten me."

She sat in a chair by the fire and he drew another close where he could sit and still reach out to capture one of her hands and

445

hold it warmly between his.

"Carmen, is there something wrong?"

"Joseph, do I always come to you when I have troubles?"

"And why should you not come to one you know cares so deeply?"

She watched him closely, possibly, after all the years she had known him, seeing him for the first time.

"You are right as usual." She laughed softly. "I must talk to you about something."

"Talk, my love, I am listening."

"Joseph, I have asked you for many favors, and you have always given them with no questions asked. You know what I have been doing?"

"Helping the unfortunate escape the Inquisition. I have known for a long time. But that is not the reason I have helped you. Carmen, you need only ask and I would do anything to help you. I do not keep a book in which I balance what I owe you or what you owe me. I care for you, Carmen, and I admire your strength. I would help you if I could."

"Then, let me tell you the story." Carmen began the talk, and as she spoke the names, Joseph's brow furrowed in a frown.

"Carmen," he interrupted.

"What?"

"This man . . . this Englishman . . . you call him Captain Burke. Would this name happen to be Reeve Burke by any chance?"

"Yes, it is. Do you know him?"

"If it is the man I think, I most certainly do. You say he is a ship's captain."

"Yes."

"Tell me, is he tall, golden-haired, rather strange eyes?"

"Yes, that is Reeve. You do know him?"

"I do, but not as *Captain* Reeve Burke. I know him as *Lord*

Reeve Burke, second son of Sir Thomas Burke. It is a remarkable story, and I imagine there are very few who know what really happened."

"And you are one?"

"I am, only because I have known his family since he and his brother Philip were boys. It is a very sad story."

"Can you tell me, Joseph?"

"Since your situation is the way it is, I feel it is nearly imperative that I do, but first, finish your story. I should like to know all the details."

Carmen went on with the complete story. When she finished it was quiet for several minutes before Joseph spoke again.

"I don't understand why Reeve did not tell them who he was. It might have gone easier."

"Will it make a difference now?"

"But of course, especially to the queen."

"Then tell me, Joseph, tell me."

"Well it goes back quite a few years. Sir Thomas Burke was not only extremely wealthy but he was nearly in direct line in the royal family. When he died, the estate was left to the two sons, Philip and Reeve. It was good because the brothers cared deeply for one another. They worked well together, and under their mutual care, the Burke estate grew both in wealth and prestige.

"Then the older son, Philip, met and fell in love with Amanda Fletcher. He did not see her as the kind of woman she was, but Reeve did, and she hated him for it. She hated what he saw in her, but she also desired him . . . him and the entire Burke fortune. She began to play on Philip's jealousy, claiming Reeve was making advances at her. At first Philip did not believe, but she continued to arrange for Philip to find them in situations Reeve could not explain without looking guilty.

"Reeve could not believe that his brother could not see Amanda for what she was. They argued and the wedge between

447

SYLVIE F. SOMMERFIELD

the brothers grew wider.

"No one knows how Amanda placed Reeve in a com-
promising situation. We surmise that somehow she sent a note
to him he thought came from his brother. Anyway, Philip
found them together in his bedroom. He would not let Reeve
explain. The brothers fought, Philip in anger and Reeve in
defense. Reeve wounded his brother. The thought that he
might have killed his own brother overwhelmed Reeve. He left
Kenton Hall, the family estate. He told his brother he would
not return. The laws of England gave Philip sole right to the
wealth, but Reeve didn't care. He left and refused to go to
Kenton Hall again. He did not trust Amanda, nor did he want to
fight with his brother. I imagine he made his own way from
there, for he dropped from sight for a long time. Then
reappeared but not in the same circles as his brother. I always
wondered why it happened so, why Philip could not see. But I
imagine it is true. Love is blind and no respecter of persons."

"Poor Reeve."

"Yes, I know the brothers loved each other. It is a shame
that a woman like Amanda came between them."

"Reeve has found much to replace what he has lost. He loves
Elana. I have got to do something to help them. I have heard
that the queen is planning to leave the castle for a month or so.
Don Francisco will move in that time. By the time she returns
the trial will be over. Rodrigo will be dead, Beatriz will be
married as well as Elana if Reeve cannot prove they already
are. Everything, the wealth and the power that goes with it will
fall into Don Francisco's lap. I have got to do something."

"Reeve cannot get to the queen?"

She explained to him about the passageways. "They do not
go to the queen's apartments. If he tries to get to her, Don
Francisco's men will kill him."

"Then . . ."

"Rafael and Catrina will try to get to the queen."

448

"If I know when, I will join them and add my voice to theirs."

"You have been here as an ambassador for a long time. Your voice will mean much. In all that has happened I had forgotten your position."

He chuckled softly. "As long as you do not forget me, you are forgiven."

"How could I forget you? I am grateful for all you have done for me. I was only a wild Gypsy girl when you took me in and taught me that there is so much more to life. So much beauty and pleasures."

"Carmen," he said gently, as their eyes met and held, "is gratitude all you feel for me?"

Carmen was completely taken by surprise. Joseph had been her mentor and friend. He had taken her from a wild, careless Gypsy life to mold her into a lady. He had opened her eyes to the finer beauties of the world. He had taught her music, art, and an appreciation of a finer life. It had been done well, for she had blended into all types of society in the pursuit of freedom for those less fortunate. Like a chameleon she had changed from one creature to another, making herself as easily acceptable in one as the other. It had never once crossed her mind that the sensitive gentle love she had searched for all her life had been before her eyes all the while, waiting for her to recognize it.

She gazed at him in wide-eyed silence as the knowledge of his emotion crashed about her. "I . . . I never knew . . . I never thought . . ."

"Of course you didn't," he replied with a look of understanding amusement. "My beautiful little butterfly, you have never stayed still long enough for me to tell you. Always you have been coming and going, trying to help all others, never thinking either of yourself or of the ones who love you."

"But . . . but you cannot love me," she said helplessly.

"Oh?" He grinned and raised one dark eyebrow. "And why

449

can I not?"

"You cannot . . . you are . . . I . . . I am . . ."

"Now, careful woman." He chuckled. "You are talking about the woman I love. And I shall tell you what you are. You are a strong, intelligent, and very lovely woman."

"I cannot believe . . . I . . . when?"

"When?" he said gently as his hand tightened over hers. "When I picked up a little Gypsy girl from the mud and washed her face and saw how beautiful she was."

He reached out to brush away the tears that escaped from the corners of her eyes.

"I cannot believe this. I cannot believe that you want me. All that I have been, Joseph, all that I am. No one has ever come to me in love. Always it has been lust, anger . . ."

He smiled. "Carmen, I wanted to give you all the world had to offer, but I saw that your heart was with people you thought needed you. You never gave a real thought to what you needed. That is why you never found what you have been searching for. Now you are ready to look around you, now maybe you have the time to see what has been lying at your feet always." His voice was quiet and he gently lifted her chin. The lips that touched hers were warm and giving. It was the first time in her life Carmen had ever tasted such sensitive possession. Her mouth trembled beneath his and tears burned her eyes and fell unheeded down her cheeks.

"I will do what you ask of me, Carmen, anything you ask of me. But when this is over, you will come back to me, and you will stay with me. I will teach you what love means as I have taught you so many other less important things. We will leave Spain and start a whole new life together. What would you say to France or Italy? I am a very wealthy man and I would love nothing better than to make you happy." His eyes held hers intently. "Promise me this, Carmen. When this is over you will come to me, and you will never leave me again."

She could hardly speak for the tears that choked her words. "I promise."

He smiled and for the first time, Carmen saw the look in his eyes she had envied so often. The look that had passed between Reeve and Elana. Warm and giving love. She made another silent promise to herself. She would give her life to this man and try to make him happy.

"I know you must go. I know you will not fully be mine until this is over and your friends are safe. I will let you go this time, my butterfly, but when this is done you will not be free to fly again."

His arms encircled her and she was flooded with the feeling that she was safe now from anything life threatened to do to her. He kissed her again, binding her to him. When their eyes met again, he could read the tumultuous emotions that swept through Carmen.

"I am much older than you, Carmen, and I have long ago learned the wisdom of patience. Now that I know you understand, I am willing to wait. It will not be long before we finish this affair. Don Francisco has made too many of the wrong enemies. We will see him finished. We will see your friends safe. Then we will begin our life."

It was the first sincere happiness in her life, and Carmen savored it.

"Before I forget all my good intentions," he said, "we had best make our plans."

Carmen nodded, still unable to trust these new and beautiful emotions. They sat before the fire and talked for over an hour until everything they planned to do was clear in both their minds.

Joseph walked to the door with her, where they shared a lingering, promising kiss.

She slipped out the door and he closed it behind her. There was no doubt in his mind that Carmen would make her way safely back to the castle. She was in her element where her wits were pitted against some adversity.

Carmen moved slowly through the dark-shadowed streets. Caution was part of her, and she practiced it without thought while her mind was on the new and beautiful thing that had entered her life and changed it so completely.

Within her was a new and deeper understanding of what Reeve and Elana meant to each other. She was distressed again at what she had tried to do to them, knowing now that Reeve could never have been hers. She meant to tell Elana and Reeve that she regretted what she had done and was forming the words in her mind when a new and much more wonderful thought came to her. She smiled to herself and increased the speed of her steps.

Soon she reached the door in the palace wall. Making sure no one saw her, she opened it and entered the dark corridors. She knew her way well and she moved as rapidly as the darkness would allow her. She marked off her steps by counting silently to herself, and after a while, she stopped in front of the panel that led to a room within the palace. She placed her eye to the small hole and surveyed the room. It was very dimly lit, still she could see the occupants.

Again, she smiled and quietly she pressed the hidden spring that slowly slid the door open. Then on catlike feet, she entered the room.

Chapter Thirty-Four

Reeve lay in the near dark room. The bed he lay on was narrow. He wondered why he could not seem to find any comfort.

He placed his hands behind his head and gave himself over to the one dream that could console his misery: Elana.

He relived every moment from the day he had agreed to come to Spain. The first time he had seen Elana. The first time he had kissed her and held her, and the golden moment when she had become his.

So many things held their lives in the balance. Whether Rafael would be able to reach the queen without being caught; whether Carmen could find a way to get help; whether Elana could hold on to her courage and the faith she seemed to have in him.

He knew the three that were locked in the room below would have to face much, just as he knew that, if they ran for freedom, Don Francisco would have no difficulty in finding them. He and Rodrigo would be killed somewhere, and Elana and Beatriz would be brought back to face whatever Don Francisco chose to do. There was nowhere to run. They had to face it out to the end.

He wished only that Elana were here, in his arms. The need to hold and to comfort her burned so deep he could hardly bear it. He rose restlessly from the bed and began to pace the floor, watching that his feet made no noise.

He knew the fear she must be feeling. He could feel it himself. He allowed Don Francisco to creep into his mind for a moment, then firmly and deliberately pushed it away. The violent emotion filled him so suddenly with the desire to kill Don Francisco with his bare hands that he actually felt his fingers curve as if they were already around his throat.

He was aware of the scraping sound of the hidden door. Carmen was coming back. He hoped she could bring some reassuring news. She had told Reeve she was going to speak to an old friend who had aided her often in the escape of others.

He turned to face the door and it was several minutes before he recognized the slim form that stepped through it.

Carmen stepped into the room in which the three prisoners were held. She could see that two slept in the bed. She looked around to find Elana, who was seated on the window seat and looking out the window.

She was unaware of Carmen's presence, and Carmen could tell she was caught up in some private dream. There was no doubt in Carmen's mind that the thoughts were of Reeve. It surprised Carmen just how much her understanding had been changed within the past few hours. She watched the door, and slowly and quietly she moved across the room to Elana's side.

Suddenly, Elana became aware of her. She spun about, wide-eyed with fear, then sighed with relief. "Carmen," she whispered, "why are you here? You could be caught. It's not safe."

"Don't worry," Carmen said with a smile. "There will be no problems. Be quiet and let me speak quickly. I have news and answers that will change things."

"Carmen, Reeve was here earlier."

"I know he was. He told me he had to see you."

"I'm sorry, Carmen, if I misjudged you."

"You need not apologize to me. I have need of your forgiveness, but that will be later. Now, I have more important words for you."

"What?"

Carmen gazed at Elana carefully for several minutes while Elana waited for her to speak. "We are nearly the same size and we have the same hair color. In the dark, I could easily pass for you."

"I don't understand."

"For a few hours, I am going to take your place."

"Take my—" Elana began, then suddenly her eyes brightened. "Reeve," she whispered.

"I will tell you how to get to him."

"I know these passages well. Tell me where he is hiding."

Carmen explained quickly and Elana nodded. "But what of you, Carmen? If they catch you—"

"They will not. I will wrap in a blanket and lie curled in the chair so they can only see my hair. They will think it is you. I can only get away with this until morning. You must be back by dawn."

"I will, I promise. Carmen, I am so grateful."

"I know." Carmen smiled as she gave Elana a gentle push toward the hidden door. Elana slipped through the hidden door and into the dark passageway.

Carmen wrapped a blanket about her and curled herself on the window seat. She folded her arms on her knees and bent her head so that her dark hair fell loosely about her. Whoever should look through the door would mistake the ebony-haired form for Elana. Carmen was content to stay so for the balance of the night. To fill the hours, she let herself plan the future she would spend with Joseph.

The wonder of this new love filled her with emotions she had never experienced before. She savored them, enjoyed them, and allowed herself to be lost to the dream.

Elana felt her way slowly along the passageways to the steps that led upward. She knew the small room was on the uppermost floor. Step by step she worked her way upward.

At the top of the last flight, she fumbled in the dark for the spring that would open the door. It swung open and she walked through the door.

Reeve stood in the dim light and she knew at first that he did not recognize her. She took two steps toward him before she saw his eyes light and his smile appear.

"Elana," he breathed softly, as if he thought she was a dream that might disappear. Then quickly he took the few steps that separated them. Strong arms swung her up against him and a hard mouth swept down to possess her.

In Reeve's mind it was as if he had dreamed her so hard that she had appeared out of the mist of his thoughts. It was only when he felt her soft body against his, her slim arms about his neck, and her warm lips parting under his that he really realized the dream was a reality.

Feverishly they kissed in wild abandon.

"Elana," Reeve whispered, "I can't believe you are really here. I'm afraid I will open my eyes and find you gone. How—"

"Carmen," Elana answered breathlessly. "She has taken my place for the night. I must be back by dawn. We have a few hours, Reeve, a few hours."

"A few hours," he repeated. He looked down into her eyes. "And a moment ago I was praying for just that, a moment, or a few hours. My guardian angel must have heard. I was praying hard enough."

"I, too, my love. Hold me, Reeve," she said softly.

Reeve tightened his arms about her and she rested her head

against his chest. With a gentle hand, he caressed her hair. He could feel her trembling cease and the soft sigh of content-ment. It was a moment of mutual peace in the center of a violent storm. Neither wanted to think about tomorrow. They would hold it at bay for these four hours they would have to share, then take the memories of these moments to sustain them over the hours of separation they might have to face.

The room was extremely small and contained only the narrow bed and one chair.

Reeve took her hand and drew her with him to the edge of the bed. He saw down and drew her down to sit beside him. "You look so tired, Elana," he said worriedly. "Have they given you food?"

"Yes."

"But you haven't eaten," he said firmly.

"I cannot, Reeve. I just wanted to know how you were, where you were." She gazed up at him. He had grown a short beard because of the inability to shave, and his eyes reflected the strain and worry he had been under the past few days.

She reached up to lay her hand against his cheek. He smiled and pressed his hand over hers, then turned his face to press a kiss in the palm of her hand. "Loving me has led you into so much, Reeve. Your life would have been so uncomplicated if we had not interfered."

"Yes," he agreed, "uncomplicated, empty, lonely, and always seeking something. I've found all here, Elana, and I would neither share nor trade it with anyone. And you, the thought that I might have missed you in my life is unthinkable. You've been the brightest, most loving thing that has ever happened to me. You've filled my life, Elana, and I would be with you, no matter what we have to face."

"And I with you, my love," she whispered softly.

Slowly, he bent his head as she raised her lips to his. Their lips met, first touching, then gently taking possession. His

457

hand lay lightly on her waist, and hers lay with the same gentle touch upon his shoulders, while their lips played upon each other, awakening all the memories of the moments they had shared.

When he lifted his head their eyes held again. Then he rose and drew her up beside him. With gentle hands, he reached to unbutton the front of her dress. She did not move but enjoyed the sensual pleasure of his touch as he slid the dress from her shoulders. Warm fingers pushed aside the thin material that stood between them.

His eyes devoured her as the candlelight touched her ivory skin with a pale glow. He breathed her name softly as again he held her close. He wanted to memorize every moment of this night. The feel of her skin, the scent of her. The pleasure of loving her that swelled within him until he could barely stand it.

They took time to slowly undress each other; time to touch, to taste and to enjoy each moment. He gazed at her slim body glazed by the candlelight. And when he saw the mark of Don Francisco's whip on Elana's perfect flesh he felt her pain and renewed anger at Don Francisco.

"My God, Elana," he breathed, "you are so beautiful—and look what he's done."

Elana's lips curved in a half smile and she reached out her arms toward him. "It does not matter now, my love. All that matters is that we are together." With a soft laugh, he swung her up into his arms and rocked her against him. For tonight they would forget all else but each other.

He moved back to the bed and sat upon it, bringing her down on his lap. He caressed her skin lightly, feeling her draw closer, warmed by his touch. His lips brushed across the soft, rounded globes of her breasts where the nipples were already rigid with passion. He heard her gasp with the intensity of her pleasure as his lips found one and then the other, drawing them hungrily to his mouth and suckling.

Their passions steadily mounted. He turned to lay her gently across the bed. Then he began to trace heated kisses on her belly and thighs until she cried out, trying to muffle her passion so no one could hear.

She slid her hands across his shoulders and lifted them to twine in his hair and draw him even closer.

It was a hunger that would be insatiable forever, a flame that grew with each touch until they were lost. Suddenly, he was within her, warm and pulsating, moving with a demand that she met most willingly. Together they were one and the promise was forever sealed.

Afterward, they lay secure in each other's arms, still defiantly holding the world and its fears at bay. They talked together in low whispers, sharing gentle kisses while they did.

"Reeve," Elana whispered, "so many times I have asked you and so many times you have taken my mind off of your answers."

"Asked me what, love?" he questioned as he lightly brushed her ear with a kiss.

"About you. Do you realize that you came into my world a mystery and though I love you beyond reason, you are still a mystery."

"I am no mystery, Elana." He laughed softly. "I am just an ordinary sea captain who has had the magnificent good fortune to find a goddess and then to fall in love and find she loves him, too."

"An ordinary sea captain? Reeve, that is not believable."

"Why?"

"First, you are far from ordinary."

He grinned wickedly. "Is that a compliment, Madam? If it is, I shall try to live up to it for the rest of my life."

She laughed softly. "Do not try taking my mind off the question," she said firmly. "You are not ordinary . . . in any way," she added swiftly and was rewarded by his warm chuckle and the way his arms tightened about her.

"Tell me," he whispered against the sensitive flesh of her throat. "Just how am I not ordinary?"

"Any ordinary ship's captain, faced with the situation you found here, would have raised his sails and left the shores of Spain a long time ago." She looked up into his eyes. "In fact, an ordinary captain would not have been asked to come here. They must have felt you were well acquainted with life at court or they never would have placed you here. Why would they believe an 'ordinary' captain would have been comfortable at court? And you were, Reeve. I watched you closely. It is a place you were well accustomed to."

"I will admit, I did business with many gentlemen, many in fact from the royal family. As a friend I was often invited to their homes. I guess the manners sort of rubbed off."

"Reeve, they are too much a part of you. I believe you were born with them."

Reeve lay back against the pillow and Elana rose on one elbow to look down at him. "What are you, Reeve Burke?" she said gently, as she lightly brushed her hands up his lean ribs to rest on his chest. "Courtier, captain, adventurer . . ."

He reached up and caught her face between his hands. The silver-gray eyes that had so mesmerized her before held her again. She could not read their depths, yet she was aware they were searching hers thoroughly. "I am the man who loves you more than the breath in my body," he replied. "I am the man who desires nothing more than to share the rest of his life with you. Does my past mean much to you, Elana? Will you be disappointed in living a life with a man who does not have riches to offer? Is my love enough for you?"

"Oh, Reeve," she cried as she bent to kiss him. "Do you think it matters? It is you I want. I do not care about riches. I will share your life and be happier than I have ever been before. But I want to share it with a man I know and understand. I love you in every way it is possible to love you."

"Look at me closely, Elana. Remember, as I do, every touch, every kiss, every sweet moment we have ever shared. Look at me and tell me that all that I am belongs to you. All that I will ever be is here before you, offering to share my life with you. When we go back to England, it will be a small house we go to. All the money I have will be earned by my own sweat and my ship. That is Reeve Burke. That is what I am."

Their eyes met and she was lost in the silent pleading she read so clearly. A fear struck her that there was something in Reeve's past of which he was afraid. It startled her to think of fear in connection with Reeve, the one who had always been her strength. She would be patient and she would give him all the love she had to give. If he needed time to conquer his fear she would give it. And she would be with him should he ever feel free enough to share his fears with her.

"I will love you always, Reeve," she said softly as she lay across him, molding her slim body close to his. She kissed him lingeringly. ". . . I shall love you always."

She felt him relax and his arms came about her so tightly it almost forced the breath from her body, but she did not mind for she sensed his pleasure at her absolute trust.

They slowly and very leisurely renewed their passion. Elana wept with the intense feeling of belonging. It was as if Reeve had pulled her deeply within him to hold forever.

For Reeve, that was exactly what he had done, for Elana had walked into a place that had been empty and filled it completely. He had pushed out all the hurts of the past, all the losses he had felt and replaced them with Elana's warm, giving love.

Elana's exhaustion was obvious when she curled against Reeve and slept. Reeve lay awake, knowing the dawn would come soon enough and he would have to give her up.

Thoughts that had not been welcome in his mind for many years came unbidden and lingered where they were not wanted. He thought back to his childhood, to the parents who had loved him and given him all that great wealth could give.

Reluctantly, he thought of his brother, Philip. The brother he had loved so much and who he knew had loved him. Philip, who had shared happy childhood years. He thought of how they had shared Kenton Hall in happiness until . . . Amanda.

She had torn their lives apart with her greed and her illicit desires. He remembered her beauty, but with it he remembered what she had done to help destroy the love between him and his brother.

He could still see the look in Philip's eyes the night he had found Amanda in his room in a state of near undress. Philip had no way of knowing that Reeve had been sent a note telling him that his brother wanted to see him.

He had been unprepared to find Amanda and even more unprepared to face an enraged brother, whose jealousy had been prodded for months by his wife.

It had been the most terrible thing Reeve had faced when his brother had drawn his sword and Reeve had wounded him in defense of his life. He had left Kenton Hall with nothing, and had vowed never to return or to take another drop of money.

He had signed on a ship and had been at sea as often as he could manage. In time he had worked his way up to captain of his own ship. But always, in the back of his mind, lingered the pain and the hunger to see Kenton Hall again and to extend his hand again to his brother in friendship.

Elana stirred and moved closer to him, seeking his warmth. He tightened his arm about her. Nothing, he thought, would separate them once they left this country . . . if they left this country.

Reluctantly, he watched the dark night sky begin to lighten. They could not endanger Carmen any longer. She needed her freedom if she were to be of any help to them.

He turned to Elana and looked down on her sleeping face. Gently, he touched his lips to hers and caressed her bare shoulders. "Elana," he said softly.

She stirred and nestled her head in the hollow between his neck and shoulder. "No, Reeve," she breathed softly, "I don't want it to be over. This night has been so short."

"There's no help for it, my love. You have got to go. Carmen might be found at any time and we need her to keep her eye on what is happening and free to carry messages if we need her."

"I know," she sighed. "I wish we were away from here and I did not have to leave."

Her body was warm and soft against his. Her arms about him made it the most difficult thing he ever did to move from her embrace and stand up. He reached down and drew her to her feet.

He helped her dress, then watched as she ran her fingers through her tangled hair to try and tame it. She, in turn, sat on the edge of the bed and watched him dress, admiring again the perfect shape of his lean, muscular body. He was a golden dream, a dream she would hold for as long as she lived.

He went to her and silently they moved into each other's arms for that final kiss. He held her close. There were no words to be said.

He took her hand and they passed together through the doors. They walked through the still dark passage until they came to Elana's room.

First, Reeve checked the room. All was well. Rodrigo and Beatriz still slept, and the form that was curled on the window seat, if Reeve had not known, could well have been Elana.

At the first sign of movement of the doors, Carmen rose quietly to her feet. Both Reeve and Elana knew she had not slept the entire night.

There was no time for them to talk. Elana entered and

Carmen touched her hand quickly as she passed. In a few seconds the panels closed and Elana stood in the center of the quiet room.

But now this time she still felt the renewed strength that Reeve had given her. She made a silent vow that she would not let the dark fear close to her again. She would have to hold the same faith Reeve had: that soon they would be free and soon they would be together.

Rodrigo stirred on the bed, came fully awake, and saw his sister standing silently in the center of the room. There was something new about her stance and he rose from the bed and walked to her side. He put his arms about her shoulder and drew her against him. He was more aware of the difference when she smiled up at him. Her eyes were bright and clear and the smile was warm and fearless.

"Elana, are you all right?"

"Yes, Rodrigo," she replied. "Now . . . I'm fine, and I shall not be afraid again."

Before Rodrigo could question her strange reply, Beatriz stirred and sat up in bed. A fateful day for all of them had begun.

Chapter Thirty-Five

Don Francisco could not have been more pleased if he had made the arrangements himself, for the events that followed.

He stood in the queen's chamber along with many of her advisors of the court.

Isabel crumpled the papers she had been reading into a ball. She was angry and there was no doubt of that in any of their minds as she flung the crumpled paper nearly across the room.

"Why cannot these stupid fools settle their differences? Why must they continue to bicker like children over foolish things?" she demanded of no one in particular. She was angry and her anger was a thing few in the room wanted to be in the way of.

When the great Moorish invasions erupted in Spain, peasants, farmers, shepherds, and city dwellers all found it necessary to place themselves under the protection of some local lord and his professional army while they agreed to pay taxes to him, and under certain conditions, to serve him.

All the kings before Ferdinand, through conquest and marriage and inheritance tried to unite them. It was a success, but occasionally, some bitter rivalry broke out. This was one of those occasions.

Ferdinand had been ill for several days, and it had fallen to Isabel to manage such affairs as best she could. She was an effective monarch, but she did not want to leave Madrid at the time . . . but Don Francisco de Vargas wanted her to.

If Isabel were gone for a week, he could hold a trial. Torquemada and tribunal had gathered and were waiting for just such an opportunity. Don Francisco did not want Isabel to get word of what he planned. He was afraid she would interfere and seek Rodrigo's freedom because of her feelings for Elana and Beatriz.

By the time Isabel could return, he would safely have Rodrigo branded a heretic, tried, and burned at the stake. He would also have Elana and Beatriz married and under control. The only thorn in his side was wondering where Reeve Burke was; wondering if he had the proof of his marriage to Elana; and, if he did, preventing him from getting to the queen.

The ways to the queen were well guarded by Don Francisco's men who had orders to kill Reeve on sight and *he* would answer the questions later.

For now, he wanted Isabel away from Madrid and was extremely grateful for an altercation that drew her attention and, he hoped, her presence. He would do all he could to encourage it.

"Your Grace," he said smoothly, "they need the fine touch of your diplomatic hand to settle their grievances."

Isabel turned to look at him and her astute gaze shook him, but he had much too much at stake to lose now. A fortune and the power it brought were at his fingertips, almost within his grasp, and he had no intentions of losing either.

Isabel had been very upset when Elana and Beatriz had been found missing, yet she did not want to believe all the stories that Don Francisco had fed to her. He had paid well to start many rumors which he had deliberately brought to the queen's ear.

No matter the rumors and how true they sounded, Isabel had loved both Beatriz and Elana and did not want to believe.

The rumors Don Francisco started about Rodrigo were even more deadly. Isabel, a devout Catholic, found it hard to push the stories aside.

Now she gazed at Don Francisco, and it occurred to her quick mind that Don Francisco de Vargas was much too smooth and seemed to her to be always within hearing distance of anything. Yet she had to admit, for the situation, he might be right. It was just that she was still waiting for news of where Elana and her brother had gone and validation of the story that Elana had deliberately defied her and run away with Captain Reeve Burke, who was not a Spaniard, not royal blood . . . and not Catholic. She wondered if he was a complete heretic.

To Don Francisco's relief, her eyes left his and she returned to her thoughts. "I suppose I must go to settle this dispute," she said more to herself than to the others.

Isabel was a woman to be reckoned with, no matter what the situation. Once her decision was made, she usually moved upon it. She did so this time, much to Don Francisco's delight, as she gave the orders that on the next dawn they would leave Madrid for a few days.

The next morning Don Francisco watched from the windows of his room as the queen's retinue left the palace grounds. He smiled as he turned to face the man who stood beside him, Torquemada, the benign, angelic-faced Torquemada, who would soon hold three lives in his hands.

"You have arranged the tribunal?" Don Francisco questioned.

"I have, Don Francisco."

"And the men who sit upon it are sympathetic to our needs?"

"The men I have chosen understand their duties well, both to Mother Church, and to you, Don Francisco. They know what must be done to cleanse our country. You need not worry. Rodrigo de Santangel will be questioned and most likely found guilty."

"Good. Then we will hold him until his sister and her friend submit to our plans. They will marry whom we choose if they think his life is at stake."

"And whom do you wish Elana to marry now that Diego is dead?"

"I have chosen another."

"Might I ask who?"

"Juan Ramerez."

"Juan Ramerez," Torquemada replied in surprise. "The man is little more than an idiot."

"You need not worry. He, despite his lack of . . . intelligence, is still of noble blood. He will be satisfied playing in his secluded castle with his swords and lances while I," he said with a chuckle, "will find it a pleasure to keep his bride amused here at court."

"And Rodrigo?"

"When Beatriz is safely married, when I know that Elana will be mine, then the court will be forced to carry out the sentence. We will be forced to burn a man convicted of heresy."

"How soon will you begin the trial?"

"The queen is gone. She will be gone for a week. Shall we begin tomorrow morning?"

"Very good, Don Francisco. I shall go and make the arrangements now."

"The witnesses I have chosen, have they written and signed the accusations?"

Torquemada smiled. "Did they have any choice in the matter?"

"Hardly." Don Francisco laughed.

"They have done what you want. They will swear to a man that Rodrigo de Santangel has committed every act of sacrilege possible."

"Good." Don Francisco turned back to gaze out of the window to watch the queen's receding carriage. "Then in a few days it will all be over, and I shall have proven to them that they should never have crossed me. It will give me great pleasure to see Rodrigo de Santangel burn at the stake."

"And I," Torquemada replied softly, "will take great pleasure in seeing that you have what you want, as you will in seeing that I have what I want."

"Yes," Don Francisco replied. "I will see that you have all we bargained for."

Torquemada bowed slightly and turned to leave the room, his feet making no sound as he did.

Carmen and Reeve sat quietly in the small room. Both were, at the moment, engrossed in their own thoughts. Both were also waiting for the word, from their network of spies, that Rafael was sighted.

The fine network of spies throughout the castle had kept them informed of Don Francisco's movements. Carmen and Reeve had walked the passageway both for the need to find something to do and to keep an eye on the three that waited in the locked room. Now, quietly and impatiently, they awaited Rafael's arrival.

"Carmen," Reeve said, "do you know the route Rafael must use?"

"Yes, of course."

"Would you tell me what it is?"

Carmen nodded and proceeded to tell him what roads Rafael would have to travel. As she ceased talking and before Reeve could ask any other questions, the small door slid open and a slim young man entered. Carmen looked at him in surprise.

"Enrico, what are you doing here? Has something happened? Has Rafael come?"

469

"No, Carmen, Rafael is not here, but something has happened and I'm sure you are not going to like it."

Reeve stood up slowly, his heart raced and a cold hand touched his mind.

"What, Enrico, what?" Carmen questioned.

"The queen left this morning."

"Left," Carmen said. "For where . . . why?"

Enrico proceeded to explain what had drawn the queen away. "But that is not all," he added.

"What more?" Reeve said.

"Torquemada," Enrico said, breathing the feared name as he swiftly crossed himself, "has called a tribunal. They are going to try Rodrigo, Elana, and Beatriz for heresy."

"When?" Carmen whispered as she watched Reeve's face grow pale and his hands clench with the depth of hate-filled anger that rose up within him.

"Today," Enrico whispered as he, too, saw the flame that leapt into Reeve's eyes. Without a word, Reeve picked up his sword from the table and started toward the door.

"Reeve! Where are you going?" Carmen cried.

"To run my sword through that bastard and rid the earth of his evil once and for all," Reeve raged. It was the first time in his life he had ever let his emotions control his head, and if it hadn't been for his fear for Elana, it would not have happened.

Carmen raced to the door, turned her back to it and faced Reeve's black rage. "No, it's sure death for you to go near him. It's exactly what he wants you to do."

"And you believe I will just sit here to save my skin and let Elana and her brother be convicted of heresy? They will burn them at the stake."

"Listen to me, Reeve! Listen to me!"

"Move, Carmen," Reeve demanded.

"Reeve, for once he has played into our hands."

"What do you mean?"

"Somehow he has persuaded the queen to leave. I don't

470

know how, but it is the best thing he could have done for us. When it is dark tonight, you will slip out of the castle. You should be able to find Rafael. Before you go, we will find out where the queen has gone, then you will go to her. You and Rafael will go to the queen, tell her the truth, and you and I both know she will return with you and bring justice with her."

"And in the meantime what will he be doing to Elana?"

"Elana is stronger than you think, Reeve. She is also sure of you. She will stand bravely in the face of whatever he plans. If you go tonight, you could be back here long before the trial is over."

Reeve's eyes held hers as he said softly, "One mistake on my part, one slip, one wasted moment could cost their lives."

"Then," Carmen replied quietly, "you must make no mistakes, and you must not waste a moment."

Carmen breathed a sigh of relief when she realized Reeve had regained control of his emotions. He relaxed. Then the glow of deep respect touched his eyes.

"Carmen, if we get out of this, someway, somehow, I must show you how grateful I am, and how grateful I'm sure the others will be."

Carmen smiled. "No, Reeve, you do not know yet, but I have already been well rewarded for anything I might have done. Fate has given me all I will ever need. When this is over, I shall explain it to you."

Reeve nodded and laid his sword again on the table to await night. As soon as it would cover his movements, he would leave the palace and begin the race for Elana's freedom.

Rafael stood by the carriage while the horses were rested. In the distance he could see the palace, but he did not want to arrive until after nightfall. That way, he and Catrina could be safely settled in the palace before Don Francisco would know it. Then he would have no way of stopping them from an audience with the queen. An audience that would bring everything to light and expose Don Francisco for what he was.

Catrina stepped out of the carriage and walked up beside him, sliding her hand into his. "Rafael?" she questioned softly. "Why do we stop here? Should we not hurry to the palace?"

He explained why they waited. "Let the horses rest. We will sit beneath the shade of a tree until nightfall. Then we shall go to the palace and do what must be done."

They did just that. Catrina sat in the soft grass and Rafael lay with his head in her lap. They spoke of things to keep their mind from the lives that depended upon what they did. They made plans for the future they would share, for the home they would have, and the children that might bless it. All with hope that they would succeed in saving the lives of the others they loved. They talked and waited for the night.

Reeve moved slowly and quietly down the dark passageway to the outer door which ultimately led him to the palace grounds. He crossed them silently, eluding the guards, and found the door in the wall that led to the outside. It opened easily under pressure and he slipped out. Like a shadow he left the palace and began to move in the direction Carmen had told him to follow.

Bright stars lit the night sky and even though it was a beautiful night, Reeve was not too happy with the bright moonlight that slowed his travel. He found the house near the town where others waited to supply him with a horse.

Once mounted, Reeve felt as if half the battle was over. It was a strong horse. He could feel the strength beneath him. He counted on that now in his desperate search for Rafael.

He followed the road that Carmen had told him about. Somewhere along its winding way he should find Rafael . . . if Rafael had gotten free . . . if Rafael had found his way there

. . . if they did not miss each other . . . if Rafael had taken the same road . . . if . . . if . . . if. It seemed to Reeve as if he had been living on *ifs* for a long time.

Once free of the city, he kicked the horse into a mile-eating run. They thundered along the dark, empty road.

Rafael had watched the moon rise. Then he began preparations to again move toward the palace. Catrina had already entered the carriage, and Rafael was about to enter when the sound of a rapidly moving horse came to them.

Rafael could only think that they might be discovered. He reached inside the carriage and took out a pistol he had placed there for safety. Holding it beneath his cloak, he waited. It sounded like a single rider. If so, maybe there was no cause for alarm. If the rider was to interfere in his plans, out of necessity, Rafael would shoot him.

Reeve rode over the crest of the hill and then pulled his horse to a skidding halt. The carriage sat before him, and in the pale moonlight he could see the figure that stood beside it. He took the chance. "Rafael!" he called. "It's Reeve."

Rafael breathed a rasping sigh of relief. He stepped away from the carriage and stood in the moonlight. "Reeve, my friend," he called. "My God, am I glad to see you!"

Reeve dismounted and strode to Rafael's side. They clasped hands in an agony of relief. "You are no happier than I," Reeve said. Before he could speak again, the carriage door opened and Catrina stepped out.

"You brought Catrina?" Reeve questioned in surprise. Rafael laughed.

"Do you think you could have gotten away with telling her to stay home? I tried, my friend."

Catrina smiled and went to Reeve to kiss his cheek. "Reeve, if my friends are in danger, I would like to help."

"I did not expect to see you here. What is happening?"

473

Rafael questioned.

In as few words as possible, Reeve explained the situation. "We need to find the queen as soon as possible. Rafael, you have the papers?"

"Yes," Rafael answered. He reached into his pocket and extended the packet to Reeve. "Let us go," he said. "There is much we have to tell the queen, also. There are many things she should know about Don Francisco."

"Rafael, I think it would be better if we leave Catrina here with the men and the carriage."

"Never!" Catrina said firmly. Rafael grinned and Reeve said nothing more about it.

"Reeve, would it not be better if we rode the horses and left the carriage here? We could make better time."

"Can you ride without a saddle, Catrina?" Reeve asked. Catrina smiled.

"Probably better than a man who is more used to a ship than a saddle," she replied.

Now Reeve had to laugh. "I suppose you are right. Shall we go?"

"Do you know where we will find her?" Rafael questioned.

"Yes."

"How far?"

"At least a day to a day and a half ride."

"It will take at least four days to get there, give her our information and get back."

"Don't remind me," Reeve said. "We have so little time. Let's not waste it talking."

The horses were mounted by Rafael and Catrina. In a few minutes they were again on their way.

Catrina made no complaint as they pushed themselves as far as the strength of their horses would allow. They stopped only to rest the horses and to eat the small amount of food Carmen had insisted Reeve take along.

No matter how hard they pushed they did not sight the

queen's entourage until early in the morning of the second day. They were halted by the guards before they could reach the queen. They gave the guards their names and waited to see if she would see them.

Within minutes they were called to her. They stood before a queen who was cold-eyed and firm-lipped. Her gaze met and held Reeve's. He returned her look with as much control as possible, but Isabel was well prepared to attack him and he knew it. There was no doubt in his mind and her first words confirmed his thoughts.

"So, Captain Burke," she said coldly, "you return to us. Have you not done enough harm within to my court?"

"Your Grace does me an injustice," Reeve said quickly. "If I could have the privilege to explain all that has happened you will see that I meant no harm then. It is others who have harmed the reputation of your court."

"He speaks truly, Your Grace," Rafael said. "I would add my voice to his in defense. If Your Grace will allow us to explain we will tell you of a plan so dark that it nearly cost all our lives."

If Reeve claimed her anger, Rafael and Catrina were two of noble lineage who could claim her attention.

"It is important that we speak quickly, Your Grace, for if we do not, innocent lives will be forfeit. Rodrigo and Elana and Beatriz will pay with their lives," Rafael said.

These words drew Isabel's attention quickly. "Who," she demanded arrogantly, "has the right to condemn such noble names to death, and why? I was told that Elana had run away with you, Captain Burke, and that her brother had seduced Lady Beatriz and joined you."

"It is not true, Your Grace," Reeve replied, "but if Elana would have done so, I would have taken her away from what you had planned for her."

"A noble marriage."

"To a man she did not love."

"A man of wealth and power," she countered.

"Who had no honor and was seeking only more wealth and power," Reeve answered.

They faced each other and for a breathless moment, all was silent. Rafael and Catrina were both wordless at the moment, hoping Isabel's anger at Reeve would not destroy any chance that she might have listened to them. Then Isabel smiled slightly and there was a glitter of curious amusement in her eyes which Rafael had never seen before.

"Sit down, Captain Burke," she said softly, "and tell me this tale of yours."

Rafael and Catrina breathed a sigh of relief, and Isabel shared a look of total understanding with Captain Reeve Burke.

Isabel did not say a word until the three nocturnal visitors had explained all that had happened from the very first moment Reeve had arrived.

The proof of all that was done was laid before her, including the proof that Reeve and Elana had been married within the church.

Rafael had added proof of the connection between Don Francisco and Don Carlos, adding what Don Carlos was supposed to do with himself and his wife, Catrina.

Isabel read each word carefully and weighed each word that had been told to her. She was alternately shocked and angered by all she had heard. She rose and paced the floor for a moment. Then she turned to face the three who waited.

"We must return immediately. We must prove once and for all that Isabel rules here." She spoke softly, but her words carried the power of the throne. "I will allow no one to play with my laws for their own benefit, and I will allow no one! No one, to use my rules and me. Don Francisco de Vargas has much to answer for."

Chapter Thirty-Six

The room in which the trial was being held was a large square room. Three sides of the room held three chairs apiece, upon which sat the nine men Torquemada had chosen as the judges.

Don Francisco stood near the door and watched the proceedings that had been going on for four days. He smiled to himself. It would soon be over.

He had watched each day as one witness after another was brought forth to accuse. Each of the three on trial had been brought in the room to be seated on a stool in the middle of the floor. There, the questions had been asked, and the accusations made.

Rodrigo could not believe the charges that had been brought against him or the witness who had brought them. He, like Beatriz and Elana, had denied everything, but he could see what was happening, and he knew they had no way to defend themselves against what had been so well planned and was being so well executed.

The three had been dragged in, one at a time, and questioned until they were exhausted. The questioning began at any time, midday or midnight, and was held until they nearly fell from the stools.

Food was withheld for the judges knew quite well hunger sometimes numbed the mind and made the tongue careless.

Rodrigo and Beatriz were both surprised at the reserve of strength Elana seemed to have. She had been afraid to speak of Reeve, in case someone was listening, yet she kept reassuring Rodrigo and Beatriz that she was no longer afraid and that they should not be either.

Elana, when brought forward for questioning, tried to remain calm, but the accusations they brought against her brother terrified her. They wanted him to be convicted of heresy and for this, he could be burned at the stake. Her real fear was that Reeve would not make it in time to save Rodrigo.

She was returned to the room now after four grueling hours before the tribunal. She sagged wearily into a chair while Rodrigo poured her a glass of water from a decanter that sat on the table. He handed her the water with an encouraging smile. She took the glass, and for a moment she gazed down into it.

"Rodrigo," she said softly, "they want to kill you. They want to eliminate you so that we will do what they want out of fear."

"I know," he replied. Rodrigo knelt before her chair. "Elana, no matter what they threaten to do to me, I do not want you or Beatriz to consider what they want. You know them . . . I know them. They will not keep any bargains they might make."

Elana smiled and laid her hand against his cheek. "I know, Rodrigo, don't worry about me. Soon this will all be over. I feel they are in for many more surprises than they might have bargained for."

Before Rodrigo could answer the door opened again and two guards entered. Rodrigo felt they might be coming for either him or Beatriz so he moved to her side and put an arm about her waist. They were both surprised when they went to Elana.

"Get up, woman, and come with us."

"Dammit man," Rodrigo said, "you've been questioning her for hours already."

Without a word, the guard struck Rodrigo across the face. "Silence, it is not for you we come but for her."

Elana rose to her feet before a furious Rodrigo could do something foolish and get himself killed before Reeve could get to them. "Rodrigo, don't worry," she said quickly, "I will be all right."

Rodrigo regained his composure and he and Beatriz helplessly watched as the two guards left with Elana between them.

Elana walked between the two guards. She was so tired that she could barely think, so she kept her mind on Reeve and the promise that he would come for her.

The only fear still holding her was Rodrigo's fate. Would it happen before Reeve could come? Silently, she prayed not. She could not see the future without Rodrigo's laughter to share it with.

She came to a surprised halt when the two guards stopped in front of Don Francisco's door. She remained silent, but her heart began to beat rapidly.

One guard opened the door and the other pushed her inside. She stood just within the room as they pulled the door shut with a quiet click that echoed through the room.

Don Francisco stood with his back to her, gazing out the window. He remained silent, hoping to intimidate a woman who was already, so he thought, completely in his control. After several minutes he turned to face her, to find her gazing quietly at him.

Despite what she had been through, Don Francisco felt she was still one of the most beautiful women he had ever seen.

"What do you want with me, Don Francisco?" she said in a voice that lacked any sign of fear.

"I would talk with you, Elana," he said softly.

"What have we to say to each other?"

He smiled and walked to her side, taking her arm and drawing her further into the room. "We have a great deal to say to each other." He turned her to face him. "It is time, Elana. You will make choices."

"I made my choices a long time ago." She lifted her chin and drew her shoulders erect. "When I chose to marry Reeve. There is nothing you can do about that."

"Is there not?" He smiled.

"No."

"You still think he will elude my guards and find a way to rescue you. You are wrong, Elana. We will find him soon. He cannot hide forever. When we do, we will kill him."

Involuntarily, she shivered. Her weariness was beginning to tell on her.

"But I have an even better offer to propose."

"What?"

"Your brother's life," he replied quietly. He grew silent, watching her slowly digest what he had just said. "You see, Elana, when you leave this room, I shall arrange for the trial to be drawn to a close. The outcome of the trial . . . the verdict . . . will be up to you. No matter what your . . . husband tries to do, your brother will already be dead. And you will watch as we tie him to the stake and light the fire. You will have a long time to remember his screams as he dies."

"No," Elana whispered, for her mind had already conjured up a vision of his description.

Don Francisco moved closer to her. "Yes, Elana. The verdict will be tomorrow, and he will die before the morning is over."

"What do you want of me!" she cried.

"I want to know where that passageway is. I want you to be married tomorrow morning as I want Beatriz de Mendosa.

480

When that is done, then you will have your brother's freedom."

"But I cannot marry again. I am already married."

"Fray Torquemada has already assured me that it will be quickly put aside. If any record of it should appear, he will see to its disposal."

"And now that your puppet, Diego, is dead, who do you have planned for me?"

"I think, since he is a distant relative of mine, that Juan Ramerez will be a wise choice."

"You cannot mean that." She was aghast. "Juan is . . . is . . ."

"I will admit he is less than most women would desire, but that does not matter. You won't be living with him, anyway." Her mind grasped quickly what he had planned. "You will be taken to my residence in Valladolid. I spend much time there when I am not at court. It is a beautiful place. You will enjoy it as I know I will."

"And what of my brother?"

"Your brother will have your best interests at heart. He will remain obedient. If he does as he is told . . . marries whom we suggest . . . he will continue a long and productive life."

"You are reaching for power, Don Francisco," Elana said. "What will you do if the queen begins to suspect your goals?"

"By the time she does, I will possess more power in Spain than she does. From there it is a small step to overthrow them."

"And making yourself king," she added in a disbelieving whisper.

Before she could speak again, he was beside her. He gripped her firmly and held her bound against him. "And you, Elana," he said, "would be queen. You would stand beside me. Together we would have all the world. You need only come to

481

me willingly and I can give you a crown. What can your poor ship captain have to offer to compare with that?" he demanded in a hoarse voice as his lips brushed her hair.

She could not fight him. There was no way her strength would be a match for his, so she stood immobile.

He pressed warm kisses against her forehead and cheeks, then tried to lift her to respond by claiming her lips, but they were cold and lifeless beneath his. In anger, he pushed her from him.

"You have asked me what he has to offer that you do not," she said. "I will tell you. He offers me the warmth of love that is not selfish. He offers me kindness, consideration, and gentleness. He gives me all I need to make life worth living. I do not want your crown, Don Francisco. I do not even want life if it is to be lived as your possession. And I believe I can speak for my brother and for Beatriz when I say I do not believe they would want their lives at such a cost. Do your will, Don Francisco. But I will never . . . never come to you willingly."

Don Francisco had never been angrier. His eyes blazed with it, but he did not move, nor did he shout. He only smiled. "Willingly or not, I will have you. With or without your acceptance I will teach you to be obedient to me. But you have condemned your brother to death, and Beatriz will be whatever I command that she be, and she will marry whom I choose. I think if she is faced with Rodrigo's death, she will be more agreeable than you to whatever I say. Go . . . go back to your brother and your friend and tell them what your foolish stubbornness has condemned them to. And when you sleep tonight remember this. I will have you . . . I will have you and you will taste all that I have planned for you."

Don Francisco reached out and gripped her arm in a brutal hold. He dragged her to the door. He opened the door and thrust her out toward the two guards who still waited. "Take her back to her room," he ordered. "Remember what I have said, Elana. Go and face your brother and tell him what you have done with his life and the life of the woman he loves."

Elana walked between the two silent guards. Hot tears stung her eyes, and her weary body made her feel as if she could barely make each step. Her tangled mind reached only for Reeve. Reeve would come, she thought. Reeve would be in time to save her brother's life and Beatriz. Reeve would take her in his arms and hold her, and all the fear and worry would be gone. Their steps echoed through the halls, echoed only one thought in her mind. Reeve would come . . . Reeve would come . . . Reeve would come.

When she entered the room, Rodrigo and Beatriz were immediately at her side. She began to weep and Rodrigo drew her into his arms. In halting words she explained all that had happened between herself and Don Francisco.

"You are right, sweet sister," Rodrigo said softly as he held her. "We do not want our lives at the cost he would ask to be paid."

It was a long and very black night for the three who sat together, waiting for their fate. Beatriz sat on the floor by the fireplace, her head resting on Rodrigo's knee. He absently caressed her hair while he gazed unseeing at the fire. Elana sat opposite them, curled deep into a large chair, her thoughts on Reeve. She held fast to the memories of all they had shared, the nights they had been together in the Gypsy caravan. It was all she had to cling to. That and the fervent prayer that Reeve would come before Rodrigo's life was forfeit.

Dawn found them numbed with the lack of sleep and food. The guards came for them when the sun had barely rimmed the horizon. Together they stood in the same half dark room to await the sentence.

When the verdict of guilty had been passed none of them were surprised. Beatriz only began to weep softly when Rodrigo was sentenced to the stake. The sentences, the angelic-faced Torquemada said, were to be carried out immediately. For a moment the entire room was silent, and the only sound to be heard was Beatriz's soft muffled tears as Rodrigo held her close for what he thought would be the last time.

There was a loud crash that echoed through the silent room when the huge double doors were thrown open. In the entrance stood Isabel whose face was pale and frozen with her anger. Behind her stood Reeve, Rafael, and Catrina. And behind them stood the queen's royal guards, swords drawn.

Don Francisco's face went from gloating pleasure to amazement, to the first touch of real fear he had ever known. It was not caused by the enraged face of the queen but by the cold look of death in Reeve's eyes. Reeve had looked once at Elana, then his eyes found Don Francisco and they did not waver from his for a moment.

Torquemada and his people could not suffer at Isabel's hands; he knew this and realized he had only to throw Don Francisco to her rage, take his people, and leave. He did just that.

"Your Highness, I did not know this was being done without your knowledge," he began.

"No one is turned over to the tribunal without the royal decree," Isabel said. "Who has given you the right to question and condemn these people?"

"Why," Torquemada said with a shrug, his eloquent face and angelic features filled with innocent surprise, "I thought that Don Francisco de Vargas had your approval or I would not have called this trial."

Don Francisco had not spoken yet. He was face to face with Isabel, and he knew he had better tread carefully or it might cost his life. The fight was not gone from him but was now tempered by his need to be extremely careful. At this moment, Isabel thought of only the ones he had tried to rid himself of. She had no real proof of treason, and treason was the only reason she could call for his death. Any other crime might mean chastisement or temporary exile from which he could still be a danger.

"Your Majesty," he said smoothly as he bowed to the queen, "I sought only to remove from your court a danger that is ever growing."

"And what danger is that, Don Francisco?" the queen said softly.

"You did not know of the secrets these people held in their past. They told you nothing of the fact that their ancestry is Jewish, and that they have only pretended the Catholic faith to be able to come to court and subvert the ones close to you. I found this out and wanted only to relieve Your Majesty of an odious job . . . of trying friends. I sought only to make it easier for you. It was Captain Burke's duty here to help them to bring more such people here."

"That," a hard voice came from behind them, "is a lie!"

They spun about to face the last people they expected to see. What had been a blank wall stood open and Joseph and Carmen stood in the opening.

Carmen had gone for Joseph as soon as she saw the queen's carriage approaching. She had a feeling Reeve was going to need more help.

"Joseph," the queen said, "how in heaven's name did you get into this room?"

"That I can explain much later, Your Majesty. For now, I will explain to you just why Captain Burke is here."

Reeve had never taken his eyes from Don Francisco. He was filled with such a black rage that he could barely hear what was going on.

He had taken in Elana's total appearance in one look. He had seen the dark shadows beneath her eyes and the exhaustion in her face. Now he could only think one thought. It was still possible for Don Francisco to escape this with his life. That, he thought grimly, was one thing he could not allow.

He moved slowly and no one realized he was doing so until

he was close to Don Francisco. Don Francisco was still pleading his case with the queen. But the words he was to say were the ones that would seal his fate.

"I am a man who takes our reputation and my honor seriously. I would die for either," he said smoothly, but the smile fled from his face when Reeve grasped his shoulder and spun him around.

"Would you?" Reeve said in a dangerously soft voice. "Would you . . . defend your . . . honor?"

"I am Don Francisco de Vargas, while you are a . . . nothing . . . a ship captain. You cannot question my honor."

With one quick whiplike movement, Reeve drew back and struck Don Francisco a blow that sent him backward several steps.

"You," Reeve said in measured soft tones, "are the scum dredged up from the bowels of the earth. You are filth. The kind of filth that preys on those weaker than you. But you do not have an ounce of courage or honor. You will abuse women, but you will not pick up a sword and defend yourself against a man." Reeve continued, in a voice as cold and detached as ice, to call Don Francisco every name his brain could conjure up and some that most people in the room had never heard.

Don Francisco's face reddened and with all the people present, he was slowly pushed to fight. It was the last thing he wanted to do. He was sure the queen would have been forced to exile him . . . but Reeve meant to kill him.

Reeve had now drawn his sword, and with a quick flip he drew blood on Don Francisco's cheek. He smiled when he knew Don Francisco could be pushed no further. With a wild curse, Don Francisco drew his sword.

"At last," Reeve breathed, "we face each other on terms a little more even."

Elana had seen nothing but the finer, gentle side of Reeve. She was shaken by the black fury that seemed to possess him.

He was like a maddened Titan as he and Don Francisco clashed.

The guards would have rushed to put a stop to the battle, but a restraining gesture by the queen held them. She fully intended that the two should settle their battle now.

The fight began when Don Francisco pushed himself away from Reeve. The two began to circle each other like cautious cats.

Again they leapt at each other. The clash of metal upon metal sounded as they lashed out at each other. Don Francisco was an excellent swordsman, and Reeve had as much expertise. They were nearly matched in strength and cunning, yet Reeve had one thing on his side. He knew Don Francisco was guilty of all he had accused him of, as did Don Francisco. Don Francisco could only see the pure rage in Reeve's silver-gray eyes, and he could feel the touch of death to the center of his soul. It was enough to give Reeve the power to defeat him.

Now it became apparent to all present. Reeve did not mean to kill him quickly; he meant to make him suffer as long as he could. Reeve's sword became stronger as Don Francisco's seemed to become weaker. Then, when Don Francisco seemed to be on the edge of faltering, Reeve's chiding and taunting voice would renew his waning spirit and strength.

Reeve's sword now was like an avenging angel. It touched like flame, drew blood, and sought another spot. He was slowly and very deliberately cutting Don Francisco to ribbons.

The battle went on, but now all the onlookers knew the outcome. It was obvious that soon Don Francisco would be lost. It came, that moment when he could not raise his sword fast enough or strongly enough to parry the last deadly thrust.

Reeve's sword drove through him, and Don Francisco's sword clattered to the floor. For one stricken moment he gazed at Reeve as if he still could not quite believe it had happened. Then slowly he sagged to the ground and lay at Reeve's feet.

Again the room was caught in that strange silence, then

Elana breathed Reeve's name softly. He turned to her, dropped his sword on the ground, and reached out to her. In a moment she fled to the sanctuary of his arms. She felt them close securely about her.

Isabel had read and listened to the entire story. She knew now that Don Francisco had been more than a threat to the young people involved. He had been a threat to her throne.

Joseph had spoken to the queen in private only because Carmen begged him to. If Reeve wanted to keep his past a secret, even from Elana, she would make sure it was kept.

Elana, Beatriz, and Rodrigo recovered quickly from the terror they had lived through. Soon happy voices of celebration filled the land as everyone celebrated the marriage of Beatriz and Rodrigo and the renewal of the vows between Reeve and Elana in the queen's private chamber.

Pedro and his whole band had been sent for to come to the palace grounds to share the celebration.

Reeve had sent a message to his ship, a long letter telling Ralph all that had happened and that he would be with them soon. They were to get the ship ready for the return journey . . . the journey home.

Party after party was given, and Reeve not only enjoyed them all, but he enjoyed the sparkle of laughter in Elana's eyes. Still he was drawn toward the shores of home and even she could understand the need that kept growing within him to go home.

As he was watching Elana enjoy herself, and as he was enjoying the wild and beautiful nights they shared, he did not realize that Elana was watching him just as closely.

They had joined the queen and their friends for a late supper. Then at the first opportunity had excused themselves for a relaxing walk in the warm night air. Then they had gone to their room.

Reeve had shared so many beautiful nights with Elana, but this night had seemed to be one made of magic. She had come to him, no longer the sweet little girl but a woman of heated blood and desires, as strong and demanding as his.

They lay entwined in each other's arms, her head upon his shoulder. It was a peaceful and contented silence. He could feel her slim body curled close to his, the velvet skin a delight which he could remember from all the dreams he had in the shadows of despair.

"Reeve?" she said softly.

"What?" he sighed contentedly as he drew her even closer.

"When do you want to go?"

He was very quiet. "Go?"

She laughed lightly and rose on one elbow to look down into his questioning eyes. "Oh, my dear husband, I love you so very much. You have stayed because you think I am afraid to leave my home and all I know."

He smiled as he reached to lay his hand against her cheek. "Can you read me so well, love?"

"Because I love you so, Reeve," she added softly.

"Would you be afraid, Elana?" he asked. "I know I cannot offer you all of this."

"With you, Reeve, I am not afraid. Let us go to your home, my love. I would like to see the place in which you grew."

Slowly he slid in his arms about her and drew her close to kiss her gently and very thoroughly.

"I love you, Elana," he whispered as she held him close and surrendered again to the rare and special love they shared.

It was over two weeks before all the final preparations were made. Elana made Rodrigo and Beatriz promise to visit her soon and to bring Catrina and Rafael. Joseph was returning to England and taking Carmen with him. He chuckled when he explained that he felt England was due for a shaking up and

Carmen was the one to do it.

The voyage to England was one trip that Reeve would never forget. Elana again became the Gypsy girl, and she captured the hearts of his entire crew, especially Ralph, whose eyes seemed to follow her in profound admiration wherever she went.

They watched the shores of England grow closer. When the ship was brought to the dock, Elana was fascinated with the color and bustle about her. But Reeve was gazing at a dark carriage that sat some distance from them. His heart leapt at the familiarity of the crest on its door.

Elana could feel the tension in Reeve and she, too, looked toward the carriage in time to see a tall blond man step out of it and walk purposefully toward them. She had only to look at him once to know he and Reeve were of the same blood. He stopped before them and their eyes met.

"Reeve," the man said.

"Philip, what are you doing here?"

"I've . . . I've come to beg you to come home, Reeve. Come home where you belong. You are needed there."

Elana could hear the pleading in his voice and see the pain in both their eyes.

"Amanda," Reeve said quietly.

"Is gone," Philip replied. "Somehow, I always believed you in my heart, Reeve. I was trapped like a fly in a spider's web. Can you forgive me and come home? I have missed you . . . brother."

"Brother?" Elana questioned softly and Philip's deep blue eyes turned to her.

"Philip, this is my wife, Elana."

"What a beauty you are." Philip grinned. "And what a lucky man my brother is. You must tell me how he came to be so fortunate."

"I don't understand," Elana began. "Reeve, you never told me you had a brother."

Reeve and Philip smiled at each other, and the years of sadness and separation seemed to melt away.

Reeve put one arm over his brother's shoulder and one about Elana's waist. Together they walked toward the waiting carriage.

"It is a long story, love, and I'll tell it to you, but for now . . . let's go home."

"Yes," Philip said laughing, "welcome home."

Elana knew only that Reeve was happy and that his brother had opened the last door to Reeve's heart.

She smiled, slid her arm about his waist, and together they started the last of the journey to home . . . to peace and to happiness.

AUTHOR'S NOTE

Do write to me at Box 45, Edinburg, PA 16116 and let me know if you enjoyed BETRAY NOT MY PASSION. No matter how busy I am I do take time to answer each letter.

YOU CAN NOW
CHOOSE FROM AMONG JANELLE TAYLOR'S
BESTSELLING TITLES!

BRAZEN ECSTASY	(1133, $3.50)
DEFIANT ECSTASY	(0931, $3.50)
FIRST LOVE, WILD LOVE	(1431, $3.75)
FORBIDDEN ECSTASY	(1014, $3.50)
GOLDEN TORMENT	(1323, $3.75)
LOVE ME WITH FURY	(1248, $3.75)
SAVAGE CONQUEST	(1533, $3.75)
SAVAGE ECSTASY	(0824, $3.50)
STOLEN ECSTASY	(1621, $3.95)
TENDER ECSTASY	(1212, $3.75)

Available wherever paperbacks are sold, or order direct from the Publisher. Send cover price plus 50¢ per copy for mailing and handling to Zebra Books, Dept. 1466, 475 Park Avenue South, New York, N.Y. 10016. DO NOT SEND CASH.

PASSIONATE ROMANCE BY PHOEBE CONN

CAPTIVE HEART   (1569, $3.95)
The lovely slavegirl Celiese, secretly sent in her mistress's
place to wed the much-feared Mylan, found not the cruel
savage she expected but a magnificently handsome warrior.
With the fire of his touch and his slow, wanton kisses he
would take her to ecstasy's searing heights—and would forever possess her CAPTIVE HEART.

ECSTASY'S PARADISE   (1460, $3.75)
Meeting the woman he was to escort to her future husband, sea captain Phillip Bradford was astounded. The
Swedish beauty was the woman of his dreams, his fantasy
come true. But how could he deliver her to another man's
bed when he wanted her to warm his own?

SAVAGE FIRE   (1397, $3.75)
Innocent, blonde Elizabeth, knowing it was wrong to meet
the powerful Seneca warrior Rising Eagle, went to him
anyway when the sky darkened. When he drew her into his
arms and held her delicate mouth captive beneath his own,
she knew they'd never separate—even though their two
worlds would try to tear them apart!

LOVE'S ELUSIVE FLAME   (1267, $3.75)
Enraptured by his ardent kisses and tantalizing caresses,
golden-haired Flame had found the man of her dreams in
the handsome rogue Joaquin. But if he wanted her completely she would have to be his only woman—and he had
always taken women whenever he wanted, and not one had
ever refused him or pretended to try!

*Available wherever paperbacks are sold, or order direct from the
Publisher. Send cover price plus 50¢ per copy for mailing and
handling to Zebra Books, Dept.* 1466, *475 Park Avenue South,
New York, N.Y. 10016. DO NOT SEND CASH.*

MORE CAPTIVATING HISTORICAL ROMANCES!

SURRENDER TO DESIRE (1503, $3.75)
by Catherine Creel
Raven-haired Marianna came to the Alaskan frontier expecting adventure and fortune and was outraged to learn she was to marry a stranger. But once handsome Donovan clasped her to his hard frame and she felt his enticing kisses, she found herself saying things she didn't mean, making promises she couldn't keep.

TEXAS FLAME (1530, $3.50)
by Catherine Creel
Amanda's journey west through an uncivilized haven of outlaws and Indians leads her to handsome Luke Cameron, as wild and untamed as the land itself, whose burning passion would consume her own!

TEXAS BRIDE (1050, $3.50)
by Catherine Creel
Ravishing Sarah, alone in Wildcat City and unsafe without a man's protection, has no choice but to wed Adam MacShane — in name only. Then Adam, who gave his word of honor not to touch his Yankee wife, swears an oath of passion to claim his TEXAS BRIDE.

SAVAGE ABANDON (1505, $3.95)
by Rochelle Wayne
Chestnut-haired Shelaine, saved by the handsome savage from certain death in the raging river, knew but one way to show her thanks. Though she'd never before known the embrace of a man, one glance at the Indian's rippling muscles made her shiver with a primitive longing, with wild SAVAGE ABANDON.

SURRENDER TO ECSTASY (1307, $3.95)
by Rochelle Wayne
From the moment the soft-voiced stranger entered Amelia's bed all she could think about was the ecstasy of his ardent kisses and the tenderness of his caress. Longing to see his face and learn his name, she had no idea that he hid his identity because the truth could destroy their love!

Available wherever paperbacks are sold, or order direct from the Publisher. Send cover price plus 50¢ per copy for mailing and handling to Zebra Books, Dept. 1466, 475 Park Avenue South, New York, N.Y. 10016. DO NOT SEND CASH.